THE
ROCKING
HORSE
OF
Tuscumbia

KIMBERLEY G. GRAHAM

D1523410

To learn more about Kimberley G. Graham,
visit www.sparrowrefuge.com and www.kimberleyggraham.com

The Rocking Horse of Tuscumbia

Wooden horse on cover created by Brent Gerdes

Photo of author by Catherine Burns
CatherineBurnsPhotography.com

Critiqued by Susan E. Richardson

Edited by Marcia Ford

The Rocking Horse of Tuscumbia is a work of fiction.
Where real people, events, establishments, organizations, or locales appear,
they are used fictitiously.
All other elements of the novel are drawn from the author's imagination.

ISBN: 978-0-9897898-0-6 (ePub)
ISBN: 978-0-9897898-1-3 (paperback)

for Nanny

Beverly McNutt Gardner
December 4, 1928 – October 18, 2009

If the blind lead the blind, both will fall into a pit.

Matthew 15:14

I am glad to take you by the hand
and lead you along an untrodden way
into a world where the hand is supreme.

HELEN KELLER

Chapter One

June 27, 1989 / Tuscumbia, Alabama

Twenty years before Mama burned the house down, I sat with my back anchored to Grandma's porch column, desperate for the earth to rise up and cave in on top of me.

It was the morning of my ninth birthday, a time when most girls are beaming with excitement. Not me. I busied myself by picking white flakes of paint off the balusters while Grandma hummed a familiar tune under her breath and poured sugar water into her planters.

After I interrupted her singing with another long sigh, she put down the watering can and scolded me.

"Amanda Reyes, get up and help your mama with the decorations. Your guests will be here in half an hour."

"I don't know why y'all are working so hard. Nobody's gonna come," I said, pulling my knees to my chest.

Mama threw open the screen door and rushed past me toward the linen-covered card tables.

"Why do you always do that, Amanda?" Mama asked.

"Do what?"

"You always think everything's gonna turn out terrible. Why don't you get up, stop your pouting, and help us get ready?" Mama shifted all her weight to her left foot and glared at me. "If I have to ask you again, you'll have to go inside while we have this party without you."

Grandma hid her water pitcher behind one of her ferns and smiled at me the way she always did when she wanted to prod me toward doing the right thing. I held my position until she went inside and let the screen door slam behind her.

I didn't see any reason to help. They'd already done a pretty good job of making things look ridiculous. It was the end of June, but from the look of Grandma's yard you would've thought it was Easter Sunday. If I could've gotten away with it, I would've run off to my favorite hiding place near the creek and spent the rest of the afternoon looking for arrowheads. Instead, I pulled the straps of my white sandals over my heels and shuffled down the front steps to where Mama was busy rearranging chrysanthemums and monogrammed napkins.

After she dusted off the tablecloth for the third time, Mama pulled a purple flower from the arrangement and tucked it behind my ear.

"You look beautiful, baby. I can't believe how big you're gettin'." Mama lifted my chin until I couldn't help but look into her dark eyes. "You know, if Helen Keller were still alive, she'd be turning 109 years old today."

"I know, Mama, I know. You never let me forget."

Mama pushed my chin aside and yelled across the gravel driveway to my little sister. "Penelope, get down from there! You're not a squirrel, you're a little girl!"

Most of the time, Mama preferred Penelope and her blonde hair over me and my auburn waves, even though I was the one who looked the most like her. Penelope loved climbing the dogwoods, but in her party dress she looked more like a bed sheet caught by the wind than a five-year-old or a rodent.

Mama worried because Penelope never played with anyone other than me. Even then, all she wanted to do was sing along with the radio as if she was Whitney Houston or pretend to be part of a marching band.

I watched as Penelope scooted along one of the branches and positioned herself to swing down.

"Don't you rip that dress, young lady!" Mama called before going back to her flower arrangement.

Penelope let go of the branch with one hand and shook her taffeta skirt free with the other. As she attempted to readjust her weight, Penelope lost her balance, slipped, and dangled helplessly before falling to the ground with a heavy thud.

"Oh, Penelope, I told you not to climb that tree!" Mama yelled as we rushed over to Pen and helped her get up. "Let me see your hands."

Penelope sobbed as tiny drops of blood rose to the surface of her skin.

"When I tell you something, it's for a reason." Mama released Penelope's hands and put her own on her hips. "Do you hear me? Stay here."

Mama rushed inside and left Pen standing there with both blood-soaked palms turned up.

"It's okay," I whispered. "Mama will be right back." As a new rush of tears came from her crystal-blue eyes, Penelope's sobs grew even louder. Feeling desperate to stop the blood, I took one of the linen napkins from the table and placed it over her hands.

"Press your hands together like you do when we pray," I said. Penelope's cries got louder and louder as I squeezed her hands around the napkin. "Mama's gonna be right back, I promise. Can you sing me a song? It's okay. Sing me a song."

The corners of her mouth turned down as she fought back more tears.

"Can you sing me the song you were hummin' at breakfast? I liked that one."

Penelope let out half a note, shook her head, and went back to crying.

Grandma held open the screen door for Mama as she hurried toward us with a damp rag.

"I'm comin'," Mama said.

When she saw the neatly pressed linen napkin stained with blood, Mama scolded me and sent me inside to rinse it clean.

Just when the blood started to rinse out, Mama came in and tossed a bloodied rag in the kitchen sink.

"Radella spent two hours ironing napkins for you. What were you thinkin' getting blood on your grandma's good napkins? Now it's ruined. You'll never be able to get that stain out in time for the party. People are gonna be here soon."

"See? It's ruined." Mama snatched the soaked cloth from my hands and unfolded it to reveal three small brown dots.

It didn't matter how hard I tried to please Mama or her friends in Tuscumbia, a nine-year-old girl has no way to compete with a famous woman—even if the woman is dead. Mama called it *my* birthday party, but really it was an occasion for her to invite all her friends and their children over to celebrate the birth date of the town's matriarch—Helen Keller.

The first person to show up was Grandma's hired help, Radella Daw, along with her husband, Sam, and their youngest son, Cecil.

"They're like family to us," Mama would say to her friends when they'd ask about the Daws.

The truth was that Grandma practically raised Sam Daw after his mother passed. Sam's mother, Ester, had worked as Grandma's maid from the time she married Grandpa until the day Ester died. They each had only one child. Ester had Sam, and shortly afterwards Grandma gave birth to my mother. I know because I've seen a photograph of the two women, one black and one white, standing together with swollen bellies.

Grandma tells people the photo is a snapshot of both of her pregnancies. But Mama sure wouldn't claim Sam as her brother. I think she cares about him, in the stiff-armed way she cares about most things, but she never allowed me talk about Sam as if he was family. Still, in my heart Sam is my uncle, and I consider Radella my aunt.

Now how two wonderful people could create such an evil little boy, I just couldn't understand.

"When are we gonna eat?" Cecil asked with a toothy grin after arriving and plopping down across the table from me.

I rolled my eyes and folded my arms across my chest.

"All we've got for you, Cecil Daw, is a little buttermilk."

"Can't taste any worse than your Grandma's cookin'." The corners of Cecil's mouth turned down, and his black dimples went flat. "Good thing my mama's always around to help."

I made an ugly face at him before slumping. "Why'd you have to come anyway? You like playin' with girls?"

"The only girl I see is the pretty one sittin' right here." Penelope laughed as Cecil poked a long index finger into her side.

"Oh, hush, both of you. Why don't you learn some manners, Penelope, and sit up straight."

When Mama told us it was time to eat, Cecil got up and piled some of everything from the buffet into a mound on his plate. He always ate like a cow with a lawn mower attached.

I wanted to sit with Ellen Johnson even though we'd only played together a few times at Spring Park while our mothers talked, but Grandma said I should sit with Pen and Cecil until cake was served. Grandma planned to join us, but she'd been assigned to stand near the food and fan the flies while the guests served themselves from the buffet. Mama didn't like that Grandma fanned with one hand while she held a cigarette in the other, but Grandma won the argument after assuring Mama that smoke helped repel insects as well.

Mama couldn't say much. After all, it was Grandma's house, and Mama was already swimming in her second gin and tonic.

Cecil took one bite of potato salad and crinkled his nose. "My word, what's in this?"

I smiled and pointed to my untouched pile of potatoes. "What's wrong, Cecil? You don't like it?"

"Goodness alive." Cecil wiped his tongue with one of the perfectly ironed linens. "Who in the world likes that?"

Penelope chuckled as she bit into a slice of ham.

"It's vinegar." I said, after unfolding my napkin. "Mama says it's a fancy way of making potato salad. She says that's how they do it in really good restaurants."

"Well, remind me to never eat in a really good restaurant." Cecil took a sip of lemonade.

I tried not to laugh; right then, Mama was passing by our table carrying a pitcher of iced tea.

"You better watch out talkin' like that when Grandma sits with us."

"Oh, I'm not afraid of Ms. Etta."

Daddy whistled above the crowd as he came toward me. "Amanda Reyes, I can't believe how beautiful you look. When I left our house this mornin' you looked like a nine-year-old girl, but now you look like a twelve-year-old princess." He stood behind me and placed a gentle hand on my shoulder. He was dressed in his usual trousers and blue collared shirt.

"Except there's one thing missin'. Now, what could it be?" he said loud enough for everyone to hear.

My cheeks turned red; everyone had stopped eating and was staring at me.

"Oh hush, Karl," Mama said as she stumbled toward us. "You're embarrassin' her."

Daddy ignored her and rubbed the place where his mustache used to be. "Could it be that she's missin' a bow? No, it's not that." Daddy pulled at the ribbon tied around my ponytail. "Could it be that she's missin' her smile?" Daddy knelt next to me and placed one knee on the ground. The smell of his earthy cologne filled the air, and I reluctantly smiled. "Nope, she's got that."

Mama folded her arms and rolled her eyes toward the guests.

"Oh, I know..." Daddy reached into his pocket and removed something hidden inside a white handkerchief. "It must be this."

Everyone clapped as Daddy dangled a long gold chain with a tiny charm in front of my eyes. I thought the charm was a diamond until it spun in a complete circle and I could see it was round. Mama must have mistaken it for a diamond too, because she let out a huff and walked away.

"It's beautiful, Daddy. What is it?"

Before Daddy had a chance to tell me, Mama stood on the porch and clapped her hands to get everyone's attention; she was not going to let Daddy steal the show.

"Excuse me, everyone," Mama called from the bottom porch step. "We just want to thank y'all for comin'. As you all know, this day is very special to us and to this city. Not only is it Amanda's birthday, but it's also the birthday of one of the most amazing women in all of history. On this day, one hundred and nine years ago, our Helen Keller was born. Without her, this nation wouldn't be what it is today." Mama paused and smiled at me. "If one day my little girl does even a fraction of what Helen did, I will be a proud mother."

Cecil's annoying grin returned.

"When Amanda was born, we couldn't believe God had given us

a child on the one hundredth anniversary of such an important day in Tuscumbia's history. Now, nine years later, we're still anxious to *see*," Mama smiled and made a quotation-like gesture with her hands, "what kind of woman Amanda's gonna grow up to be."

I wanted to cry as everyone smiled and nodded at her. Daddy put the chain in my palm and closed my hand around it to reassure me that everything was okay. As our guests started clapping, I pleaded with him to make her stop. But she just continued.

"Amanda, you have a lot to live up to. I hope one day you'll make us all real proud."

As Daddy stood, I pushed past him and ran through the field toward the creek.

I'd never be able to live up to Mama's expectations. Not ever. If I could've run all to way to Egypt, I would have.

After a hundred yards or so, I could see a break in the trees where deer came through at night to nibble at the grass along the edges of the field. Exhausting another burst of energy, I plowed through the opening until I came to where the fallen leaves were still wet with morning dew. The dampness felt good as it soaked between my toes and around the straps of my new sandals. I started to slow down, but thought about how upset Mama would be about my wet shoes so I kept running and dodging branches until I saw the embankment and heard the water moving along the rocks.

"Stop!"

At first I thought the words came from somewhere inside me, but the second time I heard them I realized Daddy was chasing me and doing a pretty good job of keeping up.

"Amanda, stop!"

I skidded to a stop and caught hold of a tree.

When he reached me, he bent over, put both hands on his knees, and gasped for breath.

"Child." Daddy stood and wiped his brow with his forearm. "I thought for a second you were gonna jump."

"I hate her, Daddy."

"Why is that?"

"Because I'm never gonna be good enough for her. Never!"

Daddy swallowed and waited to catch his breath.

"Amanda, I know it's hard for you to understand, but your mother loves you very much. She's just tryin' to make you feel special."

I wanted to run again. I wanted to run until the straps of my sandals broke. "Then why is everything about Helen Keller? Why can't my birthday be about me? Is it because I'm bad?"

"You're not bad."

"Then why doesn't she love me?"

"Amanda, sit down." Daddy reached for my hand and realized my fingers were still gripping the gold chain and tiny glass ball. "Let me see your necklace. I want to show you something." He unhooked the latch and pulled the ends until the chain made a perfectly horizontal line with the charm dangling in the middle. This time I noticed there was something inside the ball. Something tiny like a speck of sand. I held my hand behind it and tried to get a better look. When I touched the glass, the yellow speck jumped.

"What's that?"

"Sit down and I'll tell you."

I found a place near the ledge where a large root ran thick along the ground.

"I met a man at the festival who was selling these in his booth." Daddy shook the chain again and smiled as it danced. "That tiny speck is a mustard seed."

"A seed?"

"Yes. There's a story in the Bible about what happens when a seed like this is planted."

"What happens?"

"It grows and grows until it's taller than me."

"Are we gonna plant it?"

"No." Daddy fastened the chain around my neck as I held my hair out of the way. "I just want you to wear it as a reminder."

"Of what?"

"As a reminder to grow and to love. You know that seeds can't grow in soil that's hard, right?

I nodded.

"And when the dirt's hard, do you know what happens?"

"The seed dies."

Daddy tapped me on the end of my nose. "You have to keep loving so you can keep growing. Your heart is just like that little seed. Don't ever let it get hard or dry out."

"But I can't love Mama if she doesn't love me."

"Amanda, look at me. I know sometimes you feel like your mama doesn't love you, but trust me, she does. She loves you more than anything in the world. One day you'll understand."

I felt the globe again before standing to dust off my skirt. "Do we have to go back now?"

"Yes."

"Can't I wait until everyone's gone?"

Daddy slid his hands into his pockets and sighed. "I think you'd better come thank your guests. Don't worry, they'll be rushing off to the festival soon enough. Plus, you still have to blow out all sixteen candles."

I placed my hands on my hips. "I'm nine, Daddy."

He laughed and patted me on the head before turning back toward the house. "Well, not for long."

Many persons, having perfect eyes,
are blind in their perceptions.
HELEN KELLER

Chapter Two

Once the charade had gone on long enough, everyone
started to leave. Mama hurried to take everything down. While she
gathered unused flatware, Grandma stacked china dishes and thanked
the last of the guests for coming. Mama thought it was best to wait
until everyone left before I opened my gifts. That way she'd be able to
record an accurate thank-you list, and I'd be able to spend the rest of
the summer writing notes to her friends.

My assigned task was to carry the unopened gifts from the porch
to the coffee table in the living room. After my third trip, black storm
clouds began to bruise the horizon.

"I hope the festival gets rained out," I whispered to myself as I
sat on the top step.

Grandma looked up at the clouds. "Finally, the rain's coming."

After the Daws left, Grandma came and sat next to me. There
was still a lot to do, but she insisted Radella go home with her family.
As we sat looking across the lawn at the dogwoods, birds rejoiced at
the pause in the commotion and went back to plucking blueberries
from the row of bushes along the gravel driveway.

"I'm sorry, Grandma."

"It's okay, sweet girl. I'm sorry too."

"What for?"

"Oh, for a lot of things," she sighed, wrapping an arm around my shoulders and pulling me closer. "I guess right now I'm sorry your special day didn't go exactly as planned."

"It's okay, Grandma. It was fun."

Grandma knew I was lying.

"I'm glad I had my party here."

Grandma let go, smiled, and patted along the front of her blouse hoping to find her smokes and lighter. "Your mama's always been one for a celebration." When Grandma realized her cigarettes weren't hidden in her blouse pocket, she gave up the search and pulled at the bottom of her blouse to straighten it out. "Do me a favor, will you? Go inside and bring back the little white gift with the pink bow."

I recognized Grandma's gift right away; she always made bows the same way. I used to watch her fold the ribbon over itself and then use another piece of ribbon at the center to keep the bow from coming apart.

The first drops of rain threatened to escape the clouds above us. I returned to my place on the step next to Grandma and began to remove the ribbon. Penelope called for me to help her catch a frog, but I was too excited to join her. Grandma and I tugged at the ribbon until it gave way. Grandma wadded the white paper into a ball as I slowly lifted the lid. Inside was a rocking horse, no bigger than the palm of my hand.

"It was your mother's. Your grandfather whittled it for her when she was your age. Now your mama and I want you to have it."

I turned the horse over in my hand. I'd seen it on the shelf in the den, along with several other things he'd made, but I'd known better than to touch it. Holding it felt magical. I ran my fingers along its smooth surface. I was careful not to snap one of the fragile rockers while I admired his white tail and matching reins. I could imagine my grandfather sitting on the porch swing, carving bits of wood and sanding the horse as he sang. Although he died long before I was born, I'd heard stories about his love of music and his gift of woodworking. Grandma's house was full of treasures created by him over the years: the tiny shelf in the kitchen where Grandma displayed her collection of novelty jiggers, the pecan desk in his study, and even the twin beds where Penelope and I slept when we stayed the night.

I imagined his hands as strong and dirty as a lumberjack's but still gentle enough to hold a miniature as he carved away at its tiny features. Grandma said his favorite hymn was "Fairest Lord Jesus" and that he'd sit on the porch after a full day of plowing and sing as he swung and whittled.

He always had to be doing something, Mama said on several occasions. *He was always working, always creating something, always dreaming up his next creation long before he finished the first project.*

I guessed she'd somehow inherited that part of him. I wondered if he'd spent too much time doing and singing and not enough time sitting and listening. I wondered if he'd spent hours carving away at something for her while she sat alone in her room.

Mama gathered up the linen tablecloths while Daddy folded chairs and loaded them on to the back of his truck so he could return them on the way home. Mama frowned at him—the same way she always did—until she noticed Grandma and me sitting together on the porch. When she saw what I was holding, Mama pushed her red curls from her face with the back of her hand and tossed the linens into Daddy's arms.

"I want you to take real good care of that rocking horse, Amanda," she said as she headed toward us. "It's always been very special to me."

"I will, Mama," I promised.

Daddy slammed the gate of the truck, signaling that his job was done. "Well, I better get these back before the rain starts. I don't want to spend the rest of the day drying off chairs in the fellowship hall.

Amanda, do you want to ride with me?"

"She can't go with you, Karl. She doesn't need to sit in your truck while you unload all those chairs. It's ninety degrees outside."

"Well, she doesn't have to sit in the truck. She can come inside and help me set them up for tomorrow's service."

Penelope grabbed Daddy around his leg with one arm and held up her frog with the other. "Can *we* go with you?" she pleaded.

"All right, you can come, but the frog stays here." Daddy scooped Penelope into his arms. "What about you, birthday girl? Want to come with us on a chair-returning mission?"

"Actually..." I hid my hand beneath my skirt and crossed my fingers. "I was hopin' I could spend the night with Grandma."

Mama looked at her mother for approval.

"Okay, Amanda can stay here."

I shrieked with joy.

"But if you wanna open gifts, you'll have to help me pick up first."

"Can I still go with Daddy?" Penelope asked.

"Yes, but if you do, you'll miss seein' your sister open presents."

Penelope looked at Daddy and then back at me.

"It's okay. I'll show you everything after church tomorrow," I said.

Just as we brought the last of the party decorations inside, the clouds split open and large raindrops pounded the roof.

Mama made me open everything slowly enough for her to collect the tags, write down who each gift was from, and take an occasional sip of her gin and tonic. After the rain stopped, she left for the festival, and I changed into one of Grandma's old T-shirts.

Grandma turned the knob on her big box television until she found a rerun of *Lassie*. We sat together in the rocker for longer than usual and watched in silence.

The dance began as it always did, with us rocking in a spot near the window. From there we could see the side lawn and through the field to the cemetery. After a few minutes, though, the chair began working its way to the right like it was trying to escape out the front door. Grandma and I were used to watching TV that way. We never tired of the dance. We would rock and rock—every time moving a little more to the right—and eventually, without saying a word, she'd slide me off of her lap so she could go for a smoke while I pushed the chair back to its starting place near the window. When she returned, off we'd go rocking our way to the right again.

That night we rocked and returned four times before I finally fell asleep in her arms.

"Amanda, wake up." Grandma rubbed my arm. "My legs are asleep. You gotta hop up."

The room was dark. The television had those rainbow-colored lines on the screen and made an awful sound. Grandma groaned as I slid off her lap.

"Turn the TV off, will you?"

I hurried to press the knob back into place and watched as the colors shrank to the center of the screen with a snap, leaving Grandma and me in complete darkness. I felt my way to the lamp and pulled the chain.

"Oh thank you, sweet girl."

"You okay? Can you stand up?"

"Not yet. My old bones are hard sleepers. Just give me a second. I'll have to wait 'til my blood remembers which direction to go."

I sat down on the floor near her feet and rubbed my cold palms on her knees. Grandma grinned and stretched her neck.

"Do you miss him?" I asked.

"Your grandfather?"

I nodded.

"Every day of my life. It's funny the things I miss sometimes."

"Like what?"

Grandma rubbed her thighs with deep strokes and stretched out her toes.

"Oh—like having to sweep up after him when he'd come into the kitchen to grab something for lunch before taking off his muddy boots."

I smiled. "How'd he die?"

"Well, he had a heart attack, so the doctors did surgery to clear a blockage." Grandma scooted to the end of the rocker and pulled herself up. "We thought he was getting better, but before he came home from the hospital, his heart started to fail again."

"How old was he?" I asked, stepping back to give her room.

"Not old enough. Why do you suddenly want to know this stuff?"

"I was just thinking."

"About what?"

"About my daddy, I guess."

"Honey, your daddy's not gonna die."

"But what if he does?" I asked, feeling the necklace beneath my shirt. Something in my belly knew that she was wrong. I wanted to believe her. I wanted to trust her and God, but deep down, I didn't.

"Then I guess we'll have to deal with that when the time comes."

I grabbed Grandma's arm below the elbow and steadied her as she moved toward the kitchen.

"Are you hungry?" she asked. "We never ate anything for dinner."

"No, ma'am."

"Well, you need to eat something. I can't let you go home and tell your parents I didn't feed you. How 'bout a little toast?"

Grandma knew I couldn't resist her offer of warm bread, so after she pushed open the swinging door to the kitchen and held it for me, I climbed into one of the vinyl chairs at the breakfast table and waited while she dropped two pieces of bread into her toaster.

"How 'bout a little butter?" she asked without turning around.

"Sure!"

Grandma chuckled. "And jelly?"

"Yes, ma'am."

"Well, I'm glad you finally have your appetite back." Grandma grabbed the butter cube and grape jelly from the fridge and let the door slam shut while she took down a plate from the cabinet. "But you're still rubbing your fingers together like there's somethin' on your mind."

I hid my clenched fists below the Formica table.

"You wanna talk about it?" she asked.

I shrugged. "It's nothing."

The toaster made a humming sound before the bread popped up. Grandma smoothed a piece of butter on the toast until it began to melt.

"It's okay, you don't have to tell me. I just have to ask when I think something's worryin' someone I love—your mama will testify to that." Grandma drove the butter knife into the jelly and pulled out a pile of purple mush. "Want to know more about the rockin' horse?"

The thought of the horse made me smile. I wished Mama hadn't taken my gifts home with her. "Yes, please tell me more."

"Okay. Whaddaya wanna know?"

I considered a long list of questions. "How long did it take Grandpa to make it?"

"Oh, not too terribly long—a couple of days, I guess." Grandma slid the plate in front of me and opened the kitchen door to allow a little breeze to come through. The jelly covered my top lip as I took the first bite. Grandma handed me a paper napkin and pulled one of the chairs over to the linoleum sink.

"When I was a little girl I always wanted a rockin' horse, but the closest thing I ever got was that old rockin' chair." Grandma gestured toward the swinging door before pulling a cigarette from the half-empty pack near the sink. "Your grandfather knew that, so the truth is he was makin' it for me until your mama begged for it." Grandma put the cigarette to her lips but removed it before lighting the tip. "I think he would've given her about anythin' in the world if she'd asked for it."

I wiped my mouth and swallowed.

"Thanks for lettin' me have it, Grandma."

"Oh, you're welcome, but it was actually your mama's idea."

"My mama's?"

"Sure was. I wanted to start you a collection of dolls, but she said you wouldn't like that."

I made a face that let Grandma know Mama had been right.

"But you loved the doll Radella gave you."

"Until I found out Mama named her Nancy after Helen Keller's favorite doll."

Grandma laughed.

"Well then, how about a collection of rockin' horses?"

I took a bite of bread and thought about that.

Grandma, trying to hold the cigarette over the sink, leaned forward and lifted the napkin to my cheek.

"Did Grandpa make other ones?" I asked.

"Oh, sweet child, he only made the one, but there's a lot of other places to get rockin' horses. Every Southern girl ought to have a collection of somethin'. If you're not gonna go for dolls, then we'll have to come up with somethin' else."

"Rocking horses would be good. Daddy gave me a stuffed one, so I have two."

"Really?"

"He brought it from Birmingham."

"Well, see there—you have a stuffed one and a miniature. That's a pretty good start if you ask me."

"Okay. I'll start collecting rocking horses, and when I get too big to play with them, I'll make them like Grandpa did."

Grandma nodded as she released a puff of smoke toward to ceiling. "Perfect, but you have to promise me one thing."

"What?"

She ran water over the filter and smiled.

"You gotta promise to make me my very own horse one day, with nickel stirrups and a red leather saddle."

"And I could make a mane out of my gold ribbons."

"That would be perfect, and don't forget the eyes. You gotta be real careful with eyes."

I lifted my sticky hands into bearlike claws. "'Cause if you're not, they'll be blind like Helen's."

Grandma made a disapproving face as she motioned for me to lower my hands.

"No, silly, if you're not careful with a rockin' horses eyes, you'll throw the whole thing off balance." Grandma smiled and helped herself to a piece of my dinner.

"They're not like real horses, and in more ways than you think. To get a real horse to focus on what's ahead, all you've gotta do is put blinders on him. It's not like that with rockin' horses. Blinders don't do any good because rockin' horses only move in two directions, forward and backward. But if the eyes are right you can ride them all the way to heaven and back." Grandma tapped the table as she stood. "Sometimes people are like real horses. They put on blinders to help them focus. The problem is sometimes they focus on the wrong things."

I imagined a horse with eyes hidden behind black patches.

"Then there's people who live like they're cross-eyed rockin' horses. They spend a lotta time rockin' back and forth between things but never really go anywhere."

I swallowed the last bite of bread and folded my bare feet beneath the chair. "I'm not gonna be like that Grandma. I'm goin' lots of places when I grow up."

Grandma let out a belly laugh as she picked up the empty plate.

"Well, you better get your eyes right then. You start focusin' on the wrong things, and one day you'll find yourself right back where you started."

If you wish to be something that you are not,
—something fine, noble, good,—
you shut your eyes and for one dreamy moment
you are that which you long to be.

HELEN KELLER

Chapter Three

Grandma followed me up the stairs, stopping every third step to catch her breath. When we got to the top, I flipped the switch to turn on the hall light and skipped to Mama's old room. After Grandma caught up, she helped me pull back the quilted cover from one of the beds Grandpa made and pulled the curtains closed. After I settled in, she pulled the covers to my shoulders and sat next to me on the bed. "You gonna be okay up here by yourself?"

"Always am."

"Cause you can sleep with me if you want."

We tried that a few times, but between my kicking and Grandma's snoring, we didn't sleep much.

"I'm fine. I like it up here."

"All right then, don't sleep too late. We have to get up early for church."

Grandma didn't approve of the groaning sound I made when she mentioned going to church but she kissed me on the forehead anyway and whispered a blessing into my ear. When she finished praying she turned the lamp off and slowly shuffled toward the door.

I held my breath and waited until I heard the bottom stair creak. The room was dark, except for the glow from the hallway that lit the fringe of the rug beneath the bed. I stared at the light for several minutes before climbing out and drawing open the curtains again. In the moonlight, I spun the mustard seed charm between my fingers until I fell asleep.

The next morning I was awakened to the sound of dishes clanging together in the kitchen below me. The room was as bright as if it was the middle of the day, so I pulled the quilt over my head to cover my eyes. Through the sheets, I heard someone climb the stairs, two at a time, before losing balance and hammering into one of the hallway walls. After the loud thud, I threw back the covers and listened as the person recovered and pounded down the hallway toward my room. Just outside the door, the noise stopped.

I was about to ask who was there when Cecil pushed open the door and yelled for me to get up. With my birthday dress tossed over his shoulder, Cecil pretended to shoot at me with his hands.

"Get out of here!" I yelled.

"Ms. Etta says you better get up and get ready for church."

"I said get outta here!"

With that, Cecil flung my dress around like a lasso and let go. It flew into my face.

"She says you better hurry. Your mama will be here soon."

"I'm not goin' to church today."

"Well, your mama says you are, so I'm guessing you are."

I studied Cecil's dirty jeans and worn T-shirt.

"Well, you're not going."

"Daddy and I are going fishing in Ms. Etta's pond."

If I'd been wearing more than a T-shirt I would've climbed out of bed and pounded him. "Well, good luck. You know there aren't any fish in that pond."

"That don't matter."

"Then get outta here so I can get dressed."

Cecil left the same way he entered, banging and thrashing into things until he made it downstairs. I locked the door behind him and put on yesterday's dress.

Sam and Cecil were already seated at the kitchen table waiting for their breakfast when I came in. Sam folded down one corner of his newspaper and smiled at me from the other side.

"There's the birthday girl!"

Grandma greeted me with a kiss on the forehead before removing a fresh batch of biscuits from the oven.

I sat at the table and watched as Cecil struggled with a jar of Karo.

"You need some help with that?"

"Not from you, I don't."

Sam folded the paper and slid it beneath his chair. "No good reason to read the paper anymore. All they do is make stuff up."

Grandma punctured the sides of three biscuits and rolled them onto a plate for Sam. "You're right about that. Can't trust a thing they say anymore."

"One day I'm gonna write stories for the paper," Cecil said.

I was going to say something ugly, but Sam beat me to it.

"If you're gonna write anything more than a personal check, you'd better stop messing around in your English class and start payin' attention."

Cecil frowned. "I make fine grades in English."

Sam took the syrup jar and twisted the lid open. "Last time I looked you had a D in that class. If you're gonna work at the paper, you'll have to do better than that."

Cecil was a full two years older than me, but with his thin shoulders slumped over the table and his bottom lip stuck out, we looked the same age. Grandma placed our plates in front of us and warned us not to eat until after she said grace. While she poured juice, Cecil and I soaked our meals in clear Karo.

"When I grow up, I'm gonna be a wood maker," I said, although no one had asked.

Sam laughed as he added another sugar cube to his coffee.

Grandma sat next to me and unfolded a paper napkin in her lap. "You're gonna be a woodworker, honey. Only God is a wood *maker*."

Cecil smirked.

"Well, whatever—at least I can spell 'woodworker'." I returned a halfhearted grin, before Grandma hushed me, grabbed my hand, and nodded for me to take hold of Cecil's. I squeezed my eyes closed as I took his sweaty fingers.

When Grandma was through asking grace, I opened my eyes and caught Cecil looking at me. I pulled my hand from his and wiped my fingers on my dress.

Sam took a bite and washed it down with coffee. "What are you going to build?"

"Everything, probably, but I'm definitely going to build rocking horses."

"Really? Why's that?"

"Well, I'm gonna start a collection, so I figure I can make a few of my own."

"Sounds like a good plan. Your grandfather would be proud to know his granddaughter's taken up some of his skills."

Until that moment, I'd never thought about Sam knowing my grandfather. I knew he was always around, pestering my mom the same way Cecil did me, but I never thought about him with my grandfather. "You knew Grandpa?"

"Of course I did. I was here every other day with my mother.

Your grandfather was a hard-working man. He stayed in the fields most of the year, but in the winter he'd let me hang out with him in his workshop while my mama cleaned and your mama wrecked the place." Sam smiled. "Boy, your mama hated it when I got to do things and she didn't."

"Like what?"

"Like ride on the tractor or hang out in that shed," Grandma said.

Cecil pushed a piece of biscuit around on his plate to soak up the drippings.

"Why didn't Grandpa let her go with y'all?"

Grandma plopped a sugar cube into her cup and stirred. "I think your grandpa was afraid she'd get hurt. James Paxton loved her better than the stars. If somethin' happened to Tilly, he'd have died too."

Sam's cup made a clanging sound as he placed it on the table. "I think Tilly would've understood if I'd been older than her, but we're the same age."

"I didn't realize how much you goin' hurt her until after James died. We thought we were protectin' her, but we should've let her see how hard her daddy worked. If I could do things over, I'd let her chase off after James the way you did."

"Oh, Ms. Etta, you can't bang yourself up over that. You know Tilly was a tyrant. She would've gotten hurt if she'd been allowed to play in the workshop. She should be thankful she still has her fingers."

"What happened to the workshop?" I asked between bites. "Where did it go?"

Grandma slipped a cigarette from her pocket and rolled it between her fingers as she stood and eased toward the screen door. Grandma pushed open the screen with her foot and looked across the porch toward the creek. Leaning against the frame, she put the thin cigarette to her lips and lit the end.

"It used to be right there"—Grandma pointed the cigarette toward the horizon—"between the oak tree and the creek. Grandpa picked that spot because from there you can see the whole property. The workshop looked more like two shacks connected by a breezeway than it did a woodworking shop."

I leaned forward in my chair to see.

"After your grandpa died, I had the thing bulldozed. It was about to collapse anyway." Grandma sighed. "Sometimes I stand here and imagine him in the breezeway."

Sam winked at me after he took another sip of coffee and retrieved his paper from beneath the chair.

"Boy, stop playing with the sugar cubes."

The tower Cecil had been building tumbled.

"Where are Grandpa's tools?" I asked.

"I got rid of most of them, but there's a box around here some-where with a few of his things if you're interested." Grandma ran water over the tip of her cigarette and tossed the filter in the trash. "I'll try to find it this week. It's mostly small stuff, carving tools and sanding wheels."

"Oh, please find them, Grandma. I want them."

"All right, but you have to remember they're dangerous. Maybe we can find some books on woodcarving and start there."

The thought thrilled me. Even Cecil smiled and nodded in approval.

A woodworker.

I barreled up the stairs to make the bed after Grandma cleared our plates. When I'd pulled at the quilt long enough, I ran my fingers along the headboard and counted the grooves. Then I pressed my face against the cool window and tried to imagine Grandpa's workshop at the top of the hill. Mama must've done the same thing a thousand times while she waited for him to come inside.

> Whatever moves me, whatever thrills me,
> is as a hand that touches me in the dark,
> and that touch is my reality.
>
> **HELEN KELLER**

Chapter Four

Grandma did as she promised. The following week when Mama and I stopped to visit, I discovered an old shoebox waiting for me on the kitchen table along with three books about woodworking. The first book was about materials and tools and described types of woods and which tools were used to carve which materials. I decided that when I was finally old enough to carve, I'd start with cedar before moving on to something a little tougher like red oak or basswood. I didn't know where I'd get the woods, but I couldn't wait to make a mark in them.

After we started back to school in the fall, Cecil bragged that his fifth-grade art teacher allowed him to use woodcarving tools to etch linoleum blocks. He said she'd told him to hold the blade away from his body so he wouldn't cut himself and how he should press down on the block with his thumb at the corner for the same reason.

I listened, pretending I wasn't interested, as he described the bird design he'd carved and how he'd rolled thick ink onto the block before making a print on watercolor paper.

We were sitting on the front porch across from each other, waiting for Sam and Grandma to return from taking her car to the shop. I was in my usual place with my back to the column and my knees tucked under my chin. Cecil stood near the front door with his skiboard feet shoulder-width apart. After every third word he'd bounce a rubber ball against the wooden plank and catch it before continuing.

"Ms. Blackstone said." *Bounce.* "That it's important." *Bounce.* "For me to." *Bounce.*

It didn't seem right that I'd been the one researching wood but he'd been the first to carve. I'd spent the whole summer sharpening pieces of bark into miniature spears with the only tool Mama deemed safe. But lazy, bass-fishing Cecil had been the first to use a gouge. It wasn't fair, and hearing his three-word descriptions made me furious.

Anticipating the next time he'd drop the ball, I slid forward and waited for him to release it.

"And next week." *Bounce.* "We're gonna—"

When he loosened his grip and the ball began to fall toward the ground, I kicked at the area between his ankles until I felt the ball ricochet off my leg and bounce to freedom.

"Hey! What didja do that for?"

"Making ink prints with linoleum isn't woodworking, so stop talkin' about it!"

"I know it ain't wood, but I still use the same kinda tools you keep hidden in that box under your mama's old bed."

I stood and put my hands on my hips. "How do you know about that box?"

Cecil ignored my question and charged down the porch steps.

"You stay outta that bedroom!"

"I can go anywhere I like while Mama's cleaning." Cecil rounded the porch until he came to the azalea bush where the ball had landed.

"Not after I tell Grandma you're snooping around under the beds."

"I wasn't snooping."

Cecil squeezed between the shrubs and disappeared.

While he rummaged around in search of his treasure, I grabbed Grandma's watering can from behind the fern. "Didja find it?" I asked, as I began to tilt the container over his bowed head.

Cecil shouted "Aha!" and began to straighten up. Three seconds later, the first drops of water splashed the back of his neck. He screamed and grabbed at my legs through the balusters as more water rained down.

I kicked at his arms and turned the container upside down. "That's for messing with my stuff!"

Cecil abandoned his previous route and began to climb the railing.

"You're gonna pay for that, Amanda Reyes!"

I threw the can at him and ran as fast as I could through the living room and into the kitchen, hoping to find Radella cleaning dishes and watching her shows. The kitchen was empty, so I pushed open the screen door, raced across the side porch, and jumped down the steps. Unfortunately, as both my feet made contact with the earth, Cecil rounded the house and lunged for me. I stumbled and fell as I pushed him aside with my right arm and tried to break my fall with my left.

As my palm pushed into the ground, something snapped midway between my wrist and elbow. I screamed in pain, but Cecil thought I was yelling to be set free, so he kept me pinned to the ground with his shoulder while he poked at my ribs with his free hand. When he realized I was crying for help, he sat up. From somewhere inside the house, Radella heard my cries and charged down the steps toward us.

She was thick around the torso but held up by long, thin legs that grabbed at her skirt as she ran. Pain flashed through my arm, but as I watched Radella fall to her knees in front of me the pain eased a little. She examined my arm and in one strong motion lifted me from the ground and carried me back toward the house.

"You gonna be okay, baby. You gonna be okay."

She placed me on the counter near the sink and told me to let go of my arm so she could see. Loosening my grip made the pain worse, so instead of letting go, I began to cry and squeeze tighter.

Cecil stood near the door looking panicked long after Radella asked him to explain what happened. Finally, he told her we'd fallen.

"You grabbed me!" I yelled between sobs.

"It was an accident."

Radella opened the counter drawer and pulled out the phone directory. She pushed the pages around, flipping them back and forth several times before Cecil offered to help.

"Find the number for Dawson's garage."

Radella stroked my hair and shoulders until Cecil found the number.

"All right, dial the number and hand me the phone. I'm gonna see if Sam and Ms. Etta are still at the shop. You know where your mama and Mr. Karl are?"

"Penelope...piano," I sniffled.

Cecil picked up the receiver and stretched the cord until it reached Radella.

"It's okay, baby-girl. We'll get someone here who can take you to have your arm looked at," she said.

Seconds later, she was talking to someone and explaining what had happened. When I heard Grandma's voice on the other end of the line, I started to cry again.

Radella wiped my face with the palm of her hand and pressed my face to her shoulder. "They're on their way, baby. Don't you worry."

Cecil backed out of the kitchen but stayed on the porch where he could still hear.

"He didn't mean to hurt you," she said once I was all cried out. "That boy would never mean to hurt you."

"How much longer 'til they get here?" I asked, watching Cecil's shadow next to the door.

Radella let go of me and hurried to make an icepack. "It won't be long. I bet they're already on Frankfort. If we're quiet, we might hear your grandma yellin' for Sam to drive faster."

"Is it broken?" I asked.

Radella lifted me from the counter and eased into a chair with me on her lap. "Might be. Doctors will know."

"Are they gonna give me a shot?"

Radella moved the ice pack and held it between my arm and her belly. "I don't know, but don't worry 'bout that now. You just be real still. They gonna be here soon."

I nodded my head and tried to fight back another round of tears. My arm hurt enough already. I didn't want them jamming needles into it.

"Radella—" I adjusted my weight and repositioned my head beneath her chin. "Why can't you read?"

Radella turned her head. "Sometimes I have a hard time with letters, is all. And when I'm in a hurry, they jumble worse."

I flinched at the pain and saw that my arm was beginning to look fat.

"Did you go to school?"

Cecil moved a little outside the door.

"Oh, sure, I went to school—I just wasn't very good at it. When my daddy got sick, I stopped goin' so I could take care of him."

"How old were you?"

Radella smiled and rocked. "I wasn't much older than you, I guess."

"Is that why you work here instead of at a real job?"

"This is a real job, baby-girl. Matter of fact, this is a real *good* job. If it was good enough for Sam's mama, then it's good enough for me."

"I meant—"

Radella kissed me on the forehead and patted my knee. "I know what you meant."

Cecil opened the door and called in to us. "I think they're here."

Radella set me on the open chair and hurried onto the porch. I could feel Cecil looking at me and could tell he wanted to say something. He stepped toward me, but when we heard Grandma and Sam get out of the car he ran through the house in the opposite direction.

Grandma rushed into the kitchen. She looked at my arm, asked me to move my fingers, and told Sam to help me to the car. Not long after, we were pulling into Helen Keller Hospital, where my parents were already waiting.

Daddy lifted me out of the car and carried me inside.

"What happened?" Mama asked as she raced alongside us.

"I fell."

"From what, the roof?"

"No, Cecil tried to grab me and I fell."

Mama's face turned red. She looked at Sam, then back to me.

"What do you mean, he grabbed you?"

I suddenly realized I could get into trouble for pouring water on Cecil's head, so I hid my face in Daddy's shoulder. We went through the waiting room and down a long hallway.

Mama and Sam were having an argument by the time Daddy pulled back a blue curtain and placed me on the gurney. He told a nurse what he knew about my fall, and she told me to move my fingers and bend my wrist, which was hard, but I did it.

Grandma tried to stop Sam and Mama from fighting.

The nurse smiled and asked me something I couldn't hear because of their arguing. The second time she asked the question, everyone got really quiet and looked at me.

"Do you want me to ask these people to leave?"

Everyone looked surprised at whatever she said, but I still didn't hear it. "Ma'am?" I asked.

"Would you like for me to ask everyone to leave while I examine your arm?"

I nodded.

The nurse faced the others. "I'm going to have to ask y'all to go. I'll send someone to the waiting room to let you know what the x-ray shows."

Mama stepped forward and placed her hand on my shoulder.

"I'm not going to leave my child here alone." She turned to Daddy. "Y'all can wait for us outside. I'm sure this won't take long."

"I'm sorry, ma'am, but I can't do my job with all the arguing."

Mama pulled the doctor's stool from beside the bedside table and sat down. "You're silly if you think I'm gonna sit in that waiting area while you do who-knows-what to my little girl. She's been through enough for one day."

Daddy stepped past Sam and Grandma to where Mama was sitting.

"She's certainly been through a lot." Daddy reached for Mama's elbow. "Come on, Tilly, everything's going to be fine—the sooner we let this kind lady get to work, the sooner Amanda will start feeling better."

Mama jerked her arm away. "The rest of you can go, but I'm staying here."

Grandma leaned against Sam and reached down to touch my toe. "We'll be right outside, pretty girl. You're gonna be okay."

"We'll keep watch by the door." Sam smiled at me and took Grandma by the arm.

Mama straightened her blouse and smirked. "If you'd keep watch of your boy, we wouldn't be here right now."

Sam stiffened and clenched his fist. I was scared he might hit her until Daddy stepped between them and leaned down to kiss me. By the time he moved out of the way, Sam and Grandma were gone. Daddy nodded to the nurse and tried to make peace with Mama before leaving.

After the room was quiet, the nurse took a few x-rays. She was nice, but she never once looked at Mama. She acted as if she'd left with the rest of the family.

When the nurse left, I asked Mama about Sam.

"Why are you mad at him? He didn't do anything."

Mama reapplied her lipstick and tossed the tube into her purse before clicking the bag closed.

"It's just not right for him to drop off his son over there all the time. It's one thing for Cecil to be there when his mother's working, but Sam treats my mother like she's *his*."

I put my head back on the pillow. "I think that's because he does feel like Grandma's his mother. She just about raised him, right?"

Mama tugged at the sheets until they covered my bare feet.

"I'm not gonna talk about this anymore." She continued folding and pulling at the sheets until they were tucked in so tightly around my legs I couldn't move. I watched her try to make the room perfect.

"You need some water? I'll ask that nurse to bring you some. Heck, I think you're the only person in the whole hospital anyway. It's not like she has anything else to do."

Mama pulled the curtain until we couldn't see the other bed.

"I'll be right back. I'm sure the doctor will come tell us about the x-rays soon."

She waved at me through the window and went down the hallway.

I was trying to understand why Mama was so jealous of Sam when Daddy came in and sat next to me. He leaned against the bed and pushed my hair away from my face in one swoop.

"How are you feeling?"

"Pretty good. Where'd Mama go?"

"She's talking to Sam and Grandma. She'll be back in a few minutes."

"They're not fighting, are they?"

Daddy smiled and pushed back my hair again. "No, they're okay. Don't you worry about them—they've been arguing for longer than you've been alive. It always turns out fine."

"What's wrong?"

"Oh, nothing. I was just thinking about your arm."

"It's okay. It already feels a lot better."

"What happened when you broke it?"

I bit my lip. "Cecil and I were playing, and I fell is all. It was an accident."

"Why did he grab you?"

"Because he was mad, I guess."

Daddy nodded as if he understood.

"Am I in trouble?"

"No, we're just a little worried because Cecil ran off and hasn't come back yet. Radella's afraid because he's never stayed out this long after dark."

I pulled my arm to my chest and pain shot through my elbow. "I guess he's still upset about the water."

"What water?"

Tears filled my eyes. "I dumped Grandma's water pitcher on his head—that's why he was chasing me."

"Well, did he deserve it?" Daddy laughed and patted me on the knee.

I wasn't in trouble after all.

"I thought he did."

"Do you have any idea where he might have run off to?"

"Sometimes he goes to the cemetery when he's mad. There's a place in the back corner where he likes to sit. Maybe he's there."

Daddy thanked me and went to tell Sam. Seconds later, Mama appeared along with the nurse and a young doctor, who attached the x-ray of my arm to a box on the wall and pointed out the tiny fracture. Mama tried to comfort me by telling me I'd still be able to get my schoolwork done.

But my broken arm would keep me from learning to carve wood for two months. I wanted to cry.

After they set a cast on my arm and let me leave, Daddy took us to pick up Penelope. She was half asleep when he loaded her into the car beside me. Then we dropped off Grandma. The Daws were gone when we arrived, so we knew they'd found Cecil. I hoped he wasn't in too much trouble, since I'd started the whole thing.

I promised myself that the next chance I got, I'd try to make up with Cecil, even if it meant I had to apologize first.

The silent worker is imagination
which decrees reality out of chaos.

HELEN KELLER

Chapter Five

A rain-soaked fall turned into a cold winter two weeks
before Thanksgiving break. I'd gotten used to my cast. I kind of liked
the attention that came with wearing the names of all the third-graders
on my arm.

I was going to apologize to Cecil right away, but he'd stopped
hanging around Grandma's after the accident. We ran into each other
a couple of times at school, but he always pretended to be doing something else when I tried to talk to him.

Grandma said Cecil wasn't coming to her house because he was
helping Sam in the shop, but Radella's sad face told a different story.
I figured it had something to do with the argument at the hospital,
but when I asked Radella about it she acted like she didn't know what
I was talking about.

After another weekend of listening to Penelope practice her violin
in Grandma's living room, I decided it was time to get the apology
over with.

Monday morning, instead of going into the school building after
Daddy dropped me off, I waited in the rain for Cecil's bus to arrive.
By the time it stopped and he stepped off, I was a wet mess.

Cecil pulled his hood over his head and hurried toward the

building. I yelled his name.

"What are you doing out here?"

I was shaking. The rain chilled my body. "I was waiting for you so I could say I'm sorry."

Cecil looked over my shoulder and nodded to a group of older boys as they walked by. When they were gone, his eyes narrowed. "I'm not mad at you."

"Then why don't you come to Grandma's anymore?"

Cecil readjusted the weight of his backpack. "Because you don't want me there—and your mama sure don't want me there. Why would I waste my time with you when I can spend time at Daddy's shop?"

"Well, I think Radella misses you. She looks sad when I get off the bus all by myself. She likes hearing about your day first thing."

Cecil turned to walk away.

"Your mama still fills two glasses of ice every day and puts them in the freezer for us."

Cecil kept walking, leaving me in the rain again.

"She wants you to come back!"

Cecil turned and faced me before going into the building.

"I thought you were waiting out here so you could say you were sorry."

I pushed wet hair away from my face before folding my good arm across my wet jacket. *Why do I have to say I'm sorry first?* The thought made my arm itch under the cast.

Cecil pulled open the door to the building and held it as another group of kids entered.

I followed but stopped before going in. "I'm sorry, okay?"

Cecil smiled a toothy grin of victory. "I'm sorry too."

Cecil got on the bus just before it pulled out of the lot that afternoon. He looked around for a few minutes before he sat in front of me.

When we got to Grandma's, Cecil thanked the bus driver and rushed down the steps. He was almost to the house before he stopped, picked up a rock, and tossed it back at me. I adjusted my pack and hurried to keep up, but with only one arm to balance I looked like a turtle with a loose shell.

Cecil lifted the bag from my back and carried it the rest of the way. Radella pushed open the screen door and kissed us both on the forehead. After we followed her into the kitchen, she got two glasses of ice from the freezer and filled them with Coke.

"'Bout time you two started talkin' again." She put her cold hand on the back of my neck and smiled. "You feel a little warm, baby-girl. You okay?"

I took a sip of my drink before I answered. "Yeah. My backpack's heavy is all."

"Well, you two need to open those bags and get on your homework before you run off."

"You do your homework today?" Cecil asked, smiling up at Radella.

"Yes, I read the whole book over lunch."

"I've been bringing Mama books from the library," Cecil told me. He looked so proud.

"I brought you this one today," Cecil said as he opened the pack at his feet, pulled out a small children's book, and placed it on the table for his mother. A green frog wearing a top hat stared up at us from the cover.

"When are you gonna bring me somethin' that doesn't have talkin' animals?"

"When you can read as fast as me."

He quickly finished his Coke and rushed out of the room with his backpack in hand.

"I said you had to finish your homework before you could run off."

"I'll be right back!"

"That boy is wild. Where's he got to go with his bag?"

I shrugged.

Radella picked up the book from the table and looked through the pages. I opened my spelling book and started copying that week's words into my spiral notebook. Cecil came back and started doing the same thing but with bigger, fifth-grader words. He finished before me and let us know he was done by slamming his book shut and charging out the back door.

I was almost finished when Grandma came home and unloaded several bags of groceries. She kissed me on the cheek and offered me a pack of cookies before Radella put them away. I had one before I went upstairs and shut myself in the bedroom. I pulled the box of Grandpa's woodcarving tools from beneath the bed and lifted the lid. I knew I couldn't use the tools, especially with only one arm, but I still liked spreading them out on the floor and feeling the wooden handles in my hand. My arm had healed, but I still had the cast on. I wished I could use the tools to remove my cast.

I counted twenty-one tools in all. My favorite whittling knife was missing its tip. Daddy promised to have it fixed, but I liked the rough edge and dull blade. I held the tool in my hand like a pistol. I couldn't wait to use it. I wanted to make a rocking horse like the one I got on my birthday, except mine would be big enough to play with.

I put the tools back in the box, closed the lid, and lifted the skirt of the bed to slide it underneath. I pushed the box as far as my arm would go, and just then my hand brushed against something that hadn't been there the last time I'd rummaged through my hidden treasures. I reached for whatever it was and found two linoleum blocks the size of butter plates, only square.

Grandma! She always found a way around Mama's strict rules. I'd promised to hold off on my woodcarving adventures until I was older, but I hadn't said anything about linoleum.

I lifted the blocks to my nose. They smelled so good—like clay and sweet oil.

One of my books on woodcarving had a chapter about linocuts so I knew what to do. I wouldn't be able to make a real rocking horse, but it was a start. I heard the front door slam, meaning Mama was there to get me, so I tucked the linoleum squares under my shirt along with a gouge and chisel. I quickly realized the possibility of gouging out my stomach, so I removed my treasures, hid them beneath the pillow, and rushed out of the room to retrieve my bag from the kitchen. Mama was still standing at the front door, wrapped in a long wool coat, when I bounded down the stairs.

"Get your things, honey, we need to hurry." Mama folded her arms and glared at Cecil as he sat on the floor watching television.

"Yes, ma'am."

I pushed open the door to the kitchen and found Grandma and Radella sitting at the table. In front of them was a mound of green beans and a strainer where they tossed the snapped pieces. I grabbed my backpack from the floor near Radella's feet and zipped it closed.

"Why are you in such a hurry, honey?" Grandma asked.

"Mama's here. We have to go."

"Well, tell her we're in here. I need to ask her something."

"Yes, ma'am."

I started to rush through the doorway again but remembered why I was rushing in the first place. Grandma snapped another bean and tossed it in the bowl as I hurried over to her chair. She smiled as I leaned in to kiss her cheek. "Thanks, Grandma."

"For what?"

I kissed her again, making Radella chuckle. "You know. For everything."

Mama entered the kitchen as I rushed out. "We have to go, Amanda—your sister's waiting for us."

"I just have to get one thing."

Mama yelled for me to hurry as I hustled up the stairs. I dropped the bag onto the quilted comforter and got the linoleum and tools from beneath the pillow. I hid them below my school books, sat down beside the bag, and struggled to catch my breath. Maybe Radella was right—maybe I had a fever. I held my hand to my head to see if it felt warm.

Mama called for me to come, so I forgot about being sick and hurried to the car. Cecil gave me a faint wave before I left but never moved from his spot in front of the TV.

I waited for Daddy to shut my bedroom door and counted to a hundred before crawling out of bed and feeling around for my backpack. The only light came from a nightlight plugged into the outlet by my closet door. I dragged the bag over to the wall and took out one of the linoleum squares and both carving tools. I'd have to work neatly or Mama would discover the remnants the next morning when she woke me for school.

I took a deep breath before pressing the gouge into the tile and removing the first plug. After several pieces were gone, I began piling them near the wall. The process was harder than I'd thought, and working with only one hand made things worse. It took me forever to carve the outline of a rocking horse and even longer to scratch away the area inside its body. Still, I loved every second. He wasn't perfect, but his eyes were happy.

I hid the pile of shavings inside a shoe and flipped through my woodcarving book until I found the chapter about linocuts. Because the book was about carving and not printing, there wasn't much about making prints. Still, one of the photographs showed a man rolling ink onto the board. I needed thick ink and something other than notebook paper to transfer the image to.

Before I fell asleep, I thanked God for Grandma and the gift she'd given me. I knew she'd supply me with ink now that the block was ready.

I fell asleep thinking about how happy she'd be when I gave her an autographed print.

∽ 🐴 ∾

"Child, you're on fire!"

Mama held a cold rag to my head as I slumped over my breakfast. "I'm fine."

"No, you're not. You have a fever. Get back in bed."

I pushed my cereal around in my bowl and tried to force down a sip of orange juice. "I'm fine. I need to go to school."

"Not today, you don't."

"Well, can I go to Grandma's house? She'll take care of me."

Mama ran more cold water over the rag and squeezed it until it was just damp. "Take this and get in bed. Grandma doesn't want your germs."

"But—"

"Go. I'll call the doctor and see what he says."

I snatched the rag from her hand as I pushed my chair away from the table with the backs of my knees. "Can I at least call Grandma?"

"Not now, you can't. Maybe after your fever goes down."

"But I feel fine," I lied.

Mama took my bowl and cup from the table and flung them into the sink. They made a clanging sound against the ceramic. "And stay away from your sister. I don't want two sick kids."

From my room I heard Mama make several phone calls canceling the social events and good deeds that filled her day. The last call she made was to the doctor, who agreed that because of my broken arm I needed to get to his office for an examination.

I knew I was sick either because of my arm or because of standing in the rain while I waited for Cecil. Either way, Cecil was the reason I'd have to miss going to Grandma's house.

I tightened my good hand into a fist and pounded my pillow.

Before I dozed off, I heard Daddy's truck pull into the driveway. He'd gone to work early and seemed unhappy to be returning so soon. Mama loaded Penelope into the backseat of the truck. It seemed unfair—I was the sick one, but Penelope would be the one who got to spend the day with Grandma.

Sometime later, Mama woke me and helped me into the car. She'd made a little bed on the backseat with a pillow and one of the afghan throws from the living room. I stretched across the vinyl as she folded the blanket around my feet.

"You okay like that?"

I nodded, trying to ignore the pain in my throat.

The doctor told Mama I had a virus and sent me to bed for two more days. They were two of the longest days of my whole life. I felt well enough to carve the second block of linoleum but decided not to in case something went wrong when I inked the tiny horse. Grandma and Penelope stopped by a couple of times to check on me, but Mama was always around so I never got a chance to secretly ask for ink and paper.

When Friday morning finally arrived, I was awake and ready before anyone else.

Daddy sipped coffee and read the morning paper while I stood near the kitchen door with my bag. "Gettin' dressed early won't get you to school any sooner, you know."

"I'm not rushin', I'm just waiting."

Mama entered the kitchen wearing her Sunday best with her hair brushed out in perfect red waves. She held Penelope on one hip and a stack of papers on the other. She unloaded the stationery and let Penelope slide onto Daddy's lap. When her hands were free, she adjusted her gold earrings and smiled at me.

"Well, someone must be feeling better."

"I feel good. I better get to school early so I can get busy on my make-up work."

"Don't worry, I talked to your teacher. She said you could finish the work over the weekend. Sit down, we'll take you after breakfast."

"I already ate."

Daddy set Penelope on her chair and handed her his juice.

"Karl, can you take the girls this morning? I told Mary I'd meet her at church first thing so we could finish putting together the programs for the Smith-Jones wedding."

Daddy put down his newspaper. "The wedding isn't until tomorrow. Why do the programs have to be done this morning?"

Mama filled her cup with coffee and fought the glass canister back into position. "Because this is the only time Mary could help and I don't have time to fold and string ribbon through all 400 by myself."

"Don't get upset. I was just asking."

"I'm not upset, I'm in a hurry." Mama took a sip from her mug and lifted the papers into her arms again. "Amanda, I'm going to pick you up after school so wait for me out front, okay?"

"What? Why? I want to go to Grandma's."

"Not today. Janice wants to get all the moms and daughters together for tea at her house."

I dropped my bag to the floor and stomped in protest. "I hate going for tea. Why do I have to go?"

Mama pointed a long finger at me. "Don't you throw a fit. When someone invites you into their home you should accept and be grateful."

"But I don't want to go. I haven't been to Grandma's all week! Please, Mama."

"For Pete's sake, Tilly, let the child go to her grandmother's house. She's been cooped up all week. Let her do what she wants to do for one day."

Mama wrapped a piece of toast in a paper towel and pushed past me. "She's a child. She gets to do what she wants all the time. Today she's going to do this and be happy about it."

Mama bent at the waist until we were both at eye level.

"She's not the only one who's been stuck in this house all week."

The earth seemed benumbed by his icy touch,
and the very spirits of the trees
had withdrawnto their roots,
and there, curled up in the dark, lay fast asleep.
HELEN KELLER

Chapter Six

Jack Frost usually doesn't arrive in Tuscumbia until January, but the fall of 1989 was colder than most winters. If I hadn't wanted ink so much, I might've stayed in bed a little longer on Saturday morning but instead I jumped out of bed at daylight and woke Daddy so he'd take me to Grandma's. Tuscumbia hardly ever gets snow, but sometimes the ground freezes and makes the hills and hollers dangerous without a truck. Still, Mama insisted that she drive Pen and me in her car so she and Grandma could make plans for Thanksgiving.

Grandma served Swiss mocha to Penelope and me by the fire in the living room while she and Mama planned the Thanksgiving feast. I offered to help Grandma with the drinks, hoping to get her alone long enough to ask for ink, but she refused and sent me back to my spot on the floor with Penelope. I sipped patiently as they sorted recipe cards and made a shopping list. When Mama went into the kitchen for another cookbook, I whispered my request to Grandma.

"What did you say?" she whispered back.

I cut my eyes at Penelope and leaned closer. "I need ink."

Grandma coughed several times, closing her eyes and covering her mouth with her hand. "You need what?" she asked after she regained composure.

"I need ink."

Grandma leaned back against the cushions as Mama reappeared carrying several cookbooks.

When my cup was empty, I excused myself and went upstairs. If Mama came in and found me rummaging through the box of tools, she'd hide them away until I was older, so I collapsed on the bed and tried to be content knowing they were only a few feet away.

"Amanda, don't make a mess up there! We're leaving in a few minutes!"

"Yes, ma'am!"

I tapped my fingers on my stomach and stared at the ceiling. *If I could just touch them for a second...*

Quickly, I rolled off the bed and reached for the box. If I hurried, I could take a peek at the tools without her knowing.

My hands discovered the lid first. Someone had removed it and placed it on the floor near the box. When I pulled the container closer, I realized a half-empty tube of red paint and a small rolling pin prevented the box from closing.

I smiled down at my new treasures. *Grandma.*

I heard Mama's voice at the foot of the stairs so I hid the paint and roller in my pockets and returned the box. For the first time in my life I couldn't wait to get home.

On my way out the door, I hugged Grandma and thanked her. She smiled and kissed me on the top of my head. "Sleep well, pretty girl. I'll see you at church tomorrow morning."

Before I went to bed, I found two pieces of white construction paper and hid them in my closet with the linoleum shavings, but Penelope begged Mama to let her sleep in my bed instead of her usual spot on the foldout sofa so I wasn't able to roll the ink and make my first print until Sunday night.

The ink was messier than I'd imagined and filled my room with a yucky chemical smell. I tore the paper into squares and put the inked linoleum and paper between two heavy books. After standing on the book and counting to thirty, I took a deep breath and pulled away the paper. The result was a perfect red square with the outline of a misshaped horse in the middle. Each time I made a print I held it near the nightlight and admired my work. When I'd used up all the paper, I stacked the prints together and slid them into my backpack. I couldn't wait to show Grandma after school.

My hands were sticky and red, so after I hid the evidence, I crept across the hall and into the bathroom. With the door closed and locked, I used my cast to turn on the sink and wash my hands. Even with tons of soap, the color refused to wash away. I scrubbed until my fingertips were raw, but my hands still looked like they'd been soaked in Kool-Aid. Even part of my cast was smudged. I wanted to cry. Mama would know when she saw my hands. She'd know, and she'd kill me.

"Amanda, get up, we're late."

I'd slept with my hands hidden beneath my pillow, and when she pulled back the covers, I held my position.

"You have to get up and get yourself dressed right now."

Mama opened the closet door and pulled a dress off a hanger while I held my breath and prayed.

"Here, put this on and try to find some leggings and boots. It's going to rain again and you'll have to ride the bus today."

"Yes, ma'am."

"Okay, then get up. Do you know where your boots are?"

"Yeah, I'll be ready in a second."

Mama bent down to search the floor of my closet. "I don't see them in here."

"I said I'd find them!" I jumped from the bed and scrunched the pillow with both hands.

"Goodness, what's that smell?"

"I don't smell anything."

Mama looked at the ceiling vent then back at me. "Did it smell like this all night?"

"I don't smell anything."

She shook her head as she grabbed yesterday's clothes from the floor near my bed.

"I hope the heater isn't acting up again."

After she left, I hurried the dress over my head. After I got my socks and leggings on, I pushed both hands into my winter mittens, stretching the left one over my cast. It looked a little strange but would work to hide my stained fingers.

Mama slid a bowl of oatmeal to me as she hurried about the kitchen. "Hurry up and eat. You have to be out front in five minutes or you'll miss the bus."

I took a bite, hoping she wouldn't notice my gloved hands.

"Did you brush your teeth?"

"Yes, ma'am," I lied.

"Child, why do you have your gloves on?"

"I'm cold," I lied again.

Mama rolled her eyes and rushed to put the box of oats away. "That blasted heater. I'll call your dad and tell him to take a look at it after work."

"Where are Daddy and Penelope?"

"Your father took Pen to Grandma's so he could get to the store early. We have to hurry because I told the ladies at the Refuge House I'd be there before eight o'clock." Mama took a sip of coffee. "Okay, time's up. You better go."

"Can't you drop me at school on the way?"

"No, I have to run another errand first and I have a ton to do to get ready for this weekend. No one's coming into this house until

I've had time to clean it."

"This house? Who's coming here?"

"Everyone is coming here. We're having Thanksgiving here this year."

"But we always go to Grandma's for Thanksgiving!"

Mama grabbed my half-eaten breakfast and scraped them into the trash. "I know. We always go to Grandma's for *everything*. That's why I thought it would be nice to start some new traditions."

"But I love going to Grandma's. We don't have enough room to have everyone here."

Mama straightened the chairs around the table until she got to mine. "Get up."

I stood and lifted my backpack over my shoulder with my gloved hand.

"If you don't like this house, then talk your father into selling the furniture store and getting a new job. Until that happens or we win the lottery, you're gonna have to live here just like the rest of us. Now hurry up and get out there or you'll miss the bus." Mama picked up a few crumbs and tossed them into the sink. "After I clean this place, I have to go to Ivy Green. There will be lots of visitors in Tuscumbia this weekend, and no one has done a thing to get Ivy Green ready for tourists. Helen Keller would die if she saw the state her old home is in."

"She's already dead."

Mama stiffened. "Even more reason to keep the place in order."

I drank the last sip of juice as I carried my cup to the sink.

Although Mama knew everything about Helen Keller, I learned most of what I knew from the visits my school made to Ivy Green every year. Every spring, we'd load up on the yellow school bus and spend a whole day running through the grounds and listening to tour guides tell stories about Helen's first words, her teachers, and her love of books. Nothing ever changed except the moon tree. Before I was born, the tree had been planted behind Helen's house. There was something magical about standing next to a tree that had gone to the moon and back.

One day I'll take you to the moon, I thought as I tucked my mustard seed charm inside my shirt and smiled.

Cecil was already on the bus when I got on and sat in an empty seat near the front. I was shoving my mittens into my coat pocket when he switched to the seat behind me.

Cecil leaned forward and stuck his head around the seat. "I helped my daddy fix his truck this weekend. What did you do?"

"Nothin'."

"Come on."

"The usual—Grandma's house and church. Why are you botherin' me?"

"I'm not botherin' you. I'm just askin' how you are." Cecil disappeared behind the seat as I leaned against the window.

"Nice fingers," he finally whispered through the open space between the window and the seat.

I didn't answer. I just curled my hands into fists and tried to ignore him.

"I know what you've been doing."

I took off my coat and shoved it behind my head, filling in the space between us.

"Wow. I thought after all I've done for you, you might be a little nicer," he said as he gathered his things and returned to his original seat.

By the end of the school day most of the ink had worn off my hands. That was good, but stacking the papers while they were still wet had made all the prints stick together. While I waited to get on the bus after school, I tried my best to separate the prints. After the top piece of paper finally came loose, Cecil pushed past me without saying a word.

I was the first off the bus when it stopped at the end of Grandma's gravel driveway. I waited for Cecil to get off, but he continued to ignore me as we walked side-by-side toward the house. I wanted to show him what I'd made but thought I'd better just keep the print hidden inside my jacket. As we walked, I got even more excited imagining Grandma's face when I showed her what I'd made. I put my head down to keep the cold wind out of my eyes and hurried to pass Cecil.

"Hello, young lady."

Cecil walked into me as I froze with one foot on the bottom porch step.

"Hi, Mama." I knew something was wrong by the way she leaned against the column with her arms folded. "I thought you'd still be at Ivy Green." I slid my hand into my coat and pushed the print further inside my jacket before climbing the steps.

Grandma opened the door for us. In the living room, Mama grabbed the bag from my shoulder and dumped everything onto the floor. After the heavy books hit the hardwood, Radella pushed open the swinging door and told Cecil to go to the kitchen.

Mama pushed the books around with her high heel until she uncovered the mound of prints. Despite Radella's command, Cecil stayed next to me.

"I thought I'd find something like this in your bag." Mama picked up the pieces of paper. "Didn't I tell you to wait before you started using those rusty knives? Yet, you've been sneakin' around in your room at night, doing exactly what I told you not to do." Mama tossed the papers onto the floor.

Grandma grabbed Mama's arm. "Tilly, they're just drawings. She's not hurt. Give her a break."

"She lied to me! And she stole too!"

I shook my head as I fought back tears. "I didn't steal, I promise."

"Then where did you get the red ink that spilled on the floor of your closet?"

I looked to Grandma, but she just stared at the floor.

Cecil stuffed his hands into his pockets and rocked back on his heels. "I gave them to her."

Radella stepped further into the room. "Cecil, I said get in here."

Mama looked from Radella to Cecil, then back at me.

"But I thought Grandma..." I said.

Grandma frowned and cleared her throat. "Guess now I know why you've been thanking me so much lately."

Mama bent down and began tossing books back into my bag. "Oh, I should have *known*."

Radella let go of the kitchen door and stepped forward until her knees were parallel to Mama's forehead.

"Should have known what?"

Mama straightened and pushed her hair away from her eyes. "I should've known your boy was the one helpin' Amanda break the rules."

Grandma pushed her way between them and ordered Radella upstairs. "Cecil, go help your Mama finish dusting."

When they were gone, Mama dropped the bag at my feet. "Finish putting everything back in here and go to the car."

I fell to my knees and hurried to put the pile of pencils and wrinkled papers in my backpack. Grandma steadied herself against the back of the rocking chair and eased onto the floor next to me as Mama stormed off.

"I'm sorry, Grandma."

She put her hand over mine.

"Honey, it's okay. Your mama's upset now, but she'll get over it."

Tears filled my eyes and poured down my cheeks.

"No she won't. She never gets over anything."

"She's gotten over a lot in her lifetime, baby. Just tell her you're sorry and give her time."

"All she cares about is the Refuge House and Ivy Green."

Grandma pulled me into a hug and wiped away my tears. "That's not true. She loves you more than you know—maybe more than anyone else in the whole world."

"Not more than Penelope, and not more than Helen."

Grandma cupped my face in her hand.

"I think she loves you more than both combined."

One can never consent to creep
when one feels an impulse to soar.
HELEN KELLER

Chapter Seven

Mama did forgive me but not until after we spent the evening scrubbing red ink from the bottom of my closet. The top of the tube had come loose and gushed ink onto the carpet. After an hour of scrubbing, the floor still looked like the place where something had died. Mama eventually gave up and covered the stain with a pink bathmat.

Thanksgiving came and went with all of us crammed together in the living room. Some of Daddy's family came but didn't stay long after we ate. My favorite part was getting to show off my rocking horses to Daddy's favorite cousin. I still only had the one Grandpa made and the one Daddy gave me a long time ago, but Scooter promised to look for more while he was on the road. I was glad when afterwards Mama agreed that Christmas dinner should take place at Grandma's.

Daddy let me ride with him to pick out three live Christmas trees—one for our house, one for Sam and Radella's, and one for Grandma's. But Grandma refused to keep it and sent us away, saying she preferred her artificial tree. Daddy put that tree in the window of his furniture store and told me I could decorate it, so I got to spend the entire Saturday making paper ornaments and gluing together snowflakes while he helped customers. My ornaments were terrible compared to what the ladies at the Refuge House made every year, but I thought they made the store look more like a home. Daddy told me my tree was probably the reason why he sold more furniture that winter than ever before.

The day before Christmas, he came home carrying a huge gift wrapped with two different manger-scene papers. I knew right away what it was, but I decided to play along as if I didn't.

"What's that? Is it for me?"

"Might be."

"What is it?"

"Can't tell you."

"Is it a car?"

"Nope, but it's almost as fast."

"Is it a desk?"

"Nope, but you can sit on it."

First thing Christmas morning, I tore into the big gift.

Daddy laughed when he saw my face.

"I know you're too big for this type of rocking horse, but someone brought it into the store wanting to sell it and I couldn't resist."

I ran my hand along the plastic glider and pushed on its back until the metal springs squeaked.

"Do you like it?" Daddy put his hand on my shoulder and bent down behind me.

I looked to Mama for approval and was surprised to find her smiling back. Penelope pushed past me and tried to climb on, but Daddy told her I got to be the one to break him in. With one gentle swoop, he lifted me into the air and placed me on the rocking horse's back. The springs cried under my weight but quickly settled.

Daddy smiled. "Where you goin' on that horse?"

I shrugged my shoulders, making the springs sing again.

"No, silly, close your eyes."

I did as he asked. "I'm goin' to Texas."

Daddy whacked the back of the horse. "Giddyup, boy."

I opened my eyes and fell forward. Without my cast, I was able to grab hold of the pale blue handle grips before falling to the floor.

"Whoa, horsey." Daddy grabbed my arm.

"Karl, be careful or she'll break her arm again."

"My turn!" Penelope put her hand on the horse's mane, but Mama pulled her away.

"Hold on, Pen. You can have a turn as soon as your sister gets back from Texas."

Daddy gave the horse a gentle push.

"How's the weather in Texas?"

"It's snowin'! Big white flakes, like feathers."

"In Texas?" Daddy chuckled. "It doesn't snow in Texas."

Mama rolled her eyes and lifted Penelope into her arms.

"There's a big storm today. We better get out of here."

"Head for the border!" Daddy sat on the carpet beside me and put his hand on my foot. "Just keep ridin' until you see the Gulf of Mexico."

I closed my eyes again as he helped bounce me along. "I think I see sand."

"Then you're getting close. Keep riding."

I giggled and opened one eye.

Daddy smiled up at me. "Slow down or you'll be in the waves soon."

"It's time for everyone else to open a gift, Karl."

He slowed the horse to a trot. "You better let this guy have a drink of water while we open the rest of our gifts."

Penelope dumped her stocking onto the floor while Daddy helped me slide from the horse. He winked at me as Mama handed each of us a wrapped package. After everything was opened, we ate cinnamon rolls near the electric heater and loaded up the things we'd bought for

Grandma. The whole time we ate, I stared at the horse and imagined the far off lands we'd travel to next time.

Before we got in the car, I hurried to my room and hid a decorated envelope in my jacket.

Grandma's house was filled with a dozen pregnant women and children I'd never met before, all visiting from the Refuge House on the river. The women all had big bellies that looked like they were about to pop. Mama hugged the woman in Grandma's rocking chair and gently rubbed her stomach. The woman relaxed a bit and nodded. "Won't be long now."

Penelope quickly made a friend while Daddy wandered back and forth from the porch to the kitchen. While they all chatted I went upstairs and took off my coat. The envelope was a little wrinkled so I smoothed it flat again before sliding it under the bed and taking the one I knew would be waiting for me.

In the bathroom, with the door locked, I sat on the floor and unfolded the tiny piece of paper.

Merry Christmas!

I'm sad won't get your letter until after Christmas. Dad says we're gonna visit family in Birmingham and might not make it back in time to stop by. I hear you got your cast off! Is your arm really small now? I read about a man who had his leg in a cast, and when they took it off his leg was smaller than the other one. I hope not. For the 100th time, I'm really sorry about your arm. What did you get for Christmas? I hope you got a lot of rocking horses. Here's a drawing of one just in case. I hope I get a gun so I can go hunting with Dad.

Hope you like it! See you soon.

–Cecil

I laughed at the little rocking horse he'd sketched in the margin. Pretty soon he'd open my letter and find the print I'd saved the day Mama discovered the mess in my room.

The pregnant women were leaving when I finally returned to the living room. Daddy helped them load their things while Mama hung the ornaments the women made for Grandma.

The only thing I knew about the women who lived in the Refuge House was that they stayed there until their babies were born and then went away. I never saw the same person twice. Grandma said that sometimes God gives babies to people who need help caring for them. She said that's why she and my mother help them out until they can leave and take care of themselves.

For some reason, Penelope found it easier to play with those kids than she did her friends at school. Still, Mama was careful not to let us get attached to anyone.

Grandma closed the front door and leaned against the frame. "There are too many people livin' in that house."

Mama hung the last ornament and wiped her hand along her pleated skirt. "But they seem happy."

"No, I was there yesterday. Kids are sleepin' on the floor."

"Maybe there should be a rule against bringing children."

Grandma pulled a cigarette from her apron and headed for the kitchen. "If someone gets the flu, they'll all get sick."

"Was that girl sick?" Penelope asked.

Mama removed a package from Pen's hands before she had time to shake it. "No, honey, she's not sick."

"But she said her mama's dying."

Grandma laughed as she steadied herself against the chair. "She's not dyin', she's just carryin' a nine-pound baby around in her tummy. Probably feels a little like dyin'."

I slid across the arm of the couch and fell into the cushions. "How big was I when I was born?"

Daddy pushed open the kitchen door.

"What are you ladies talkin' about?"

Mama lifted me up by the shoulders and sat in the spot where my head had been. "Amanda wants to know how big she was when she was born."

"You were the size of an ape and had as much hair." He lifted his hands and clawed at the air. "When they handed you to me, I thought your mother had given birth to an orangutan."

"Daddy!"

"It's true. You were all fat and red, with a head full of auburn fur."

"What about me? Was my hair red like Mama's too?" Penelope pulled at Daddy's belt. He patted her blonde hair before lifting her into his arms. He didn't answer her question.

Grandma went into the kitchen, leaving my parents to sort through the details.

Mama stood to follow her. "I better help Grandma get dinner ready."

Pen smoothed Daddy's collar. "What kinda animal did I look like?"

Mama left before he had a chance to answer her question.

"You looked like an angel—a little angel fresh from heaven. Your mama couldn't stop holdin' and kissin' you. She hardly gave any of us a chance to get near you, but the second I lifted you into my arms like this"—Daddy flipped Pen over like a baby and shook her until she giggled—"I knew you were my monkey too."

After dinner Pen and I opened our gifts from Grandma. My favorite was a book on how to draw horses. Grandma said all I'd have to do was put rockers on their feet. She was right. I stayed up all night sketching horses and adding half-moons to their hooves.

By the time spring came, I'd gotten pretty good at drawing rocking horses. Finally, by mid-March it was warm enough to sit on Grandma's swing and draw after school. Cecil knew to leave me alone, so he'd sit on the top step and watch the birds return to the yard.

I was almost finished sketching a saddle horse when he broke the silence. "Pretty soon there'll be tadpoles in the creek again."

I erased one of the hooves and started again. "Won't be long."

"This year I'm gonna take some home and watch them grow legs."

"Why would you do that?"

Cecil shrugged. "I think it'd be neat to see somethin' sprout legs. Kinda like watchin' babies grow inside a tummy."

"That's gross. I don't want to see that."

"Well, I do. I might be a doctor one day and help ladies give birth."

I closed my pencil inside my sketchbook. "You're nasty, Cecil Daw. You don't even know what you're talkin' about."

"It's not nasty. It's amazing." Cecil stood and hobbled down the steps. "Matter of fact, I'm goin' right now to see if the tadpoles are back."

"It's too cold. You won't find anything."

"Wanna bet?"

I stood and followed him down the steps. "Sure."

"Okay. If we find a tadpole, I get to look through your sketchbook."

I tucked my hands into my pockets and hurried to catch him. "And if we don't?"

Cecil thought for a second. "If we don't find tadpoles, you can look through my math folder."

I turned and headed back toward the house.

"Okay, okay. You can *have* my math folder."

I stopped and put my hands on my hips. "If we don't find a bunch of half-frozen tadpoles, you gotta do somethin' in front of my Mama that you know she'll hate."

"No way—I ain't crazy. Your mama already hates me."

I laughed and hurried in the direction of the creek. "Well, that's the deal."

We stopped running when we arrived at the edge of the trees. Even if it was too cold for tadpoles, we both knew snakes were nearby. Cecil picked up a branch and jabbed at the ground while we made our way through the woods. He told me about how some frogs lay eggs in the trees above creeks, and when the rain comes the tadpoles drip down into the water. He talked about webbed feet and frog teeth. He talked about everything until we arrived at the edge of the embankment and looked down into the dry riverbed.

There were a few places where the water stood, but the creek was mostly empty except for red sand and flat rocks. I smiled, knowing Cecil had been defeated.

"See, there's not even enough water for a frog to swim. No way there's eggs down there."

As if the clouds had heard me, thunder cracked above us.

Cecil moved along the edge looking for a way to climb down. "There's plenty of water. We just have to see if anything's swimmin' around in it."

"There's nothing down there. I want to go back before the rain starts."

"I'm not hurryin' back so I can get slapped by your mama, at least not until I have a good look."

Cecil grabbed the root of an oak tree and eased his way into the creek bed. I crossed my arms as he tiptoed his way to the first pool of water.

"See anything?" I called as he squatted, resting his elbows on his knees.

Cecil pushed at the top of the water and looked up at me. "Oh, yeah, there's a ton of 'em."

"Liar." The thunder cracked again and a wind pushed the trees around. "Come on. We have to get back."

Cecil clawed his way to the top of the ridge and brushed his hands on his jeans. "You really gonna make me do something you know Mrs. Tilly will hate?"

I warmed my fingers under my arms and smiled. "Mama's not even picking me up today."

We ran toward the house without saying a word. When we were to the place behind Grandma's house where the field stopped and grass grew, I grabbed Cecil by the elbow and bent over to catch my breath.

I was about to say something when we heard Grandma call for us from the back porch. We rounded the side of the house and found her standing with Daddy. "Where have you two been? We've been calling you for fifteen minutes."

Cecil apologized and explained about the tadpoles while Daddy shook his head and ushered us inside. "Sam's having car trouble, so we're gonna take Cecil and Radella by their house on our way home."

Once we were inside, Radella handed Cecil his bag and sent him to the truck.

"What's wrong, Mama?"

"Nothing's wrong, boy. I just wanna get home so I'll know everythin's all right with your daddy."

All life is divided between what
lies on one hand and on the other.

HELEN KELLER

Chapter Eight

After I kissed Grandma, I took my bag from the kitchen table and rushed to Daddy's truck. Heavy drops of rain pounded the hood before we pulled onto the pavement at the end of Grandma's driveway. Cecil sat beside me with his long legs crammed against the passenger seat.   "Whoa, it's coming down hard." Daddy used the back of his hand to wipe the fogged glass.

I held tightly to the green vinyl and peered over Daddy's shoulder to see the road. We moved slowly as rain beat against the windshield, making it impossible to tell the difference between the asphalt and the grassy embankment. Daddy held the wheel with both hands and leaned forward. I could tell he was nervous, but he was still trying his best to keep up the conversation with Radella. She nodded at something he'd said as she pulled her purse closer to her tummy.

"I haven't seen it rain like this in a long time." Daddy readjusted his grip and leaned forward again. "Why don't y'all buckle up, just in case we start slidin'."

Cecil helped me loosen my lap belt and held the buckles in place while I clicked them together. When they were fastened, he tightened the strap for me.

"That's too tight. Are you tryin' to put my legs to sleep?"

Cecil laughed and fastened his own belt.

Daddy stopped at a red light and relaxed his shoulders a bit. Several cars passed through the intersection as Daddy turned the radio dials.

Radella squinted towards the sky. "It'll probably pass through in a second."

Another clap of thunder shook the truck and made me scream. I covered my ears. Daddy turned in his seat and gave me an ugly look. When the light turned green, he eased forward.

"Radella, would you mind if Amanda and I stayed at your house 'til this storm's over? I don't wanna be on the road if this thing turns into a tornado."

"Of course."

"But Mama," Cecil interrupted.

"But nothin', son." Radella apologized for not having a phone we could use.

"I'm sure we won't be there long."

Daddy's tires split the pools of water as he drove.

I was settling in next to the small window when I saw the yellow lights of a truck top the hill in front of us.

Daddy pressed down on the brake as the eighteen-wheeler fishtailed.

Radella screamed and lifted her purse to shield her face as the headlights shifted right, exposing the broad bed of the truck. I looked at Cecil, who was yelling something that I couldn't hear. I reached for Daddy, but Cecil pulled me down next to him in the seat. Tiny pieces of glass flew across my back as the truck pushed Daddy's truck across the gravel. I closed my eyes and screamed for it to stop, but the truck kept pushing and pushing until we jammed against something and flipped.

"Amanda! Amanda!"

Rain pounded against my face as I tried to force my eyes to open. "Amanda!"

A thousand needles stabbed at the back of my arms and neck as my shirt soaked up water from the ground.

"Amanda, please!"

I opened my eyes and saw Cecil kneeling over me. He cried and moaned as he rocked back and forth while patting my hand.

"Daddy?"

Cecil leaned close to me, and for a second I thought I saw him smile. A man fell to the ground beside me and pushed back my wet hair.

"Daddy!"

Cecil moaned as the man forced my shoulders back to the ground.

Cars stopped along the roadside, and people rushed down the grassy hill toward us.

"Cecil, where's Daddy? Where's Radella?" I lifted a bloodied hand to my chest and felt around for my necklace. Nothing.

Cecil closed his eyes and rocked harder.

"Where's Daddy?"

A woman knelt above me with her umbrella. "Honey, everything's just fine. Don't you worry—the ambulance will be here in a minute. You just stay right there."

"Is my daddy okay?"

"Yes, honey, your daddy's fine."

A man wrapped his coat around Cecil's shoulders and tried to pull him away.

The woman leaned closer. "Look at me, sweetheart. Look at my eyes. That's good. What's your name?"

I answered her and tried to move my legs. The man pressed a piece of white cloth against Cecil's forehead, but Cecil never took his eyes off me. As the woman asked more questions, I realized other people were busy working on my legs and feet. After a fire truck tossed red shadows on the trees, a crew of emergency workers rushed to our side.

The woman backed away and whispered something to a fireman as an ambulance skidded to a stop behind the fire truck. I cried as the men loaded me into the back. Smoke was everywhere.

Daddy's truck was upside down and looked half its normal size. Firemen had already pulled a big sheet over the passenger side to block the rain and were using a loud machine to tear at the metal.

"Daddy!"

If Daddy was okay, why wasn't he with me? If Radella was okay, why wasn't she with Cecil? I cried out for answers, but everyone ignored me and hurried to bandage my legs. A short woman with dark hair grabbed my arm and inserted a needle.

Mama was hunched over in the chair beside the hospital bed with her forehead pressed against the mattress when I opened my eyes again. For a second I thought she was sleeping, but then I heard her praying.

"Mama."

She jerked her head back and leaned closer to me. "Oh, baby, are you okay?"

"My leg. My leg hurts."

Mama stood and pressed a button on the wall before kissing me on the head.

"You're gonna be okay. Your leg is broken, but you're okay." Mama lifted the sheet and looked underneath. "You are a fighter, sweet girl, and you've been fightin' really hard. I'm proud of you."

"Where's Daddy?"

Mama straightened the sheets near my shoulders and dropped her face to my chest. As she sobbed, warm tears rolled from the corners of my eyes and pooled behind my ears.

"Where's my daddy? Where's Radella?"

When I woke up Grandma was smiling at me. She was singing and running her gentle fingers along my arm.

When I woke again, Cecil was the one beside my bed. He was wearing black trousers and a white button-down shirt with the sleeves rolled up. He sat with his shoulders slumped and his hands folded together in his lap. Before I spoke, I looked around the room to see if we were alone. I was surprised to find Mama sleeping on the blue couch with her back to us.

Cecil didn't say anything. He just took a folded piece of paper from his shirt pocket and put it in my hand.

I swallowed and tried to speak, but my throat felt like it had been mopped dry. Cecil reached for my water cup but knocked it over and spilled it onto the floor. Mama got startled and jumped to her feet.

Cecil grabbed a box of tissues and hurried to clean the mess. "I'm sorry, Mrs. Tilly. I was just tryin' to help."

While Mama moved around the bed to where Cecil was dabbing tissues at the pond of water, I tucked the note beneath the sheets.

"Don't worry about cleaning it, Cecil—just go find a nurse and tell her we need a mop and another glass of water." Mama turned to me. "How are you feelin'?"

I swallowed and tried to move my leg. "Better."

Cecil hobbled toward the door. When the door closed behind him, Mama sat on the bed beside me.

"Is he okay?" I asked.

"I think he and Sam are havin' a hard time."

"No, I mean, is he hurt?"

"Oh, he's okay. He had to have several stitches, but you're both gonna be fine." Mama adjusted the pillow behind my head. "You're comin' home today."

I blinked back tears. "I don't want to go home without Daddy. Please let me go to Grandma's."

"I understand."

Sam gently lifted me from the car and carried me inside while Cecil held open the screen door.

Grandma had a full table set for us in the living room. "I hope y'all are hungry. People have been dropping off food all day."

Pen came over and touched my hand. "I'm glad you're okay," she whispered before returning to her favorite spot on the sofa.

"I'm sorry, Grandma, but I just want to go to bed," I said.

Before Mama had a chance to argue, Grandma pulled me into a hug and promised to make biscuits for breakfast. I tried to get to the staircase, but Sam lifted me into his arms again and carried me to Mama's old room.

"You okay, baby-girl?" he asked after pulling back the sheets.

"Yes, sir."

Mama pushed her way between us and tucked me in. "You need to get all the rest you can, but if you're hungry I'm sure Sam will bring somethin' up."

Sam tucked his hands into his pockets and nodded.

"No, I'm fine—just tired."

Mama pulled the curtains closed and moved the lamp to where I could reach it. "Sam, can we have a little privacy for a few minutes?"

I waved to him as he left the room.

"If you need me, I'll be across the hall. Just yell if you need to go to the bathroom. I'll help you up." Mama left the room and returned with a glass of water. "Do you need to go to the bathroom now?"

"No, ma'am."

"Then get some sleep, okay?"

I nodded and crossed my hands over my chest.

"Lights on or off?"

I closed my eyes and tried to hold back the tears. "Off."

Mama turned off the lamp. "Pen's going to sleep with me so you don't have to worry about her bothering you. Just call me if you need anything."

I nodded in the darkness.

No child ever drank deeper of the cup
of bitterness than I did.

HELEN KELLER

Chapter Nine

Light came in through a tiny slit between the curtains before I opened my eyes the next morning. Twice during the night Mama helped me to the bathroom. Both times I'd woken up scream-ing, and both times I'd fallen back to sleep crying. She promised things would get better, but she also cried.

In the morning, I heard Grandma and Mama talking in the kitchen but couldn't understand what they were saying. My smocked dress lay on the other twin bed—a reminder that we'd soon bury Daddy and Radella. My leg throbbed, but I ignored the pain and held still, listening to the clang of dishes Radella would never scrub again.

I wanted my Daddy. I wanted to hold him and smell him. I wanted him to make me laugh and tell me things would be okay. If he told me that, I'd believe him.

I trusted Daddy.

Penelope pushed open the bedroom door, smiled at me, and darted off again. I was surprised that Grandma was the one who returned to help me take off my PJs and pull the pink dress over my head. Before we stood up, she pulled me into her chest and stroked my head. She didn't say anything, just kissed my hair and wiped my tears. She smelled like Halston and cigarettes and warm bread.

The church-house was full during the service, but there were only a few people at the graveside.

Cecil sat between Grandma and me in the white folding chairs next to Daddy's grave. The three of us were silent as Mama hugged people and thanked them for coming. When they lowered Daddy's body into the ground, Mama and several family members tossed in roses and whispered sad goodbyes. When it was my turn, I limped over to the grave and tossed the note Cecil gave me in among the dirt and petals.

Actually, what Cecil gave me wasn't really a note. It was a drawing of a horse—not a rocking horse, but a regular horse running through a field near a two-story house like Grandma's.

I think it was his prayer for me. I prayed the same for him.

Grandma seemed weaker as the day went on, so Mama insisted she sit down. I don't think she minded being forced to rest, but Mama had also asked her not to smoke.

Weeks went by, it got warmer outside, and getting around Grandma's house got a lot easier. Because of my injury, the people at school agreed to let me do my work at home. Mama did less volunteering and instead kept busy doing Radella's chores. Grandma appreciated the help, but I think she missed having the house to herself at times.

In the mornings when Mama would leave for her prayer time with the ladies at the Refuge, Grandma would sneak out to the porch for a cigarette while I looked through my carving tools.

Cecil still rode the bus to our house most afternoons and seemed to be getting back to his normal self. Cecil couldn't bring books to his Mama anymore, but he still enjoyed bringing me things.

I was sitting on the back porch watching the evening sky turn orange when I saw Cecil hurrying across the field with a glass jar held to his chest.

"What's in there?"

"It's time!"

"Time for what?"

Cecil removed the lid.

"Don't even think about pouring that muddy mess on me, Cecil Daw."

"I wouldn't do that. It would kill 'em." Cecil held the jar in front of me, reached inside, and removed a small black speck. "Pretty soon these guys will have legs."

"That's nasty."

"They're not nasty—they're tadpoles." Cecil replaced the lid and handed me the jar. "Promise me something."

I frowned as I watched all the tadpoles bump against the side of the jar. "What?"

"Promise me that once those tadpoles begin to sprout legs you'll go to the stream with me to see their friends hop around."

I lowered the jar to my lap. "I can't walk that far."

"You haven't even tried. Come on. You have to leave this house some time."

"I leave this house plenty while you're at school. I go to a different doctor every day, so don't go on thinkin' all I do is sit around."

"I'm just sayin' it would be good for you to stretch your legs."

I pushed myself up from the swing and knocked on the cast on my leg. "How can I stretch my leg? It's in a cast, Cecil Daw—just like my arm was after you broke it!"

Cecil snatched the jar from my hands and stormed down the steps. After he disappeared around the side of the house, I grabbed the swing's chain so I wouldn't fall.

"He's right, you know." Mama pushed the screen door open with her shoulder and stood there toweling off a plate from dinner.

"No he's not."

"He's worried about you—we all are. I'm beginning to think keepin' you outta school was a bad idea."

I eased myself onto the swing and lifted my broken leg until it was horizontal in the seat next to me.

"You were sitting out here before dinner, and now you're out here again."

"I've always done this."

"You used to sit out here and sketch and laugh. Now all you do is watch the clouds change colors."

I crossed my arms and chewed on the inside of my cheek for a few seconds while Mama stood staring at the side of my head. "What do you want me to do?"

"Anything but rot out here on the porch all day."

I thought about my sketchbook and my carving tools. "Can I use my tools to carve something?"

"No."

"Why?" I dropped my leg to the ground and turned to face her.

She stopped whipping the dish and tucked it under her arm like a purse. "Because—"

"Because you're afraid I'll hurt myself? I'm already hurt."

"No. I just think it's dangerous, and on top of that I don't want you to start a bunch of carving projects and forget about the rest of the world."

"I'm not the one busy with a bunch of projects."

"You're not even ten years old, young lady. Don't talk to me like you're eighteen."

"Well, I'm almost ten, and you said I could use the tools after I turned ten."

Mama let the porch door slam behind her after going back into the kitchen. "You keep moping around, and I'll make it eleven!"

That night, I saw that someone had put the jar of tadpoles on my bedside table. After Grandma tucked Pen and me into bed, I lowered myself to the floor and searched the box of tools for another letter.

"What are you doing?" Penelope whispered through the darkness.

"Nothing. Go back to bed."

Pen's feet hit the floor with a loud thud.

"I said go back to sleep."

"Are you okay?" she asked, flipping on the light switch.

I gave up the search and started to get up when Mama opened the door and found me lying on the rug.

"Oh, honey, what happened?" she asked, rushing to my side.

"Nothin'."

"Did you fall?"

"No, I thought I dropped something."

"Like what?"

"I thought I dropped...a pen, but I guess it's downstairs."

Mama grabbed me under my arm and lifted me until I was standing with all my weight on my good leg.

"Why do you have that jar of muddy water in your room?"

"They're tadpoles."

"Frogs?" Penelope asked, leaping back into her bed and making a grossed-out face.

"Not yet. I promise that once they become frogs I'll carry them down to the creek and let them go."

Mama helped me get back into bed. "I think that sounds like a great idea."

Two months later, the bedside table that once held a lamp instead held a twenty-gallon aquarium filled with gravel from Grandma's driveway, a shallow pool of water, and six tiny frogs. I kicked back the sheets and sat up to greet my favorite green friends. Pen's bed was empty, so I wasted no time pulling back the curtains and making my bed.

Mama had sold our house, so my room at Grandma's was finally filled with all of my favorite things. Pen's side was covered with books and musical instruments, and my side was decorated with over two dozen rocking horses.

I placed a few of my stuffed horses on my pillow before leaving the room. The frogs would have to wait for their breakfast until Cecil arrived to help me set them free. Grandma was busy taking homemade biscuits from an iron skillet when I limped into the kitchen.

"Good morning, Grandma."

"Good mornin', honey. How did it feel to wake up without a cast?"

"Great. Where's Mama?"

"Oh, she went to Ivy Green to help get things ready for the festival."

"But she said she'd take me shopping for my birthday gift."

"I'm sure she'll be back in time. Anyway, don't you have plans to get rid of your dreadful amphibians with Cecil?"

"Yes, ma'am."

"You're not going to kiss them before you let them go, are you?"

I made a kissy face and opened the fridge.

"I already poured you a glass of juice. It's on the table with your sister's, but before you sit down go find Penelope and tell her to get in here."

I pushed open the kitchen door and yelled for Pen. Grandma rolled her eyes. While we ate, Grandma chewed a piece of gum and sipped coffee just like she'd done every morning since the day Mama found her hidden cigarettes. Grandma gave up the fight, but I knew she still enjoyed a few smokes while Mama was at the furniture store. I guess she knew she'd have to quit as soon as Mama sold the store. She'd sold our house in no time.

Mama said it was all a bunch of junk anyway and that we'd be better off with the cash than we would a bunch of old furniture.

I missed my daddy.

Cecil and I loaded the frogs into a bucket and hurried down the stairs. I did my best to keep up, but my leg was still weak. Doctors said it would be a while before I was able to run the way I used to.

We rushed past Grandma and Sam as they sat reading the paper at the kitchen table. Pen was waiting for us on the porch when we pushed open the screen door. She jumped from the swing and chased us into the yard.

"You can't come, Penelope."

"Yes I can.

I stopped following Cecil and turned to face her. "No you can't."

"Those are my frogs too."

"No they're not."

"Well, they've been in my room."

Cecil called for me to hurry.

"Go back to the porch, Pen, or I'm going to tell Grandma."

One of the frogs leapt from the bucket as Cecil waited.

"Just let her come." Cecil grabbed the frog and placed him back into the container. "I can't keep these guys waiting forever."

Penelope smirked at me.

"Fine. Let's go."

When we reached the embankment, Cecil used a tree root to lower himself while Pen and I made sure the frogs stayed put. When he got to the bottom, I used a stick to lower the bucket to him. Pen was the next to climb down. The water was knee-deep in some places, but there were still several rocky places where we could stand without getting our shoes wet.

Cecil removed the first frog and handed it to me. "You gotta kiss it before you let it go."

Penelope giggled.

"I'd kiss you before I kissed a frog, Cecil Daw."

Cecil looked away as the frog kicked free and plunged head-first into a small pool of water. Penelope clapped as her amphibian friend pushed himself back to the surface.

When the bucket was empty, the three of us sat together on a fallen tree, took off our shoes, and pushed our bare feet around in the red sand.

"One day I'd like to build a house right there," Cecil said.

"In the creek bed?" I asked.

"Not in it, beside it. Maybe up there near the clearing." Cecil pointed up toward an area where sunlight came through the trees. "One day I'm going to ask your Grandma to sell that piece of land to me."

I stood and waded through one of the pools. "By the time you save up enough money, you'll have to buy it from me."

Cecil tossed a rock at my feet, splashing water onto my knee-length shorts. "I'll just ask Pen for it. She'll probably give it to me."

Penelope was busy pulling pieces of rotten bark from the fallen tree. "Give you what?"

"Will you give me that little piece of land up there so I can watch over all of these frogs for you?"

Pen shrugged her shoulders. "Sure. You can have it."

Cecil tossed another rock at my calves.

I found a large rock and stood on it like a queen. Green moss tickled my toes while sunlight warmed my back. I closed my eyes. It felt good to have my body back—to be restored. I lifted my arms and reached toward the sky. When I opened my eyes again, I found Cecil staring up at me.

"What?" I asked, lowering my arms.

"Nothing."

"If you'd been covered in plaster all year, you'd be doing the same thing."

"I know. It's not that."

"Then what?"

"You're smiling again. It's nice." Cecil tossed another pebble in my direction. "You look pretty when you smile."

People were overwhelmed with amazement.
"He has done everything well," they said.
"He even makes the deaf hear and the mute speak."

Mark 7:37

They laid their treasures at my feet, and I accepted
them as we accept the sunshine
and the love of our friends.

HELEN KELLER

Chapter Ten

June 25, 1996 / Tuscumbia, Alabama

"**A**manda Reyes, you look like a movie star!"

I stood at the foot of my bed with my arms out like a gorilla. "It hurts, Mama."

"What hurts?"

"The beads hurt. There must be a million of them. How am I supposed to look good if I can't put my arms down?"

"I know this dress wasn't your first pick, but it looks fabulous." Mama pushed my arms down to my sides and moved a curl away from my face.

"Can't I just stay in the bathroom all night?"

"No. It's your sixteenth birthday. You're the star. If you hang out in the bathroom, we'll have to join you—and I don't think Billy Mayfree would like that very much."

I pushed my lips out and scratched the top of my knee where the dress fell against my scar. "I don't like Billy."

"Well, he sure likes you. I can tell by the way he gets that meek little grin on his face when you walk in the room. You should give him a chance. He's a good boy from a good family."

"No way."

"Stop scratchin'."

"Now I'm definitely spendin' the night in the bathroom."

"Suit yourself, but if you do I'll tell everyone it's because you have digestive problems."

"Mama!"

"Your choice."

I adjusted my earring and rested my hands on the heavy beading around my waist. "Fine. I think there's only one bathroom in that place anyway."

Mama knocked over one of my rocking horse figurines as she picked up her glass of wine. "That place? Do you know how many people get to have their sixteenth birthday party at *that place*? None. No one has ever had a birthday dance on the Ivy Green stage."

"There's a reason for that."

"Yes, because no one from Tuscumbia ever shared Helen's birthday before, and nobody else's mama gives as much of their time to *that place*."

"No, Mama, it's because no one ever thought it was a good idea to stand outside in hundred-degree heat wearin' twenty pounds of beads."

"Oh, honey, try to smile. I promise you're going to have fun."

I pulled at the white fabric near my chest and tried to loosen its grip.

"And put on a little more lipstick—you look washed out."

She turned to leave.

"Hurry down. We have to go in fifteen minutes."

Penelope sat in a folding chair beside the stage with her violin on her lap. "When's everybody going to get here?" she asked as I plopped down in the seat next to her.

"It won't be long, I'm sure."

Pen ran the bow across one of the strings. "I wish Grandma was here."

I put my arm around her shoulders and gave her a hug. "Me too. I know she'd love to watch you play tonight."

Pen straightened up. "Mama said she'd be watching from heaven."

I looked away so Pen wouldn't see the tears welling in my eyes. "She promised me she always would."

"Then she's probably gonna be singin' along as well."

The thought of Grandma singing with angels made me smile again. "Are you nervous?"

"Nah."

I watched Mama as she rearranged the food tables and directed the caterers. She loved a party more than anything in the world, and this seemed to be the one she'd been waiting for her whole life. The stage really was beautiful. She'd spent the entire week cleaning the set and hanging lights, even though she knew she'd have to take them down before tomorrow night's performance of *The Miracle Worker*. The bad part was that because of all the permanent props for the play, the stage provided only enough room for the DJ. It took Mama weeks to find someone who could assemble a temporary dance floor between the first row of bleachers and the latticed stage-front.

"What song are you going to play?"

"It's a surprise."

When Billy Mayfree rounded the corner, Mama put her hand on her hip and motioned for me to stand up so my dress wouldn't wrinkle. When I stood, I noticed a woman moving in the darkness a few yards behind the top row of seats. I squinted and lifted my hand to my forehead, but when I did she turned and disappeared into the trees. I'd seen her before. She always wore a shade of purple and had her blonde hair pulled in a bun. But who was she, I wondered? And why was she hiding? I wanted to ask Mama, but I was interrupted by the squeal of arriving guests.

Cecil came with a group of senior boys but left before I could say hello. All he seemed to care about was football and hanging out with the team. Sometimes he'd show up on Saturday mornings to take Pen and me fishing, but we'd have to listen to the radio the entire time because heaven forbid he miss a second of whatever sport was being played.

Mama was right. The dance went much more smoothly than I'd expected, and for the first time in a lifetime of Helen Keller-themed birthday celebrations, I had more friends in attendance than Mama did.

Tammy was by far the prettiest girl in school and she knew it, but that didn't stop her from hanging out with me, Megan, and Rachel. We'd gotten pretty tight the summer after seventh grade, when our mamas forced us all to take etiquette classes from a lady in Sheffield. We got in a ton of trouble the day we skipped and went down to the river instead. We would've gotten away with it too, if it hadn't rained. And if I hadn't slipped on the way back and gotten mud all over my fancy dress. That's why they brought me a poncho and rain boots instead of a regular birthday gift.

When Mama brought out the cake, Pen surprised me with a well-tuned rendition of "Happy Birthday." I felt pretty special as everyone sang along. It was a good party. Daddy, Grandma, and Radella would have loved it. Thankfully, Sam was there to twirl me across the make-shift floor a few times.

"Baby-girl, you are sumpthin'. I didn't know you could move like that. Aren't you the girl who was supposed to walk with a limp for the rest of her life?"

I curtsied and winked. "No more limping over here."

"You know, your grandma used to shake her hips like that too."

I laughed. "Really?"

Mama removed the last tray of food from the table as Sam leaned over for another handful. "Less chips, more dancin'," she said before she walked away.

Sam rolled his eyes.

"It's true about your Grandma. When I was a little boy, she'd turn up the radio in the kitchen and dance with me and Tilly until we'd fall out."

"My mama, dancing? Are you sure?"

"Oh, I'm sure. I'm sorry Cecil didn't stick around long enough to learn a few moves from you."

"Me too. It kinda makes me mad."

"Well, we've forgiven him for bigger things than skipping out on a party early, so we'll have to do the same thing this time." Sam patted me on the back and gave me a sideways hug.. "I'm real proud of you, baby-girl. Your daddy would be proud of you too."

"I know," I said.

"I bet he and Radella and your grandma are all lookin' down from heaven and swelling up with joy over the young woman you've become. Just keep on being yourself and everything's gonna turn out fine for you."

"Good morning, birthday girl."

I rubbed my eyes and sat up in bed.

Mama handed me a card. "You don't have to wake up yet. I just wanted to tell you happy birthday before I left." Penelope pulled her covers over her shoulder and rolled toward the wall. "Watch your sister until I get back."

"What time will that be?" I yawned.

"I don't know. I'm returning your dress, then heading to the festival to help the ladies from the Refuge House sell ornaments. You can bring your sister to the festival if you want."

I fell back into my pillow and covered my eyes. "No thanks."

"Okay, but don't watch TV all day."

Pen and I slept for two more hours before we got up to fix ourselves a bowl of cereal.

"What're we going to do today?" she asked, her mouth full of Cheerios.

"I don't know." Spending my birthday with Pen was not exactly what I had in mind.

I stood to rinse my bowl when I heard a truck pull into the gravel spot near the back porch.

Pen slid from her chair and pulled back the curtain. "Cecil's here."

I put my bowl in the sink and adjusted the hot water.

As Pen flung the door open, I removed her bowl from the table and considered whether I should tell Cecil how disappointed I was that he'd left the party early. I didn't look up when I heard his footsteps on the porch.

Pen pushed the screen door open as I washed her bowl. "Good morning, Cecil!"

"Good mornin' to you, and good mornin' to the birthday girl."

"You didn't seem to care that I was the birthday girl last night."

Cecil leaned against the doorframe. "You mad at me?"

"Did your daddy send you?"

"No, I wanted to bring you this." Cecil stepped toward me and held out a tiny package.

"Apologies don't come in little packages, Cecil Daw."

"Okay, I'm sorry. Now open it." Cecil pushed the package across the counter.

I tore off the polka dot paper as Pen waited excitedly.

"What is it?" she asked after watching me fumble with the paper.

Cecil winked at Pen as I removed a gooey purple lure.

"Gross."

"It's not gross. Matter of fact, the big fish we're gonna catch will think it's pretty yummy—'til the hook we'll add snags his big lip." Cecil made a fish-face at Penelope.

"You got me a purple worm?"

"But that's not all." Cecil snapped his fingers above his head before darting from the kitchen.

When Pen and I got outside all we could see of Cecil were his legs and feet dangling over the side of his truck.

"I also got you this." Cecil jumped back down and held out a long pole as if he was a knight presenting a sword. "Your very own fishin' pole."

"I already have a fishing pole."

"Not like this, you don't." Cecil climbed the steps two at a time and hurried to show me all the special features.

I pretended to be amused as he flipped the line-release and cast into an imaginary lake.

"Well, are you going to take me fishing?"

Cecil dropped the handle grip to the ground and gently held the thin end of the rod out to his side. With a grin, he opened his arms. "All day if you want."

Penelope smiled and let the screen door close behind her. "Gotta take me if you go. Mama said."

At the edge of the pond, Cecil lowered his tackle box to the ground. Seasons of drought and fungus had taken its toll on the water. I couldn't imagine how anything could live beneath the surface of green slime that ran from the shady spot where I sat to the place on the other side where Pen was busy chasing a grasshopper.

Before long, I was ready to give up.

"We're never going to catch anything here. I thought you were taking us to the river."

"Are you kidding? There are huge fish out here. My daddy caught a six-pound bass once."

"That's not true."

"It is true. I bet there are even bigger ones still around."

"Then how come you two never fish here anymore?"

Cecil shrugged his shoulders and plopped down next to me as he fiddled with the lure. "I don't know. I think it's still kinda hard for Dad to be here—especially now that your grandma's gone."

"He's probably afraid Mama will run him off."

Cecil cast the line into the water.

When the spool was set, he handed it over to me. "I'm afraid your mama will run *me* off."

I nudged him with my shoulder. "Well, I say that you can fish this lake anytime you want—as long as you take me with you."

Cecil pulled his knees to his chest and folded his arms around them.

"The ground's kinda hard. You want me to find somethin' for you to sit on?"

"No, I don't mind."

Cecil rested his chin on his sleeve and watched me reel.

"Am I doing it right?"

"Perfect."

When the bait clanged against the tip, I turned and found Cecil watching me. Not watching me fish but watching me move.

"What?"

"Nothing." Cecil blocked the sun from his eyes and looked toward the horizon. "I was just thinking about last night."

I opened the bail and made a wimpy cast into the mud.

"About what? About leaving before you said a word to me?"

Cecil took the rod from me and worked carefully to clear the backlash.

"No. I was thinking about how pretty you looked in that white dress."

"If that's what you thought, why'd you leave?"

"Jealous, maybe."

He made another cast and smoothed the line between his fingers.

"Jealous? Why?"

"I don't know. I guess because when we were kids I didn't have to fight for your attention. Now I have to share you with everyone else."

Cecil made another cast and handed me the rod.

"I feel the same way about you and your football buddies."

Cecil lifted the tip of my rod before brushing his hands on his jeans and calling for Pen to stay close.

"Then why don't you spend some time with just me?" he asked.

"What do you mean?"

"I mean like without our parents, or Pen, or our friends. Like we used to do when we were kids. How about we go for a walk together—just the two of us?"

"A walk? Where?"

"Down by the creek."

"No way. There are too many bugs and snakes down there."

Cecil stood up. "That's not what you used to say when we were kids."

"I'm a lot smarter now."

Cecil took my hand and pulled me up. "Please. Just walk with me."

I tried to hide the burning in my cheeks by spinning the line and stepping closer to the water. "When?"

"Tonight."

"I'm sure not going to the creek at night."

"Come on, it'll be fun. I'll bring flashlights."

"And there's no way my mother will let me go anyway."

Cecil slammed the tackle box closed and flipped the latch. "Then don't tell her."

"You're asking me to sneak out with you and wander around in the woods at night?"

"No, I'm asking you to be with me when no one is around to interrupt."

Cecil put the box in his truck and closed the tailgate.

I fastened the hook to the pole and followed him.

"Why are you angry? You have all of my attention now."

As if on cue, Pen ran up to us and held out a fist full of grasshoppers.

"Look! Can I use these to catch a fish? I bet a fish would love these."

"Toss them in the water and see what happens. If a fish jumps, we'll use live bait next time."

When she was gone, Cecil helped me put my rod with the others.

"Let me think about it, okay?"

"Okay."

"If I do decide to meet you, what time will you be waiting for me?"

"I'll wait for you near the cemetery at midnight. If you don't show up, I'll understand."

80 🐎 ○8

Mama didn't get home until almost midnight. I pretended to be asleep when she came in to kiss Pen and me goodnight. When she put her lips to my cheek, I breathed in the sweet smell of alcohol. It didn't take long for her to stumble to her room and fall asleep, but it was already one o'clock in the morning when I finally summoned enough courage to tiptoe through the kitchen and out the back door.

I swallowed hard and started toward the cemetery when I noticed something move in the darkness near the oak tree. "Cecil?"

"I thought you weren't coming." He moved toward me.

"Mom didn't get home until late. I thought we were meeting at the cemetery."

Cecil took my elbow and pulled me into the shadow.

"I waited for over an hour. When you didn't show, I walked over here to make sure everything was okay."

"I'm fine, but I really don't want to go to the creek."

"There's nothing out here to be afraid of. Just walk with me to the top of the hill so we won't have to whisper. You'll still be able to see the house."

I glanced back toward the porch light as Cecil knelt down and gathered several things into his arms.

"What's all of that?" I asked as we made our way through the darkness.

"I was afraid I wouldn't get you any farther than the yard, so I brought something for us to sit on."

"Did you bring a flashlight?"

"Yeah, but we don't need it. Just stay close to me."

A breeze shifted and filled the air with the earthy smell of Cecil's cologne. I followed closely, amazed by how fearlessly he moved across the abandoned furrows. When we made it to the open space between the creek and the house, Cecil spread the blanket across the ground and sat down.

"Are you thirsty!"

Cecil emptied the contents of a canvas sack, revealing a flashlight, a couple of canned drinks, and a small notebook and pen.

"What's all of this for?"

"The beer is to drink." Cecil flipped on the light but immediately turned it off again.

"The paper is so I could write you a letter and hide it under your bed if you didn't show."

"And how exactly did you plan on getting into my room?"

"It's easy. You sleep harder than you think." He waited for the thought to turn over in my head a few times before he admitted he was joking. "I promise I haven't been in your room in a long time, although I miss your letters."

"I miss yours too."

"Then how about we start writing again? You can tell me about your day, and I'll write to you about mine."

"What happens next year when you're at college?"

I watched Cecil's silhouette change against the distant backdrop of forest as he looked up toward the stars. "I promise I'll keep writing." Cecil opened a beer and held it out for me.

"You know I don't drink."

"You will when you get to be my age."

"I hope not. There's enough drinking going on at my house these days."

Cecil took a sip. "Your mom's having a hard time?"

I nodded.

"Okay, then I won't drink either." Cecil turned the can upside-down and let the earth drink the rest. "Let's just talk."

"About what?"

"Tell me what you think about when you're drawing all those rocking horses."

"Nothing, I guess."

"Come on. You have to think about something."

"Sometimes I think about the future and what I'll do when I get old enough to leave this place and finally start making horses of my own."

"Why do you have to leave before you start? Most people start before they leave."

I shrugged in the darkness and pulled my knees to my chest. "I think Mama would rather me do something else with my free time."

Cecil was silent for several seconds. "Do you ever think about anything else?"

"I think about God."

"God?"

"Yeah. You know. It's like when I'm drawing sometimes I can hear Him better."

Cecil started to open the second can but stopped short. "What does He say?"

"I don't know. Nothing really."

Cecil laughed. "Yeah, I've had that same conversation with Him, several times. He never says anything to me. I don't think He likes to be bothered."

"Maybe He's just not that into football."

Cecil shoved my shoulder so hard I almost fell over in the dirt. "Very funny."

We spent the next hour talking about school and friends. Cecil admitted he was afraid to go off to college and leave his father behind. He told stories about things I'd forgotten. And he told me other things I was certain he'd never shared with anyone else. I wanted to ask him about the night of the accident. I wanted to know what he'd seen, but in the end I decided to save my questions for another night.

Cecil walked me all the way back to the porch and waved as I slipped back inside.

The fishing pole had been an okay gift, but spending the night with my best friend had been the best gift ever. As I tucked myself in between the sheets, I thanked God for Cecil and for all the things He'd brought us through.

I walked in the stillness of the night,
and my soul uttered her gladness.

HELEN KELLER

Chapter Eleven

Cecil and I met on the hill three more times that summer. We'd lie on our backs and talk about our dreams. He knew the secret longings of my heart and agreed I should make rocking horses even if my mother thought I should give it up.

"It's your life, and you should do what's on your heart."

"But no one's ever made a living by piecing together rocking horses."

Cecil fell back on the blanket and folded his arms behind his head. "Maybe that's because no one's ever tried."

I smiled in the moonlight and pushed myself up on my elbows. "There's probably a good reason for that."

"Have you told your mama you want to take shop class next year?"

"No, and I don't think I'm going to."

"Not going to take the class?"

"No—not going to tell her. It'll be Christmas before she figures out I'm the only girl playing with electric saws during third period."

Cecil swatted a mosquito and sat up again.

"I don't understand why she won't encourage you."

"Me neither, but I think it has something to do with my grandfather."

Cecil pulled apart a blade of grass and tossed it on the ground near his feet.

"Maybe one day she'll understand you the way I do."

I took in a heavy breath and tucked a loose piece of hair behind my ear. "I hope so."

Cecil and I agreed to pass notes through the owl hole in the old oak tree. That way we wouldn't have to worry about Mama or Pen finding them. When Mama wasn't around, I'd carry a note out to the tree and place it inside the hole. Then, sometime during the night, Cecil would take the note and leave one behind for me. The exchange became easier after our yard man quit and Mama agreed to hire Cecil to mow. Mama knew Cecil wouldn't do a very good job of mowing and raking leaves, but she was willing to help Sam bring in extra cash.

Cecil's landscaping abilities proved to be lacking but not because he couldn't do the work. He didn't do well because he spent the whole time making faces at me while I watched from the porch swing.

After he went home I knew I'd find a new letter in the tree—just like he knew he'd find one when he arrived.

In the fall, Cecil started slipping notes into my locker. He wrote to me about football plays I didn't understand and his excitement about upcoming games. On Friday nights I'd stand alone at the game with my fingers woven around the metal fence. I watched his every move and prayed the way Grandma used to pray for us. And it worked too. God protected Cecil and kept him strong all the way to a 9-0 season, making Deshler High School the fourth-ranked football team in the region, with a chance to win the state championship.

The week before the semi-finals, I curled up in Grandma's chair to study for a history test. I had just started reading when I heard a truck ease to a stop near the front of the house. I put my books on the floor and stretched my legs. Through the window I could see it was Cecil's truck.

"When did you start parking out front?"

Cecil smiled as he climbed the porch steps. "Just thought I'd try something new this time."

I kept the screen door closed between us, embarrassed that I was wearing sleep pants and an old T-shirt. "I'm studying for a test."

Cecil stopped at the door and looked down at me through the screen. "Can I come in?"

I swallowed. "No one else is home right now."

Cecil turned and headed back toward his truck.

"Wait."

Cecil stopped on the bottom step and faced me as I pushed open the door.

"Of course you can come in. Are you thirsty?"

Cecil removed his ball cap and jacket before sitting at the kitchen table. I placed two chilled glasses filled with ice in front of him. He nodded as he wrapped a strong hand around one of the glasses. "You still do this?"

I popped open a can of Coke and divided the contents between us. "You mean freeze ice-filled glasses?"

"Yes, just like Mama used to do for us after school."

I pulled my chair away from the table and sat. "I still freeze one for you and one for me, but Penelope drinks from yours a lot."

Cecil lifted the glass to his lips.

"You okay?"

He put the glass back down and dropped his chin until all I could see was the top of his head.

"What's wrong?" As I moved to touch him, he slid from the chair and put his face on my knees. I couldn't tell if he was crying, but it was obvious he was upset. In all of our nights on the hill, he'd never come close to touching me. The feeling both excited and frightened me. I cautiously put my hand in the spot between his shoulder blades and felt his heart quicken. "Are you nervous about the game?"

"It's not the game." Cecil lifted his head and slid my chair across the floor until I was almost on top of him. "It's you."

I swallowed hard as he rose to his knees and pushed my hair away from my shoulders.

"I can't think about the game because I can't stop thinking about you. How am I supposed to go off the college knowing that you're here? It doesn't matter how often you write, it won't be enough."

I closed my eyes and tried to breathe.

"Amanda, I've loved you my whole life. I don't think I can leave."

"You have to go. I promise—"

Cecil rested his head on my shoulder. I swallowed and felt his lips near my neck, then my ear. "Promise you'll wait for me? You'll join me when you finish school?"

I closed my eyes and breathed in his cologne. I'd wanted him to kiss me a thousand times, but I knew it would change everything between us. We weren't kids anymore, and as much as our families cared for each other, they wouldn't like us being together.

Cecil squeezed the back of my shirt and let the tip of his nose touch mine. "Amanda, if I kiss you, are you gonna stop sitting with me at night?"

I felt his heart pounding in his chest as he pulled me closer but I didn't say anything.

Cecil let go of my shirt and lifted my face to his with both hands. He was gentle at first, allowing me time to relax and find a way to kiss back. I gasped as he slid me off the chair and onto his lap but relaxed again as his kisses softened. I wanted to stretch over him—to cover him and kiss him until Mama came home and found us in each other's arms.

I was surprised at how comfortable I was in his arm. "Cecil, you have to go."

He kissed my neck again. "Please."

I stood and pulled him up with me. "You've got to go. Mama will be home soon."

Cecil stepped toward me and wrapped his arms around me again. "One more?"

Before I could answer, his lips were pressed against the corner of my half-opened mouth. "I love you, Amanda Reyes. I always have, and I always will."

When Mama and Pen came home, I was in bed, pretending to read.

"Amanda!" Mama called from the bottom of the stairs. "Come down if you're hungry. I brought you somethin' from the Refuge."

"No thanks, I'm fine." I pressed the book to my chest and imagined the kiss one more time.

Pen opened the bedroom door and pulled her violin case from under her bed. "You missed it. There's a woman at the Refuge House who can play the cello like an angel. Mama said she can teach me. I'm goin' over there after school tomorrow so we can play together."

Pen opened the case and frowned at me. "What's wrong with you?"

"Nothing. I'm just tired is all."

Pen lifted the instrument to her shoulder and pushed out a wretched note.

"Don't do that in here."

"I have to practice."

"Fine—just not in here."

Pen made a face before continuing to play.

"Just go downstairs and practice. I'm trying to read."

Pen continued to play as she paced the floor.

"Leave, Penelope!" I flung my pillow at her. Pen tossed her violin onto her bed and stormed off.

In the quiet of the room, I pulled the covers over my head and imagined Cecil's lips against mine again, his hand on my back. I wished I hadn't sent him away so soon. I wondered when we'd be together again.

On November 22, the Friday of the semi-final football game against Cleburne County High School, all of the kids left early so they could make the three-hour drive in time to see kickoff. Mama knew I was afraid to drive, but she refused to let me ride with my friends which meant I had to endure the ride with her and Pen.

When we finally arrived, the parking lot was filled with screaming, half-painted Deshler students. I saw Rachel and Megan and said hi but hurried off to the edge of the field so I could see the team warm up.

Cecil seemed nervous. I watched as he ran between rows of players, stopping every few feet to yell something at a cardinal-colored helmet. I closed my eyes to pray but felt someone leaning next to me on the fence.

"Don't worry, baby-girl. That boy's gonna be fine."

"You think we're gonna win?" I asked Sam.

Sam chuckled and looked up toward the stadium lights. "Now I don't know about that. All I know is, either way he's gonna be fine."

I gripped the chain-link fence and rested my chin on my gloved hands. "I just want God to keep him safe."

Sam nodded. "Next year's gonna be a lot rougher than this one. He'll be up against boys twice his size at Jackson State."

I let go of the fence and tried to make sense of what Sam said. "Jackson State?"

Sam slid his hands into his pockets and rocked back on his heels.

"I thought you knew. Cecil left the house a few days ago determined to tell you."

I guess he forgot to mention that while he was kissing me.

"He's gotta go to college, baby. Might as well go somewhere where he can play ball. Jackson offered him a scholarship and promised to find someone to help with his classes. You should be proud of him."

"I am." There was no way Mama would let me go to Mississippi to see a college game at an all-black college.

Sam put his hand on my shoulder. "Amanda."

I watched Cecil hug a teammate, patting him hard on his back. "Yeah? I mean, yes, sir?"

"You in love with that boy?"

I wiped my chin with a cold sleeve and ignored his question.

Sam slipped his hand back into his pocket and scanned the crowd. "Oh, Lord."

"I'm not, okay? I'm not. It's just that he's like a brother to me. I'm just upset because my brother is leaving."

"I'm gonna kill that boy."

My cheeks flushed and the need to run like I did when I was a girl returned. "He hasn't done anything wrong, Sam. He hasn't!"

I heard the crowd hush as I darted toward the darkness behind the bleachers. After I'd run as far as my legs would allow, I nestled into a dark corner of Cleburne's baseball field where I could still hear the game and see the scoreboard.

The game seemed to go on forever, and not just because I'd sat with my back against the left-field fence all night. No one scored during the entire first half, but Deshler gave up seven points during the third quarter. They tried to come back, scoring six points during the fourth, but missed both field goal attempts. I knew Cecil would be heartbroken.

When the crowd thinned, I found Mama and told her I was ready to go.

"Where have you been? And why is there dirt all over your new jacket?"

"Sorry."

"I've been lookin' for you. Penelope's been ready to go for an hour. Sam said you were upset about somethin'."

I walked ahead of her. I just wanted to get to the car.

"Get back here when I'm talkin' to you!"

"Mama, please. I said I'm sorry. Let's go."

"First tell me what happened."

"I'm just upset we lost."

Pen took my hand. "Are you sad because of Cecil?"

"No." I pulled her toward the car. "I'm upset because football's over."

"The announcer said Cecil's gonna play next year. I'm gettin' his autograph before he's famous."

Mama smirked at me across the hood of the Oldsmobile. "Yep, he's gonna be a big star in Jackson."

I buckled into the passenger's seat and leaned against the door. "What's that supposed to mean?"

"Oh, nothin'." Mama shook her head as she turned the ignition. "I just think it's ridiculous that Sam's gonna let that boy run off to a second-rate college just so he can watch him play ball for a few more years."

"Cecil *wants* to play football, Mama. Sam's not making him."

"Cecil's a kid. It'd be better if Sam made him hang up his helmet so he could get an education and a real job."

"But they're giving him a scholarship."

"Yes, and with it will come half a degree and a body full of broken bones." Mama put the car in reverse. "Sam should know better. He made the same decision when he was Cecil's age—whole lotta good it did him."

"What are you talkin' about? Sam seems perfectly happy at the hardware store. He complains less about his job than you do about volunteering."

Mama slammed on the brakes and turned to face me. "Hold on for one second! I don't complain about what I do—*you* complain about what I do. I'm perfectly content with how I spend my life, and I'm sorry if that bothers you. I do a whole lot of good for a whole lot of people, Amanda. If you weren't thinking about yourself all the time, you'd realize that."

I rubbed my eyes until they burned and muzzled a scream with my scarf.

"Let's just find a place to eat. I think you girls will feel better after you get some food in your stomachs."

Mama stopped at a diner just short of Birmingham and finished two glasses of wine before the waiter brought us our food. When he offered a third glass, she accepted.

"If you drink another glass, I'm gonna have to drive home. Please, Mama, I've never driven that far at night."

"Don't worry, honey. I'll be fine. I'm just tryin' to take the edge off after an intense game." Mama took a sip of water and chased it with a mozzarella stick. "Sorry about what I said back there. I'm sure Cecil's makin' a fine decision. He played pretty well tonight, didn't he, Pen?"

My sister nodded.

"Did you even watch the game, Amanda?"

I shrugged. "Some of it."

Mama tossed another bite into her mouth. "Well—" She swallowed. "I better not find out you were under the bleachers with Billy Mayfree."

Pen stopped chewing and waited for my response.

I wanted to crawl to the bathroom and throw up. Nothing was further from my mind than Billy.

"What is wrong, child? You disappeared for the entire game, and you've been pouting for an hour." Mama wiped her mouth, tossed her napkin into her lap, and motioned for the waiter to bring the check. "My goodness, it was just a football game."

Mama paid the bill while Pen and I went to the car. As I fastened my belt, Pen pointed out the Colbert County school buses parked at the gas station next door. Before I had time to cover my face and slump down in the seat, Cecil descended the stairs and jogged over to us.

I pretended not to notice until he tapped on the window.

As I rolled down the window, the hurt of finding out from Sam that Cecil was leaving subsided.

"Hey." Cecil knelt and rested his arms on the window frame. "I didn't see you after the game. You okay? You plannin' to drive all the way home?"

I gripped the wheel with both hands. "I'm fine. Just sorry we lost."

"Me too, and I'm sorry they made that announcement. I didn't know that was gonna happen. I wanted to be the one to tell you."

"Then why didn't you?"

Pen rolled down the back window and congratulated Cecil on his scholarship. "You promise to still take us fishing?"

Cecil said he would. I looked over at the restaurant and saw a man holding the door open for Mama.

I pushed his elbows away from the door and told Penelope to roll up her window. "You better go."

Mama stumbled toward us, digging in her purse for something. "Cecil? Where'd you come from?"

Cecil pointed toward the buses. "The drivers stopped so we could get something to eat before we head back."

"You guys will probably clean that place out like a bunch of boll weevils." Mama snickered at her wittiness and dropped her purse on the hood of the car. "Oh wait, you have the keys. I thought I lost 'em. Okay, slide over, I'm driving. Sorry about the game, Cecil."

I didn't let go of the wheel.

"Mrs. Tilly, why don't you let Amanda drive? It'll be good for her."

Mama shooed him aside and opened the door a little. "If she won't drive at nine on Sunday, she's sure not gonna drive for two hours on the interstate."

I adjusted my grip on the wheel and swallowed my fear.

Cecil stepped between me and the open car door. "Then I'll drive y'all home. Coach won't mind."

Mama stiffened and tucked her purse under her arm. "You'll get back on that bus, Cecil Daw, and you won't say a word to Coach Mothershed." Mama stepped back and pointed at the bus. "Amanda, scoot over."

"Mama."

"Right now, Amanda."

Cecil rested a hand on the car. "Mrs. Tilly, I'm sorry, but if you've been drinking, I'm not going to let you drive."

"Not going to let me?" Mama laughed and laid a hand on her chest.

I pushed Cecil out of the way and slammed the door shut. "Mama, just get in. I'm fine to drive."

One of the coaches called for Cecil to hurry.

Mama glared at us as Cecil knelt down and put his hand on my shoulder. "You're a great driver, Amanda. Just keep your eyes on what's ahead, okay?"

I wiped my brow and flipped on the headlights.

"Amanda." Cecil pushed my hair from my shoulder. Mama cut through the light in front of the car as she made her way around. "It's not going to happen again."

The coach called for Cecil as one of the buses pulled away.

"Just follow us, okay?"

I nodded nervously. "Okay."

It makes me happy to know much about
my loving Father,
who is good and wise.

HELEN KELLER

Chapter Twelve

Mama didn't say a word the whole way home, even after Penelope fell asleep. I stayed a healthy distance from the bus, knowing Cecil was probably watching me from the other side of the exit door. When the bus turned onto Woodmont, I waved at the darkness and pointed the car toward home.

Mama helped Pen to bed and tucked her in without speaking to me. When the house was quiet for long enough, I tiptoed down the stairs and onto the kitchen porch. A frigid breeze filled the heavy blanket wrapped around my shoulders and chilled me to my socked feet. I was more than exhausted, but something was calling me onto the porch—something deep inside me. I sat down on the swing and bundled the blanket around my legs. Inside my cocoon, I began to warm up again.

The moon looked like a perfect crescent that hung in the branches of the oak tree. I watched the shadows of leaves dance around until the horizon exploded with light, then died to darkness again. Headlights. Someone had turned off the main road and parked in the open field.

I held my breath as I waited.

He was coming for me.

"Amanda, get up. You can't stay in bed all day."

I pulled the quilt over my head and moaned. "Why not?"

"Because you have to help me finish putting the Christmas ornaments away. After that, we have to move all of your things out of your
sister's room. You promised we'd have everything done before New
Year's Day, and now it's two days after."

I quickly remembered our new sleeping arrangements and fanned
both legs out to fully enjoy the large bed where Mama used to sleep. It
took a long time to convince her to take Grandma's room downstairs,
but she'd finally agreed to do it. That meant I could move across the
hall so Pen and I would each have our own space.

Mama pulled the curtains open and busied herself by picking up
clothes and pushing things to the wall with her foot.

"If you're going to stay in here, you have to do a better job than
this of keeping the place up. Gross. What is this?"

I peeked over the covers and found Mama standing at the foot
of the bed holding a half-eaten bowl of cereal.

"You know you can't eat up here!"

"Sorry. It was late, and I was hungry."

I ducked beneath the covers again, welcomed by the lingering
smell of Cecil's cologne. I breathed him in, wanting to hold him again
like I had a few hours before and at least twice a week since the night
of the last football game. My grades suffered toward the end of the
semester due to my absolute exhaustion, but I'd done well enough on
my exams to pull them up before Christmas break.

Mama said something else before slamming the door and
pounding down the hallway, but I was too engrossed in thinking about
Cecil to care. I closed my eyes and imagined his mouth on my neck
again, his hands in my hair. We both longed for the day when the
weather warmed up and we could sit together on the hill and watch
the stars, but the winter air gave us a good excuse to bundle up together

in the back of his truck.

I placed my hand on my thigh and remembered how he'd felt next to me. I moaned at the thought and pushed back the covers. I loved him more than anything in the world, but if I was going to make it through another long day of not talking to him, I needed to get busy helping Mama with the chores.

I reminded myself that when she finally drank herself to sleep, I'd be able to creep back into the cold darkness where I knew he'd be waiting for me. I smiled at the thought and tightened my robe around my waist. Just twelve hours without him—surely I could survive that long.

After Easter had passed and it was warm enough to visit the creek, Cecil packed two lunches and took me on a picnic. When we finished eating, he sat on the fallen tree and watched me kick around in the shallow water. "If you keep kickin' like that they'll never become frogs."

I laughed and kicked water in Cecil's direction, but the spray fell short. "I just like to watch them scatter."

Cecil grinned. "You're getting more on your dress than anywhere else."

I kicked the water again—this time hitting my target.

Cecil wiped the droplets from his face. "Okay, you've done enough damage for one day. Come and sit with me."

"I can't sit. It feels too good out here!" I did a little jig that made him chuckle and shake his head. "Come dance with me."

Cecil slipped off his shoes and rolled up his jeans. "Okay, but just remember whose fault it is when there aren't any frogs to catch in a few weeks."

Cecil put his arms around my waist and kissed me on the top of my head. Tiny pieces of sunlight warmed his shoulder, making a perfect pillow for my head. With our feet in the water, we swayed to the sound of rustling leaves.

"I love you, Amanda Reyes."

I slid my hand into the back of his shirt so I could feel the warmth of his soft skin. "I know you do."

Cecil lifted me into the air and carried me back to our abandoned picnic blanket. I closed my eyes as he eased me to the ground. After he settled beside me, he put his hand on my knee and ran his fingers along the place where my leg had once been broken. "I've always loved you."

I lifted my chin to allow room for his mouth on my neck. "I love you too."

Cecil's hands trembled as he put his forehead on my chest. "Come with me to Jackson."

I lifted his fingers from my thigh and kissed the inside of his palm. "I can't go with you. I have to finish school."

Cecil pulled his hand away and used it to move the strap of my dress. "But I can't leave you. I can't breathe when you're not around." Cecil pressed his mouth to my shoulder and pulled himself on top of me.

"Cecil."

I felt his heart pounding inside his chest, his lips on my shoulder again. He fought to steady his breathing. I could feel his warm breath on my skin. We stayed like that for a long time, with his face on my shoulder and me looking up at the trees. He started to kiss my neck again.

"If you tell me to stop, I will."

I opened my eyes and felt him move against me. I listened to him pant. I wanted him as much as he wanted me, if not more. I wanted to share everything with him.

Cecil lifted his head and kissed me as I ran my hands along the back of his shirt and relaxed against the blanket. When I slowed my breathing, he did the same. When I kissed harder, his breathing quickened.

Another breeze pushed the trees above us. He whispered those words again. "If you tell me to stop, I will."

I didn't.

The day that school ended I wanted to crawl under our latticed porch and die. It was over. I would never see Cecil between classes again. I would never bump into him in the halls or feel him watching me from across the cafeteria. It was all over. After a lifetime of being near him, everything was going to change. As far as I was concerned, everything that mattered in the world had ended. I was alone, with only a few friends, a crazy mother, and a sister I had nothing in common with.

Cecil seemed happy enough—excited about playing football at the college level but not so excited about leaving me behind. When we were together I tried to hide my desperation over losing him, because I didn't want him to feel guilty about leaving. On the inside, however, I felt nauseous and scared.

Cecil worked long hours at the shop with Sam that summer. When he got home after locking up the hardware store for the night, he'd call my house and let the phone ring once to signal that he'd made it home safely.

Mama stayed busy with the Refuge and Ivy Green, and taking Penelope to music practice, so Cecil and I were able to be together during his days off. My drive home from the football game gave me enough courage to drive across town in the car Grandma left to me, so every chance I got I'd sneak off to be with Cecil. He never stopped finding ways to slip notes to me—another treat I knew I'd miss in the weeks to come. When I was certain Mama wasn't looking, I'd wander into the yard to check the tree.

That's how I knew which nights to meet him on the hill.

That's how I knew he'd be waiting for me.

With only two weeks left before Cecil's departure, the pain growing inside me became almost unbearable. I wanted to cry and lash out at the world, but there was no one to share my hurt with. No one knew our secret. I'd considered telling Mama a thousand times, hoping she'd find a way to understand and accept our relationship, but I wasn't willing to risk losing the little amount with time Cecil and I had left. What if she forbade us to see each other again? What if she made us break up? Then I'd have nothing.

The morning of August 6, 1997—a date I'll never forget—I awoke to the distant sound of hammering and Mama yelling.

I crawled out of bed, pulled back the curtain, and looked into the front yard but didn't see anything. I put on a pair of jeans and hurried across the hall to Pen's room, where she sat on the windowsill with her face pressed against the glass.

When Pen saw me, her eyes widened. "Oh, you better come see this."

I hurried to pull my hair into a bun and leaned over Pen. "What's going on?"

Pen laughed.

My eyes took a few minutes to adjust to the sunlight, but when they finally did I was shocked to see Mama standing in the backyard with both hands planted on the hips of her cotton robe. I squinted and leaned closer to the glass so I could see what all the commotion was about.

Mama yelled something toward the hill and waved her hands.

"What's she doing?" I asked.

Penelope pulled at my shirt until I was low enough to see through the oak tree.

At the top of the hill—in our special place—Cecil and several other boys were busy unloading something from the bed of his truck. Mama turned and looked up at us before storming toward the house.

I fastened the last button of my blouse and raced into the kitchen where Mama was tearing off her robe.

"What's he doing?" I asked as I followed her into her bedroom.

"You tell me. I was enjoying a quiet cup of coffee when he and a truck full of other boys tore through the field and set up shop." Mama pushed her legs into a pair of sweats and tightened the drawstring around her waist. "That boy is crazy. It looks like he's building something."

I followed Mama back through the kitchen and into the yard.

"Cecil Daw, what in the world are you doing? Have you forgotten this is private property?" she said.

Without looking up, Cecil slid a heavy two-by-four from his truck, allowing it to fall onto a pile of others as it hit the ground. "No ma'am, I haven't. I'm just settling an old bet."

Mama's eyes widened. "And what bet is that?"

Cecil straightened, adjusted his hat, and grinned at me. "Well, that's between me and Amanda."

I gasped as Mama turned to me. "I didn't make a bet with him!"

Cecil went back to work and signaled for the others to do the same. "Yes you did. It was a long time ago, but you were right—there were no tadpoles in that half-frozen stream."

Mama raised her hands to her hips again. "What are you talking about?"

My cheeks flushed as I remembered Cecil's promise to do something my mother hated if we didn't find tadpoles in the stream that year. I remembered how cold it'd been when he climbed down the embankment to search the water and how our lungs burned after we raced back to the house and found Daddy and Grandma waiting for us.

Cecil wiped his brow and pulled his cap down over his eyes. I felt a sudden tightening in my chest.

"That was the day of the wreck, wasn't it?"

Mama hustled toward the truck and leaned over the side. "Will one of you please explain to me what all of this is about?"

Cecil opened the aluminum bed-box and removed a tool belt. As he fastened the heavy belt around his waist, I slid in behind him and put my hand on his back. "What are you doing, Cecil?"

Mama tightened her jaw and scanned the faces of the other boys as Cecil straightened up and pushed past me. "Settling a bet is all."

"Cecil—"

"Cecil Daw, you will not put one nail in a board until you tell me what you think you're doing!"

"I'm building Amanda a workshop."

Mama crossed her arms. "A *workshop?*"

"Yes, ma'am. She needs a place to build her horses, and there's only so much she can do from the confines of the porch swing."

I covered my mouth with my hand and tried to stifle a smile.

"Well, we bulldozed the last workshop that sat on this hill, so I don't know what makes you think we won't do it again."

Cecil stepped over the pile of boards and handed a hammer to a boy I recognized from school. "I guess if you do that, we'll have to start over again."

"That's enough—I'm going to call your father."

"He knows where I am. I've been saving all summer so I'd have enough money to buy the wood from him."

"Why in the world didn't you ask me if this was okay?"

Cecil ignored the question, so I answered.

"Because you would've said no, Mama."

"How do you know? You two didn't even give me a chance to say yes."

I wiped my brow with the back of my hand and tried to look at her. "We all know the things you approve of and the things you don't."

Mama's eyes blazed as she mumbled a swear word under her breath and stomped off toward the house.

"Mama!"

"Get away from me, Amanda!"

"Will you just listen to me for one second?"

"Why in the world would I listen now?" Mama threw open the screen door and let it smack against the kitchen window.

"Because I need to explain to you—"

Mama turned and pointed at me. "You want to explain now? *Now?* Get out of my kitchen!"

I blinked back an angry rush of tears and turned toward the back door, but she grabbed me by my jeans and pulled me toward the living room. "Go to your room."

We practically fell through the swinging door, nearly knocking Pen off her feet.

Pen tilted her head and looked puzzled. "What's wrong?"

Mama's face turned a shade of red I'd never seen before. "Both of you, go to your rooms!"

In my room, I pushed my dresser in front of the door and fastened the curtains with a hair clip. If I was going to be trapped inside for the rest of the summer, then I was going to do it in complete darkness. Maybe I'd starve to death. The thought sounded appealing. I threw off my shoes and got back under the covers.

Just when I thought Mama had settled down, I heard her in the kitchen, yelling at someone on the other end of the phone. *Poor Sam.*

The hammering and sawing continued into the late afternoon, but because my bedroom window faced the front of the house, I couldn't see what Cecil was doing.

I would've given anything to be back in my old room.

When darkness fell, I heard Cecil's truck on the gravel driveway. He didn't even slow down before pulling onto the pavement and riding off into the night. If he had, I might've been tempted to leave my room and check the tree.

Several times, I heard Mama in the hallway outside my door, but it wasn't until after she tucked Pen into bed that she tapped on my door and asked me to let her in. I wanted to ignore her but knew better than to do that.

With all the strength left in me, I slid the dresser back into place.

Mama looked smaller and more fragile than ever before, and the hurt in her eyes threatened to break me in half. When the door was completely open, I fell on my bed and covered my face.

Mama sat down next to me and put her hand on my back. "Amanda, are you in love with Cecil?"

I folded my pillow around my face to soften the sobs.

"Amanda, why?"

"It's just a workshop, Mama. He's just trying to do something nice for me before he leaves."

"I know that's what you think, but what he's really doing is building an altar so you'll have a place to remember him when he's gone."

"I don't need something new to help me do that, Mama. Cecil is a part of every piece of this house and land."

He's a part of me.

Mama rubbed my back before lying down next to me and breathing the scent of alcohol across my neck. "Why didn't you tell me?"

I felt another rush of anger as I sat up. "I wanted to, but I knew you wouldn't approve."

Mama rubbed her eyes with the palms of her hands, swung her feet over the edge of the bed, and stood up. "Amanda, I love you, but—"

"But you don't love Cecil."

Mama stopped pacing. "I do love Cecil, but you're my daughter, and it's my job to help you make good decisions."

"Why is being with Cecil a bad decision?"

"Cecil's not a bad boy, Amanda, he's just not right for you."

"How do you know, Mama? Maybe he's exactly right for me. God doesn't say anything about people not falling in love because of the color of their skin."

Mama came over and knelt between my knees. "I'm not upset because Cecil's black, and I'm not upset because Cecil's poor. I spend most of my days serving poor, pregnant black women. I'm upset because you, Amanda Reyes, are special. I'm upset because I don't want you to look back in twenty years and realize that you're just like one of your silly horses."

"What does that mean?"

"Amanda, if you marry that boy, you'll spend the rest of your life rocking back and forth between things but never going anywhere. I don't want your life to be like that, baby." Mama wiped my face with the palm of her hand. "I don't want you to be like me."

"Then who do you want me to be like? Helen Keller?" I pushed her hand away from my face. "Because asking me not to love Cecil is like asking me to be blind and deaf."

Mama pursed her lips, stood, and headed for the door. "I don't have to ask you to be blind and deaf, because you're already both of those things." Mama started to leave, but she stopped before the door closed and leaned back into the room.

"Don't ruin everything for the sake of a boy. If you ever want to be free of me or this house, consider for a second what being with Cecil would mean."

In the darkness of my bedroom, I considered whether or not Mama was right. What if waiting for Cecil and marrying him would trap me in a town that I wanted to leave? What if marrying him and having his children kept me from following my dreams? Was I really content to live my life in the shadow of my mother and her obsession with the town's matriarch?

I wrapped my arms around my stomach as another wave of nausea came over me. I wanted to sleep. I needed to sleep, but my nausea kept one thought pushing its way to the forefront of my mind.

What if I was pregnant with Cecil's baby?

I rolled over on my side and begged for that not to be true. If it was, I knew Mama would send me away to live in the Refuge House with all the other pregnant vagrants.

When the nauseous feeling in my gut bumped up against my guilt, I rushed to the bathroom and gagged into the toilet. As I choked, I imagined Mama standing over me shaking her head. I imagined Sam and Cecil's disappointment when they found out their football-hero dreams had ended.

And, as Mama suggested, I imagined what my life might be like in twenty years.

The next morning I awoke to more hammering.

I sat up and rubbed my swollen eyes before buckling over in pain from an empty stomach.

On the bedside table I found a cup of milk, three slices of toast, and a honey dipper. I scooted across the mattress and took a gulp of milk before coating the toast with honey. When all the bread was gone, my stomach begged for more. The sound of an electric saw screamed as I practically staggered down the hallway to the bathroom. I wanted to see Cecil's progress but not until I'd showered and dressed.

As the water pounded my back, a cool burst of air circled the curtain and sent chills down my legs.

"Pen?"

"Are you okay?"

"Shut the door, I'm freezing."

The bathroom door clicked, and the room quickly filled with steam again. Penelope pulled back a corner of the curtain. "Mama's gone. I just wanted to make sure you were okay."

"Where'd she go?"

"I don't know—the Refuge House, maybe." When I turned off the water, Penelope sat down on the toilet lid and pulled her legs to her chest.

"Did she say when she'd be back?"

"No, she just said we better not step foot out of this house. What happened yesterday?"

"Nothing."

"Did she find out about you and Cecil?"

I wrapped a towel around my torso, pulled back the curtain, and stepped out of the shower.

"What about us?"

"That you sneak off with him at night and when she takes me to music practice."

I hushed her even though we were alone. "How do you know that?"

"Promise you won't get mad?"

"I'm already mad!"

"Never mind then." Pen jumped from her perch and reached for the door, but I held it closed with a stiff arm.

"Okay, I'm not mad. Now tell me."

Pen's shoulders dropped. "I read your letters."

"What letters?"

"The ones you keep in the box under your bed."

"You read my letters from Cecil? Did you tell Mama?"

"No, I promise, but she already knows."

"What! How?"

"I don't know. I think she found the letters while you were sleeping. She took the whole box with her when she left."

I pushed Pen aside and ran down the hallway.

At the side of my bed, I fell to the floor and reached for Grandpa's toolbox. Gone. Mama had taken the whole overstuffed box. I'd saved all the letters—all the way back to the first one. They were my most valued possession. I loved them more than all my rocking horses combined. If she destroyed them, she'd destroy a part of me.

Penelope stood in the doorway and watched me as I moaned. I couldn't stand up. I couldn't breathe. I could only curl into a ball and sob.

"She's trying to kill me."

Pen knelt down next to me and put her head on my back. "I'm sorry."

I pulled the corners of the towel to my eyes. "I hate her."

"You're not supposed to say that."

"You don't understand. She doesn't love me like she loves you."

Pen smoothed the towel against my back. "She loves you the most, probably."

I swallowed Pen's good intentions and lifted myself to my feet. "I need to get dressed."

"You're not leaving, are you?"

The electric saw let loose another cry. "No, not yet."

Remember that you, dependent on your sight,
do not realize how many things are tangible.

HELEN KELLER

Chapter Thirteen

I stood near the kitchen window and watched Cecil put the finishing touches on what appeared to be nothing more than a double-wide outhouse with a tin roof. I wished he'd chosen a better way to expose our secret.

Pen woke me from my daze when she slid the metal chair along the kitchen floor so she could reach a jar of peanut butter.

"Here, I'll help you." I let the curtain drop into place.

"I can't wait any longer for Mama to come home. I have to eat something."

"Get down. I'll fix you a sandwich."

"Are you gonna eat one too?"

My stomach turned to knots as I twisted the jar open. "Sure. I'm starving."

Pen opened a box of saltines and placed an even number on each plate. While she spread peanut butter on the crackers, I poured us a Coke.

"Why aren't you using the frozen glasses?"

"I'm just not, okay?"

When the glasses were full, I sat across from Pen and bowed my head. After a few seconds, I lifted it and began eating.

"You're not gonna say grace out loud?"

I broke the corner off a cracker and placed it on my tongue. "No, you go ahead."

Pen reached for my hand but stopped as something behind me caught her attention. I started to turn but recognized the familiar sound of Cecil's shoes on the porch.

The screen door rattled but refused to open.

Pen lowered her head and pulled her plate to the edge of the table. "You want me to open it?"

"Amanda? Can I come in?"

Pen removed her plate from the table and disappeared into the living room.

"Amanda? I can see you. Can I come in?"

I pushed my chair away from the table and unlatched the heavy door. With only the screen door between us, I could smell the hours of sweat he'd poured into his building project. I tried not to look at him and wished he couldn't see me. My eyes finally settled near the bottom of the screen. "I can't let you in."

"Then come outside and let me show you what we've done."

I shook my head and grabbed my midsection. "No."

"Please, come outside. Pen isn't gonna tell."

"I can't open the door, Cecil."

"Why? Because your mother told you not to? Open the door, Amanda." Cecil grabbed the handle and rattled it against the frame.

"Cecil, please."

"What did she say to you?"

"Nothing."

"What did she say?"

"Nothing. She's been gone all day."

"Did you tell her about us? Did you tell her we're going to get married and start a family?" Cecil rattled the door again. "Did you tell her there's nothing in the world she can do about it?"

I wiped away fresh, burning tears. "She took my letters. She took them, and now she's probably somewhere reading them and tossing them into a fire."

"Who cares? They're just letters. I'm going to write you a million more. You can start a new collection today. Hand me a piece of paper. I'll start right now."

"No."

"What do you mean, no?"

I straightened and looked into his sad eyes. "This isn't what I want, Cecil."

"What? The workshop? Fine, we'll light it on fire and roast marshmallows in the flames. I don't care about the workshop, I care about us."

"That's not what I mean."

"Amanda, I love you. Please, just come outside and talk to me. I promise everything's gonna be fine with your mother."

While he tried to reason with me, I stepped away and closed the door. I could still hear him calling for me as I pushed through the swinging door to the living room and found Pen eating crackers in front of the TV. She didn't turn around. I climbed the stairs to my room.

After darkness covered the house, Mama parked her car in the gravel spot out front. While the voice on the TV sang about discounted school supplies, I rocked myself in Grandma's chair and waited for her to open the latch. After several minutes, Mama still hadn't come inside.

Penelope waited near my feet and quietly combed Barbie's hair. "She's probably gone to tell Daddy."

I released the breath I'd been holding and agreed. Anytime Mama was upset about something, she'd storm off to the cemetery to tell our father. After Grandma died, she spent several hours a day out there, crying and yelling at Daddy's grave.

When a half hour had passed and Mama still hadn't come inside, I decided to wait for her on the porch swing. I pushed at the floor with my foot until I saw her shadow moving through the yard.

"I thought I told you not to leave the house."

"You didn't tell me, you told Pen to tell me. I was still asleep when you left."

Mama climbed the steps and sat next to me on the swing. "Is your sister still awake?"

"She's watching TV."

Mama repositioned her legs on the swing. "It looks like Cecil made a lot of progress today. Have you been out to see the shed?"

"No. This is the first time I've left the house."

Mama pursed her lips. "You mean it's the first time you've left the house *today*. I can tell from your letters that you've left the house quite a bit over the last few months. "

"Don't worry, Mama. I'm not gonna see Cecil anymore."

"Well, it sounds to me like the two of you are engaged. Cecil sure talked a lot about his plans for you after graduation—marriage, building a house by the creek, starting a family together."

"You had no right to read my letters."

Mama crossed her arms and closed her eyes. "You had no right to sneak off with your...boyfriend."

"That's not how it started. If you read the letters then you know that."

"Oh, Amanda! How can you be so stupid? That's how it *always* starts."

"Well, if I'd thought for one second that you'd approve, maybe things would've been different."

"Oh, don't you dare try to blame this on me. I'm a good mother, and I work hard to take care of you and your sister."

I tried to act unfazed.

"Amanda, when Cecil shows up tomorrow I want to sit down with both of you to discuss what's gonna happen from this point forward."

"No, Mama. Please. I already told him it's over."

"And you think one slap in the face is going to keep him away?" Mama stood and walked toward to the door. "Maybe you don't know him as well as you think you do."

"Amanda, I need you to get up and come downstairs." My bedroom filled with light as Mama threw open the curtains. "Cecil's waiting in the kitchen. He understands he can't finish the shed until we all have a chance to chat."

I covered my eyes and turned away from the window. "Is Sam here?"

"I suggested that, but Cecil doesn't want to involve Sam."

Mama pulled the sheets away and shook me by the shoulder. "Come on, wash your face and get in the kitchen."

I tried to lift myself out of bed but buckled under the nausea of another missed meal. When my face was washed and my teeth were brushed, I pulled my hair into a bun and hurried to get dressed.

In the kitchen, Cecil sat with his back to the porch while Mama served toast with eggs and bacon. She smiled when I pushed open the door and told me to sit across from Cecil. "Can I get the two of you some juice?"

I declined as I pulled the chair away from the table.

"Okay, then I'll pour you both a glass of water. Cecil, I know you have a full day ahead of you if you're going to finish anytime soon."

"Yes, ma'am. We're hoping to finish today."

Mama smiled and tossed a red curl away from her face. "Well, that's good. I'm sure you'll have to work double shifts the rest of the summer in order to pay back your daddy for all the wood."

Cecil glanced from Mama to me and nodded. "Yes, ma'am."

Mama removed her apron and folded it over the back of the

chair before sitting down. "That's great because I've been thinking." She lifted her coffee cup to her lips and took a sip before continuing. "You're going to be workin' really hard next year to keep your grades up and still play football, right?"

Cecil nodded.

"Well, I want you both to consider giving your relationship a rest until Amanda graduates."

Cecil fiddled with his fork before responding. "Ms. Tilly, I know you're upset, and I'm sorry for that, but I love Amanda and I'm not gonna break up with her."

"I appreciate your loyalty, but I'm not really asking." Mama set her cup on the table. "I know what's best for Amanda."

I looked down and tried to remain calm.

Cecil pushed his glass around on the plastic coaster. "Have you asked Amanda what she wants?"

Mama looked back and forth between us. "As a matter of fact, I have."

For the first time, Cecil seemed nervous. "Amanda?" I thought for a second he might push past Mama and fall to my knees the way he had the first time we'd kissed. "Amanda, please look at me."

I pushed a tear back and looked into Cecil's eyes. "I don't want this, Cecil. I already told you that."

"Fine." Cecil stood, making the chair bounce against the window frame before it hit the floor. "Then come with me, and we'll figure out what you *do* want."

Mama stood as a barrier between us.

"No, Cecil. Please just leave me alone."

With one movement Cecil moved past Mama and lifted me into the air.

"Cecil, if you take her out of this house, I swear I'll call the police."

My foot knocked over the water as he swung me around and

headed toward the door.

"Go ahead and call."

All of his crew stood in stunned silence as Cecil hurried across the field with me in his arms. I relaxed against Cecil's chest and tried to shield my face.

"Why are you doing this?" I asked.

When we reached the passenger side of his truck, Cecil put me down and opened the door. "You know why."

"I can't go with you. She really will call the police."

"Okay, then we can talk right here!" After Cecil scanned the group, everyone went back to work. "Amanda, I know you're scared. I'm scared too."

"I'm not scared. I'm sixteen! I still have two years of high school."

"I know. I'll come back every chance I get."

"Don't you see, I just want a normal life? I don't want you to come back for me."

Cecil lifted me into the truck and pushed my bare feet out of the way before slamming the door.

"Where are you taking me?"

Cecil hurried to the driver's side. "I want to show you something."

"Please, let me go back in. If you don't, we'll both get in a ton of trouble."

Cecil started the truck and grabbed my hand, holding it as we bounced through the open field. Near the tree line he eased the truck to a stop and turned to me. "This is the spot I've been dreaming about since I was a boy."

I leaned forward to see the clearing. "This is where you want to build a house? It's not anywhere near our spot."

"No, but we could be there in seconds—all I'd have to do is build a bridge to the other side. Our spot is just around the curve."

My stomach clenched in pain again. "Cecil, I don't feel well. Please take me home."

"Okay, but I have to show you something first."

Cecil got out, circled the truck, and helped me to the ground. "Do I need to carry you?"

I brushed his hand aside and followed him into the clearing.

When we were in the middle the circle of trees, Cecil smiled and wrapped his hands around my waist.

"This is where I want to spend the rest of my life with you. If I save every penny I earn over the next two years, I'm sure your mother will sell it to us. I even thought we could get married right here after you're finished with school. We could set up tents and folding chairs. You said you wanted to get married outside. What about right here?"

I looked at the dry ground and envisioned our guests sitting under the hot sun, melting into their seats—white people on one side, black on the other. "Cecil."

"Just think about it, okay? We have a long time before we have to plan anything." Cecil kissed me on the nose. "I just want you to know that I love you and that I'll always love you."

When he put his hand against my back, a sharp pain burned through my thighs. Cecil placed his hand on my cheek and pressed his lips against mine. I wanted to fold into him and wrap my arms around his shoulders, but the pain in my back pushed me toward the ground. Something was wrong.

Cecil eased me to a shade tree and helped me sit with my back against its trunk. "Are you okay?"

"I think I'm just dehydrated. Do you have any water?"

Cecil ran to his truck and threw open the tailgate. After he climbed in and slid a round water cooler to the edge, Sam's red truck pulled up behind his. I saw a quick exchange of words before Sam helped his son lower the cooler to the ground. Within seconds they were both standing over me. Sam held a damp cloth to my head while

Cecil helped me drink from the open spout.

When the pain began to ease and drift toward my abdomen, they helped me back across the field.

"You go on home, Cecil. I'll take Amanda back to Tilly."

"But Dad—"

"Don't you argue with me!" Sam's forehead furrowed into a thousand layers. "You're in enough trouble already."

Cecil lifted me into Sam's truck and kissed me on the temple. "I'll call you in a couple of hours."

I shook my head, trying to push through the pain and nausea. "Give me a few days, okay? I need to make things right with Mama."

"But I have to leave in a week."

"Please, Cecil, just give me some time to think."

Lead out those who have eyes but are blind,
who have ears but are deaf.

Isaiah 43:8

Once I knew the depth where no hope was,
and darkness lay on the face of all things.
Then love came and set my soul free.

HELEN KELLER

Chapter Fourteen

Friday, June 13, 2008 / Memphis, Tennessee

I could feel the wave of guilt and sadness run through my body just as it had so many times before. Somehow, in a moment of silence, it had found me in the stillness and ripped open my chest again. All the emptiness inside my heart slowly filled with heavy darkness, and the weight of it pulled me down into the water.

I relaxed my shoulders and felt the water rise over my head. Its warmth tickled my ear lobes and pushed into the corners of my mouth. I took what I imagined was my last breath and pushed myself further into the bathtub.

I felt my hair soak up some of the water and hated myself for cutting it. In a moment of misjudgment, I'd decided my long hair wasn't helping me look the way a sophisticated wife and mother of two should look, so I got my hair cut short on Mother's Day—two hours before Frank and I were scheduled to have dinner with his friends at some new restaurant that served only the organic foods he insisted on.

I thought Frank would like my shoulder-length style, but I soon realized no man really wants his twenty-seven-year-old wife to have the same haircut as Harry Potter's redheaded companion.

"Amanda Reyes Crosby!" he gasped when I walked into the kitchen that evening. "Who cut your hair?"

I tried to act as if I loved it, but the truth was I'd cried the whole way home, barely watching the road because I couldn't stop looking in the rearview mirror and pulling at the hair on the back of my neck. Frank must have seen right through me, because after a few minutes he started laying on thick compliments, as if they were going to stretch my hair down to the middle of my back.

My lungs began to tighten and ache as I pressed my feet hard against the cold porcelain tiles and anchored myself under the water. My body began to beg for air, but the weight of my heart lashed out against it.

I heard the water drip from the faucet as air began forcing itself out through my nostrils and up toward the surface of the water. I closed my eyes, fought the urge to breathe, and clamped my fingers against the bridge of my nose.

How many times will the water drip before Frank comes home and finds me?

My lungs burned for oxygen.

If Frank's cancer gets worse, who will take care of our kids?

Large pockets of air pushed free through tiny slits in the corners of my mouth.

What will they—

My body gave in to my need to breathe before stubbornness allowed my head to breach the surface. I gasped for air, but instead I took in liquid. Soapy water burned the back of my throat as I coughed and begged for oxygen.

After my breathing began to relax, I sat for several minutes taking in deep breaths of warm air. I wished I could stay there naked and daydreaming all day, but that wasn't a possibility for me. Not that day or any other day for that matter. I hated being dragged around by my responsibilities. Still, I couldn't escape them.

Rushing to rinse my hair, I heard a low, dull hum coming from the room next door. *The phone.* After the third ring, I turned off the shower to ensure that no additional noise would disturb my two hours of peace.

I knew most likely it was Mama again.

We hadn't finished our conversation earlier that morning about the wonderful thing Penelope had done for the Women of the Presbytery when she'd played "the most beautiful contemporary Christian music I ever heard," only to be politely applauded by the old women in their little white shantung hats.

I smiled, imagining the shock on Pen's face as the women gave much less than a standing ovation for another one of her failed attempts to bring Tuscumbia into the 21st century.

Shortly after college, Memphis, Tennessee, became my home, but I've always thought it was better suited for Pen than me. After all, she's the musician, and Memphis is alive with music twenty-four hours a day. Still, Pen chose to stay in a town known as "The Birthplace of Helen Keller" when she could easily live near me in "The Birthplace of Rock 'n' Roll."

After I towel-dried my hair, I hurried to finish some of my daunting tasks. I picked up a few dozen toys from around the house, paid a few bills, and unloaded the dishwasher. In the midst of my chores, I almost forgot to brush the last coat of polyurethane on my latest rocking horse—a blue one with pink flowers. A woman in New York City ordered it after she found out the baby growing inside her was a girl.

If I didn't finish soon, the baby would arrive long before the horse did.

I pulled on my favorite jeans and a yellow T-shirt before I headed out the back door and down the steps toward my studio. The horse had been sitting on my work table for over two weeks, patiently waiting for me to add his last coat of sealant and send him off to the Big Apple. I knew my deadline was quickly approaching, but painting required joy, and I didn't even have the amount needed to roll on clear lacquer.

Halfway through the backyard, I remembered the naptime caller and thought that I better turn the ringer off in case they called again. Like so many times before, I abandoned the idea of finishing my rocking horse project and hurried back inside. I listened to the phone message as soon as I got inside.

"Amanda, it's your mother—call me as soon as you get this message."

I knew by her tone that something was wrong, but it was the fact that she'd referred to herself as "mother" that scared me. Tilly Paxton Reyes hadn't called herself anything other than "Honey" since the day Christopher, her first grandchild, was born. She said the name suited her because of all of the sweetness and love she was going to pour out on our children. Frank and I laughed, secretly agreeing that it was a better indication of how she'd likely stick around for longer than we wanted.

After the second ring, I began to get impatient. "Come on, Mama, pick up!" My coaxing through the phone helped but not until after the fourth ring.

"Hello," she said, sounding equally frustrated.

"Mama, it's me. What's wrong?"

"Amanda."

"What's wrong, Mama?"

"It's Cecil."

The feeling that tried to drown me in the tub weighed heavily in my chest again.

"There was an accident in the river. Cecil was fishing. It's bad."

"But he's all right?" He's not—" I asked.

He's alive, but it's not good. There were two other boys with him.

Tears pushed their way into the corners of my eyes.

"They can't find one of the boys."

"Haven't found him? You mean he's—"

"I hope not. They think Cecil almost drowned trying to save him."

"How did you find out?"

Mama hesitated. "Sam called."

I could tell there was more. "What else, Mama? Tell me what else Sam said!"

I heard Mama slide the kitchen chair across the floor. "He asked for you."

"Cecil?" I asked. "What did he say?"

"Sam said when Cecil woke up, he said your name." Silence. "He's unconscious now, because of the meds. Pretty soon he'll go into surgery."

"Why?"

"He has several broken bones. Sam had to go, so I didn't get all the details."

"Did Sam tell you to call me?"

"Yes."

"Does he want me to come home?"

"I think Sam would do anything to make Cecil better right now, but you better stay in Memphis. Frank needs you."

"Will you call me when you know more?"

"Yes, I promise. But, Amanda..." I heard Mama pull back the curtain. "You need to be very careful. All you can do is pray. Guard your heart and pray."

I held the receiver to my ear and closed my eyes.

"Amanda?"

"I'm here."

"Remember, it's taken you a lot of years to get over what happened."

I let my thumb slide across the disconnect button before saying goodbye. Years hadn't given me the ability to get over what happened that day. They'd only given me the ability to hide the truth.

I think of days long gone,
flown like birds beyond the ramparts of the world.
HELEN KELLER

Chapter Fifteen

Mama called every day before Frank came home from work to give me updates about Cecil's surgeries. She said he'd only been conscious for a few minutes since the accident and that he had a tube in his throat to help him breathe. Of course, I wanted to know if he'd asked for me again, but Frank was home the last time Mama had phoned, so we didn't talk specifically about the accident. It felt good talking to my mother every day. Finally, my need to know things aligned with her need to continually offer her opinion.

The boy who escaped uninjured—a teenager from Sheffield—told police that the three of them had been fishing near an inlet when another boat sideswiped their Javelin and threw them into the river.

It took the rescue crew four days to find the missing boy.

I read his obituary online. Nineteen-year-old Raymond Beard: star football player, loved by everyone who knew him. Described in the same way Cecil would've been remembered twelve years earlier—as someone with a bright and promising future in sports.

Friday morning, as I lay in bed wishing Frank would hurry up and leave for his appointment with his new doctor at UT Medical Center,

I listened as he planned out the weekend with Christopher and Lilah. The familiar clang of silverware told me breakfast was already underway, so I pulled the bed sheet over my head and tried hard not to listen to the noises coming from downstairs.

Getting up in the mornings had become more and more difficult over the previous week. I'd lie there and try to imagine what Cecil was going through at that moment. It was as if I could walk into that hospital room, through the quietness of the early morning, and lie down, not just next to him but *into* him. Like I was being absorbed by his body in a way that allowed me to feel what he was feeling and hear what he was hearing. I liked being close to him again. I liked listening in. I liked feeling as if I was still part of him. I liked that lie. It felt good there, so warm, so safe, and at the same time so wrong. Even in my deepest thoughts—in the mysterious place between sleep and awake—that *thing* inside me found joy in throwing the gavel down on my heart.

Most mornings, I would just lie there lifelessly and cry, wishing I was a child again. Wishing I could go back to a time when life had no boundaries, no regrets. To a place where I was free of guilt, free of God.

As I lay there with the sheets pulled tightly over my head, I imagined what people in the hospital room were saying to Cecil. I wondered what his wife was saying as she held his hand. How much did she cry? What did she do to pass the time? Was she praying for him, or was it up to me to beg God for his life?

I threw the sheets back and kicked them until they landed at my feet. Folds of white fabric gathered around my ankles like a sail fallen from its mast. I slid out of bed and in one motion clutched the sheets in my hands and stretched them toward the headboard until they were smooth again. My frustration was building. I tucked the loose ends underneath the mattress and smoothed the sheets flat with my forearm. It was a trick I'd learned from watching Radella, except she touched everything with love. I pulled and tugged until the fabric obeyed. Radella would've smoothed the wrinkles of cloth into thick cream with just the purr of her voice.

I hurried down the steps and past the children eating breakfast. The coffee pot was still full of yesterday's coffee, so I dumped out the old grounds, filled the pot with water, and poured in the whole beans.

"Good morning, sunshine." Frank had crept up behind me and slid his arms around my waist.

"It's raining." I motioned toward the tiny specks of moisture bouncing off the kitchen window. "I don't see any sunshine."

"Aren't you going to say good morning to your beautiful children?"

I slid a chair over to Lilah and kissed her on the back of her neck. "Good morning, Lilah. How's your cough? Did Daddy give you your medicine?"

Christopher held out his cup for me. "I need more juice, Mommy."

Before I could respond, Frank leaned over me and took the cup. "I'll get it."

I smoothed out the curls along Lilah's neck while Frank took the cup into the kitchen and opened the door to the fridge. He moved with greater ease than he had over the past several weeks.

"More orange or do you want apple?"

Christopher swallowed. "Orange."

I leaned back in the chair and stretched my neck. "What time are you meeting with the oncologist?"

"My appointment isn't until 10, but I need to go by the pharmacy first and help Ginger organize some new medications."

"Why can't she do it by herself?"

"She does it by herself all the time. When I can help, I need to be there."

I helped Lilah scoop some oatmeal onto her spoon as Frank filled Christopher's glass with the nutrient-infused juice he'd bought to replace my favorite concentrated brand. As he poured, Frank steadied himself against the refrigerator door.

Instead of bending over to put the juice back in the fridge, Frank bent his knees to reach the bottom shelf. Before he shut the door, he turned some of the containers so their labels faced forward. "We're almost out of yogurt. Be sure to get some today?"

I nodded.

"But not the kind you got last time. Get something better."

I nodded again. "I'd go with you to the doctor, but with Lilah still coughing I don't want to leave her with a sitter."

"It's okay. I'll call you after lunch. When are you leaving for Tuscumbia?"

I helped Lilah down from her chair. "Not until Sunday."

Frank placed the cup in front of Christopher. "You're not leaving until after church, I hope."

"Are we going to Honey's house?" Christopher interrupted.

I cut my eyes at Frank. "After Sunday school—I have to teach."

Christopher pulled at my robe. "When is Sunday? How many days?"

"Today is Friday, so y'all are goin' to see Honey in two days!"

"Are you coming, Daddy?"

Frank knelt until he was eye level with his son. "I can't go, buddy. I wish I could, but I'm still too sick."

"When are you gonna get better, Daddy?"

The rain quickly changed from a few drops to a thunderous downpour as I fixed myself a cup of coffee and listened over my shoulder as Frank explained to Christopher again why he couldn't do all the things he wanted.

Everything has its wonders,
even darkness and silence,
and I learn whatever state I am in,
therein to be content.

HELEN KELLER

Chapter Sixteen

Sunday morning, I decided to honor my commitment to teach but skipped both morning worship services. It was a decision I felt completely comfortable with until I told Frank, who quickly reminded me that "Sunday is a day of worship."

"It's also a day of rest," I said, "and my lesson on Judges to a bunch of teenagers will certainly erase any possibility of that."

In all honesty, I wanted to have plenty of time to pack. I was planning to leave as soon as Lilah swallowed her last bite of lunch. Mama called on Saturday to tell me that Cecil was beginning to stay awake for longer periods of time and that the doctors had removed his breathing tube. She said he was even talking some.

Footsteps thundered through the ceiling above my head as I rushed to pack some of the children's favorite toys into a duffel bag. "It's time to go, kids!" I zipped the bag closed, lifted it onto my shoulder, and raced toward the back door. My shin caught the corner of our wooden coffee table and toppled over a photo of Frank and me on our honeymoon.

Two days before that photo was taken, I'd stood in front of a couple hundred witnesses and repeated the words "from this day forward, for as long as we both shall live." And I had meant every word of it. But for two years now, we'd been facing the grim reality of what those vows really meant.

Frank and I were blindsided by the discovery of Frank's cancer. Lilah was only a few weeks old. I was so consumed with the stress of childbearing that I didn't notice the physical changes Frank was going through. He and Christopher loved to wrestle in the backyard when Frank got home from the pharmacy, so when he began complaining about back pain, we chalked it up to age, fatherhood, and years of lifting heavy boxes of medications. We even laughed it off as sympathy pains from seeing me carry around forty extra pounds of baby weight for two years.

I wish he'd gone to the doctor earlier. I wish I hadn't gotten frustrated with him when he told me the pain was so bad that he couldn't get up in the middle of the night to give the baby a bottle. I hated what I thought was laziness, but mostly I hated seeing the man I fell in love with grow weak and needy.

When we first met, I thought Frank was the most handsome and brilliant man I'd ever known. I had moved to Memphis to begin nursing school after college, and Frank was a guest lecturer in one of my classes. He was, as I learned later, almost eighteen years older than me, but his dark hair and big blue eyes made him look like he was only thirty. It was truly love at first sight and second sight, and by the time we got to third sight I could already hear wedding bells sounding in my ears.

I never really wanted to become a nurse, but after I finished college the one thing I felt certain about was that I was not ready for what Mama called the "real world." So my solution was to attend more school. Mama agreed that it was probably a good way to meet and marry a doctor.

Frank and I met during my second semester of nursing school.

The fact that he was a pharmacist rather than a doctor didn't bother me. In fact, Frank's job was better than a physician's. Being a pharmacist allowed him to be home every night for dinner.

What I didn't know was that after only a few years of marriage and the birth of two children, we would discover three cancerous tumors the size of golf balls attached to his spine. After several weeks of testing and x-rays, the doctors told us that surgery was the best option in order to save his life but that removing the tumors would render him paralyzed from the neck down. Frank never considered life as a paraplegic an option. Instead, he began very aggressive chemotherapy in addition to other painkilling and hair-removing drugs.

Over time, the monthly treatments became part of our routine—as well as the short, seven-day recovery period between them. For two years we tried to kill the cancer living inside Frank, and for two years it tried to kill us.

If I'm bitter toward God, it's because over and over again He gave me great things—and then took them away. He took my father, Radella, Grandma. Even my first baby. And the moment I began to believe things were getting better, Frank was diagnosed with cancer.

"Surely this God who created me and knew my name even before I was born hates me," I once said to Frank. "And Reverend Harper says He 'predestined every day of my life.' Right."

Frank believes in a God who doesn't feel contempt. I swear, only men called by God can lie as close to death as Frank and still praise Jesus for it.

My faith moves round like the wind. I'm weakest during the times when Frank is the sickest. When he first began his treatments, he always wanted me near him. So, night after night, I would lie beside him watching him shake and sweat. Then after he'd drift off, I'd have to get up to feed or console a baby. That's how it went for almost a year, until we settled into survival mode—an even darker place, where you know the end result but pretend that everything is going to be fine.

I loaded the suitcases into the car as Frank stood behind me and watched. When I was done, he kissed me on the cheek and told me he loved me. "Call me as soon as you get there and let me know you're safe."

"I will," I said, slamming the trunk of my gray Accord.

Frank fastened the kids into their car seats. "I love you, kiddos. Take care of your mama, okay?"

Frank straightened the mirror on the driver side door as I rolled down the window and buckled my seatbelt. He forced a smile and lowered himself to eye level. "Are you gonna be back in time for us to celebrate your birthday?"

"Well, you know I don't want to be in Tuscumbia for the festival, but I bet Honey's gonna want us to stay until Saturday and go with her. She's always wanted me to go on my actual birthday."

"Your mama loves you. You should go along with her plans this time. If nothing else, it'd be fun for the kids to go to a festival on your birthday. Maybe even have some fried food." He winked at me.

"I prefer we not celebrate it at all," I said, cranking up the engine.

"Well, I've already got you something. I'll save it for you until you get back."

"I don't want any gifts."

"I know. You tell me that every year."

"Then you should listen."

Frank lifted my hand to his lips and kissed it as if he were playing the role of a hero in an old black-and-white movie. "I'll never be content with acting as though you were never born."

The kids waved to him as we backed out of the driveway. As we slowly pulled away, I watched Frank steady himself and inch toward the house. He'd been pretty quiet since his appointment on Friday, only saying that he was looking forward to a restful week in Memphis.

If the eye is maimed, so that it does not see the
beauteous face of day,
the touch becomes more poignant and discriminating.
HELEN KELLER

Chapter Seventeen

Three hours after leaving Memphis, we finally arrived in Tuscumbia. As we got closer to my childhood home, I realized it had been years since I'd visited during the summer. Because of Frank's cancer diagnosis I'd only visited during Christmastime when all the trees in Grandma's yard were bare and frosted over with a thin layer of ice. While holiday carols played on a small radio in the kitchen window, I had stood motionless, gazing out at the old oak tree and the abandoned workshop. I'd watched the top branches of the tree bend and creak as Frank rested in Grandma's rocking chair.

When I turned down the long gravel road toward my family's home, I leaned forward in my seat and looked past the row of shrubs and picked-over blueberry bushes that lined the dirt driveway. I smiled, seeing the oak tree full of leaves and the two special additions Mama had made to its heavy branches.

I shook Lilah a bit to wake her from her nap. "Look. We're here, and Honey has a surprise for you!"

Lilah rubbed her eyes and looked around.

"Look at the tree. Look!" I parked around back and pointed through the car window toward the century-old tree.

Christopher's eyes grew wide. "There's two of them, Mommy! One for Lilah and one for me!"

Underneath the tree hung not just one but two rope swings. From one of the golden lassos hung a little red chair—the perfect size for Lilah —and the other rope held an old rubber truck tire. The tire hung so low I worried it might drag under Christopher's weight.

We hadn't even opened the car doors when Mama and Pen came running through the screen door. They waved with excitement and hurried down the steps toward us. The slam of the door startled me as I put the car in park and stepped onto the gravel. The Southern-pitched squeals of joy scared crows from the tree, while the sound of the car and the slamming door had hardly got their attention.

Christopher yelled "Honey!" as Mama—wearing a lime-green shirt, pink pants, and flip-flops—ran through the damp gravel and threw open the car door.

"Christopher, you are humongous!" she said, struggling to free him from his seatbelt.

My sister was already busy removing Lilah from the car when I got to their side. Within seconds they were both twirling and laughing.

"When I have kids, I hope they're just like you, Lilahbell."

I was stunned to hear Pen suggest she might want children of her own someday. I'd gotten used to the idea of Pen forever remaining quirky and alone. Maybe her job at the Refuge House was finally rubbing off on her.

I hugged Pen and kissed her on the cheek. "I've missed you, sis."

"Yeah, yeah, I've missed you too." She looked at my long neck. "I almost didn't recognize you with short hair."

"I hate it. Don't even talk about it. I can't wait for it to grow out."

Honey carried Christopher over to join us.

"What in the world did you do to your hair?"

"I cut it. I told you that weeks ago."

Mama frowned. "Boy, you sure did."

"Thanks for the compliment, Mama." I rubbed my hand along the back of my neck. "Aren't you the one who's been dyeing her hair red for the last thirty years?"

"It's my color," she said as she pushed her stiff hair into position. "Don't worry, your hair will be fine after it grows out some more."

"Let's swing!" Christopher yelled, squirming free of Mama's arms.

"When did you hang the swings?" I asked as we hurried after the children.

"Billy did it last week."

"Billy Mayfree? That was nice of him."

"No, not Billy Mayfree. He's been in jail for years. Billy Arbuthnot—he teaches American history at CHS."

Pen blushed and glanced at Mama as she said Billy Arbuthnot's name. I almost expected to find their initials carved inside a big heart on the oak tree.

"U.S. history? Wow! Did you tell him you've never been any farther than Memphis?" I tried not to smile.

"As a matter of fact, I did not. And you better not either." Pen pushed Lilah in the swing like a cat swatting a ball of yarn.

"Your sister invited Billy to dinner tonight," Mama said. "And I expect everyone to behave."

Christopher called out for me to give him a push. As I pulled back the heavy tire, I glanced toward the top of the hill at my old workshop. I wanted to leave them all swinging while I wandered out to the shed, but I'd promised myself a long time ago that I wouldn't go back inside. And I promised myself I wouldn't check the tree anymore either. I'd been disappointed too many times.

Mama and Pen kept talking about dinner plans, but I couldn't stop thinking about the workshop long enough to listen.

"Does that sound good to you?" Mama asked, startling me.

"Does what sound good?"

Mama took her turn pushing Lilah in the swing. "Did you hear anything we said?"

I shook my head and gestured toward the hill. "I thought you would've bulldozed that thing by now."

"I started to, but I figured I'd give it a few more years and let it fall over by itself."

One grilled pork chop, two helpings of mashed potatoes, and a side of green bean casserole later, I led Lilah and Christopher upstairs to bed. It felt good to be free of the food regulations Frank enforced. He would've insisted I only eat half my pork chop, so I made certain I didn't leave anything on the bone.

The kids cleaned their plates too, and after they ate some of Mama's angel food cake, they agreed to go up to bed. The excitement of being at Honey's house made the long process of bedtime preparation a complete nightmare. Lilah cried and complained that she "no wan go nite-nite," while Christopher slowed the process down with his refusal to wear pajamas.

Normally, I would've had help from Mama, but she was having too much fun drinking wine and visiting with Billy to follow us upstairs. Billy spent most of the evening talking about his fascination with the Chickasaw Indians, who had lived on our land hundreds of years earlier. Mama jumped at the opportunity to tell him about the cemetery and even offered to walk him there after dinner, but he nervously declined.

I closed the curtains and tucked the children into the twin beds. The room was filled with my things; Mama had turned my room across the hall into a guest room after I left for college. Christopher tucked a stuffed rocking horse under his arm and pushed the horse's mane out of its plastic eyes.

I could hear Pen laugh in the kitchen below us. I pulled the lamp string to turn off the light.

"Mommy, will you read to us?" Christopher asked in a last attempt to stop me from leaving.

"How about a song instead?"

"Will you sing 'Jesus Loves Me'? That's what Daddy sings."

"Well, that's Daddy's favorite song," I said, sitting back down. "I'll sing something else. How about 'Jingle Bells'?"

It was the middle of summer, but they seemed delighted by my song. When I finished, I ran my fingers across Lilah's back until she fell asleep. Tiny beads of sweat collected at the nape of her neck.

Part of me wanted to lie down next to her and go to sleep, but the other part wanted to know what Mama wasn't telling me about Cecil. I had hoped she would tell me right away—at least pull me aside while Pen and Billy were talking—but instead she'd spent the whole night playing hostess and acting as if nothing was wrong. Regardless, I didn't intend to go to bed without knowing every detail of what happened on the river. And more than anything, I wanted to know why Cecil had asked for me.

The joy and excitement that had filled the kitchen moments before died as soon as Billy left and I entered. I was not happy that Pen was going to be around to hear the things Mama had to tell me. It didn't matter that we were both grown women. Pen was still my little sister, and I didn't want her attempting to coach me through something she could never understand. Most likely, Mama had a full lecture prepared anyway about guarding my heart, doing what's right—putting God first.

During my last two years of high school, my relationship with Mama remained turbulent, but after I went to college, she changed a little. She stayed off my back at least. I wondered if it had something to do with me being gone, but Pen assured me that wasn't the case.

Mama still spent lots of time at Ivy Green and the Refuge, but Pen said she also spent more time reading and praying with friends.

As I entered the kitchen, I saw both women silently pass glances back and forth before settling into their dishwashing routine.

I broke the silence in an attempt to lighten the mood. "So what's wrong with him?" I asked.

Pen glanced over her shoulder toward me then focused her gaze on the side of Mama's head. Clearly she'd misunderstood who I was asking about, so I added, "What's wrong with Billy? Something has to be. He seems pretty nice...kinda wimpy, but nice."

"He is a catastrophist," Mama replied without turning to face me.

"Mother!" Pen gasped.

"A catastrophist? What's that?"

Mama held back a smile as she continued to wash. "He thinks the Big Quake's gonna happen tomorrow."

"Mother!" Pen groaned at the absurdity and the truth of what Mama was saying. "That's not completely true!"

"Not completely?" I asked.

"Oh yes it is," Mama continued. "And the quake is gonna cause a big flood, and at the same time we're all gonna be bombed by terrorists."

"Mother! Stop it! That's not true. You just made that up." Pen turned off the faucet. "He's a great guy. He's just a little high strung, is all."

I grabbed the drying towel from Mama's shoulder. "He's a *lotta* high strung, if you ask me."

"Well, nobody asked you." Pen huffed.

Mama tossed a few leftovers into the garbage.

"Heaven forbid we ever have another tornado come through Tuscumbia like last year. We'll have to peel his claws off the ceilin'."

"He's not a cat, Mother." Pen's face tightened.

I tried not to laugh, but the second I started thinking about Billy hissing and hanging from the ceiling everything inside me started to bounce and chuckle. "I don't think catastrophist is the right name for someone who—"

"She just made that up!" Pen snapped. "Everybody knows there's no such thing as a catastrophist."

Mama rung out the sponge as she laughed. "Well, then you tell me what it's called."

Still holding the damp rag in her hand, Pen stood staring at Mama in disbelief. "He's called Billy, okay? Just Billy." A smile started to lift in the corners of Pen's mouth.

"Go on," Mama said. "Tell your sister some of the things he's done."

Pen threw the rag into the sink and crossed her arms. As she shifted her weight around on her feet, she tried to hold back a smile.

"Okay, so maybe he freaks out a little when something unexpected happens."

"Well, lots of people do that," Mama said. "But not everyone made a classroom of twenty kids crawl under their desks after someone pushed over a set of lockers in the hallway."

"What happened?" I stacked some plates and chuckled.

"Oh, okay." Pen finally gave in to our amusement. "Some kid pushed over a row of lockers at school, and Billy overreacted a little."

"Get Down! Hurry! Save yourself!" Mama's imitation of Billy must have been accurate, because Pen burst out laughing.

Pen blotted her eyes with her sleeves.

"Last week we parked his truck out by the pond, and somehow we must've put the thing in gear because before we knew what happened, we'd rolled into the water. We didn't even notice until water started coming in underneath the doors. When he started yelling, I thought it was because his truck was being immersed in water and mud but then"—Pen gasped for breath and covered her mouth—"then Billy yelled, 'Get the raft!' Before I could say anything he reached behind the seat and pulled out a life raft. I yelled for him to stop, but it was too late. He pulled the string and inflated the raft right there in the seat between us."

Mama and I held onto one another to keep from falling to the floor.

"It was worse than being hit with an airbag. I had to open the door and crawl head first into the mud."

With that visual in mind, Mama let out a laugh that sounded like the air being let out of a balloon. It was as if someone had released a toxic mixture of laughing gas into that room and we'd all fallen prey to its effects.

It felt good, laughing together. Pen was still my quirky little sister, but for the first time in her life, she was falling in love.

After we regained our composure, I asked about Cecil.

Mama put the last dish away and closed the cabinet door. "Let's sit down. I can finish the kitchen in the morning."

Like every child in the world, I knew that when your mother asks you to "sit down" what follows usually isn't going to be good.

"Mama, just tell me."

"Good news first." Mama took a sip of water and leaned forward. "Sam called today and said he's glad you're home."

"And?"

"And he said the doctors have been amazed at how much Cecil has improved over the last couple of days. He's struggling to move the fingers on his left hand, but they say that's most likely because they operated on that arm, not because of complications or anything like that. They expect him to make a full recovery."

"Well, that's great news, right?" I felt confused.

Mama leaned back in her chair.

"Sam also said that Cecil saw something while he was under the water trying to save that boy."

"He saw something? Like what?"

"Cecil won't talk about it now, but Sam thinks that when Cecil was under the water"—Mama ran her fingers along the side of her glass—"Sam thinks he saw *you*."

"Under the water?"

Mama nodded. "That's what he said."

That couldn't be true. Cecil must have said something ridiculous because of the trauma. I wasn't in the river. I was in—

It was silly to feel like I needed an alibi, but I still tried to remember where I'd been the morning Cecil went fishing with those boys. I had been at home. I was hundreds of miles away.

I covered my face with my hands and saw myself running water into the bathtub the day of the accident. I wasn't in the river. I was in Memphis—wishing I could end the pain of losing Cecil and our baby by drowning myself.

"Amanda, what's goin' on?"

I shook my head behind my hands. "I tried to drown myself."

"What did you say?" Mama asked as she pulled my hands away from my face.

"I tried to drown myself the day of Cecil's accident."

"What? Why?" Pen asked. "Because of what happened to Cecil?"

"No." I wiped my tears on my sleeve. "I didn't even know about it yet. I didn't really want to drown. I just wanted to make the hurt stop. I just wanted everything to stop!"

"You mean with Frank?" Mama asked.

"I mean with *everything*!" I yelled.

Mama got the picture and backed away from the question. She knew I wasn't going to talk about the past with Pen in the room.

I closed my eyes and lowered my head to the table. Mama tried to comfort me by placing her hand on my back, but instead her affections turned my hurt to anger. Before she had a chance to say anything, I pushed the chair back and stood up.

"Where's Sam?"

I wanted to pound my fists against something. I wanted to run into the yard and kick the tree. I grabbed the door handle and pulled, expecting it to open right away, but each time I jerked it, the knob the door refused to open. The feeling of being trapped infuriated me, so I kicked at the door.

"It's locked. Back up."

"Locked? Since when did you start locking the stupid door?"

Mama pushed her way in front of me and turned the lock. I growled under my breath as I stepped out onto the porch. *How could Cecil have seen me when I was more than a hundred miles away? It wasn't possible. It was absurd.*

I never should have come back here.

I hurried down the steps and into the darkness. *God, I hate this place.* My foot caught hold of something, and I tumbled to the ground in the same spot where I'd fallen as a child and broken my arm. My knees hit the ground before I had time to put my arms out, so at least there was no chance I broke it again.

As I tried to get up, headlights burned across the oak tree. I knew that in a matter of seconds a car was going to whip around the side and park on top of me.

"Get up!" Mama yelled as I flipped over and scurried backwards toward the steps. The headlights grew wider and brighter. I tried to get out of the way.

As I reached the bottom step, the car eased to a stop.

Joy deserted my heart and for a long, long time
I lived in doubt, anxiety, and fear.
HELEN KELLER

Chapter Eighteen

I tried to shield my eyes from the bright headlights. I knew whoever was visiting us at that hour and was driving around to the back wasn't just a passerby.

As the headlights dimmed, I turned to my mother, who was still standing in the doorway. "Who is it?"

"It's Sam," she said as if she'd been expecting him the whole time.

I felt weak when I realized she'd asked him to come. Staring into the darkness that pooled around the bottom step and poured onto the lawn, I wiped my face with my sleeve and waited for him.

When I heard the car door open and the familiar sound of heavy work boots step onto the grass, part of me wanted to get up and run to him. I wanted to wrap my arms around his neck. I wanted him to tell me everything was okay, but I was afraid too much time had passed since the last time I saw him. I didn't want him to be disappointed in me. I didn't want Sam to reject me.

As he came closer, I closed my eyes.

Deep inside me, I knew the closest thing I'd had to a father since Daddy's death was standing in front of me, but I couldn't even look at him.

The gravel crunched under Sam's feet as he stopped at the bottom step. "Hey, baby-girl."

With my chin still lowered to my chest, I stood and lifted my arms. The boards beneath my feet moaned as if the weight of my heart might cause them to break. I couldn't speak, so instead I wrapped myself around him and laid my head on his shoulder.

Mama finally broke the silence and asked him if he'd like to come inside for coffee and angel food cake.

"No, but thank you, Tilly," Sam said as he let me go. "I thought if Amanda wanted to, we'd go for a little ride." Sam opened the passenger door and held out his hand for me to join him.

I started to ask where he was taking me, but I decided I didn't care. Sam smiled as I climbed into the car and fastened my seatbelt.

Pulling off the gravel and onto the pavement, I realized how clean and new the car smelled and how funny a 200-pound man looked while driving it. The last time I saw Sam was the day he drove me home in the red Ford pickup. I'd held onto that image for more than a decade, and the car didn't seem to fit well with it. I leaned against the door and watched Sam force his body behind the steering wheel.

I wondered if he knew as little about that day now as he did then.

Sam exhaled and tugged at the bottom of his shirt to allow more room for his massive belly. The moss and ginger smell of Sam's cologne began to fade and was soon replaced by a powdery scent.

"Sorry about the car," Sam said as if he'd read my mind. "Merle took a load of flowers home from the hospital today, and now this car smells like a flower shop."

Mama told me he'd married a woman from Birmingham named Merle who she didn't like very much. I hoped the slick car belonged to her.

"Is this her car?" I asked.

"Now you don't think I'd drive this thing around all of the time, do you?"

I smiled a little but didn't want him to know how truly relieved

I was that it wasn't his regular form of transportation.

"Where are we going?" I finally asked.

"We're gonna get a burger. I'm starving."

I set my gaze on the open fields as they flew past the window. It looked like someone set a heavy sheet of black velvet across the horizon, making it impossible to tell where the thin row of trees began and where the sky started. I could've drawn a map of each valley ten years ago, but as we got closer to town every half mile of what used to be cornfields had been replaced by freshly landscaped subdivisions.

"How's Cecil?" I asked, turning back toward Sam.

He squirmed in the seat again. "Stupid car." He adjusted his belt and ignored my question.

I wished I'd asked how *he* was or even how Merle was before I jumped to Cecil, but it was too late—the question was already floating around the dashboard.

Sam bent forward and squinted his eyes. "How's this?" he asked, turning into a familiar parking lot.

The car jerked and bounced as we pulled off the pavement and into the decaying, asphalt lot of Patmos Diner. I pressed my face against the coolness of the car window and looked up at the same neon sign that'd been swinging from its iron anchor for over four decades. As I got out of the car, I expected to find at least one familiar face in the crowd of young people who stood at the entrance, but I didn't know anyone. Not only did I not recognize them, but they didn't so much as glance at me.

Sam ordered for both of us before we even opened the laminated menus. "I'd like the BB Burger with no mustard, and she'd like a strawberry milkshake."

As the waitress walked away, I caught Sam's full gaze. His eyes were red in the corners and turned down just like his frown. I hoped he'd answer my question about Cecil, but I refused to ask it again. I hunched over and pretended not to notice his disapproval while I closed my lips around the end of the straw. The jingle of the bell that hung on the entrance door broke his stare. I welcomed the intrusion. As I glanced over my shoulder toward the entrance, I was again surprised not to know the person who entered.

"The doctors say he's gonna to be fine, but I'm afraid right now he's experiencing something even worse than physical pain." Sam's tone told me not to interrupt with questions. "I told Tilly he asked about you, but I didn't tell her everything."

"She just told me about—"

"—about what Cecil saw in the water? He won't talk about it now. All he told me was that he knew the other boy was trapped under the boat and wanted to find him or die tryin'."

"How could he swim with a broken arm and leg?"

"We don't know. Doctors think he broke his arm tryin' to flip the boat over, and we guess the boat broke his leg when it flipped. I don't know how he survived, but I swear I'll praise God for the rest of my life because he did." Sam took a long sip of water. "Cecil said he kept grabbin' in the darkness for the boy, but he couldn't find him. Said he could feel the air squeezing out of his lungs but refused to go up for more. He knew he was gonna die, and that's when he saw somethin' in the water."

I swallowed hard. "Well, if he said he saw me swimming in the Tennessee River, then he must have just mistaken me for a mermaid or something."

Sam didn't smile. Not even a little.

"He said he saw you and that you were holdin' something." The waitress returned and placed our orders on the table. Sam leaned back in the booth and thanked her. When she was gone, he opened the ketchup container and emptied it onto his burger.

I sipped the milkshake and tried to hide the fact that I was drowning at that very moment—right there across the table from Sam.

"Did he tell you what I was holding?" I finally asked.

Sam shook his head. "No." After another bite he added, "Do you know that Cecil and his wife are expectin' a baby?"

The word *baby* made my cheeks burn. I wanted to lean forward and yell at the top of my lungs. I wanted to ask him to excuse me while I used the pay phone near the restroom to call my mom and yell at her for her inexcusable lack of information.

Instead, I fought the overwhelming urge to scream, took a deep breath, and hoped the redness in my cheeks would translate as concern.

Sam leaned toward me and poked out his bottom lip. A long breath escaped from his nostrils as his brows pushed together. "I don't know how to tell you this, and Lord knows I've questioned whether or not I should, because I know 'bout your husband bein' sick."

Sam took another sip of water and cleared his throat.

"I'm really sorry this has pulled you away from your family, because I know they need you. But"—Sam searched for the right words as the waitress placed the bill on the table—"Baby-girl, I can tell some part of my boy is dying *again*...and somethin' tells me you're as much a part of it now as you were last time."

"Last time?" I asked, pretending I didn't know what he was talking about.

I swallowed, but the taste of milk and strawberries remained in the back of my throat. Choking back tears, I rolled the berry seeds against the top of my mouth. It would've been easier to cry, but I preferred the acrobatics of holding back the pain I felt. I took another sip of the shake, closed my eyes, and resisted the urge to jump up from the table and run to the hospital.

I wanted to tell Cecil I was sorry for walking away—for hurting him.

The only part of Sam's story that mattered was the part that crept up from deep within and wrapped its fingers around my heart.

Cecil was going to be a father.

I placed my hand on the back of my neck and rubbed the tight knots under my skin.

"The last time you left you took a part of Cecil with you. It took a while, but God finally filled that hole. Now that this has happened, the hole's back."

"Well, I'm sure God will fill it again."

Sam leaned back in the booth and looked around the dining area as I ran my fingers back and forth along the tops of the sugar packets.

"Can I ask you something?" Sam spoke with the ease and calmness fathers often use when it's time for the truth to be told. "What happened?"

"It's not my place to tell you. If he never told you, it must be because he doesn't want you to know."

Sam wiped the corners of his mouth. "He told me some."

"He did?" I dropped my chin and began pulling the sugar packets out of the small rectangle container. "What'd he tell you?"

Sam reached over and put his hand on top of mine so I'd stop fumbling with the condiments. "He told me about the baby."

"There was nothing we could do. It just happened. I didn't even know I was pregnant."

"Did your mama tell you not to tell Cecil?"

"No. That was my decision."

"And you thought he wouldn't find out?"

"No. I wanted to tell him, but the truth was that I was glad I lost the baby. I was only a kid. I didn't want to live at the Refuge House with all those homeless, knocked-up prostitutes, the women my mother took pity on every day while I raised my little sister. I wanted a life, a normal life. And when Cecil was gone and the baby was gone, I had my chance again."

Sam looked around at the other customers. "And how's that workin' for you now?"

I pushed the milkshake around with my straw and considered his question. "I love my husband, and I love my children."

"Can I tell you the story about when Cecil came home after two years of college ball and told me he wasn't going back? It killed me, because I knew he could do more than come home and sell nails like his daddy. It took a long time, but I finally realized that him quitting was the best thing that ever happened to me."

I didn't understand what he meant.

Sam pushed his uneaten burger aside and leaned forward again.

"When he came home, he was broken and hurting. He'd hit rock bottom and had no desire to climb out. That's when we learned that being the best and working the hardest is nothin' if you're doin' it for yourself."

"I don't understand."

Sam tapped the table three times. "I realize that."

"Are you saying Cecil didn't believe in God until then? Because we had plenty of talks about God."

"I'm tellin' you, Cecil didn't *need* God until then. He was so puffed up on who he was and what he was doin' that he never stopped to think about who'd given him all that strength and ability. I know that's my fault, but I can't change the reason why he didn't go back to school any more than you can change the reason why he came home. "

"Why did he come home?"

"He said he wanted to work with me and take over the shop one day, but I think he was buyin' time until you came back."

"And then he heard I was getting married?"

"Yep. So, a few weeks later, he woke up one morning, put on a tie, and went to church. I let him go by himself a few times, but then I started to worry people would think poorly of me, so I started going with him."

"Did you go to our church?"

"No, we started going to a little church in Sheffield. There were only about fifty people at the time, but then he started gettin' involved with some of the kids and playin' football with them on Saturdays. Now there's so many kids we could form two full teams and have just as many cheerleaders if we wanted to."

I tried to be happy for Cecil. I wanted my heart to jump for joy at all the wonderful things going on in his life, but deep down I longed to be a part of it.

"Is that where Cecil met his wife?"

"Yes. She comes from a rough background, but under the surface she's a good girl. She reminds me of Radella."

"And the boys in the boat? Were they from the church?"

"They were both members of the youth group. I think that's part of the reason why Cecil's hurtin' so bad right now. He was tryin' to help those boys."

Sam pulled out his wallet and placed a bill on the table. I thanked him for the shake as we waited for the server to return with his change.

"I don't know what I'm supposed to do. I want to help Cecil, and I know there's a lot between us that's gone unsaid." I took a second to consider my words. "But I can't see him. If I go there, I'm afraid I won't be able to leave."

Sam stood up and offered his hand to me. "If you don't intend to see him, why'd you come home?"

"I'm here to visit my mother and sister." I grabbed Sam's hand and slid out of the booth.

Sam laughed and pulled me into a hug. "Then I better get you home so you can help Tilly get ready for the festival."

"You know I'm not going to the festival." I forced a smile.

"Yeah, I know, but you've gotta help your mom with the preliminary stuff. I'm sure Tilly has a long list of things for you to do."

For we live by faith, not by sight.

2 Corinthians 5:7

God is love, God is our Father, we are His children;
HELEN KELLER

Chapter Nineteen

When I got home, Pen's car was gone and Mama was already sleeping. In the kitchen, I found a note letting me know Frank had called to check on me and the kids. After ten minutes of feeling my way around in the dark, I finally found my purse hanging on the hook near the front door. My phone showed that Frank had called three times while I was gone. I stepped out to the porch and dialed half our number before realizing that if I called and told him something that didn't match Mama's story, he'd be concerned about what I'd been doing. I turned off the phone and put it in my front pocket.

A light rain began to fall as I sat on the porch swing. I listened to the delicate sound of a thousand leaves awakening to the unexpected shower. It was the most peaceful thing I'd ever heard—the way the crickets hushed and listened to tiny drops of water fall from the clouds above us.

I thought about Frank and the sad fact that I hadn't called to let him know we'd made it to Tuscumbia. I closed my eyes and listened to the storm grow stronger.

Poor Frank.

I tried to pray and thank God for him, but every time I began to soften, my mind would drift to a dark and unforgiving place.

The tips of my toes were the only things touching the painted rafters below the swing. I used them to push myself to the rhythm of the rainfall. I pictured myself riding on the back of one of my rocking horses. In my imagination, I held onto the reins and leaned over to look at the ground below me. The grass blew in the wind as the horse rocked north then south. The heavy wooden rockers pushed the grass deep into the earth. With every rocking motion the horse sank deeper and deeper into the earth.

I lifted my foot and placed it next to the other one on the porch swing and felt the swing slowly come to a halt. If I was going to move forward in life, I knew I'd have to stop teetering in one direction and then the other. I'd have to get off my horse and learn to walk again.

"Hello! Dad-dy. Hello-o? Da-Da."

I strained to open my eyes as sunlight blinded me. My eyes felt like they were connected to the nerves along my spine. With every blink, a new part of my body screamed with pain.

"Daddy!"

Lilah pushed the swing back and forth as I tried to pull myself up into a sitting position. Once I was up, I realized she was wearing nothing more than a diaper and one pink sock, and that she was speaking into a cordless phone.

I took the phone out of her hand and placed it to my ear. My first attempt to speak came out not in words but in a long *grr* that I mistakenly directed into the receiver.

"Amanda?"

"Good morning," I murmured, wishing I hadn't let last night's milkshake build a fortress of muck inside my mouth.

"Are you okay?" Frank asked.

"I must've fallen asleep on the porch. How do you feel?"

"Better today than yesterday," he said, knowing that he'd continue to feel better for another six days—until he began his next round of chemotherapy.

That's the cruel reality of the drug and the disease. When you finally begin to feel like yourself, one or the other attempts to kill you again.

"So, did they lock you out or did you choose to sleep in the open air?" I was thankful he didn't sound upset with me. He could've criticized my decision to sleep outside. He could've asked why I hadn't called the night before, but he seemed happy to hear my voice. "Honey told me about all the things she has planned for you this week."

"Oh, she did? Well, I can't wait to hear for myself."

"Yes, and she told me I could come join y'all if I wanted to. That way I wouldn't miss the motor vehicle show or the live music or the outdoor play—"

"I think the kids and I are going to skip all that fun and just hang around here."

"Come on. You should check it out. Maybe you'll decide to rent a booth next year and sell some of your rocking horses."

"Yeah, and I might as well just buy myself a stage and invite everyone I know to walk by and laugh at me."

"Your horses are amazing. I think all of your old friends would be blown away by them."

"Okay, I'll think about it."

"Good. Now you have to promise me one more thing."

"What's that?"

"Promise me you'll find something healthy for the kids to eat while you're there."

"You know I will." I was more than ready to hang up.

The aroma of homemade biscuits filled the air. It was the same smell that filled the kitchen every Sunday. Every Sunday…and *always* on the first day of festival week.

"You know what today is, right?" Mama asked as I entered the kitchen carrying Lilah.

"Yes, and I'm not going."

Mama turned to look at me. "Okay."

I waited for her to reason with me about why I should go, but she said nothing.

"No, really, I'm not going."

Mama nodded. "Okay."

"Come on, Lilah, it's time to get dressed." I grabbed a biscuit as I reached for her hand.

"Put her in something nice, please."

"We're not going!" I pinched off a corner of the warm crust and placed it on my tongue. Before we reached the top of the stairs, the entire piece had melted like butter against the top of my mouth.

Lilah and I entered the bedroom and found Christopher exchanging his favorite Spiderman pajama bottoms for the same khaki shorts and dress shirt he'd worn the day before.

"No, sweetie, that's for church. Just put on a T-shirt."

"But Honey told me to put on something nice to show her friends."

I should have known. She no longer cared if I went. She was much more interested in taking her grandbabies. I had one of two choices: Either I could let her take the kids while I sat at home or I could swallow my pride and go.

Maybe it would be nice to go to the festival.

If I didn't know anyone at the diner, maybe I wouldn't have to act friendly at the festival either if nobody recognized me. I knew the children would love the parade and the magical tent where the women from the Refuge House sold ornaments.

I made up my mind—if she insisted on taking them, I'd have to go as well.

After I got dressed, I hurried downstairs and found Lilah and Christopher taking turns in the rocking chair.

Mama pushed open the swinging door. "Let's go. We're late."

When Mama was no longer in sight, Pen darted through the living room and charged up the stairs. A minute later she hustled down carrying two Santa hats.

"Better get the kids out here or Mama's going to throw a fit."

"Tell her I'll bring them in a little while."

Pen skidded to a stop. "You're going?"

I rolled my eyes. "Just tell her, okay?

"Okay. We're gonna drop off all these biscuits at the bake sale, then hurry over to Christmas Village. Just meet us there."

"Okay."

As we loaded into my car, Christopher asked me about the Refuge and the women he'd heard so much about since our arrival. I'd only visited the riverfront mansion at the end of Montgomery a handful of times, but in recent years Pen had starting working there fulltime.

Before we were born, the Refuge House was donated by the widow who once lived there with her seven adopted children. Her dream was to leave behind a safe-house where women could stay until their babies were born. My mama and sister spent most of their time making sure that woman's dream was being fulfilled.

The sign on the front door of the house had a verse from 2 Samuel painted across it: *My God is my rock, in whom I take refuge.*

The word "refuge" circled round and round in my mind as I buckled Lilah into her seat. When she was fastened, I looked in the direction of the cemetery and closed my eyes, remembering my rock— and it wasn't God.

Toleration is the greatest gift of the mind;
it requires the same effort of the brain
that it takes to balance oneself on a bicycle.

HELEN KELLER

Chapter Twenty

The streets of Tuscumbia were packed with more out-of-town visitors than locals, people who'd traveled from all over the country to take part in the festivities. There were hundreds of vendors selling jewelry, paintings, handmade clothes, and every fried food imaginable. Mama thought of it as heaven. I didn't.

My attempt to park in the lot behind Food Mart was a complete disaster. A Wonder Bread truck blocked the exit and filled my car with the smell of Memphis. It's remarkable how in a city the size of Memphis, the Wonder Bread factory has the ability to break through the thick clouds of smog and noise and fill you with a hunger so potent you have to fight hard against the urge to pull off Monroe Avenue and beg for a sample of freshly baked bread.

I recognized the irony of the situation as soon as the frustration of being blocked by the truck occurred to me. As my fingers gripped the steering wheel, I realized I'd spent the entire morning basking in the smell of my mother's homemade biscuits. I savored each bite as it melted in my mouth and momentarily felt at peace with being at home again. Her bread was the poison that softened my resolve long enough to agree to come to the festival.

Sitting in my car less than an hour later, here I was, cornered by a bread truck that filled me with a longing for my Memphis home.

I placed my head on the steering wheel and closed my eyes. "God, help me."

"Mom, I'm hungry."

"Hungry, Mommy," Lilah added.

"Mom, we're really hungry," Christopher said again.

"Okay! We're gonna eat as soon as this truck moves out of the way."

"But we're hungry."

After the third cry, something inside me snapped and sent me into an unexpected rage. "Well, I'm hungry too, but there is nothing I can do about it right now!" I turned to find both kids staring at me.

"I'm sorry. I'm hungry too. As soon as the truck moves we'll go and find some lunch."

I was hungry, that much was true, but mine was different from my children's hunger.

"Am-an-da Reyes! Girl, what are you doin' here?"

I didn't need to search the crowd for very long before I found the source of the Southern drawl. Before I could blink, Mrs. Towner was holding me by both shoulders—the same way she had at the end of every Christmas recital. She had the same short haircut that she'd had when I was a kid singing in her choir but with a larger gray tuft near the front. Even in June she wore a sweater tied across her shoulders.

"Mrs. Towner, you haven't changed a bit."

"Oh, come on." She gave me a light tap on the arm before bending down to greet the children still strapped in the double stroller. "Aw, and who are these two beautiful children?"

"This is Christopher and Lilah. Children, can you say hello to Mrs. Towner?"

Both children responded to my question by staring at her with a glazed-over look.

Mrs. Towner didn't seem to find their reaction the least bit surprising. I guess she'd gotten used to that look after so many years of asking a roomful of children to sing, clap, and smile at the same time.

"They're just precious, Amanda. I know your mama is so proud of you. She talks about you and her grandbabies every time I see her. Oh, and I'm so sorry about your husband. Girl, I know you must feel like yer candle is burnin' at both ends. I'm gon be prayin' for you."

She didn't know the half of it.

"Thank you, Mrs. Towner. It was so nice to see you. Now I better find these kids some lunch before they have a meltdown."

I was relieved when we finally made it through the crowd of people without running into anyone else from my past.

The kids were busy eating their corndogs and rubbing mustard into their cheeks when we finally made it to Christmas Village. Mama was dressed in the same red shorts and white shirt she'd been wearing when she left the house, but she'd added a red Santa hat and sequin earrings.

"You made it!" she hollered as if she was seeing me for the first time in weeks.

On the outside, Christmas Village was nothing more than a white tent with walls draped in the same canvas material as the roof—the kind of tent people use for outdoor weddings, professional golf tournaments, and makeshift firework "stores" set up in parking lots before the Fourth of July. A passerby can't really grasp the magnificence of the place until they step inside.

Mama and I wrestled the children from the stroller and wiped the condiments from the fronts of their white shirts. Lilah was covered in streaks of red and yellow.

Mama cleaned Christopher's face and cut her eyes at me. "You couldn't find something less messy for them to eat?"

"You're starting to sound like Frank."

"I'm not sayin' it has to be organic. I just wish there was less on their clothing."

Crossing through the opening of the tent and arriving inside the massive space was like walking into a sanctuary for the first time and feeling overwhelmed by its vastness. There were no tables in the makeshift room. Instead, the roof and walls were woven together with grape vines, Virginia creepers, and miles of stripped kudzu vines; every inch of the interior tangled around itself. The women at the Refuge House spent two months every spring weaving the walls with ivy and tiny strands of Christmas lights.

I watched as Lilah took it all in. Her little face glowed with eager delight. She reminded me of myself as a child—blinking and struggling to understand what she was seeing.

Overhead, tiny angels made from corn stalks, homemade glue, and bamboo leaves danced and twisted in the breeze of a box fan. The room was filled with children, as well as several women who were clearly from the Refuge House, their bellies all swollen with child.

Christopher carefully made his way to one of the walls and ran his hand along a thick vine until its path was blocked by one of the tiny lights. "Mommy, are we inside a tree?" he asked.

I knelt down beside him. "No, sweetie, this place was made by most of the women in this room. Every year they work really hard to braid and weave it all together. Then they make these ornaments for people to buy and hang on their trees at Christmastime."

"Can I have one?"

"Yes, you and Lilah can each pick out one to take back to Daddy."

Lilah twisted out of my arms and toddled toward the wall behind her brother. They touched every ornament that hung at eye level.

When I was a child, I hated to see people take the ornaments down and buy them. I wanted them all to stay inside that magical place. When I was five, Mama let me pick out a small Mother Mary made of silver glitter and pale blue yarn. She had the most beautiful face, with her eyes drawn as crescents that made her look so peaceful. I was so proud of my selection that I could hardly wait to get it home and place it on the shelf in my room until winter, but the second I left the tent the magic of it was lost. In the hot sun, I could see all of Mary's imperfections. A piece of glitter hung from her mouth, and glue licked across her forehead as if she'd been run over by a snail.

Christopher called to me from the place where we'd entered the puzzling vineyard.

"I want this one! What's it say, Mommy?" He pointed to a small metal sign that hung to the left of the entrance.

I hoisted Lilah into my arms, much to her dislike, and walked over to where Christopher was standing with three of his fingers resting on a tin sign the size of a Post-It note. The tiny metal plate was decorated with bead-strung wire and red ribbon.

"What's it say, Mommy?" he asked again.

Painted on the front in thin white letters were the words "I am the vine, ye are the branches." I read the words aloud, expecting that he wouldn't understand and would move on in search of something else.

"What's that mean?" he asked, never taking his eyes or hand off of it.

"It's from the Bible. It was written to remind us that Jesus is the vine and that we are the branches."

"Is that Jesus?" He pointed to the withered vines along the walls.

"No, sweetie, it just means that we are all small and weak and that we can't do anything without God." The words caught on my tongue and hung there—lifeless and dead. I'd heard my mother say that to me a thousand times, but now the verse from the book of John made my heart ache. I knew the rest of the verse said something about remaining in God in order to be fruitful. I swallowed hard, hoping to bury the thought. I knew how far from God I'd traveled. I could almost feel Him moving in the darkness behind me.

"Can I have this one? Please?" Christopher asked.

I helped him untangle the wire from the vine and gently placed it in the palm of his hand. "Let's show Honey." On our way out, I pulled one of the angels down from the vines above our heads and handed it to Lilah. She touched the angel's paper wings and decided that would be her gift.

As we left the tent, Lilah and I were forced to pause for several seconds in order to allow our eyes to adjust to the sunlight. I squinted hard and was relieved to see Mama and Christopher checking out his newfound treasure in a shaded spot near the road. I recovered the stroller and placed Lilah back into her seat. Strapping her in was usually a difficult task, but her unwillingness to cooperate was eased by her distraction with the angel.

I pulled a few loose bills from my pocket and paid for the ornaments as a police car pulled onto the curb and raised a cloud of dust into the air. An officer got out of the car and scanned the crowd. My first thought was that someone must have recognized one of the pregnant mothers as a wanted felon.

I covered my mouth to keep from inhaling the dust and realized the officer, one of Daddy's old friends, was rushing toward Mama.

Lilah bounced around as I pushed the stroller through the crowd as quickly as possible.

By the time I got to Mama, the officer had taken her by the arm and was helping her to the car.

"What's wrong?" I asked.

Pen ran up beside me and asked the same question.

"The house is on fire!" Mama yelled before jumping into the passenger seat and slamming the door.

"What?" I asked, turning to Daddy's uniformed friend.

The officer hurried around to the driver's side. "I'll get her back to the house. Can you get back on your own?"

"Go with her!" I yelled to Pen as I grabbed Christopher's hand.

Pen jumped into the backseat and slammed the door.

The car was gone before I got Christopher fastened into his seat.

We could never learn to be brave and patient,
if there were only joy in the world.

HELEN KELLER

Chapter Twenty-one

When I got within a mile of the house, I could see thick smoke above the trees and knew it wasn't going to be the small brush fire I'd been praying for. I pressed the gas pedal and sped along the rough pavement. When I turned onto the road that ran along the upper field, I could see three fire engines fighting a blaze that had already consumed the back of the house and was moving along the roofline.

The car skidded to a stop on the gravel at the end of the driveway. I had parked far enough away to keep the kids safe but close enough to see Mama in complete panic. She kicked the ground and yelled at the blaze. I left the car running and yelled for the kids to stay in their seats before I jumped out and ran toward her. When she saw me she dropped her head into her hands and began to cry.

I put my arms around Mama and held her tight. Even from a distance of fifty yards, the blaze and smoke burned our eyes. The heat of the inferno felt like 300 degrees on her back. I held her and stared up at my childhood home in disbelief.

"I did this," she mumbled, turning toward the house again. "Oh, my God! How could I do this?" Mama's face looked as if it had caught fire as well.

I had no idea how to respond. It was clear the fire had started in the kitchen, which most likely meant she'd left something on after cooking the biscuits.

"I was the last to leave, Mama. I should've noticed the oven was on."

I pulled her back as the windows on the porch began to billow smoke. Even the firefighters backed away as the house began to creak and moan.

Penelope's face was red and soaked with tears as well. "It's nobody's fault," she said.

A fireman in full yellow gear waved for us to move, so we went to sit on an iron bench in the corner of the yard.

We sat in disbelief. Everything was lost. We watched and cried as the curtains in the living room caught fire and dissolved as if they were made of paper.

All of the things Mama had collected over the years were gone. The things my grandfather made. Grandma's rocking chair. My first rocking horses.

I wanted to say something to ease the situation, but everything seemed anemic as we sat with the heat of the blaze still dancing at our feet.

Mama sobbed into Pen's arms, the Santa hat still fastened to her head.

"Well, too bad the fire didn't get the hat." The second I said it, I regretted it.

Pen cut her eyes at me and began to laugh. Mama sat up and slid the hat from her head and used it to wipe her face. Black mascara streaked the fluffy white trim like tire tracks in the snow. We laughed so hard that some of the firefighters turned and looked at us as if we were delusional.

After a few minutes, Mama stood and walked toward the house. With the Santa hat still in her hand, she knelt down and picked up some of the gravel.

Mama put the rocks into her hat and tossed it onto the porch. She stood there for a long time—any longer and I would've been afraid she was planning to run head-first into the blaze. Instead, she turned and walked to the car.

I got behind the wheel as Mama closed the passenger-side door and Pen squeezed between the kids in the back seat.

"Where are we going?" I asked as I started the ignition.

"I need to tell your father."

A minute later we topped the hill next to the workshop. I slowed the car as we pulled past and got a good look at the rotten wood. One match could've turned the shed to ashes. When we were past it, I looked into my rearview mirror and watched a cloud of dust fill the space between the workshop and me.

Mama got out of the car after I parked beside the entrance to the cemetery. The field was bone dry, but inside the white picket fence, lush grass covered a dozen graves. I hadn't been to the cemetery in years, but it looked as though someone had gone every week to cut the grass and groom the tiny azalea bushes that hid behind every headstone.

Pen and I watched as Mama went through the archway covered with wisteria vine. She didn't look up as she closed the gate.

Pen leaned forward and put her hand on my shoulder. "Why don't you go with her, and I'll take the kids back to the Refuge House. There will be plenty of other children for them to play with there."

She must have known that part of me wanted to go—and that another part was scared to death of what I might feel once I entered that gate.

"Go on."

I nodded my head and lifted the car handle. Penelope was climbing across the armrest and into the driver's seat by the time I finally placed both feet on the ground.

"They'll be fine," she added before closing the door and driving away.

I waved to the children through the car window and blew them both a kiss. Once they were gone, I followed Mama's path through the arch and into the cemetery.

I couldn't believe how beautiful it was. She must've gone there every day to trim the grass and prune the flowers. I imagined her carrying buckets of water from the nearby ditch and sprinkling it across every inch of the grassy area.

Mama was right where I knew she would be. She sat with her legs crossed and arms in her lap on top of Daddy's grave.

She looked my age sitting on the ground cross-legged. The visual reminded me that Mama had been visiting Daddy out here since she was my age.

I joined her and sat in the same position.

Mama ran her hand back and forth across the blades of the grass like she was petting an animal. Her eyes were closed, but she found my hand anyway and held it tight. Tears ran down her face but she didn't wipe them. She just let them flow.

I stared at the headstone.

Karl Dexter Reyes, December 4, 1948–March 8, 1990.

"I'm so sorry, Mama."

Mama stopped praying and opened her eyes. "No, I'm sorry. I'm the one who destroyed everything."

"You know, I've never really liked that house much anyway."

Mama frowned. "Why is that, Amanda? Why don't you like this place?"

I pulled a blade of grass from beneath me and ran it along the palm of my hand, gently tracing the lines and creases. "It's just hard to come home."

"But you loved being here when you were a child." She lowered her head and tried to break my stare. "I know it hurts to be reminded about the baby, but you have to let it go."

"I did let it go—for a while. Or at least I ran from it pretty well, but when Frank got sick all of the hurt came back times twenty." My lungs swelled in my chest until they felt tight around my heart.

"Baby, I know you still care about Cecil, but you don't love him. You love Frank and your babies."

"Cecil and I had a baby once too." I choked as the words left my mouth. "And I do love Cecil. I've always loved him.

The sun burned the back of my neck as I searched for the right words. Words that would finally show Mama how much she'd hurt me.

"You said I'd have to leave home if I ever saw him again. I'd just had a miscarriage, and you said that to me. I was just a child. I was scared, I didn't want to lose anything else."

"I never said that."

"Oh, yes you did."

"Well, if I did it was because I was a scared mother who couldn't bear the thought of losing anything else either. You weren't the only one who was suffering! I lost your father too, and I was still trying to get over losing my mother to lung cancer when I found out you'd been sneaking around behind my back and having sex with your boyfriend."

I dropped my head and closed my eyes.

Mama grabbed my hand and held it between hers. "Losing that baby was horrible, but you can't keep blaming yourself for it. It wasn't anymore your fault than the wreck that killed Karl and Radella."

"I don't blame myself." I jerked my hand back, pushed off the ground, and dragged myself to my feet. "I blame God."

I walked across the narrow row of graves and knelt in the corner near the fence.

Hidden beside one of the posts was the rock I brought up from the creek the week my baby died. I lifted the stone and rubbed a thin layer of mud from the bottom to reveal the place where I'd etched a tiny horse—not a rocking horse but a galloping mare.

I could feel Mama's eyes on me as I cradled the rock in the palms of my hands.

Mama came over and knelt beside me. She held out her hand, and I gave her the rock. Then, without a word, she stood, placed one foot on the ledge of the wooden fence, and started climbing.

In a matter of seconds she'd scaled the three-foot-high fence and was running across the field, two-pound rock in hand.

"Mama!"

I lifted myself over the wooden two-by-four and took off after her. "Mama! Stop!"

"I've been gardenin' around this rock for too long! I'm not gonna do it anymore!" She gained speed as I fell farther and farther behind.

"Mama, please stop."

She slowed to a jog as she reached the line of trees at the edge of the field.

When I got close to her, she took off into the woods, dodging branches and hurdling broken limbs until she got to the embankment.

I skidded to a stop behind her. She faced me and held the rock over the ledge. "It's time to let it go, Amanda."

"Don't even think about throwing that into the creek."

"Fine," she said as she grabbed my wrist and slammed the rock into my hand. "Then you do it!"

I turned the rock over in my hand and looked down at the shallow water.

Mama knelt down, grabbed a piece of rotten limb, and held it out to her side. "I know you think if you let go of the rock it will be like sayin' you didn't love her or you didn't care. I felt the same way about your father for a long time—even before he died." Mama looked at me and then back to the piece of wood. "Karl, you old rotten branch, from now on I pledge to cling to the Vine!"

Mama closed her eyes and swung the branch into the ditch with all her strength. When she heard it crash against the trees and fall to the water, she opened her eyes again.

I looked down at the rock. I wanted to run, but I also wanted to be free. I'd given my baby a name the day I'd placed the rock in the cemetery, but I'd never said her name out loud.

I closed my eyes and tried to find the strength to let her go. "Suzanne—" I listened to the name echo through the trees. "You are a heavy stone, but you are not my foundation!"

I heard the stone bounce twice and break apart after I tossed it. If it hadn't, I probably would've jumped in after it.

And that faith,
the rock not fashioned of human hands,
be the stability of our triumphant, toiling days.

HELEN KELLER

Chapter Twenty-two

I knew what I had to do, and that *knowing* was what drew me up from the ground and allowed my feet to carry me back across the field. The stone wasn't the only thing I needed to let go of. I had to let go of Cecil as well, and that *knowing* was what led me across town, after I dropped Mama off at the house of a church-friend, and into the lobby of Helen Keller Hospital.

After stopping at the nurses' station to ask directions, I found Cecil's room and quietly opened the door. The nurse was right—he was alone and resting.

I eased the door closed and crept closer to the bed.

Cecil's eyes were closed, but I still felt like he was watching me. Everything inside me wanted to reach out and touch his dark skin. I missed the feel of his hands, the taste of his lips—the way he kissed my neck.

God, are You really through with us?

I watched Cecil's chest rise and fall.

If it's over, then let it be over. Help me not love him anymore.

I moved the doctor's stool closer to the bed and sat down, but the stool was too low so I repositioned myself in a chair near his feet.

For some reason that made me think of the Bible story about Ruth sitting at Boaz's feet, so I went back to the stool.

All of my fidgeting caused Cecil to open his eyes. When he saw it was me, he turned his face away.

"Hi."

Cecil kept his gaze focused on the window. "Why are you here?"

"Why do you think I'm here?"

"Who told you?"

"About the accident or about what you saw in the river?"

Cecil blinked twice before looking at me. "I didn't see anything in the river, so you can go now."

"Okay, I just wanted to make sure you were all right."

Cecil was clearly in pain. "Where is everyone?" he asked.

"I don't know. No one was here when I came in. It's close to dinnertime, so maybe they left to get something to eat." I looked around the room until my eyes settled on a cup of water beside the bed. "Can I get you anything? Some water, maybe?"

"No. Thanks."

The nurse in me took over. I started to straighten the sheets on his bed, without thinking of it as anything more than a task. Cecil stopped me and took my hand. I couldn't let go. Neither, it seemed, could he. Each of us seemed to be waiting for the other to break the connection.

I pulled my hand away as the door opened and a nurse entered the room. She introduced herself and busied about as she asked him questions and checked his monitor.

I welcomed the few moments her entrance gave me to compose myself. When she finally left, Cecil turned and faced me again.

"I'm glad you came."

"Should I leave now?"

"I know you're going to leave. I know you have to."

I slid my hand back into his. "I wish we could talk longer. I have so much to ask you. There are so many holes in our lives—so many missing pieces."

I stopped and reminded myself that I hadn't come here to catch up.

"Tell me about Lilah and Christopher."

It was the first time I'd heard him say the names of my children. His words quickly settled into an empty place in my heart. I wondered if he'd ever imagined them the way I did—as his children, as our children.

"Oh, Cecil, I'm so sorry. I'm so sorry that I hurt you and that I left you and especially that I never said goodbye."

"I'm sorry I didn't fight for you...and that I let you go."

I cried the entire way to the Refuge House.

Cecil didn't tell me what he saw under the water the day he almost drowned. Sam said he'd seen me holding something, and I was desperate to know what that something was. I allowed myself to believe that he'd seen me holding a baby and that he had survived because seeing me with our daughter gave him a reason to live.

I wiped my face and pounded the stereo button until the music turned off.

The Refuge House came into view after I turned onto Tenth Avenue. The house was surrounded by large groaning trees that seemed anchored into place by tall clumps of monkey grass. Even the house seemed to bulge as if it was planning to give birth.

I parked my car on the street and entered through the front door. Inside, I found the kids eating grilled cheese sandwiches, fresh sliced peaches, and butter pickles. Pen was talking with several of the women I'd seen at Christmas Village. I kissed Lilah on the head before she joined another child in the makeshift play area.

Pen cleared the kids' plates from the table. "We have an empty bedroom upstairs that we'd love for you to stay in."

"What about Honey? Where's she going to sleep tonight?"

"Some of her friends from church are helping her settle into the mission house. She wants us to leave her alone tonight but said she'll come by in the morning."

I accepted Pen's offer and settled the kids into a spare room at the top of the stairs. After they drifted off to sleep, I found a quiet spot in the front yard and stood staring at my cell phone. I needed to call Frank and tell him about the fire, but I struggled to press the numbers. I wanted to scream. I didn't feel any better, and I was almost certain that Cecil didn't either. Finally, I made the call.

Frank answered after only the second ring. I quickly got through the story of the fire, assuring him every few minutes that we were fine and filling any silence with questions as to how he was feeling. I was grateful when the conversation ended. At that moment, a group of women erupted into laughter on the porch.

As I climbed the steps, the three of them stopped laughing and asked me to join them. One of the women, a Hispanic woman with long black hair and dark eyes, rocked in one of the rocking chairs. She rubbed her abdomen as if she was trying to settle her baby.

I joined a large African-American woman on the swing before noticing the small leather Bible and a spiral-bound notebook she held in her lap. She introduced herself as Beeny, which sounded to me like a name that should belong to someone half her size.

Beeny's hair was wrapped in a beautiful African scarf, and she'd already settled into a long white nightgown with red appliquéd flowers across the chest. She had kind eyes, but something about them seemed to ache.

Beeny settled the swing as I sat down. "Your sister is one special lady, Mrs. Amanda."

"Yes, she is." I noticed a pink scar on Beeny's chin that seemed to have just recently healed. "Pen really loves her time here. I know she's learned a lot from all of you."

"Yeah, we tried to teach her some stuff, but she got a long way before she's gonna be good at dancin'."

I laughed and assured them that I'd spent many years trying to show her how to move to the music, to no avail.

The front door opened and out stepped Pen. "What's so funny?"

"Oh, nothing," Beeny chuckled.

Pen crossed her legs and sat on the floor near our feet. "I thought you ladies were about to have your devotional."

I realized what the Bible and notepad were about and began to excuse myself when the Hispanic woman grabbed my hand and asked me to stay. Without her touch, I probably could have gotten past them and back into the house before they could stop me, but her resolve forced me back into my seat.

Beeny opened the Bible and began leafing through its worn pages until she found the place she was looking for—a page covered with inscriptions and writing along both margins. It reminded me of Frank's Bible, the one his mother gave to him when he was young. The one he reads every morning before the kids and I wake up.

Another woman never moved until Beeny said her name. "Emma Sue, do you remember what part of the Bible I said I'd be readin' from tonight?"

The woman was startled at the sound of her name and tucked a long black curl behind her ear. "My name's Thumper," she whispered, cutting her eyes at me. "Just call me Thumper."

Pen put her hand on Thumper's back. "I think she said we were going to read from 1 Samuel, Chapter 2."

Beeny straightened and jolted us both into a bouncing motion before she began speaking again.

"We've been talkin' 'bout one of the best mothers who ever lived—the mother of the prophet Samuel. She was a barren woman whose husband loved her. She begged God for a child and promised if He gave her one that she'd give him right back."

I planted my feet on the porch in order to ground us.

"Tonight, we're gonna read what Hannah prayed after God blessed her." Beeny wiped sweat from her top lip and read with a deep voice. "Then Hannah prayed and said: 'My heart rejoices in the Lord; in the Lord my horn is lifted high. My mouth boasts over my enemies, for I delight in your deliverance. There is no one holy like the Lord.'"

Beeny lifted her hand into the air and continued reading. Each syllable burst forth like thunder as the women settled into their chairs and listened.

"'There is no Rock like our God. Do not keep talking so proudly or let your mouth speak such arrogance, for the Lord is a God who knows, and by him deeds are weighed.'"

When she finished she closed her eyes, bowed her head, and waited for us to do the same.

Beeny began to speak, but this time her voice was low and hushed.

"Father, You gave us these words, and You gave us this wilderness. Lord, there is no Rock like You. Show us Your way through the power of Your Spirit, and give us the strength to give everything over to You. Amen."

Emma Sue sat quietly the whole time and pulled at the tips of her fingernails. If she'd not been so far along in her pregnancy, she probably would've drawn her knees up under her chin and held her legs close to her chest. Instead, she sat hunched over with her hands tucked beneath her pregnant belly. She turned away when she realized I was looking at her.

Love always finds its way to an
imprisoned soul, and leads it out into the world
of freedom and intelligence.

HELEN KELLER

Chapter Twenty-three

After everyone was asleep, I crept into the kitchen looking for something that contained either chocolate or alcohol. I would've preferred a little of both, but because pregnant women are usually advised to stay away from both, I had to settle on a small bag of potato chips instead. When the bag was half-empty, I sensed Beeny enter the room behind me.

"I thought you'd gone upstairs," I said with more surprise than I'd intended.

Beeny arched her back and let out a long moan. "Well, I had, but I thought I heard you shufflin' 'round. Guess I was right."

"It's always hard for me to settle in somewhere the first night." I stretched my neck. "And now I feel like I've had two first nights in a row."

As Beeny came closer to me, I stiffened and turned to face her. She must have seen my uneasiness, because she stopped in midstride.

"Well, I'm glad I found you in here 'cause I was hopin' maybe we could talk." She pulled two of the wooden chairs from underneath the kitchen table. "I seen somethin' in you out there tonight. It was like lookin' in a mirror, Mrs. Amanda."

I wondered how a 200-pound black woman could look at me and see any resemblance.

Beeny sat down at the kitchen table. "Sit down with me. I'm gonna show you what I been thinkin' 'bout lately."

As I approached the table, she shifted her weight from one side to the other. I pulled the chair farther away from the table and sat with both elbows on my knees. I don't remember her grabbing my hands, but within a few seconds she was holding them and rubbing her thick fingers along the back of my wrists and knuckles.

"There it is!" she said, as if she had found exactly what she'd been looking for. "There it is. Just like mine—your knuckles are white as chalk."

"What are you talking about?"

"Mrs. Amanda, your knuckles are white like mine 'cause you're holdin' on tight to somethin' that ain't yours. I know how you feel—I got a baby growin' inside me that I want to keep more than anythin' in the world, but I believe that God's wantin' me to let her go." The pain between us moved like electricity between our fingers. "Just like the story we were reading on the porch—me and you are beggin' God for somethin' that was never intended for us."

I took back my hands. "You seem like a nice lady, Beeny, so I don't understand why you're here."

Beeny leaned back and put her heavy elbow on the table. "Mrs. Amanda, I'm not gonna tell you my story. But I am gonna tell you that I believe in a God who only gives to open and empty hands."

"And you think that mine are closed tightly around something?"

She patted my hand and stood. "And I believe that God doesn't just show us a way out of darkness. He allows us to taste it so we'll draw closer to Him.

"I think He's waitin' for you to open up your hands. That's the only way you're gonna get to know Him."

"I know who God is, Beeny. I've known Him my whole life."

Beeny ran water into a cup and took a sip before heading for the door.

"Maybe you've heard Him, but I don't think you've seen Him."

When I woke the next morning the children were no longer sleeping in the bed next to me. I could hear laughter and music downstairs. Commotion filled the hallway as women hurried past the bedroom door.

I had to lie down on the bed in order to zip up the clean pants Pen gave me. The shirt buttons pulled so far apart I was afraid they might come off if I sneezed. Still, it was good to have something to wear that didn't smell like soot. I needed to go somewhere and buy a few things for myself and the children. I dug through my purse, hoping to find a piece of gum to tide me over until I could get to the store and buy a toothbrush.

There was movement outside in the hallway again. I recognized a few of the voices and was headed toward the door when it flew open and in came Lilah, covered with flour and wearing a dress that looked like it'd been handmade twenty years earlier. The fabric was burgundy with thousands of tiny turquoise flowers. The capped sleeves puffed out like balloons that could have lifted Lilah off the ground had they been filled with helium.

"Oh, Lilah, what a lovely dress." I complimented her by raising my right arm and bowing the way an English gentleman would.

She held her arms up high and revealed a mouthful of pancakes. The sight of her lifted my spirits, so I grabbed her hand and gave her a twirl.

I gathered the few things we had left and headed down the long, narrow hallway. The walls were covered with photographs of women, children, and small babies. It was a portrait hall like you'd find in the home of any Southern family, except this family didn't just cover generations; it covered races, state lines, and denominations. Each photograph had been taken in the foyer downstairs. I identified the exact spot by the rich damask wallpaper in the background of every photo. Their faces were filled with sadness, longing, peace, and some-times joy—either for the new place they were heading or for the child they were leaving behind. There were hundreds of photographs, which meant that hundreds of women had spent some part of their lives in the Refuge.

Suddenly, I realized the number of lives my mama and sister had touched.

One woman smiled back at me as if she was listening to my thoughts and considering each one of them. Her eyes matched the blue wallpaper, and her hair was pulled into a loose bun behind her right ear. She wore a purple sash around her neck and matching lavender earrings. She couldn't have been much older than thirty, but something about her clothing and hairstyle made her seem older. I wondered where she was now. Had she gone home? Had she taken her baby with her? There was no way to know for sure. The Refuge House didn't keep any record of the girls' names or even the sex of the babies. The only way to know how many women had lived there was to count the number of faces that lined the hallway or count the birthdates carved into the walls of the prayer porch.

In any case, I was sure the numbers wouldn't come close to lining up.

The walls of the small screened porch that led to the grassy area behind the house were covered with the birthdates of each child born at the Refuge, but the porch had endured many rainstorms and had been repainted a time or two over the years. Some of the names were hard to read.

I looked back at the photo and blew a thin layer of dust from the bottom of the frame. With my index finger, I pushed the corner of the frame up so it hung level with the others. Before I went downstairs,

I closed my eyes and thanked God for the blue-eyed stranger in the photo and her decision to find help.

When I entered the kitchen, Mama called to me from behind three other women. "Amanda, would you like some coffee?"

It was almost 10 a.m., but because Mama had no other place to lend her all-too-eager hand, she had arrived early to help the women who were assigned to cooking breakfast, while the others drowned their pancakes in Karo syrup the same way Cecil did when he was a boy.

I figured out right away that every task at the Refuge was designated, assigned, and taught to the women by Pen on a rotating schedule. That was her favorite part of the job. Helping the women with labor and counseling them through the heartbreak that came with putting their babies up for adoption was not.

Mama handed me a large coffee mug that read "Alexander Printing Company." I took the cup and read it aloud, recognizing the name as the one my friend had taken when she married her college sweetheart. "Is this the company Rachel and her husband started?"

"Yes. Rachel's so sweet. She gave us all kinds of stuff they couldn't use after they changed their logo." Mama handed me a pile of sugar packets. "Can you believe she has four babies? Her mama is so proud of her. I saw them last week at the tire shop, and she said to tell you hello. Why don't you call her and let her know everything's okay? I know she'd love to catch up."

"Mama," I said, with the same authority I'd always shown her in the midst of this type of conversation. "I am glad everything's going well with Rachel, but we're just not that close anymore."

"Sweetie, she and the other girls are your friends. Why don't you call them? Megan would love to hear from you. She's gettin' married again."

"We talk a couple of times a year, and that's plenty."

"You should call them right now. Tammy's doing a show in New York, but the others are in town, chasing kids and whatnot. You should call them and go do something."

"Great idea." I rolled my eyes. "'Hey, did ya hear my husband's dying and the house burned down, but come on girls, why don't we get together for lunch? I'll get out the old poncho and rain boots and we can slide on down to the river again.' Great idea!"

The other women began to either excuse themselves from the kitchen or pretended not to hear us.

"Oh, give me a break! You know this is hard on me, too. I just lost everything, and my son-in-law is fighting for his life while my daughter takes care of the kids and tries to pay the bills by selling rocking horses."

"Are you kidding me?" I wanted to slam my hand against something. "I make beautiful pieces of art that sell all over the country. I'm not trying to support my family, I'm just trying to be who God created me to be."

Mama closed her eyes and shook her head. "You make me crazy!"

Pen came in and gave me an exasperated look before I had a chance to remind Mama that she'd been crazy longer than I'd been alive. "I'm too old for this."

Mama huffed and went back to washing dishes.

When the other women began mingling again, I noticed Emma Sue sitting at the kitchen table. She was hunched over her untouched pancakes with her curls draped over the edge of the table.

Beeny had followed my sister into the kitchen and was singing something about Jesus until she noticed Thumper at the table. "Get on up and sing, Emma Sue, 'less you're gonna eat something."

Emma Sue pushed her chair away from the table and left the kitchen. I helped clear her cup and plate, and apologized to Mama before handing her the dirty dishes.

Pen agreed to watch the kids while I ran a few errands. I needed to buy some toiletries even though I was hoping to leave town as soon as possible.

After pulling up to Alisha's General Store, I adjusted the rearview mirror so I could see my eyes. They were wrinkled with age and still had tiny pieces of black mascara smudged around the bottom lashes.

Great. Now I'm sure I'll see everyone I know.

Thankful that my list was short and all I needed were the essentials, I blinked and pushed my eyebrows upward hoping to appear younger, but I decided to just wear my dark glasses.

Inside, a woman sat on the floor refilling the lotion shelf. "Let me know if ya need anythin'," she said without looking up.

I passed by the more expensive brands of makeup and stopped once I reached the section I knew and loved as a child—Hot and Spicy. I tossed several items into the basket. I even decided to try the glittery golden eye shadow, creatively named "Glittery Golden Shadow for Eyes."

Before searching for underwear, I grabbed some deodorant and three toothbrushes. I'd never bought panties at Alisha's before, but I knew they'd have them. They had everything. I even saw a ridiculous variety of pet-themed slippers near the entrance.

"A-man-da?"

No.

Rachel opened her arms and scampered in my direction. "Megan, come over here. It's Amanda!"

God, no. Why?

"Hey, Rachel. How are you?"

"I'm fine, but I just heard about your mama's house! I am so sorry! Are you okay? My mama said you were there when it happened but that the kids were okay." Rachel wrapped her arms around me.

"Well, I wasn't actually there, I mean, I was in—"

We were interrupted as Megan rounded the corner, carrying a basketful of puppy-faced bedroom shoes and red nail polish. "We were just talkin' about you! Are you okay?"

"I'm fine, thank you."

Megan put down her basket and wrapped her arms around me too. "I can't believe it. I mean, I. Am. So. Sorry. How's your mama? It must've near killed her. To lose everything in one moment. I would die. And how's your husband? I'm sure he's just the nicest man ever. Except for my Westley—he's really the nicest man ever. Do you know I'm gettin' married again?"

Rachel laughed and rolled her eyes. "Megan, you've got to stop making everythin' about Westley."

"Well, I'm sorry, but he's wonderful."

"As all chicken farmers are, but for the love of fresh poultry. Amanda's old house just burned down, and her husband is sick. Can we talk about that for ten seconds without hearin' about Westley?"

I smiled watching their exchange. *Maybe mama was right.*

Megan let out a familiar burst of laughter that made us all laugh.

"Oh, please come to the weddin', Amanda. Please."

Standing in the aisle at Alisha's General Store, my friends caught me up on all the news about town. Tammy, who was once the fourth wheel of our group, was indeed making it big as a star in New York City. They were a little upset that she no longer answered emails or called home, but I couldn't blame her—she'd probably given them more of her time than I had over the last several years.

Megan said the slippers were for a wedding shower they were giving a friend that night. They invited me to stop by, but I declined.

"Amanda, we miss you, and we'd love to spend time with you. I hear your children are beautiful. I'd love to meet them."

I hugged them both after loading my purchases into the car.

I felt grateful and ashamed all at the same time. Before going our separate ways, we promised to plan a trip to see each other. I was glad to see them, half certain that my mother had called to tell them where to find me—but, still glad all the same.

I am not discouraged, nor am I afraid.
HELEN KELLER

Chapter Twenty-four

The mission house shares a fence with the parking lot of First Presbyterian Church. Sooner or later, everyone in Tuscumbia steps through the tall white doors of First Pres. They worship there, marry there, or are carried from there in a big pine box—some people have the privilege of all three. That's how it was for Daddy.

He loved worshiping there and let Mama squeeze us into her favorite pew, the one where Helen Keller sat with her family when she was a child. Other parishioners knew better than to sit in *our* pew.

After picking up the kids from the Refuge, I drove to the mission house to drop off a few things for Mama. She agreed to take the church up on its offer to house her until she found somewhere else to stay, even though most of the time the mission house was reserved for church leaders and missionaries. I was beginning to realize that Mama was a little bit of both.

The Share Shack is what the regular churchgoers call it—not only because so many people have shared it, but also because Share was the name of the family who owned the house before the church bought it several years earlier. When the Shares lived there, it was a two-bedroom, two-bath cottage with no landscaping and only a small chain-link fence separating it from the church parking lot. Since then, the house had grown by two bedrooms and been given the most beautiful landscaping in the whole city. And in addition to the extra space, they'd added a red-brick porch complete with two gorgeous Harkins chairs. Whatever gift I have for building rocking horses, Greg Harkins has for building chairs—times a thousand.

I parked on the street near the driveway. Lilah loved the tall red and white impatiens lining the broken sidewalk. Lilah rarely ever came home from being with Frank when she didn't have some type of half-dead annual hanging from her barrette. It didn't matter if they were in a restaurant parking lot or taking a meal to someone they'd never met, Frank always let her pick a flower for her hair.

We knocked twice on the red door. Two young pastors greeted us. The first—a short, balding man—welcomed us while the other stood cautiously examining us out of the corner of his eye. After introducing themselves, they showed us through the house and into the backyard.

The house was just as I remembered it: clean, crisp, and slightly outdated. Every inch was filled with donated furniture in various shades of blue. There was at least one wing-back chair in every room, and the walls were covered with odds and ends like Duck Stamp prints and wooden crosses. Cross-stitched pillows were thrown on every couch, chair, and bed. The largest pillow—the one tucked into the corner near a television—read "Sometimes God calms the storm, sometimes He lets the storm rage and calms His people instead."

And sometimes He lets everything you own go up in flames, I wanted to add.

We found Mama in the prayer garden. She was sitting on a small metal bench praying with a tiny, gray-haired woman wearing a loose-fitting dress made of purple linen. The woman whispered prayers as Mama nodded and mumbled something every few seconds. I motioned to the kids to stay close to me and keep quiet until they were finished praying.

Mama thanked the woman before they turned to welcome us. Mama introduced the kids first and then me. I shook the stranger's hand and squinted at the familiarity of her fragile face—and her radiant blue eyes.

"Tilly's told me so much about you." The woman spoke in gentle phrases. "We pray together every week for you and your family. Just last week we were rejoicing over all of the things God's doing in your life."

From any other mouth, the word "rejoice" would have felt like sand in my ears, but from her it sounded like a piece of a song that I had forgotten.

I thanked her and turned to face Mama. "We brought you a few things from the store that we thought you might need." I handed her the small plastic bag.

"Lotion, granola bars, gum, a toothbrush—" Mama knelt down to the children as if she was investigating a Christmas gift. "Oh, and look at this...some nail clippers and some gold eye shadow. How lovely." Mama made a silly face at Lilah, who returned her gesture with a perfect chuckle.

"Do you like it?" Christopher asked, grinning from ear to ear.

"I love it! Y'all sure were sweet to bring me this stuff. Now run and look at all of the pretty roses, but don't touch because then they might get you!" Mama tickled Christopher's tummy before he ran along the rocky path toward a beautiful bed of roses.

When the children were gone, the woman took us both by the elbows and led us back toward the house.

"Amanda, I've told your mother that she's welcome to stay here as long as it takes. We don't have anyone scheduled to live in this house until after the holidays. We'd love to have her help us keep watch of things until then. When are you going back to Memphis?"

"I was planning to stay until the end of the week, but now I think we should head back tonight."

Mama's shoulders dropped as the woman started speaking.

"I thought you might've gone to see Cecil by now."

Her comment rippled the foundation I was standing on. No one knew that I'd been to the hospital. Mama and I hadn't even discussed it. But something told me that this woman knew lots of things no one had told her. I watched Lilah sniff a rose as she and Mama patiently waited for me to respond.

"Yes, ma'am. I saw him yesterday."

"How did that go?"

"Ok, I guess." She waited for me to continue. "It had been a long time since we'd seen each other."

The woman smiled as if she understood. "Did you ask God to break the tie?"

"What tie?"

"The promise that you made to each other when you were young."

I pushed the tips of my shoes around in the rocks. "Not really."

The woman glanced at Mama and then back at me. "He's going to get better, you know."

"Yes."

"And then what?"

I took a long breath and considered my answer before settling on a response. "And then my husband's going to die, and Cecil will have a baby, and I'll be alone."

"Is that why you're here? You're afraid of being alone?"

"No, I'm here because the man I've loved my whole life almost died and because when he woke up he called for me."

"Would you have come back if Frank was healthy?"

"I don't know," I said.

"Do you know what love is, Amanda?" The woman touched my arm.

"Love is being willing to give up everything for someone, I guess." I stepped out of her reach. "But I can't do that. I can't leave my life now."

"God doesn't want you to leave your life, and I'm certain He doesn't want you to leave your husband either. I promise you that

God will never ask you to do anything different from what He asks you to do in the Bible. The Bible gives us a pretty good description of what love is."

"Yeah, I know. Love others as—"

"No. You don't have any problem loving others as you love yourself. The problem is, you don't love yourself. The Bible says that 'Love is patient, love is kind. It does not envy, it does not boast, it is not proud, it is not rude'—and, Amanda, it is not self-seeking."

"You think I'm self-seeking?"

Mama crossed her arms, making me think for a second that she might ask the woman to give it a rest.

"What I think is that you're on the fence, just like you've been for a long time, and that you're quietly waiting to run in and devour everything in sight just for the sake of self-preservation. And what I'm afraid of is that if you don't learn what love *truly* is before your husband dies, then you're gonna come back one day and foil the blessings God's given to Cecil...and to you."

I listened to her describe me as an animal waiting to devour its prey. I wanted to lash out at her and dismiss everything that she was saying, but I knew deep down that it was true—all of it.

"Until you understand how much God loves you, you're never going to love others the way He intends for you to."

I sat on the bench and watched the children play while Mama walked the woman to her car. When she returned, Mama sat next to me and put her arm around my shoulders.

I used my thumb to pull my shirt collar to my face and wipe a slather of makeup and sweat from my cheek.

"Who was that lady?" I finally asked.

Mama sighed as she stroked my back. "Oh, she's just an old friend of mine. We've been praying together for a long time. Since before your Daddy died."

"She looks familiar. Have I ever met her before?"

"I don't think so, but she's lived around here for a lot of years."

Mama blotted the makeup smear on my borrowed shirt. "Let's go inside. People from the church have been dropping off clothes and food all day."

"I'm a wreck, right?"

"Come on," she said, standing up. "We'll find something great for you to change into."

I grabbed Mama's hand. "No, I'm not talking about my clothes. I'm talking about my heart."

Mama pulled me up. "We all need a heart transplant, Amanda. I know you feel like yours has turned to mush, but the truth is that your heart's turned to stone. Don't worry though. God promises to give you a new heart and put a new spirit in you." Mama drew me into her arms and held me close. "That's what He did for me."

We found some clothes that seemed a bit more fitting for me and the kids before filling our stomachs with pimento cheese and crackers. The kids found a quiet spot in one of the bedrooms and rested for a bit in front of the TV while I called Frank and updated him on how things were going. He told me about the long list of people in Memphis who were praying for us. I wasn't surprised at how quickly the news had spread.

Frank sounded lonely. He usually felt lonely only during his off week, when he wasn't taking his chemo pills. He described his loneliness as the burning feeling he gets when he finally starts to feel *alive* again. When he's at the height of his treatment, he feels too bad to care, but when his body begins to heal and recover from the medicine, he begins to long for other things.

I know that feeling—the one that accompanies pain and

discontentment. For a moment, I hated that I wasn't with him.

What if this was his last good week? What if the new doctors and tests at UT Medical showed that what we were doing wasn't enough to stop the cancer?

"I miss you." His voice was low and cut a sliver of flesh away from the wall around my heart.

"I miss you too," I said. "I'll be home tonight."

"I know Honey needs you. Why don't you stay, and I'll come to Tuscumbia?"

I shifted my weight from one leg to the other and decided to leave the room where Mama could hear me. I found a quiet spot in the prayer garden and listened to his plan for joining us.

"Some of the neighbor's friends are headed to Corinth tomorrow, and they said I could ride with them. Can you pick me up there in the morning?"

I wished for a couple more days to fix the damage that I'd done at the hospital. "I guess, but you know we're staying in a borrowed house and wearing borrowed clothes. I can't imagine why you'd want to be here."

"I can bring you some of your things. I..." he paused, clearing his throat. "I just want to be with you."

"Are you sure you feel like being here?" I bit my lip and waited for his decision.

"Please," he said. "Let me come and spend some time with you and the kids. I should've gone with you on Sunday. I'm sorry you've had to go through this on your own."

A few minutes later, I hung up the phone and went inside. It was getting dark, and the kids needed a shower. I needed a soak.

Christopher and Lilah were excited to stay with Mama at the mission house. It was quiet there—peaceful and calm. We played cards with the kids for a long time after dinner and settled them into a room filled with bunk beds. Before I left the room, I kissed each child on the forehead and thanked God for their gentle hearts.

Surely there are hearts and hands
ever ready to make it possible
for generous intentions to be wrought
into noble deeds.

HELEN KELLER

Chapter Twenty-five

I tossed and turned for two hours before finally drifting off to sleep. Then, at midnight, I woke again to the creaks of the mission house. Lights from passing cars flashed around on the walls only twice during the time that I lay in bed, staring at the blank ceiling. The woman in the garden kept appearing in my mind.

Who was she, and why did she look so familiar?

The embarrassment from my outburst at the Refuge House also weighed heavily on me. It was too late to call Pen and apologize. I should've done that earlier. I should've apologized to her when I got back from Alisha's General and told her how sorry I was about the scene I'd caused in the kitchen with Mama. Instead, I'd just grabbed the kids and left. *Typical Amanda.*

After dinner, I had swallowed enough pride to tell Mama I was sorry for my behavior. I even told her I loved her, but as soon as the words crossed my lips, I remembered the way the strange woman had questioned whether or not I had any understanding of love at all. Her words ran circles in my mind, digging ruts into my temples. I begged for sleep and tried to make my body give up the fight, but her words forced their way into the front of my mind. "Love is patient, love is kind." I knew the verse. I had even taught the verse to the kids in Sunday school, but lying there alone in that room, I couldn't remember how it ended.

"Love is patient, love is kind. It does not envy, it does not boast, it is not proud. It is not rude, it is not self-seeking." *What is the rest?*

I rolled over again and buried my face in the pillow. Who cares? Just go to sleep!

I was on my feet before I knew it, rummaging through the drawers of the bedside table. The house was designed for missionaries. Surely there was a Bible around there somewhere.

No luck finding one in the bedroom. Maybe in the living area, near the entry hall. I tiptoed past the bunk room and toward the front of the house. There were angels of all shapes and sizes, and two stacks of devotionals, but after several minutes of searching, I still couldn't find a Bible.

Exhausted, I sat down on the couch and held one of the embroidered pillows to my chest. My body needed sleep.

I put my feet on the coffee table, being careful not to bump the crystal vase and flowers, and sank into the creases of the couch cushions. That's when I saw a small Bible tucked under a figurine near the front door. I pushed the pillow aside and went to the door. The white cover of the Bible was almost completely hidden by the object resting on top of it.

I turned on a lamp. The ceramic piece on the Bible was a tiny bench like the one in the garden, except on this bench sat a disproportioned yellow rocking horse. Its rockers were red and worn, and the saddle was like the one I was working on in Memphis, with tiny pink roses painted against a blue background. Wisps of brown paint gave the illusion that the mane, tail, and forelock had been combed and braided.

I ran my finger along its cold face. His eyes were missing and his ears too. Vacant white holes sat below the horse's brow. I imagined that diamonds once sat in the empty sockets, but someone had cut them away and pawned them. The horse was small, no bigger than a silver dollar, but he was huge in proportion to the bench. I realized they hadn't been sold together, so I pulled at the bench and tried to separate it from the rocking horse. Neither would budge.

I wanted to keep it, to tuck it away in my pocket and put it on a shelf when I got back to Memphis. I promised myself that I'd put it somewhere safe where no one else could reach it—somewhere it wouldn't burn.

I gave up, put the figurine down, and opened the Bible to the 1Corinthians 13. The tiny pages felt like silk in my hands. Bits of the double-fan binding chipped free and then settled again in the grooves of the page. I scanned the beginning of the verse and then slowed down once I reached the part I remembered.

"It is not self-seeking...it is not easily angered, it keeps no record of wrongs. Love does not delight in evil but rejoices with the truth."

"It is not easily angered." I whispered the words and thought about the fight I'd had with Mama. I was so quick to anger and filled with hate and dissatisfaction. The words bounced around in my gut as I continued reading: "It keeps no record of wrongs."

Maybe love doesn't keep records of wrongs, but I sure do.

I shut the Bible and placed it back on the table. I picked up the ceramic bench and rocking horse and cupped it with both hands. It wasn't perfect, and neither was I.

Sleep finally came after I prayed and swaddled myself like a baby. I felt more certain of God's presence than ever before. He was in that house with me. I could feel Him watching and waiting for His plan to unfold. God had withheld sleep so I'd go to His Word, and He had arranged the meeting with the woman in the garden as well.

In the darkest hours of the night, He'd held me like I'd held the horse and bench. I felt safe in His arms—not alone like in a dream, but full of Him, full of His Spirit. I begged that the feeling would stay and not get smothered out like a flame.

I liked the way He burned inside me.

His fire was real.

Morning crept into the room like a mouse, and I was waiting to pounce on it. I was excited that Frank was going to be joining us soon. I missed him, and I welcomed that feeling.

I let my feet hang out of the end of the covers the way a child does. The hum of the air conditioner muzzled out the sounds coming from the yard and blew a cool wind across my toes.

I remembered my dreams. In the first one I was a child running around in a forest filled with flowers. The flowers were heavy with moisture and hung toward the earth. Vines and branches blocked out the sky, except for occasional blues and shades of orange that pushed through the leaves and danced around below me. I wasn't alone. I could hear the laughter of other children, but I couldn't see their faces. We were playing a game with a rope and a ball. A little girl with dark skin laughed and tossed the ball to me. I knew, somehow, that her name was Martha.

In the second dream, I was one of the women at the Refuge House. My belly was big and round, and I could feel a baby move between my ribs the way Christopher had when he was growing inside me. In my dream, I was wearing the same clothes I'd borrowed from the mission house, except the T-shirt constantly rolled up my pregnant belly. No matter how many times I pulled it down, it would roll back like a window shade. It felt ridiculous walking around the house with my belly exposed, but the other women didn't seem to notice. They just moved about, laughing and singing. Then the dream ended.

I sat up in bed when I heard Mama walk by the door and head

down the hall toward the kitchen. I got out of bed and followed her, stopping at the children's room to pull the door closed. A few seconds later, I found Mama in the kitchen, busy making coffee.

"Good morning," I said, nearly scaring her to death.

She jumped and gasped for breath.

"Sorry," I whispered.

"I'm just not used to other people being around this early."

I thought about how quiet the old house must've been for her in the early mornings. I couldn't imagine a morning of waking up and starting the day without the constant chatter of children.

Frank always wakes up before the rest of us. That's when he talks to God. It's when he prays. Even when he's the sickest, he starts his day with prayer. I asked him once why he thought the Lord listened better in the morning. "God doesn't listen better," he said. "I listen better."

I knew exactly what Frank was doing as Mama and I shuffled around the kitchen looking for coffee beans—he was sitting in his overstuffed chair talking to God.

"When're you goin' to meet Frank?" Mama asked while she poured water into the coffee pot.

"I'm not sure. I'll call him after the kids get up."

"I'd like to take them to Ivy Green to see everyone rehearse for the play if that's okay."

I took a deep breath.

"The play" is a theatrical performance called *The Miracle Worker*. It's a reenactment of the struggle that Anne Sullivan faced when she first began to teach Helen Keller how to communicate. Every year during the festival, children from Tuscumbia perform *the play* in the outdoor theater behind Ivy Green where we celebrated my sixteenth birthday. Not only has Mama never missed *the play*, but she's also never missed the rehearsals.

Mama opened a cabinet, pulled down two coffee mugs, and placed them on the counter beside the sugar jar. We discussed what time the rehearsals would start, along with other things she needed to do regarding the house. She had a lot of phone calls to make and wanted me to deliver some food to the Refuge. I was thankful for the excuse to visit Pen. I wanted to tell her how sorry I was for my outburst the day before.

Mama sat down at the kitchen table and opened some of the letters people had left when they dropped off food—way too much for us, which was why I was taking it to the Refuge. She asked me to grab a notepad and pen from the drawer below the phone and join her at the table.

"Do you want me to write down who they're from?"

"That would be great. I can't imagine the number of thank-you notes I'll have to write before all this is over."

"Why do you have to write thank-you notes? I mean, you're the one whose house burned down. Can't you just skip the notes, for crying out loud?"

"No, I can't. Not in this part of the country!" She chuckled.

I wrote down the names of the people and what they'd brought as Mama passed me the empty envelopes.

"Also write down Lada."

"Is that the woman I met yesterday?"

"Yes. Her name is Lada Prudence." Mama stood up, walked back over to the coffee, and poured two cups while I finished jotting down the rest of the information.

When she came back to the table, I asked her about the horse.

"I found something last night that I'd like to keep, if it's okay with you." I went to the living area and got the ceramic bench and horse from the shelf where I'd placed them the night before.

When I handed it to her, she squinted at it and lowered her reading glasses to the bridge of her nose.

"Oh, wow," she said, looking it over by turning it around in her hand. "Well, it's no wonder you want it. I'll ask Lada about it. I'm sure the church won't mind. Everything in this house was donated by people looking to get rid of stuff. I doubt there's any real sentimental value to it."

Mama handed it back to me as the rotary phone began to shake before finally purring out a dull ring. Mama answered, said a few words, and handed the receiver to me.

"Good morning, Sunshine," Frank said. "Your cell phone went straight to voicemail, so I had to call the house."

"The battery must be dead. Are you headed this way?"

"Not yet. I imagine they'll come get me around lunchtime. I'll let you know when we leave so you'll know when to head toward Corinth. Can you pick me up at the Shell station on 72?"

"Okay. See you soon."

"What's the plan?" Mama asked as I hung up the phone.

"I'm going to leave here around noon to go get him."

"Great! Then you'll be able to go with us to see *The Miracle Worker* before you leave."

"Mama, I've seen it a million times. Please don't ask me to go again."

"If you've been a million, then I've been three times that many. It's still fun."

"Don't you have the whole thing memorized by now?"

Mama held out her arms as if she was Juliet and I was Romeo, awaiting a dramatic hug. Then she placed her palms together and drew them in close to her chest. She took a deep breath and fixed her eyes somewhere on the ceiling above my head.

"Love is something like the clouds that were in the sky before the sun came out. You cannot touch the clouds, you know; but you can feel the rain and know how glad the flowers and the thirsty earth are to have them."

"Is that Shakespeare?" I jokingly asked.

"Dear child—that is Anne Sullivan."

Suddenly curious about the women's lives, I asked Mama if either

Anne or Helen had married.

Mama laughed and took an orange juice container from the fridge. "Oh, now you want to know more about Anne and Helen, huh? Well, it's about time."

"Okay, never mind."

"No, no. I'm sorry, I'll tell you anything you want to know. Anne married, but I don't think it was a very good marriage."

Mama pulled a few eggs from a plastic container and placed them next to a metal bowl near the sink.

"Okay, now ask me something else. I love answering questions about Helen, especially when you're the one asking."

"Are you ever going to get married again?"

"That's not about Helen."

"Come on, Mama. Do you ever think about that?"

"I'd get married if I ever fell in love, but I don't think that's ever gonna happen."

Mama cracked an egg and began beating it with a fork. She looked so young, standing there making breakfast for me.

"Maybe you and Ms. Prudence are like Anne Sullivan and Helen Keller."

"Heaven help me if they bury me next to Lada."

"Did they bury Anne next to Helen?"

Mama turned and pointed her yolk-covered fork at me.

"How do you not know this stuff? Did you not grow up in this town? For almost thirty years you've been saturated in this town and the history of its people. How do you not know anything about your roots?"

"I know plenty about my *roots*, Mama. I know I'm the granddaughter of Etta Sue and James Henry Paxton and born to Tilly Paxton Reyes and Karl Dexter Reyes on June 27, 1980. And I know I'm the older sister of Penelope Grace Reyes."

Mama poured milk into the eggs and began beating them again, but it was too late—I'd already seen something flash in her eyes, something that told me what I'd said wasn't exactly true.

"What?" I asked, suddenly fearful of what she was holding back. "I swear, Mama, if you're about to tell me you're not really my mother, then please don't! I don't want to know. I'm too tired to learn anything else about how messed up my life is."

The woman in the garden appeared in my mind again—the familiarity of her face.

"Mama, look at me."

She tossed the fork into the sink. "I'm your mother, Amanda. Get a grip."

"Then what is it?"

Just then, Christopher walked into the room and wrapped a big hug around my legs. "What're you talkin' about, Mommy?" His big eyes looked up at me.

Mama picked him up under his arms and squeezed him tight. "Oh, your mommy's just being silly." She planted a series of kisses on Christopher's cheek.

"Guess what?" she said, leaning back. "Honey's gonna take you to a play!"

"What's that?"

Mama kissed him again. "It's like a movie, except the people are right in front of you."

He liked that answer. "Lilah!" he yelled, squirming free of her arms. "Honey's gonna take us to a *pay*!"

I knew my suspicions were probably fueled by the fact that everything seemed to be unraveling, but I still couldn't ignore my uneasy feeling.

What was it I'd seen in Mama's eyes when I rattled off my family history?

I think if this sorrow had come to me
when I was older, it would have broken my spirit
beyond repairing. But the angel of forgetfulness has
gathered up and carried away much of the misery and
all the bitterness of those days.

HELEN KELLER

Chapter Twenty-six

Beeny held open the door at the Refuge House as I staggered through carrying some of the food from Mama. Her eyes were red and swollen, as if she'd been crying when I knocked on the door. She took two loaves of bread out of my arms and led me to the kitchen. The house was quiet—not filled with the usual commotion of women and children.

"Where is everyone?"

"Most of 'em are outside." Beeny removed a large bowl from the pantry and filled it with the apples and oranges. "A nurse lady's here. She's tellin' them 'bout how to nurse and feed a baby. I couldn't watch her hold that plastic baby up to her chest no more, so I came inside."

Beeny took one of the apples and cleaned it with her shirt. "Your sister's out there if you wanna see her."

"I'd like to tell her I'm sorry about yesterday. How long do you think they'll be out there?"

Beeny didn't respond to my question. Instead, she took a huge bite of apple and started pushing it around in the sides of her mouth.

When she reached for a cup, I got a better look at the scar that ran from the back of her ear to the nape of her neck.

"Do you think it's okay if I go out there?" I asked.

"Sure, but go out the front and go 'round. There's some people on the prayer porch who's pretendin' not to listen."

"Why don't they want anyone to know they're listening?"

"Well, Mrs. Crosby"—she swallowed another bite of apple—"if you don't plan on feedin' your baby, there ain't much use in learnin' how to do it."

Her words sent a chill down my spine. I'd forgotten that some of the women wouldn't be taking their babies with them when they left. I went to the car to get another load of food.

When I got back, I placed the things on the counter and watched Beeny wash her hands in the sink. I'd never seen someone wipe a piece of fruit on their shirt and wash their hands afterward. Maybe Pen should do a demonstration on pesticides and germs.

Beeny and I found a place to hide the things away before I walked out the front door and around to the side gate. Just as Beeny promised, a path cut along the side of the house and around to where the women were sitting.

Pen noticed me right away and motioned for me to join her on a picnic blanket. I sat beside her and whispered about the extra food. I listened as the nurse explained to the group what types of foods were appropriate for young children and which ones weren't. Then, with great surprise, the woman began acting as though the plastic baby was choking. Some of the girls began laughing, but the woman seemed unfazed as she pulled the baby from its highchair and faced the crowd.

"What do you do if your baby starts to choke?"

"You call 911," blurted a woman at the front of the group.

Another yelled, "Tell it to hold up its hands!"

After the laughter died down, the nurse gave instructions on how to dislodge food from a child's throat. I leaned over to Pen and told her I had to go because of the play.

Pen gave me a surprised look. "You must feel like you're choking."

"You know I do."

I turned to look at the group of women sitting in the screened porch. I could only make out the silhouettes of a few bodies. The one I recognized belonged to Emma Sue. She sat with her head bowed as usual and her hands tucked under her tummy.

"Why's Thumper not gonna keep her baby?"

"I'm not sure. She won't talk about it with any of us."

We watched as the nurse laid the doll across her lap and pushed on its back. Pen grabbed my hand and helped me up.

As we walked to the porch, I told Pen I agreed with Beeny about the doll thing being weird.

Pen laughed. "It reminds me of the doll you used to carry around all of the time when we were little."

"That was the only doll I ever played with. What was her name?"

Pen winked at me. "It starts with an N."

I wiped the sweat from the back of my neck as I tried to remember.

When we got to the porch, we climbed three large steps and opened the screen door. The women looked up—all except for Emma Sue, who kept looking down at her swollen toes.

"Why don't y'all go inside," Pen suggested. "Amanda brought y'all some food."

After they were gone, Pen and I sat where we could see the women sitting in the grass.

"You're a nurse. You should come teach this group sometime," Pen said as she rocked back and forth in her chair.

I ignored her comment while I tried to remember the name of the doll I'd loved so much as a child.

"Nancy!" I snapped, glad that the name had come back to me after so many years.

Pen laughed and rolled back in her chair again. "Of course it was Nancy. Remember how much you loved that doll? That is, until you found out Mama named it after the doll Helen played with when she was a little girl."

I searched my memory but came up empty.

"How's Mom?" Pen finally asked.

"She's okay, I guess. Right now it's kinda like being on a strange vacation."

"Maybe it's good for her to be rid of that house. Maybe it will help her not miss you and Daddy so much."

The white paint was beginning to crack and peel off the chair I was sitting in, so I scraped off a piece with my nail and dropped it onto the floor.

"Pen, do you know a woman by the name of Lada?"

"Why would you ask me that?"

"Because when I got to the mission house yesterday, she and Mama were praying together."

"Yeah, they do that a lot."

"Well, I know I'm not around much, but how can Mama do something *a lot* that I don't know about?"

Pen rubbed her hands along the arms of her chair, as if the wood might soak up some of the sweat from her palms. "I don't know."

"Well, who is she? I know her, but I can't remember how."

The fan spun circles above our heads making a shrill sound with every turn. I looked around at all of the marks on the walls of the prayer porch. There weren't just hundreds of birthdays drawn on the walls—there were thousands.

"Did she ever live here?" I asked.

Pen closed her eyes for what seemed like an eternity before opening them again. Finally, she looked past my shoulder to the chair rail that ran at waist level around the perimeter of the porch. Sliding off the end of her chair, she touched the wood.

As Pen ran her fingers along the board, the sickening feeling in my gut began to swell. When she reached the place she was looking for, she stopped without looking up.

"These are Lada's markings."

I pushed her fingers out of the way and leaned over so I could read what was left of the inscription. The numbers were hard to read at first, but after a moment or two I was able to see them clearly. Right away, I recognized the date. I'd celebrated it for as long as I could remember. My whole life I'd decorated cakes with candles and attended parties in honor of that special day and the person born on it.

"Pen?" The numbers came to life on the wall and almost pulled me down to where she sat looking up at me. "That's your birth date."

"After I found out, I asked Mama and Lada not to tell you."

I tried to find the right words, but naturally the wrong ones poured from my mouth in a slosh of sadness and emotion.

"You're not my sister?" I asked.

"Well—" She pulled her hand from mine and looked around as if someone else had interrupted our conversation. "That's what I was afraid you'd think."

"How long have you known?" I asked with the regret of my last question still lingering in my mind.

"A couple of years. I've always felt drawn to this place, but Mama never wanted me to spend time here. Then she asked me to help start serving the Sunday dinners. One of the girls was so proud of her new home that she invited me upstairs to see her room. That's when I noticed the photograph—the one that looked just like me."

The photograph of the woman with blue eyes flashed in my mind again. The morning I'd woken up in the Refuge House, I'd looked into her familiar eyes, and later that day I'd done the same thing in the rose garden.

"Pen, you'll always be my sister. Nothing can change that." I felt the fan begin to blow cool air around our heads. "I've loved you for as long as I can remember."

"I know. I wanted to tell you, but I couldn't figure out how to do it."

Of course she couldn't. I calculated the timeframe in my head. She probably discovered the truth at the same time we discovered Frank's cancer. I was so busy panicking about my own life I didn't notice the shambles hers was in.

"Pen, I'm so sorry that I've been so caught up in my own world that I haven't taken any time to ask you about yours. I'm so proud of you and everything you're doing."

After I saw her begin to smile, I got up and sat in her lap. Pen winced as I curled my legs into a ball and kissed her on the forehead. "I love you, little sister."

"Get off of me."

Our laughter caused a commotion in the yard as the session outside ended.

"Pen, thank you for telling me."

The witchery of love is in rock and tree.

HELEN KELLER

Chapter Twenty-seven

I resisted the urge to feel angry, but I'd been lied to for so long. I knew myself well enough to know that if I went to see Mama at Ivy Green, I'd probably cause another scene.

Slow to anger, I reminded myself.

I couldn't remember a time when Pen wasn't running around the house with her musical instruments, but I also couldn't remember Mama being pregnant.

Why would a woman like Lada, who seemed to have her life together, hand her baby over to my mama? I couldn't imagine, but I was overwhelmed with gratefulness that she had. Pen was after all *my* sister. Finally, I was beginning to come to terms with the idea of a woman giving up her baby. It helped that I was the recipient of such a perfect blessing.

As I drove along Highway 72 toward Corinth, I felt grateful that I wasn't an only child. Memories of our childhood bounced around in my mind. I'd taken for granted the fact that Pen was always a part of my life. I needed her, and it was suddenly obvious that she needed me too. I tried to flip through our old photo albums in my mind. So many photographs were lost in the fire. I wished I could look back through our childhood. Surely this time I'd notice that there were no photos of Mama with Pen growing in her belly.

I looked out at the hills and valleys and watched as the trees danced and swayed in the wind. I'd driven that route a hundred times and never tired of the horizon.

I'd be arriving earlier than we'd planned at the place where Frank would be. I didn't let Mama know I wasn't going to make it to the rehearsal, but I figured she'd dismiss my absence anyway, knowing that I didn't really want to go in the first place. If she worried, I knew she'd call Pen looking for me. At least that would give Pen the opportunity to tell Mama that I knew about Lada.

Twenty miles east of Mississippi, I ignored a call from Mama and pulled my car off the road. The landscape was breathtaking, and every tree seemed to point toward heaven. I could have stayed there all day watching the trees bow and bend against the breeze.

When my grandmother was growing up, Old Highway 72 passed right through the heart of Tuscumbia. Now it bypasses Old Lee Highway and Main Street so travelers don't drive through downtown anymore. Most people go around my hometown and never stop to enjoy it. I guess for a long time I was like that highway. I found it easier to go around my past rather than straight through the heart of it.

I walked around to the passenger side, leaned back against the door, and watched the sunlight fade into the tops of the trees. Purple light seemed to rise up like a cloud of smoke along the edge of the horizon. I breathed in the beauty of hill country.

The highway stretched out for miles in both directions. To the west it would take me underneath the Natchez Trace and through the northern tip of Mississippi toward Tennessee, and if I followed it northeast through Alabama far enough, I'd eventually end up in some part of Tennessee again.

I knew God was calling me home. I just didn't know where home was. I knew where I was from, and I knew where I lived, but I knew nothing about *who* I was. I had lied to myself and others my whole life—just like my mama had.

I bent down, picked up a rock, and looked out at the trees again.

I love you, Suzanne.

I closed my eyes and felt the afternoon sun burn the skin on my cheeks and shoulders. The piece of gravel felt like it was wrapped in a blanket of sandpaper. I rubbed my finger hard against its surface and closed my eyes even tighter.

Eighteen-wheelers zoomed past me and blew my hair in every direction. I was thankful for the breeze they brought but resented the cloud of dust that they left behind. As they passed, I kept rubbing the rock. Like the other one, I wanted to scratch a tiny horse onto its surface.

You have forgotten God your Savior, you have not remembered the Rock, your fortress.

The words poured out of me from some sacred place, a place where only memories live. I knew who they were from, but I refused to stop rubbing the rock.

God, why did You take my baby? I would have stayed if You had let my baby live. I would have stayed and loved You—and Cecil. Now You're going to take Frank too, aren't You? If You love me so much, why do You keep taking the people I love from me?

A caravan of cars flew past and kicked dust into my eyes and mouth. I licked my lips, swallowed deeply, and continued my questioning.

Why don't You answer me? You never answer the hard questions!

I put the rock into my pocket and got back into the car.

I knew I should've laid it down, but I wanted to keep it. I wanted to feel it in my pocket. No one ever went to jail for stealing a rock from the side of a highway, I told myself. I put the key into the ignition and turned it over as hard as I could. The vehicle jumped and sputtered, then settled into a deep roar.

Lay it all down, Amanda.

I gripped the steering wheel a little tighter and pressed my foot against the accelerator. It's just a rock!

I am the Rock, Amanda.

I turned up the radio a little louder and listened as the '80s group Kansas sing "Dust in the Wind." The guitar strummed out the same melody I'd heard a thousand times before.

Same old song. Just a drop of water in an endless sea. All we do crumble to the ground though we refuse to see.

I rubbed my palms hard against the wheel. Dust in the wind—all we are is dust in the wind.

Is that it? Am I just dust in the wind?

The pull of the road felt good under my wheels. I was in control. I could've run off the road if I had wanted too. The temptation to scoff at God filled the emptiness in my heart. Dust in the wind. Yeah, right.

I could've stayed in Tuscumbia if I had wanted to. I'm not dust, I'm a person—a woman who decided to leave for something better. Something real. And I'd found that something—at least for a little while.

I'm not dust. I have two beautiful, healthy children and a husband who loves me. I made a good choice. I'm not dust!

For dust you are, and dust you will return.

The words came from no conceivable place and sent chills up the nape of my neck.

I turned down the music and tried to listen again.

Nothing.

I wanted to call out to the voice, but instead I eased my foot off the gas and allowed the car to slow down. I didn't want to die, I just wanted answers.

Is that it? Am I the one who's going to die?

I said the words in my mind at first, but then I said them aloud.

"Am I going to die?"

Silence. No inner feeling or knowing. Just silence. I felt stupid, confused.

I put my hand into my pocket and felt the rock again. I wasn't going to throw this one away.

Not ever.

Corinth, Mississippi, is a congestion of small businesses and fast food restaurants—a place where people stop to put gas in their fancy cars on the way to their weekend homes along Pickwick Lake. Most of my wealthy friends have either a home on the lake or a condo at the beach; some have both. My guess is that very few of them travel any farther than Corinth on Highway 72.

I pulled into the gas station where Frank and I agreed to meet and parked my car in a spot near the door. After a few minutes, I went inside for a cup of coffee. Three old men crowded the corner booth. All of them were smoking cigarettes and puffing about the upcoming football season. They stopped and watched me pour powdered cream into my coffee. I noticed their stares, so I smiled and nodded in their direction.

"He's a heckuva quarterback."

"Gonna be the best one we've had since Manning."

"Aw, heck, I don't know about that."

Their banter continued as we took turns looking back and forth at one another. While my coffee cooled, I scanned the drink section for some organic juice to tide Frank over until we got back to Tuscumbia. I knew well enough that he would pack his own variety of granola bars and whole grain crackers, but I thought it'd be nice to offer him something when he arrived.

I managed to find one item—a small bottle of cranberry juice that didn't contain added sugars.

After the clerk handed me my change, I waited in an empty booth. The seat had been lazily repaired with duct tape. As I waited for Frank, the tape clawed at the backs of my thighs. I looked at my watch; he would be here soon. Probably in ten minutes, based on the time we'd projected during our last phone call. That would give me enough time to finish my coffee and figure out how to tell him about Pen and Lada.

I took the rock out of my pocket and placed it on the table. The sun sent little lines of light through the large window and made the pieces of sand on its surface shine like diamonds.

"Do you collect heart-shaped rocks?"

I jumped before realizing the question came from one of the men in the corner. He had come over to the end of my booth and was looking down at me. I covered the rock with my hand as I looked up.

"Do you collect rocks like that?" he asked again. "My mama used to collect heart-shaped rocks."

I opened my hand and noticed for the first time that the rock was in fact shaped like a little heart. "Um, no," I finally answered.

He was a tall man with gray hair and a scruffy little beard that only grew in a few spots along his chin and cheeks. He wore a hunter's orange shirt and khaki pants held up around his waist by a large belt.

"My mama had jars and jars of 'em. Every time we'd go somewhere she'd pick one of those rocks up and bring it home with her. I think she started doing it after my brother died in the war." He held out his hand. "Can I see it?"

I didn't want to give it to him, but I placed it in his hand.

"Yep, that's a good one," he said as he held it up to his face and inspected it as if it was a diamond. "Do you have children?"

"Yes."

"How many?"

"Three," I lied.

"Pretty girl like you with three children. Whoa. I hope you've got a good husband too."

"Yes sir, I do."

"That's good. I've got one son and three grandbabies. My son's a good daddy, too." He put the rock down on the table and slid it back to me. "Well, you have a good day."

When he told his buddies he was leaving, I glanced over my shoulder and felt relieved to see the others weren't interested in our conversation.

"Um, sir. What did you do with them?" I asked as I put the rock back into my pocket.

"With what?" he asked.

"With the rocks. You said your mama had jars of them. Do you still have them?"

He squinted at me a little and slid his hands along the sides of his hips like he was looking for something. Pulling a large set of keys out of his pocket, he looked past me toward the road.

"I've never told nobody this, but after my mama died I took every one of them jars out to Pickwick Lake, got in a boat, and went way out into the middle of the water. Then one at a time, I skimmed those rocks across the water." He jangled the keys in his hand.

"I hated those stupid rocks. I was her boy, the one who stayed here and took care of her, but all she cared about was a bunch of dried-up dirt and my dead brother." The man tipped an imaginary hat in my direction. "You have a safe trip, ma'am."

I watched as he shuffled to his truck and climbed into the driver's seat. I thought about what Lilah and Christopher would do with a jar of rocks I'd collected. I wondered if one day they'd think I had loved "dried-up dirt" more than them.

An unfamiliar car pulled to one of the pumps, and out stepped Frank. I grabbed my things and on my way out the door said goodbye to the men in the other booth. Next to the door stood a garbage can. I tossed my empty cup into it and reached into my pocket. The rock felt smaller in my hand than it had earlier. I looked down at the rock before I made eye contact with Frank, who stood smiling and waving at me. He was wearing his favorite red baseball cap, a blue collared shirt, and jeans.

Even though he was sick, he was still handsome. He pushed the cap back on his bald head and smiled the biggest Southern smile I'd ever seen. Even from across the lot I could see in his eyes the joy and love he felt for me.

I smiled back and pushed the rock into the cigarette-littered sand on top of the trashcan.

People are better than rocks.

...there is no Rock like our God.

1 Samuel 2:2

I never fight, except against difficulties.
HELEN KELLER

Chapter Twenty-eight

While I drove, Frank talked about the family he rode to Corinth with and their generous invitation to stay in their lakefront home at Pickwick anytime we liked. He went on about their son and his interest in one day becoming a pharmacist like Frank. I tried to listen, but my mind kept drifting to Cecil.

When Frank realized I wasn't paying attention, he slid his hand between my back and the seat. I felt the warmth of his hand through my shirt and was thankful for his touch.

"I bought you this juice," I said, handing it over to him.

Frank thanked me and turned the bottle around so he could read the label. Without ever opening it, he placed the cranberry juice in the cup holder and pulled another container of red liquid from the bag at his feet.

"What's wrong with the juice I bought you?" I asked.

Frank shrugged and took a sip from his container. "Nothing."

"Well, something must be wrong with it, or else you wouldn't have been drinking that other stuff."

"Nothing's wrong with it. I just thought I should finish this bottle first."

I rolled my eyes. "Let me guess—too many sugars?"

"Nothing's wrong with it, Amanda. I said thank you. Are you

okay?"

"I'm fine, but I can tell that you don't like the juice. I just want to know why."

"It's not a big deal. I just don't want to drink juice that has that much salicylic acid in it. Sometimes people can have a reaction when they mix too much salicylic acid with aspirin, and I took an aspirin on the way here."

I couldn't believe what I was hearing. "You're a pharmacist! You feed people pills all day long, but you're worried about the effects an aspirin mixed with juice might have on you? That's crazy."

Frank slouched and reached for the container. "Maybe if I'd been more health-conscious before, I wouldn't have cancer."

I cracked the window to allow some fresh air into the car. Anytime we hit on the topic of Frank's cancer, he would find some way to bring up the idea that if he'd done something different during his younger days, he wouldn't be in this situation.

I wondered if he felt the same way about marrying me. I wondered if maybe he thought about how much better he'd be cared for if he'd married someone with an exceptional ability to read labels or calculate calories.

After a few minutes of silence, Frank put his hand on my back again and gently rubbed the area between my shoulder blades. "I'm sorry," he said, massaging the nape of my neck. "Thank you for thinking about me. I know you were trying to help."

I wanted to close my eyes and enjoy his touch, but instead I bent over and opened up more room between my back and the seat. With that invitation he pulled up the bottom of my shirt and slipped his fingers between the back of my jeans and the elastic of my new, general-store-bought panties. His touch reminded me of the clothes I was wearing, and suddenly I felt insecure about how I looked.

"I'll be so glad when I finally get to wear some of my own clothes again."

Frank smiled and moved his hand along my spine. "I kinda like these new clothes," he said, leaning toward me.

His hand on my back made something inside me tingle—and he knew it. I glanced away from the road for a minute and smiled at him.

"I love you." He pulled his hand away and touched my hair instead.

"I love you too. I'm really sorry about the juice."

Frank tucked a piece of hair behind my ear. I could feel his eyes taking in the lines of my face and the curve of my shoulder. After a few minutes, he admitted to what he was thinking. "Let's not go straight to see the kids."

"Where do you want to go?"

"I don't know. Let's go somewhere we can be alone."

I grabbed his hand and wove my fingers into his. "I guess we could go to the river."

Intimacy was another one of the things his treatments robbed us of. I could close my eyes and forget that he was bald or sick, but he couldn't. Those were the times when he seemed the saddest, when no matter how much he wanted to, he still couldn't get his body to do the things his heart most desired.

I tried to focus on the road and bury the longing that was building inside me. It was better to act as if I didn't want to be with him than to ask for something he couldn't provide.

Frank withdrew his hand and readjusted his red baseball cap. "Isn't there a place we can go for a couple of hours so that we can be together?"

I laughed, a little unsure of what he was asking.

"I've been feeling pretty good the last few days, and I'd like to hold you." Frank reached over again and put his hand on my thigh.

I felt my cheeks flush. "There's a hotel on the edge of town."

"Perfect."

Frank went inside the Cold Water Inn and paid for the room while I parked the car and collected a change of clothes from the bags he brought. The hotel looked like something that should have been in downtown Memphis, not in rural Alabama. Two large wooden staircases graced the hotel lobby, and every corner was filled with heavy drapery and exotic bird feathers.

Frank took my hand and led me up the stairway and down the long hallway to our room. He slid the electronic key into the slot and pushed the door open. Once we were inside, I walked over to the bedside table and put down the pile of clothes I was carrying. While I was turning off my phone, Frank walked up behind me, placed his hands on my shoulders, and kissed the back of my neck and arms. I closed my eyes and enjoyed his touch.

Frank sat on the bed and watched as I undressed. He pulled me over to him. He kissed my stomach and ran his fingers along my hips and sides. I sat and slipped the brown loafers off his feet. After he was undressed, he pulled back the bed sheets and motioned for me to get in.

I did as he asked.

We lay there for a long time, enjoying the way our skin felt next to each other.

God, please heal him.

My prayer caught in my throat as if I'd said it out loud. I prayed that short prayer again.

Frank lifted his head from my stomach and pressed his lips against mine. "I love you," he said, trying to catch his breath before kissing me again.

His body against mine made my heart moan. I closed my eyes again, but a tear escaped the corner of my eye and fell onto his hand.

"Amanda, look at me."

Frank caught a second tear with his finger and turned my chin toward his face.

"Amanda, please look at me. I love you more than anything in the world. Please, open your eyes and look at me."

I opened my eyes and looked into his. They were blue like Christopher's, only older and wiser. He closed his eyes and pressed his lips against mine again. I wanted to tell him how much I loved him, but I couldn't speak. Instead, I wrapped my arms around him, pulled him close, and opened my mouth to his.

Frank and I listened to a thunderstorm roll across the Tennessee River as we lay there looking at each other. He ran his finger along my arm. "I want to make love to you like that every day for the rest of my life."

I tucked my hands under my face. "Me too."

Frank smiled, but for a flash of a second I saw sadness in his eyes. He slid his hand down the back of my legs and pulled my knees over until they touched his.

"I don't want to be sick anymore."

"I know. I wish it was me instead of you."

"I mean, I don't want to take that medicine anymore."

I sat up, pulled the covers over my chest, and tucked the sheets under my arms.

"That medicine is the only chance we have to beat the cancer."

"It's not working."

"It *is* working. It's just going to take more time."

"No, Amanda. It's not working."

"It's going to work. Don't talk like that!"

Frank reached over and took both of my hands into his. He rubbed his thumb back and forth across the top of my wedding ring. I could see him searching for the right words.

I wanted to pull away from him and tell him he was being ridiculous. I wanted to run.

"It seems like it was only yesterday when I slipped this ring onto your finger." He spread my fingers out over the palm of his hand and gently ran his over the top of the ring again. "I don't want to die sick and bald. I want to go to heaven in your arms, like we are right now."

"Well, I want you to go to heaven when you're old and gray. That's why we're going to keep fighting this!"

He sighed and looked up at me. That's when I realized what he was trying to tell me.

"Amanda. I got the results from the tests. The medicines aren't working."

"What are you saying?" I pulled my hands away. "If they're not working, then we'll try new ones. Isn't that what the doctors said we should do?"

Frank grabbed my hands again and sat up on his knees.

I tried to pull back. "We're not going to let this beat us! The doctors said with the right meds we could reduce the size of the tumors and maybe operate."

"They're not getting smaller."

"They will. We'll try something else." I kicked, trying to get free of the sheets and of Frank. "I'll call the doctors. I'll talk to them."

"Okay, but first talk to me." Frank caught hold of my ankle and pulled, sending me flat onto my back. I kicked again, trying to sit up, but he wrapped his arm around my waist and pinned me to the bed.

"Get off of me!" I said, throwing my elbow into his ribs. "Let go!"

Frank winced in pain as my elbow caught him a second time.

"Oh, God, I'm so sorry." I realized what I'd done and wanted desperately to take it back. "Are you okay? Where did I hit you? Are you okay?"

Frank rolled over onto his stomach and buried his face in the pillow.

"Are you okay? I'm sorry."

He lay there for a long time, quietly fighting his anger. His ears were red with heat and rage, like an exhausted child's after a tumultuous fit. While I rubbed his back and begged for forgiveness, I watched his spine rise and fall. Somewhere, hidden among his vertebrae were three murderous tumors. I pressed two of my fingers into the small of his back and watched as his shoulders loosened a bit. As I pressed, he gathered the pillow around his face and let out a small whimper. Gently, I released the pressure, closed my eyes, and felt along his spine until I found a small knot between his shoulder blades. I opened my hand and placed my palm over that area and began to cry. I could feel the tumor under his skin. Quiet sobs came from the pillow as I closed my eyes and began to silently pray.

God, please. Please make them go away. You can do anything. Now please, do this for Your son. If You love him, heal him.

The second I finished praying, Frank sat up as if he knew I was done pleading my case.

"What are you doing?" he asked.

I suddenly felt ridiculous for praying. "I was asking God to heal you."

Frank wiped the tears from his face and put his hands on my shoulders. "God has already healed me."

"Then how come I can feel the tumors growing inside you?"

"Because healing me has nothing to do with my body. Why don't you listen to me?"

"I am listening to you. I'm listening to you cower and quit. I'm hearing you give up!"

Frank took my cheeks into his hands and pulled me up until we were both on our knees. "If you won't listen to me, then listen to God."

"God doesn't talk to me anymore, and He doesn't listen either."

Frank lifted my face again until my neck felt like the skin around it was being stretched. "God's talking to you, but you've closed off your heart to Him. He hasn't closed off anything to you. You're the one who's stepped away." Tears filled Frank's eyes and began to pour down his face. "Open your heart to Him, and you'll be able to hear. I promise you. He hasn't forgotten you."

I grabbed Frank's wrists and tried to loosen his grip, but instead of letting go he closed his eyes and pressed the tips of his fingers against my ears. Suddenly, the hum of the room and the noises from outside the window were silenced. All I could hear was the beating of my own heart and my own staggered breathing. I pulled at his wrists, but with every pull his fingers went deeper into my ears.

"Stop, Frank."

His eyes softened, but his hold on my face stayed strong.

"Please let go."

His lips began to move, but I couldn't hear what he was saying. Rage filled me as fear settled in. "You're hurting me. Let go!"

I felt the vibration of his words as his lips moved again.

Finally, I gave up my struggle and loosened my grip, hoping he'd do the same. I let go of his wrists and sat there, listening to the inner grumblings of my own body and looking at the ceiling, my arms limp by my sides.

A few seconds passed before he put his cheek to mine. I felt his sobs as he lifted his fingers from my ears. He kissed the side of my face and the lobe of my ear. "Be opened, Amanda," he whispered. "Be opened."

I do not remember when I first realized that
I was different from other people;
but I knew it before my teacher came to me.

HELEN KELLER

Chapter Twenty-nine

Tiny drops of rain began to fall as Frank and I walked quietly across the empty parking lot behind the hotel. Before Frank opened the car door for me, he put his hand into mine and lifted it to his face.

"I love you," I told him as I got into the car.

As I turned down Woodmont and headed toward the mission house, I realized that telling him I loved him was easier than ever before. It felt natural, like an honest outpouring from my heart—a reaction to how I genuinely felt about him and not just something to say.

The rain began to ease up as we passed by the rolling hills of Spring Park where people visiting the Helen Keller Festival were taking cover under the vendors' tents. I felt something begin to grow and swell in my chest as we entered downtown Tuscumbia. It was like God had begun to chisel away the hard places inside my heart. The old buildings that lined the streets didn't look as bad as I remembered. Instead, everything seemed alive and hopeful.

"I'm glad you're here," I said as we turned onto the street in front of First Pres.

Frank leaned toward the windshield and looked up at the stained-glass windows and red brick steeple that towered above us. The old bell chimed and welcomed us.

Frank held his hand to his brow to shield the sun as we circled the church on our way to the mission house.

"We should've gotten married in that church," Frank said.

"I'm glad we got married in Memphis."

Frank sat back in the seat again. "Yes, but a Southern lady is supposed to get married in the church she grew up in—not in the church her husband grew up in."

"I'm glad we got married in the church our children are growing up in," I said as we pulled to the curb in front of the mission house.

I thought by the time we arrived everyone would be back, but the house was empty. The front door was unlocked, so we decided to unload our things from the car. As Frank carried in the bags, I imagined what he'd selected for the children. He loved to dress Lilah in the elaborate handmade dresses his mother smocked for her. And poor Christopher—Frank would still dress him like Little Lord Fauntleroy if I'd let him.

In the kitchen, we found a note from Mama telling us she'd decided to take a picnic dinner down to the river. She asked us to join her and the kids as soon as possible so we wouldn't miss Pen playing her cello for the group. On the back of the paper, Mama said she loved us and left directions about where to find a trail through the kudzu near the Refuge House.

Frank and I unpacked some of the bags before we left. It was as I expected. He'd packed three handmade dresses—a blue one that had been hanging in her closet since Easter and two others that would need to be ironed before Lilah could wear them. He'd done pretty well packing for Christopher, though.

I folded their clothes over my arm as we headed out the door. Darkness was already settling into the crevices along the horizon. If we didn't find the trail through the woods before sundown, we'd never find it.

Frank found the trail before I did, but he wasn't thrilled about following it down the slope toward the river. From the top of the hill, it appeared as if someone laid a green swaddling cloth atop a mound of dying trees. I held onto the tips of Frank's fingers and led him into the thick vines. The kudzu climbed every living bush and tree. Daddy once told me the banks of the river hadn't always looked that way, but when his father was alive someone planted the vines along the river to stop erosion. At first the plan appeared to work, but kudzu grows at the rate of about a foot a day and smothers the life out of everything it touches.

We ducked our heads and felt our way through the thicket. Birds chirped and sang the news of our arrival. The last rays of daylight shot flashes of color through the top of the branches. After only a couple of steps into the vines, we began to hear the muffled laughter of people a few hundred yards below. As we moved closer, the voices hushed and the heavy hum of a cello began to vibrate through the trees.

I couldn't make out the song Pen was playing until the voices quieted and the movement of the river pushed the music toward us. I could feel each chord vibrate within me as the bow crossed each of the cello's four strings. I recognized the song. It had always been one of Pen's favorites.

Frank grabbed my elbow and swatted a bug from his face. The quickness of his movement almost caused us to lose our balance and go plummeting down the embankment. I held tight to one of the thick vines and repositioned my feet in the dirt.

The cello continued to purr as we descended the hill, and with it came Pen's delicate voice. The words poured from her and sent a current along my skin.

She continued to sing as we got closer to the foot of the hill.

Suddenly, the words of the song came back to me from a long-forgotten memory: "Thou burning sun with golden beam, Thou silver moon with softer gleam. O praise Him."

Frank stopped for a moment and listened. He closed his eyes and breathed in the verse. "This is my favorite."

We didn't want to make any noise, so we crept toward the edge of the trees. After we reached the opening and stepped out onto the sandy embankment, we could see Pen standing beside a small fire. She held the cello to her left shoulder and sang to the group of women seated in front of her.

Pen tipped her chin and continued with her slow, graceful singing. "Ye who long pain and sorrow bear, Praise God and on Him cast your cares. O praise Him. O praise Him. Alleluia." The sun slowly disappeared behind the trees as the women from the Refuge listened to Pen, who looked beautiful in the glow of the fire and the shadow of the orange horizon.

Frank and I stood at the edge of the trees until she finished. I watched as Mama gently rubbed Christopher's hair and kissed him on his head. He and Lilah sat quietly, captivated by the music.

What a gift, I told myself. *My sister is a gift.*

To the left of the group sat a woman with her back to the crowd. After a few minutes, I realized it was Beeny. She sat with her arms crossed in a kind of fitful way. She didn't turn to look at us, even after Pen finished playing and I began introducing Frank to some of the other women.

The children were overjoyed to see that their father had finally arrived. Christopher told Frank about all the things that had happened since we got to Tuscumbia.

"Honey burned her house," he announced.

Mama kissed Frank on the cheek before leading him around and proudly introducing him to each of the women. She never made eye contact with me, which assured me Pen already told her what I knew about Lada. Still, I didn't plan to say anything because I hadn't told Frank and I wanted to talk to Mama first.

I walked over to Pen as she loaded the large instrument into its leather case. She closed the lid and stood to hug me.

"That was amazing, Pen. It's been a long time since I've seen you play like that."

"I love to come down here and play. There's something about the sound of the river and the wind in my hair that makes my soul want to sing."

"If I could sing like that, I'd be down here every day."

Pen smiled and hoisted the case onto its side. "Thanks, sis."

"What's wrong with her?" I asked, motioning toward Beeny's back.

"She doesn't like to stay out here after dark. She got mad when no one would walk her back to the house." Pen winked at me and called to Beeny over her shoulder. "We're goin' back up now. If you don't want us to leave you, then you'd better come on."

"Why don't y'all just leave me down here so I can die!"

"Maybe we will!" yelled one of the other women, making the rest of the group roar in laughter.

Beeny stiffened and lifted her large pregnant body out of the folding chair. "I hate every one-ah you. Y'all promised to have me back up that hill by dark. Now somebody's gotta go get a boat, 'cause I ain't goin' back up that hill in the dark!" She swung her fist around in the air as the others continued to laugh at her. "Y'all keep on laughin' and see what happens. A snake is gonna bite one of you, and then I'm gon' be the one laughin'." Beeny turned down the corners of her mouth and chuckled sarcastically at the crowd of women.

I led Frank over to meet her. Beeny frowned and looked him over from head to toe. Frank waited as she checked him out.

After a couple of seconds Beeny's face began to soften. "I was just prayin' the Lord would send a big black man down outta those hills to come save me from this crazy buncha women and all them hungry snakes."

She sniffed in a quick breath of river air and folded the chair up with one quick movement of her hip.

"You ain't exactly what I had in mind."

Frank smiled and took the chair from Beeny. "I'm not looking forward to climbing back up in the dark either, so let's eat and then I'd be delighted to escort you up the hill."

Beeny looked over at me before tipping her chin back in Frank's direction. "Well, it's 'bout time a gentleman showed up 'round here."

Beeny and Frank walked over to the women crowded around a cooler of food. Mama handed out foil-wrapped sandwiches and bottled water to the group. The sandwiches were pulled pork, topped with slaw and grape jelly. Lilah didn't like the selection, so instead of eating her sandwich, she licked the jelly from the inside of the bun. Within a matter of seconds, her hands and face were covered with a thin layer of sticky jelly and river sand.

After they were through eating, the women turned on tiny flashlights that hung from a strand of yarn around each of their necks. Frank and Beeny walked side by side into the trees as the other flickers of light quickly fell into step behind them.

Christopher twirled his light around in a thousand directions as he shouted the words to his favorite song. Lilah thought his silliness was the greatest thing she'd ever seen. We gathered the last of the supplies as they danced and sang with their little lights bouncing below their chins.

Pen quickly pushed dirt over the fire and smothered the remaining flames while Mama closed the lid to the cooler and began dragging it across the ground toward the trail. We climbed the hill toting two kids, several folding chairs, a large cooler, and a cello. Breathless, we stopped in front of the house and looked up at the magnificent old building.

Mama stayed with Pen and the other women while Frank and I returned to the mission house to bathe the children and put them into bed. It was after ten o'clock by the time Frank went to sleep, but I was determined to stay awake in my bed until Mama came home. I tried to pass the time by returning to my first memories of Pen, but the earliest I could remember was when she was around the age that she started walking.

I had a long list of questions for Mama, and no matter how long she avoided me, she'd eventually have to answer them.

Thus I came up out of Egypt and stood before Sinai,
and a power divine touched my spirit and gave it sight,
so that I beheld many wonders. And from the sacred
mountain I heard a voice which said.
"Knowledge is love and light and vision."

HELEN KELLER

Chapter Thirty

The next morning, I was already awake and sitting at the foot of the bed when sunlight pushed through the heavy curtains and filled the room with a yellow glow. I'd fallen asleep before Mama came home, but I knew somehow that she'd come in during the night. I felt her close to me. Near me. But she wasn't the only one. I could feel Cecil too.

Grandma once told me that if a person really wants to know who their idols are, all they have to do is pay attention to who or what they think about first thing in the morning. Not the person they think about throughout the day, but the person or thing that surfaces before their feet hit the ground.

"For some people, it's their job or maybe their family," she said. "That's why Papa put his Bible on the bedside table. He said it was to remind him of the commandment God gave to Moses about having no other gods. You gotta remember God first."

I sat near the footboard and tried *not* to think about Cecil. I tried not to think about him alone in his hospital room. I tried not to fall back onto my pillow and let my mind go, but the more I prayed, the more my mind wandered.

After giving up, I slid my legs into the jeans and tiptoed down the hall to the living room. The tiny rocking horse was still waiting for me on the shelf where I'd left it. I removed it from the ledge and gently combed its porcelain hair with my index finger. I took the horse with me out to the garden.

The damp grass caused brown specks of earth to settle between my toes. Near the back fence, I placed the horse on the edge of a bird fountain and crouched down to where it watched little bugs jerk and kick their way across the top of the water.

"Are you thirsty?"

The words almost scared the life out of me. I spun around to find Frank. He held a glass of water.

"You scared me to death!"

"Sorry. I looked out the window and saw you bent over the fountain. Looked to me like you were about to drink from it." Frank held the glass out for me.

"I'm not looking at the water." I took the glass from him and sipped. "I'm looking at this." I pointed at the rocking horse and stepped back so he could see.

"Oh, I see. You're playing in the fountain." Frank picked up my tiny treasure, turned it over in his hand, and held it out for me the same way he'd held the glass.

I grabbed the horse, walked past the long row of roses, and sat down on the bench. Frank joined me and wrapped his arm around my shoulders.

"Sorry. I guess it's too early for jokes."

I leaned into his chest and put the figurine on top of his knee. We sat together and watched the garden come to life in the morning sun.

Frank broke the silence and sent a tiny bird off its perch in a nearby tree.

"I think I know why you like that rocking horse," he said.

"Why?"

"Because you're a lot like him."

I laughed under my breath before sitting up and taking the horse from his knee. "How is that?"

Frank pulled a long strand of leatherleaf from a nearby plant. He ran the fern through his fingers and watched it curl. "You just are. You're like a rocking horse with its eyes and ears cut away."

"Are you kidding me? I can see, and I can hear pretty well too." When I tried to hand the glass of water back to him, some of the water spilled onto his lap.

"I can't believe you'd suggest I'm like a blind and deaf rocking horse. You know who you're starting to sound like? Mama. She told me once that I was rocking back and forth between things but not going anywhere, so let me just warn you about saying something like that."

I put the glass down and stood up to go inside. "I didn't stay in Tuscumbia like everyone else, so don't tell me I didn't go somewhere. And no, I'm not blind—or deaf."

I stood in the shower and allowed water to pound against the back of my neck. Frank's words made me want to scream. I lathered the soap into my hands as the bathroom door opened and sent a gust of cold air over the vinyl curtain. After I rinsed the soap from my eyes, I could see Frank through the curtain.

"Can you hand me a towel?" I asked, turning off the faucet.

"Why do you always do that?"

"Do what?" I jerked back the curtain and grabbed the towel from him.

"Why do you always storm off every time I try to talk to you?"

I wrapped the towel around my body and pretended to ignore him.

"I was just trying to help you see some of the things I think you struggle with."

"I don't need you to help me see."

"Okay then. I'm sorry."

"I can see perfectly fine." I brushed wet hair from my face and looked at myself in the mirror. "What did you plan to do? Were you going to poke your fingers into my eyes like you did my ears?"

The second the words left my mouth, I hated myself for saying them.

Frank turned and left the bathroom without saying another word. He didn't have to speak. I could already see defeat written over his entire body.

After I finished drying my hair, I found Frank and Lilah watching cartoons in the den. I stood in the doorway and watched Lilah thumb the buttons on her father's shirt while she smiled at the glowing screen. Frank adjusted Lilah's weight on his lap as a brown bear danced across the screen and made the sound of the letter B.

I went into the kitchen, started a pot of coffee, and sat at the breakfast table. The notepad and pen were still sitting on the table where I had left them the day before, so I tore out a blank page, scribbled down a few words, and tossed it into the garbage can. Then, after a few seconds, I scribbled out another note, folded it, and slipped it into my back pocket. When the coffee was done, I poured a cup for Frank and sat next to him in front of the TV.

When I handed him the mug, he didn't look at me. He just took it and placed it on the coffee table in front of him.

"I'm sorry," I whispered, trying not to disturb Lilah.

Frank glanced at me and then kissed the side of Lilah's head.

I pulled the note from my pocket and held it out for him to see. I watched as he read it: *Honey is not Pen's mother.*

Frank stared at me in disbelief before sliding Lilah off his lap. I folded the paper and put it back into my pocket. He grabbed my hand, pulled me up, and led me into the kitchen.

"What do you mean?"

"Just what I said. Pen told me yesterday that a woman named Lada is her birthmother."

"You found out yesterday, and you didn't tell me?"

"I wanted to talk to Mama first, but I can't get her alone long enough."

"Does she know that you know?"

"I think so, but I'm not sure."

Frank put his arms around me and pulled me to his chest. "I'm so sorry."

I felt my whole body stiffen. I wanted to tell him I was sorry for my outburst, but instead I let him hug me.

He let go and leaned back to see if Lilah was still watching television. "Why do you think Honey kept it a secret for so long?"

"I guess because she's crazy. I swear, if I grow up to be anything like her you'll have to fish me out of the river."

I poured myself a cup of coffee while he paced the floor and rubbed his bare head.

"When Christopher wakes up I'll take the kids into town so the two of you can talk." Frank grabbed a banana and began peeling it. "But first I want you to promise me you'll listen to her story and not get angry. Honey loves both of you, and whatever her reasoning is, explaining it to you will be harder than anything else she's been through."

After Christopher woke up, I dressed the kids and loaded them into the car. Frank was okay to drive but only for short distances, so I encouraged him not to waste time looking for an organic restaurant. He agreed that McDonald's would be fine just this once.

Once the house was quiet, I tiptoed back to the bedroom. I couldn't tell if Mama was sleeping or playing possum, so I stomped my feet as I walked down the hallway to the front door.

"I'm coming!" I yelled into the empty driveway before I shut the door and tiptoed into the kitchen. I wanted Mama to think the house was empty so she'd get out of bed.

Quietly, I pushed back one of the chairs from the kitchen table and sat with my back to the window. As I waited, I thought about what Frank said about me being like a rocking horse. His words were similar to what Mama said after she found out about Cecil and me.

As I waited for Mama to wander into the kitchen, I prayed that God would not let me fall back into a life of going nowhere like Frank had mentioned. I didn't want to be like one of my rocking horses. I wanted to live and grow and move forward. I wanted to hear Him again.

What I heard instead was the sound of Mama coming toward the kitchen.

When we walk in the valley of twofold solitude
we know little of the tender affection that grow
out of endearing words and actions and
companionship.

HELEN KELLER

Chapter Thirty-one

I listened as Mama tiptoed to the living room window
and pulled back the shades. After she saw that our car was gone, she
gave a sigh of relief and allowed the plastic blinds to snap back into
place. In the kitchen, I watched her open the cabinet and pull down
an empty coffee mug from the top shelf.

"Good morning."

Mama grabbed her chest and gasped for air. "Why do you always
do that?"

"I was just sitting here."

She put her mug down and poured coffee into the cup until it
overflowed onto the countertop. Mama mumbled something under
her breath and began cleaning up the spill with a damp paper towel.
"I thought you were gone," she said, dabbing hot coffee from the
bottom of the mug.

"You *hoped* I was gone."

Mama lifted the lid to the garbage can and tossed the wet towel
in. I watched and waited for a reaction to my comment as Mama bent
over and pulled a piece of paper out of the can. I realized it was the

first note I'd written to Frank, telling him about Pen—the note that I'd decided not to show him. The second note, the one that I'd shown to Frank, was still hidden in my pocket. The one that she'd found was worded a bit differently. It said, "Pen is not my sister."

Mama closed the lid and put the note down in front of me.

"This isn't true."

"Yes it is. Pen told me yesterday." I swallowed hard and fought back tears.

"No, it's not true. Pen is your sister." She shook her head and continued. "Only she didn't come from my womb."

"I know she'll always be my sister, but Lada gave birth to her." I took in a deep breath and tried to follow Frank's advice not to get angry. "How come you never told us?"

"Because they asked me not to." The thin lines on her forehead thickened as she hunched over in the chair.

"Who is 'they'? The people at the Refuge House? Why would you adopt a baby from there and keep it a secret? I would've loved her just the same." I considered the possibility that maybe my birth date was also carved into the walls of the prayer porch. "Am I from that place too?"

Tears fell down Mama's cheeks and onto her cotton nightgown.

"Who told you to keep that secret?" I asked again.

She looked at me with tear-filled eyes. "Lada…"—she sniffed once and took in a staggered breath—"and your father."

"My father?" The mention of Daddy startled me.

Then I knew.

Lada and my father.

I closed my eyes and tried not to believe her.

Mama must have understood my reaction, because she immediately reached over and put her hand on my arm.

"Daddy and that woman had an affair?" I asked.

Mama nodded her head and continued to cry.

I scanned the tabletop in search of answers. "How did you find out?"

"He told me. But as we were trying to piece our lives back together, Lada called and told him she was pregnant."

"And you forgave him?"

"I'd already forgiven him for the affair when we found out about the baby."

I pulled my arm from her and wiped a thin layer of sweat from my face and neck.

"How could you forgive him for making a baby with another woman?"

"He asked me to. I still felt angry but more at myself than anyone else."

"That's it? He asked you to forgive him so you did? And then you decided to give the baby a home? Sorry, but I don't understand. And now you and that woman are best friends! Are you kidding me?"

"Amanda." Mama took a sip of coffee and looked through the window to the empty driveway. "Lada's not a bad person. She is a woman who fell in love with the wrong man, the wrong man because he was already my husband. It took me a long time to understand what happened, but now that I'm older I've started to understand how God uses those types of things for His good."

"Well, then, please tell me. Help me understand."

She searched for the right words before speaking again.

"Lada wanted to have an abortion after your father refused to run away with her. And, to be honest with you, some dark part of me wished she'd go through with it. As miserable as our marriage was at times, I still wanted my life to go back to the way it was before the affair, but the truth was that your daddy had loved Lada for a long time. That's what hurt the most.

"After Karl told me Lada planned to get an abortion, I waited for her until she left work one day. I scared her to death. It took all I had to keep from smacking her across the cheek. Instead, I asked her to get into my car."

"And she did?" I was shocked.

"For whatever reason, she agreed, so we drove down Montgomery toward Sheffield. She told me later that she thought I was going to drag her out to some desolate place along the river and throw her in."

"Why didn't you?"

"I'd heard about a place where pregnant women were living, so I drove up to the front of the Refuge House, grabbed her by the arm, and dragged her to the front door.

"The woman who answered didn't ask me any questions, she just welcomed us in and ushered us into the living room. I handed the woman every bit of money I'd saved over the previous few years and told her I'd be back the following week. The woman tried to explain that there was no need for money, but I refused to leave Lada without paying for the burden your daddy caused."

"Did Daddy know you were going to do that?"

"No, but I didn't care."

"What did he say when he found out?"

"He wasn't happy. I told him about how Lada cried the whole time I talked with the woman. I wanted to slap Lada's face and storm out, but instead I bent down and sat on my knees. She was so scared she couldn't even look at me. I made her promise she'd stay there and take care of herself until the baby was born. After she promised, I left."

I held out my hand to Mama and listened as she continued to tell me about the weeks that followed her initial visit to the Refuge House. Mama took food to the house while Lada was living there. During those visits, the woman who answered the door started telling them about God's forgiveness and His willingness to heal their pain.

"Did Daddy ever go with you?"

"No. I didn't tell him where I was going."

"Well, how often did you go?"

Mama wiped a tear from her chin with the back of her hand. "I went every week for about seven months, I guess. During my visits the woman who worked there would talk to me about God. She helped me begin to understand things I'd never understood before. She helped me *truly* forgive your father. She helped me see that at first I'd forgiven him because I was afraid I'd lose him, but then she helped me forgive your daddy and Lada for the sheer fact that Jesus had forgiven them."

"Where's that woman now?"

"She died not long after Penelope was born. She'd been sick for a long time and had been praying for God to send someone to take over when she was gone. Lada was the answer to her prayers."

I leaned back in my chair, trying to make sence of it all. "What was her name?"

"Her name was Esther. She taught us that people are the only ones who think some sins are greater than others. God sees all of our sins the same. That's what she said the first time she sat Lada and I down and began to pray with us. Seven months later, Lada called to tell me it was time."

"Time to have the baby?"

"Yes. Your daddy knew nothing about the Refuge House then. For all he knew, Lada was miles away, and the baby was long gone."

"Why didn't you tell him?"

"Fear, I guess. I didn't want him to leave with Lada and I didn't want him to tell me I had to stop going to see her. I had to wake up every morning and make a decision to forgive Karl—like God had forgiven me. On days when I thought I might go crazy, I tried to make myself useful by spending all of my time serving other people. Ivy Green was the place where I really felt like I could get away and think. Being there made me feel like I was living someone else's life." Mama leaned forward. "Amanda, I'm sorry for the times I made you feel like I didn't want to be around you."

"All of these years, I thought it was me. I thought I had done something to make you angry."

"I'm so sorry, baby. As much as I wanted things to be okay, they were still a mess most of the time. I was a mess."

"Why didn't Lada keep Pen?"

"I thought she was going to, but a couple of days after she was born, Lada told me she wanted Penelope to live with us. She wanted Pen to have the family she never had, so I agreed. A few days later, your daddy came home and found me rocking Pen in Grandma's chair while you played at my feet. He fell to his knees and thanked God for saving his baby. And we never talked about Lada again."

Mama shifted in her seat and wiped her eyes again.

"There's a verse that surfaces when Lada and I pray together. It's from John 15 and says, 'No one shows greater love than when he lays down his life for his friends.' That's the kind of love Lada and I have for each other. Lada laid down her life for me—for all of us. She didn't have to stay here and watch her child grow up in someone else's arms. She could've easily terminated the pregnancy, destroyed my marriage, or even given birth to your half-sister and disappeared forever. Instead, she chose to live quietly along the sidelines. She's loved us in the best way that she could."

I wondered how Lada managed to stay quiet for over two decades. She probably looked familiar because I'd seen her at Pen's music recitals and plays. I didn't remember her specifically, but I remembered her clothing.

"Why does she always wear purple?"

Mama laughed. "You should ask her."

"That's not ever going to happen."

Mama and I watched through the window as a long brown car with a dented hood and missing rearview mirror pulled into the driveway.

Mama went to the back of the house to change out of her pajamas while I poured our cold coffee into the sink and watched Beeny climb out from behind the steering wheel. I was surprised to see one of the women from the Refuge House driving a car. I guess I thought they all stayed locked in the house, with the exception of an occasional walk to the river.

I wiped dried tears from my face with a wet rag and went to the door to welcome Beeny. She was holding three Mason jars on top of her pregnant belly and smiling from ear to ear.

"Hi, Mrs. 'Manda," she said as I took some of the jars from her. "I used up some of the apples you brought to make y'all some apple butter."

The jars were still warm and sticky. "Oh, thank you, Beeny. I wish I knew how to make apple butter."

"Well, maybe when we get back to Memphis I can show you." Beeny looked at me as if there was something else that she wanted to say.

"I didn't know you were from Memphis."

She wiped her hands on her skirt. "You never asked."

I wanted to know if she'd changed her mind about giving her baby up for adoption, but Mama walked into the room and interrupted our conversation.

"Hi, Beeny, come on in. Did you bring us some of your famous apple butter?"

Mama was delighted to see the jars in our hands.

"Did you know Beeny's from Memphis?" I asked.

"Yes, I did. Now Beeny, you gotta tell Amanda what part of the city you live in. I bet y'all know some of the same people."

I bet we don't, I thought.

I could see Beeny wishing she'd just placed the apple butter at the front door and left. "I grew up a couple of blocks north of East High School in Binghampton."

I knew the area. I had to pass through there on my way downtown. It's a neighborhood filled with starter homes built by young white families in the 1950s. Now the neighborhood is primarily black and filled with gangs, drugs, and violence.

"I know that area. It's over by Chickasaw, right?"

Immediately, I felt embarrassed by the landmark I'd chosen. Chickasaw is a fancy country club that backs up to Binghampton. Beeny didn't seem to notice my fumbling.

"My grandmama's house sits at the corner of Nathan and Holmes. I grew up lookin' out at that golf course. I used to have big dreams 'bout workin' there one day."

"Well, maybe I can call someone and get you an interview."

"Nah, I got a good job waitin' for me when I get back." Beeny laughed and headed for the door.

"Okay, just let me know if you change your mind."

Beeny eased herself down the front steps toward her car. "I ain't gonna change my mind 'bout that, and they don't want me hangin' round Chickasaw any more than I want to be there. I caused a lot of trouble for them when I was a kid."

I laughed. "I hope I get to hear about it one day."

Beeny got back into her car and cranked down the window. "That'd be fun. If we run into each other one day, you remind me to tell you."

I tried to remember how far along Beeny was in her pregnancy.

"How long 'til you're back in Memphis?"

Beeny put on the brakes and rubbed her tummy for a few seconds while she calculated a date. "I think I only have 'bout two weeks 'til the baby comes."

"Well, take care of yourself. I'm gonna call Pen and find out how you're doing."

Beeny smiled and waved as she drove down Cave Street. I liked Beeny. She was feisty, but there was a calm hidden beneath her deep voice. I wanted to know more about how a girl from Binghampton ended up pregnant and hiding out in Tuscumbia.

> Any teacher can take a child to the classroom,
> but not every teacher can make him learn.
>
> **HELEN KELLER**

Chapter Thirty-two

After Frank returned with the kids, Mama stayed busy the rest of the day making phone calls to insurance agencies and friends. While she talked to whoever was on the other end of the line, Mama organized all the cups in the cabinets and turned everything in the fridge until the labels faced forward. I wondered if perhaps she was turning into Frank.

During lunch, I kept my eye on her and tried to piece together parts of her conversation while I spread apple butter onto the kids' peanut butter sandwiches. It wasn't until after the kids went to bed that Mama finally stopped milling around and decided to join Frank and me on the front porch.

"Is it always this quite around here at night?" Frank asked.

Mama leaned back in her chair. "At night it is. Even in the city."

A dog barked in the distance as I leaned my head against the porch column and closed my eyes.

Frank and Mama talked for a while about political figures neither one of them knew anything about. They'd just blurt out someone's name and try to piece together little bits of information. I sat on the top step and watched as they continued to dance between "Did you hear...?" and "Well, I heard..."

I was glad they enjoyed each other's company, but watching them together made me miss Sam, and missing Sam led to me missing Cecil. I wanted to know how he was doing. I wished I'd told him goodbye when I had had the chance instead of promising I'd return. I wondered if the kindest thing would be to pick up the phone and call to tell him goodbye—forever. The more I turned the idea of a phone call over and over in my mind, the more it sounded like some kind of junior high breakup.

When we'd had enough of the mosquitoes nipping at our flesh, the three of us went inside and finished a bottle of wine. Frank went to bed early so Mama and I could talk, but Pen called to tell Mama about her date with Billy. She went on and on about the band they saw in Spring Park, but I knew Pen was really calling to check on us. When they were through talking, Mama handed the phone to me so I could hear about the date firsthand.

Mama listened to the exchanges Pen and I made, and I knew what she must have been thinking. I was thinking the same thing: Pen and I would always be sisters, no matter what.

A few hours later, I was lying in bed and begging for sleep to overtake me. I'd tried all my usual tricks, but eventually I allowed myself to drift off into a memory of Cecil. It wasn't actually a memory—it was more like the ending to a love story that we never really lived. I tried to push the thoughts to the corners of my mind, but every time I relaxed enough to fall asleep I found myself in the arms of another man.

I had to tell him goodbye.

You have to tell him goodbye.

"Come to me, all you who are weary and burdened, and I will give you rest."

You can't leave him again.

I can't wait to get away from this place.

Are you really going to leave? You can't just walk out on him again when he's hurting. You're only thinking about yourself.

"I am your refuge."

I put my foot on the brake pedal, shifted the car into neutral, and pushed my foot against the concrete until I felt the wheels begin to roll backwards down the driveway. Once they rolled over a couple times, I put my leg back into the car and quietly shut the door. The car gained momentum as it reached the end of the driveway and rolled far enough into the street to allow me to turn on the headlights without flashing them into the windows of the mission house. My heart pounded in my chest, forcing me to take a deep breath before starting the car.

As I drove down Cave Street, I realized it made me feel young again to be sneaking off in the middle of the night. I rolled down the car windows and let the summer air blow my hair out of my face. I tried to find something to listen to on the radio, but by the time I settled on a good song I'd already circled the parking lot of Helen Keller Hospital twice. I knew a third lap would draw unwanted attention, so I parked the car in the middle of the lot and walked toward the side entrance of the building where I knew there'd be very few people at night.

I was right. I slipped through without seeing a single person.

There was a young nurse on the elevator who wore a wedding ring on her left hand and carried a tray of food with her right. Her ring told me she had at least one person at home who was missing her while she plugged away during the late shift. When the nurse pushed the button to the second floor, I pushed the one to the fourth. Cecil's room was on the second, but I didn't want her to know where I was going, and I certainly didn't want her to ask me any questions.

I held the elevator door for her as she stepped off and used her exit as an opportunity to glance down the narrow hallway toward the nurse's station. When an older nurse saw her coming with food, she stood and followed her out of my line of vision. I tiptoed down the hallway toward the desk and listened to them chat while they divvied up the food. When it seemed as if they both had their backs to me, I crouched down and slipped past the desk without making a sound.

Room 211 was the last room on the left. I held my breath as I opened the door. If there was anyone else in the room, I'd have to make a speedy exit before they recognized me. In the darkness, I could see Cecil sleeping with his hands held together on top of his chest. I stood at the foot of his bed and watched his chest rise and fall.

I couldn't see anything below waist level, so I had to feel my way around until my foot bumped against the doctor's stool.

When I touched his hand, he opened his eyes and looked at me.

"Don't sit up," I whispered. "I just wanted to see you again before I left." I smiled at his beautiful brown eyes and touched the side of his face with my hand.

He didn't say a word as he put his hand on top of mine and closed his eyes.

"I will always love you, Cecil. I'm not ever going to stop, but I have to go home now. Please forgive me for hurting you."

The corners of his mouth turned down as he pressed my hand against his face and opened his eyes. I knew if I didn't leave soon, we'd both run the risk of dissolving into one another. I felt his soft skin in my hand and breathed him in.

One last kiss—no one will ever have to know.

I will know...and Cecil will know...and God will know.

He wants you to kiss him. Then you can go back to Frank and fulfill your vows.

Jesus, help me to do the right thing.

"I have commanded you to flee from temptation, but you have disobeyed my command."

But I love him. He may not be my husband, but he'll always be my friend.

"This is my commandment, that you love one another as I have loved

*you. Greater love has no one than this, that someone lay down his life for his
friends. You are my friends if you do what I command you."*

I thought I heard something move in the corner, near the sofa.

Friends don't leave if one of them is hurting.

Just one kiss.

"Why are you here?"

The voice came from behind me in the darkness and sent chills
down my spine.

Before I could focus my eyes on her, out of the darkness came
a force like I'd never felt before. Felicia, Cecil's wife, pulled back her
arm and swung at me, catching my left eye with the inside of her wrist.
Her bracelet cut a tiny sliver of skin near my eyelid while the rest of
her hand connected with my ear and forced me off the stool and onto
the hard linoleum floor. My knees slammed against the tiles before my
nervous system told me to brace for another hit.

Felicia towered above me as I knelt eye level to her pregnant belly.
Cecil shouted for her to stop as he pressed a button on the bed and
turned on the overhead lights.

When I was certain she wasn't going to hit me again, I pulled
myself up and wiped a spot of blood from my face.

Looking into her eyes made me realize who I was. I was the woman
in Proverbs 7 who was leading a man astray—and I was the woman at
the well in John 4 who was thirsty.

I was a sinner in need of a Savior...and something in her eyes
told me I was the other woman.

Blood flowed through my veins with such force that it washed
out all the sound in the room, but I knew Cecil was saying something
behind me. Everything blurred and pounded in my head as shame and
self-disgust began to bear down on me. All I could do was stand there
and stare into her dark brown eyes. Then something flashed inside
her—a sudden movement that shocked me back to my senses.

I positioned myself to make a break for the door, but again

something flashed across her face.

The second time, I recognized her expression as pain.

Felicia placed her hand on top of her pregnant belly and balanced herself against the foot of the bed. That opened up a clearing between the door and me, and everything inside me told me I should run.

Run, Amanda. Run!

I took two steps toward the door.

Get out while you still have the chance.

I saw Cecil reach for her as more pain shot through her body.

See what you've done?

I took another step.

All you do is cause problems.

I opened the door to the hallway as she whimpered in pain. Turning back, I saw her bend over the bed and grab her swollen belly again.

Leave them. They don't need you. You've done enough.

"Nurse!" I yelled down the hallway hoping one of the nurses would come running down to the room.

Felicia cried out with a combination of pain, fear, and pure hate.

"Get out of here! Get away from my husband!"

"Nurse!" I yelled as loudly as I could before rushing back to the bed. Cecil's wife flinched and covered her face as I got closer to her.

"I'm not going to hit you! You need to calm down while we wait for help," I said.

I searched the bed for the call button until I found it attached to a cord near Cecil's knee. I pressed the button repeatedly, hoping someone would get the message.

Felicia cried out for someone to help her.

"You see what you've done? This is your fault!" Felicia swatted in my direction and tried to catch hold of me again. "Cecil told me about you. I know who you are!"

I tried to ignore her and focus on getting help as quickly as possible. I knew that removing the finger monitor from Cecil's hand would trigger an alarm, so I grabbed hold of the cord and pulled his hand free.

"You need to calm down."

After I called for help again, I realized what I was doing. I was calling out for someone with the same training as me.

When it was clear no one was coming, I grabbed Felicia by the shoulders and eased her onto the stool while Cecil pushed the red call button as fast as a kid playing a video game. I wanted to wheel her into the hallway so we could find a doctor, but she must have thought I was trying to choke her, because the second I put my arm around her shoulders, she started pounding me on the back of my neck with her fist. With every hit she pulled out more of my hair. I tried to make her stop by grabbing at her wrists, but every time I grabbed she pulled and punched a little harder.

Finally, I let go and pushed a mess of hair from my face.

"I'm trying to help you!"

"Go away!"

"I can't just leave you here! If I do you're going to lose that baby!"

"You wish!" Felicia grabbed her belly again.

I looked over to Cecil, who looked more afraid than I'd ever seen him before.

My left eye started to throb, and I could feel fluid begin to fill the corner of my eye. "Please let me help you!"

Felicia pulled herself onto the bed next to Cecil.

"Are you bleeding?" I asked.

She shrugged her shoulders and began to cry.

"I need to know if you're bleeding. Can I check?"

Felicia covered her face with her hands and pulled her body as close to Cecil as she could.

"Let her look, Felicia. She's a nurse. She can help you!" Cecil ran his fingers through her thick hair and nodded. After I pushed back her gown, I was relieved to see there was no blood. I tried to act calm, but on the inside I was screaming at God and begging Him to let their baby live. I wanted Him to let me die right there if it meant saving the baby.

I wanted to lay down my life for my friend.

Felicia needed help, but it wasn't coming, so I did the most ridiculous thing I'd ever done. From the second floor of Helen Keller Hospital, I picked up the phone and called 911.

The 911 operator told me to push the call button on the bed. Well, we had already been doing that; Cecil had been pushing it nonstop while I was on the phone.

Seconds later, a team of medical personnel flooded the room.

No one, not even Cecil, noticed as I backed into the hallway. I waited downstairs until one of the ER nurses came down and assured me that everything was fine with Felicia and the baby. I recognized the nurse from school in Memphis, but couldn't remember her name.

"The baby looks fine on the ultrasound," she said, "but Mom's blood work shows she's severely dehydrated."

I was relieved.

"They're giving her fluids and telling her to stay in bed for a while, but their baby girl is going to be fine."

Baby girl. I repeated her words in my heart.

"You know," she added, "if she'd been sleeping she probably would've woken up tomorrow morning in full-blown labor. In another couple of hours she could've lost that baby."

I smiled at the woman and thanked her for telling me more than the Department of Health & Human Services would have ever allowed. I turned down her offer to get some ice for my eye and walked through the automatic doors.

"Good thing you were there," she called out as the doors closed between us.

Yeah, good thing.

When I was a child, I spoke and thought
and reasoned as a child.
But when I grew up, I put away childish things.

1 Corinthians 13:11

> I little dreamed how cruelly I should
> pay for that birthday gift.
>
> **HELEN KELLER**

Chapter Thirty-three

If I was going to make it home and back into bed before the sun came up, I needed to hurry. Exhausted, I slid behind the wheel of the car and studied my bruised eye in the rearview mirror. My eyelid was already swollen at the base of my lashes, so I knew my left eye would soon be swollen shut.

How am I going to explain this?

I tried to start the car, but the engine just clicked twice and died. I turned the key again, but the car still wouldn't start. If my face hadn't hurt so badly, I would've banged my head against the steering wheel. Instead, I threw the keys to the floorboard, got out of the car, slammed the door, and started walking.

Halfway across the parking lot I remembered I needed the keys in order to sneak back into the house, so I turned around, went back to the car, and snatched my keys off the mat. Before walking away, I decided to try to start the car one more time.

Nothing happened.

God was laughing; I was sure of it.

The walk home was nice—for the first mile.

A couple of cars passed by, but unlike the way I felt on the few late-night walks I'd taken in Memphis, I never felt scared. It was actually kind of peaceful. Quiet. I ran my fingers along the chain link fence at Deshler High School and looked out at the empty football field.

When I made it to North Commons a red pickup slowed down and pulled up beside me.

"Amanda, get in." Sam leaned across to the passenger door and pushed it open for me.

"No, thanks. I think I'll walk."

"Just get in the truck. I know what happened, and I'm not gonna let you wander around out here all night."

"I'm not wandering. I'm walking back to the mission house."

"Well, there's no use in that either. Get in."

Sam drove me the two remaining blocks and stopped a hundred yards short of the mission house.

"What are you gonna tell 'em?" he asked, looking at my swollen face.

"I don't know. I guess I'll tell them the truth."

Sam looked at me with a combination of concern and anger. As he started to pull forward, I put my hand on the door handle.

"I better walk the rest of the way."

"Why didn't you drive?"

"I did, but my car died at the hospital." I ran my hand through my hair and wiped away the sweat from the back of my neck. "So much for lying and saying I got into a bar fight."

I wished Sam would smile, but he didn't.

"I can jump your car and get it back to the house before anyone wakes up."

I was thankful for his offer but knew I had to refuse. "Thanks,

Sam, but I'm tired of lying. I just wanna go home and try to get some rest. I think it's time for me to grow up."

Sam shifted into first gear. "Okay, baby-girl," he said as I shut the door. "But don't forget about us."

I held back tears as Sam drove away in the direction of the hospital. The last time I rode in that truck, he was returning me to Mama. This time he was returning me to my husband and kids.

The golden glow of daylight began to fill the sky as I stepped onto the porch of the mission house and pulled the keys out of my pocket. Quietly, I slipped them into the lock, but as I began to turn the latch something inside me stopped.

I took a deep breath and put the keys back into my pocket. Tucking my shirt into my jeans, I tried to muster up as much courage as possible. I licked the tip of my index finger and tried to wipe away smears of makeup from my face, but the pain of touching my eyelid proved to be unbearable. After I felt that I'd done everything I could to clean myself up, I pushed my shoulders back and pressed the doorbell.

As a crowd of feet barreled down the hallway toward the door, I closed my eyes and took a deep breath. Voices called out from within the walls until finally the locks were unbolted and the door flung open. Frank and Mama both stood in the doorway and stared at me in confusion and disbelief. I waited as they studied my face.

"Are you okay? What happened?" Mama asked as she pulled me into the house.

Frank just stood there, not quite knowing what to say as Mama hurried me into the house and examined my eye.

"I'm sorry."

Frank stared at me with a look of both concern and disbelief.

"Frank! Say something to her!"

After he refused to speak, I walked past them, pulled the rocking horse down from its resting place, and hurried through the house toward the backyard. I let the screen door snap closed as I charged down the path toward the rose garden. Beneath a magnolia tree, I found a soft patch of earth and began digging at the dirt with my fingers. Mud filled the space beneath my nails and stuck to my knees. I knew Frank and Mama were watching me, but I didn't care. I kept clawing at the ground until I felt like I'd dug deep enough. Once I was done, I stopped to examine the porcelain horse and bench one last time.

With my last bit of strength, I broke the horse free from its chair and tossed it into the hole. Seeing it inside the grave made something inside me break free as well. It was different from the feeling I had when I threw the stone into the ditch, and it wasn't like placing the heart-shaped rock into the dirty ashtray either.

As I dropped the first handful of dirt into the hole, Frank knelt beside me in the cool grass. Gently, he took my hands and made me stop.

"I need to do this," I told him as he brushed the dirt from my fingers.

Frank dropped his chin and looked over at the half-buried horse. "If all you do is bury it, one day you'll crawl back out here during a moment of weakness and dig it up again."

"Then what should I do? I don't know how to get away from it."

"Give it to me," he said, holding out his hand.

"Give it to you? What're you going to do with it?"

"I'm going to give it to God," he said, moving his open hand closer to me. "You don't have to carry your burdens alone, Amanda. Let me help you give everything over to Him."

"How?" I asked, as both half-asleep children eased through the back door.

Mama quickly shooed them back inside and let the door close behind her.

Frank waited until they were gone before he continued. "We can pray every day and ask God to replace the things of this world with the blessings of what He's promised us in heaven."

"And what will I do after you leave me to go to be with Him? What will I do after you die?"

"You'll keep on praying and living your life for Christ until we see each other again."

"I can't do that. I don't know how to be alone."

"You'll never be alone, Amanda."

Frank lifted his empty hand.

"I can't take it away from you. You'll have to give it to me. You'll have to hand it over."

"What are you going to do with it?"

"If you're ready to get rid of it, why do you care?"

I shifted in the dirt and considered his question. "Because it's mine."

"No it's not."

He was right. Just like Cecil, the horse didn't belong to me.

I rescued the horse from its grave and placed it into Frank's hand. He covered it with his fingers.

"Whatever has been keeping you from God isn't your burden to bear alone. Not anymore."

I felt so cold, I imagined I should die before morning,
and the thought comforted me.

HELEN KELLER

Chapter Thirty-four

"**I**'m gonna get some ice for her eye," Mama said, disappearing from the bedroom as quickly as she'd left the garden. I could tell she was silently panicking—the way mothers do when they know their children have gotten themselves into a world of trouble. She was gone only a few minutes before she reemerged holding a cotton dishrag and a Ziploc filled with ice.

"She needs to put this on her eye."

Frank pulled the covers over my shoulders. I jumped as he eased the pack onto my face.

"Tell me what happened," he said once the air in the room began to settle. "Did you wreck the car?"

"The car isn't here," Mama whispered, as if my ears had been injured instead of my eye.

I removed the ice long enough to give her an unhappy look. She read my expression and excused herself, leaving Frank and me alone in the bedroom.

"Where'd you go?" The hurt in his voice told me he already knew. "Were you alone?"

I swallowed hard and pressed down on the cloth as if the pressure might keep me from crying. "I just decided to go for a ride. That's all."

"And where did you end up?"

"The same place I always end up—somewhere between hell and home."

"What does that mean? Tell me. Tell me what happened to your eye. Tell me what happened to our car. Is someone else hurt? Did you hurt someone?"

"Yes."

"Yes, what?" he asked. Frank, suddenly concerned, pulled my hands away from my face and told me to sit up. "What happened? Are you in trouble?"

I pushed myself up and sat with my back against the wall. "Yes, Frank. Okay? Yes! I'm in trouble. I'm a stupid, thoughtless woman who is always in trouble. And, yes, someone always gets hurt when they're around me."

Frank's eyes narrowed.

"Did you go to see him?"

I tried to lift the pillow, but he grabbed it and tossed it across the room before I had time to hide my face.

"Why would you do that? Why would you leave me in the middle of the night to go see him?"

"Stupidity, I guess."

"But you're not stupid."

"Sometimes I am."

"No you're not." Frank rubbed his cheeks with his hands in an attempt to calm his anger. "You're just lost." He took in a deep breath before pounding his fist on the bed. "And blind—and deaf!"

"I'm not like you! You're good and kind, and you always make the right decisions. It's not that easy for me. I can't be like you."

Frank studied my eye again. "Did he hit you?"

I was shocked that he'd even consider that a possibility. "No, of course he didn't hit me."

"Then what happened to your eye?"

I considered lying, but something inside me knew it was better to go ahead and tell him the truth.

"His wife hit me," I said after I gained enough courage to be honest.

Frank's body stiffened as a word slipped through his lips that I was certain had never crossed them before.

"I never asked you to be like me."

All of his concern for me drained from his face as he stood and searched the floor beside the bed. "I just want you to love me," he said as he pulled a clean shirt out of his duffel bag.

"Where are you going?" I asked.

"I'm going for a walk."

"You can't go for a walk. You're sick."

"I need to think."

Frank stepped into his loafers and grabbed his hat and Bible from the bedside table.

"Get some sleep," he said, opening the bedroom door and looking out into the dark hallway. "When I get back, we're leaving."

I'm not sure how much time passed between the time Frank left and the moment the loud tapping on the front door startled me awake. The awareness of my bruised eye immediately surfaced and erased the peace I'd felt as I dreamed. I waited for someone to answer the door, but after several minutes I realized I was the only person left in the house.

The tapping stopped for a few minutes, making me think the visitor had left, but soon it continued even harder than before. I pulled myself up to the window and peered through the latticework.

Even through the overgrown ivy and wooden slats, I could tell the woman standing at the door was Lada, wearing yet another plum-colored outfit.

What does she want?

I buried my head beneath the covers and tried to ignore her pounding.

"Amanda?"

How does she know I'm here?

"Are you in there? I need you to come to the door."

Don't you run this place? Surely you have a key.

I threw back the sheets and sat up.

She probably wears that color because Jesus did. She probably thinks she's some kind of royalty.

I jumped out of bed, stumbled down the hallway, and jerked open the front door.

"Why do you always wear that stupid color?"

Lada pushed past me. "Because I like it."

"Why are you here? Obviously, Mama's gone."

"I know. Your mama told me to come get you."

Panic set in as I realized something might have happened to Frank or the kids.

"Why? What happened?"

"Your mama needs you to come right away. One of the girls at the Refuge House has run off, and she needs you to take the kids so she can go looking for her."

"I thought something might've happened to Frank. I can't leave until he comes back."

Lada rushed into the bedroom and began pulling clothes out of my bag and holding them out for me to wear.

"Frank's fine. He's riding around with Beeny. They're looking for the missing girl."

I didn't like the way she was pushing me around like I didn't have any choice but to follow her. When she was through piling clothes into my arms, I tossed the items onto the bed and stood with my hands on my hips.

"Why didn't my mother just bring the kids here?"

Lada glanced at the pile of discarded clothes and then back at me. It felt like an eternity passed while the two of us stood there glaring at one another. I could tell she was getting a good look at my eye and trying hard not to shake her head.

"All I know is that your mama said something about your car not being available."

"Did she tell you what happened last night?" I asked, snatching a pair of jeans off the floor.

"No, but I've pieced together enough to know you're in trouble."

"Not with you I'm not. You're not my mother."

Lada rolled her eyes. "Thanks, Amanda. I've waited my whole life to hear someone say that." She brushed past me on her way out. "I'll be in the car."

⚜

We rode in silence most of the way to the Refuge House until I started feeling guilty about the way I'd acted.

"Ms. Prudence," I said, sounding more like a child addressing her math teacher than a grown woman trying to offer a kind word to a stranger. "I'm sorry. It's just been a long week."

She kept both her hands on the steering wheel and pretended to ignore me. After we entered Sheffield, Lada eased the sedan off the asphalt and turned to face me.

"And I'm sorry about what happened between me and your father, but that was a long time ago. Even if it hurts you as if it happened yesterday, I assure you it was a lifetime ago for me and your mama."

Whose lifetime? Pen's lifetime? My daddy's lifetime? I wanted to ask those questions and more, but I held my tongue.

I crossed my arms and leaned against the passenger door.

"Did you love him?" I asked after my heart rate steadied a bit.

"I thought I did at the time, but now I think I was just looking for any love and attention I could get."

"Did you know he was married? Did you know about me?"

Lada tucked a piece of graying hair behind her ear before she answered.

"Yes. He talked about you all the time. He loved you very much."

"Then how could you do it? How could you try to take my father away from me?"

Lada laughed. "The same way you're willing to destroy everything so you can be with Cecil, I guess. I was selfish, and all I could see were my own desires."

Lada's words unnerved me.

"I don't want to destroy anyone," I argued. I turned to look out the window but instead caught a glimpse of my bruised and swollen eye. "Honest, I don't."

"Well, you're very blessed to have a husband who loves you. I'm sure he can help. I didn't have anyone to help me make decisions. I was more alone than you can ever imagine."

"I'm not sure Frank will ever forgive me for what I've done."

"That doesn't sound like the man Tilly talks about."

"I'm not sure I deserve forgiveness."

"That's the beauty of grace, Amanda. Because of God's grace, we don't get what we deserve. If we got what we deserved then we'd all be burning in hell. Thankfully, God forgives us when we ask—and Frank will forgive you, too."

Whenever I enter the region that was the
kingdom of my mind
I feel like the proverbial bull in the china shop.

HELEN KELLER

Chapter Thirty-five

Lada pulled into the driveway at the Refuge as Mama finished sweeping something into a metal dustpan near the front steps. After she saw us she leaned the broom against the porch and met us at the end of the walkway. Tiny bits of what was once a huge clay pot littered the path and spilled out into the yard.

"What happened here?" I asked.

"A man came looking for Emma Sue. He didn't like it when your sister told him she'd called the police."

"Did he take her with him when he left?" Lada asked.

"No, she must've gone out the back door when she saw him kicking 'round the landscaping. Pen's not just worried because that idiot's lookin' for Emma Sue, she's also afraid because the girl's due date is soon."

"Has Pen gone looking for her?" I wanted to know.

Mama nodded. "Pen is with two police officers. They've gone looking for her at the festival, in case she hitched a ride into town, and Frank and Beeny are driving around looking too. I was gonna go, but maybe it's better if I stay here and clean up this mess."

"Why don't you go for a walk and see if you can find her?" Lada suggested, patting me on the back as if I was an old friend. "I'll stay here and help your mama with the kids and the cleanup job."

"But it's so hot," I said, pulling my shirt away from the part of my stomach where it was already beginning to cling to my sweat.

"That's another reason why we need to find her," Mama said as she handed me an unopened bottle of water.

I set off down the winding road behind the house, water bottle in hand, and tried to imagine which route I would take if I was nine months pregnant and trying to escape a crazed lunatic. The breeze from the river was blocked by tall trees, heavy overgrowth, and an occasional house, so walking along the pavement felt more like being trapped in a hot parking garage than strolling along an empty street.

I refused to wander aimlessly while yelling "Thumper" into the open air. People would think I was searching for a rabbit.

It didn't take long to realize that leaving my purse and phone in Lada's car had been a huge mistake. After only twenty minutes of walking, I was already soaked in sweat and wishing I could call Mama and ask her to pick me up.

I hoped Emma Sue was smart enough to escape the heat. I wanted to believe she'd taken shelter, but I remembered how nervous she was around me and the other women. Now, pieces of Thumper's life were beginning to come together. If this guy is the father of her unborn child, no wonder she cowers every time someone speaks to her.

Out of the corner of my eye, I saw something move in the bushes beside a shed.

"Thumper?" I called out, breaking the promise I'd made to myself. "Thumper! Is that you?"

After no one replied, I crept closer and found a path leading down through the woods behind the shed.

"Thumper? If that was you, please don't hide. That man is gone now. All I want to do is help you get somewhere safe."

Still no reply.

I slapped a mosquito and called out for her one more time, even though I wasn't sure if I'd actually seen her or just a shadow. I found a path near the spot where I thought she'd gone and knew it would eventually come out near Riverfront Park, so I took a sip of water and headed down the hill into the heavy brush.

"Thumper!" I yelled again, trying to comfort myself with the sound of my own voice. "Please don't make me chase you."

Wishing I'd chosen something cooler to wear than blue jeans, I turned the water bottle up and took a gulp. As I struggled to replace the lid, I lost my footing, fell to my rear, and slid until I stopped at a ditch filled with leaves and debris at the foot of the hill. I kicked at the bottle as the last drops of water spilled out and were quickly absorbed by the earth.

This is the worst week of my life.

I stood, brushed the dirt and leaves from my jeans, and realized I'd found the road leading to Riverfront Park—actually, I'd almost rolled right into the middle of it.

I was still trying to wipe some mud from my hands when a car sped by. The brown clunker squealed to a stop after Beeny realized that it was me she'd almost run over.

"What are you doing out here?" Frank asked after they backed up and offered me the backseat of the Buick.

"The same thing you are. I'm looking for Emma Sue."

Beeny cut her eyes at me over the vinyl seat. "Looked to me like you was rollin' in the dirt."

"I was following a path through the woods when I fell and nearly rolled into the street. I thought I saw Thumper, but now I think it was just a mirage caused by this heat."

"What happened to your eye?" Beeny asked, trying to drive and investigate my face at the same time.

"That's what happened the last time I went chasing something that didn't really exist," I confessed, reaching over the seat and putting my hand on Frank's shoulder. I was certain he was still mad, but I wanted him to know I was sorry.

After a long minute passed, he grabbed the tips of my fingers and kissed the top of my hand.

For almost an hour Beeny cruised up and down the few streets in Tuscumbia that weren't blocked because of the festival.

"This is pointless. We ain't never gonna find that girl," she said, slapping the steering wheel.

"Well, we have to keep looking," Frank insisted.

I strained my eyes and tried to sort through the crowd of people.

"Is that her?" Frank asked for the tenth time as he pointed toward a tall blonde woman.

Beeny scrunched up her face, "That girl ain't even pregnant."

"Stop the car," I said.

"Why? Did you see her?"

"No. Just stop the car. Beeny's right; this is pointless. We're not going to find her by driving around all day. I'm going to walk through the festival and look for her." I opened the door and stepped out. "Can I borrow your hat?"

Frank handed me his favorite Redbirds hat through the passenger-side window. "Where do you want us to pick you up?"

"I'm going to walk through Spring Park and then up the hill from there. I don't have my phone, so let's plan to meet at the corner of Main and Third in a half hour."

Hundreds of people crowded the craft booths and food stands in the grassy areas on both sides of the lake. Spring Park is the home of Cold Water Falls, the world's largest manmade waterfall built with natural stone. My friends and I used to study near the spot where the water spills into the lake.

I watched a man and woman standing at the water's edge lean in and kiss each other. Something about the way they looked at each other reminded me of Cecil. Maybe because they were young, or maybe because they seemed to have their whole lives ahead of them. I swallowed hard and tried to force my thoughts toward something else. I still wanted to know what Cecil saw under the water the day he almost drowned. What had I been holding?

As I passed through a row of white tents, I prayed God would help me to focus on finding Thumper.

Slow down, you'll never find her if you keep running through the crowd like someone's chasing you.

I stopped near a booth where a man was busy making baskets.

"Come on in," he said without looking up from his handiwork. "Welcome to one of the few craft fairs in the South that actually has electricity. Come cool off by this fan if you'd like."

"No, thank you, sir. I'm not shopping—just looking for my friend."

"I didn't ask you to shop. I only asked you to cool off." The man began to hum as he continued to weave heavy cords of willow through thick rattan.

"I'm sorry, I'm just worried about my friend." I went over to where he was working and lowered my face to the fan. "She's pregnant, and she has no business being in this heat."

He nodded his head and reached beneath a covered table. Still holding the basket with his right hand, he pulled a small cooler into the open with his left.

"Here, when you find her give her this." The kind man handed me a bottle of frozen water. "Don't worry, it won't take long for it to melt out here."

"Oh, thank you." I wiped the cool condensation from the bottle and pressed my hand to my face. "Hey, you haven't seen a pregnant woman come through here have you? She's about my height with long, curly brown hair."

The man stood and looked at me with his cloudy eyes, "Ma'am, I haven't seen anyone in almost forty-three years."

I rushed through the last of the tents and finally reached the foot of Main Street, where the edge of downtown meets Spring Park.

Orange cones blocked both sides of the road from oncoming traffic, so I walked down the middle of the street in order to see in all directions. My gut told me I was getting closer and closer with every step. As I walked down the streets, my heart warmed to the idea of being home. The buildings were beautiful. I remembered pieces of what Mama told me about each structure. I remembered something about the Sutherland building being one of the oldest retail structures in the state and about Fifth Street once being called Commercial Row.

As I listened to the sounds of the festival, pride for my hometown began to wash over me. I wished Frank was healthy enough to walk with me. He would have loved to hear about the Sutherland brothers and the closing of their business in the1800s, seeing the building and hearing how one brother moved to Texas and wrote a book after witnessing the fall of the Alamo.

I passed by the place where Helen Keller's father ran his newspaper and then stepped inside a law office to use the phone. Mama assured me the kids were fine but that Thumper hadn't come back to the house. I told her we were still looking and that we'd come back to the Refuge if we didn't find her soon.

As I hung up the phone, I recognized Thumper's long, dark curls as she passed by the window.

I knew there were obstacles in the way;
but I was eager to overcome them.
HELEN KELLER

Chapter Thirty-six

I followed Emma Sue for a while to see where she was going. She made her way over to a group of men standing beside the open hood of a refurbished car that was on display. She spoke to one of them as if she was the most confident woman in the world, not like the pregnant woman who had sat hunched over at the Refuge.

Emma Sue seemed much more Thumper-like as she pushed her hair off her shoulder and laughed. The man nodded and touched the top of her arm. When another man joined them, she mouthed something in his direction. I imagined she was asking for money, but the man pulled a pack of cigarettes from his shirt pocket and seemed obliged to give her one. I wanted to ask the man what he was thinking giving a pregnant woman a cigarette, but I didn't have time. Emma Sue walked away before I could reach them.

I was afraid to call her name as she wove through the display of cars. I didn't want her to run off again, and I knew if she continued in the same direction, she'd eventually end up in the spot where I was scheduled to meet Frank and Beeny. My plan was to wait until I saw the Buick before approaching Emma Sue.

One block short of the meeting place, Thumper stopped, lit the cigarette, and ducked behind the Abernathy House. She had spotted me. I thought she'd throw down her smoke, but instead she kept on puffing away as if she'd known I was watching the whole time.

"Emma Sue, you shouldn't be smoking. You know that, right?"

"That's not my name. My name is Thumper," she said, showing a flash of anger.

"I'm sorry, but you must've told someone that your name was Emma Sue. Otherwise, people wouldn't be calling you that."

"Your sister said I couldn't stay unless I gave my birth name, but nobody's called me Emma Sue since my daddy died." She took another drag. "I buried that name when I buried him."

I wondered how literal she was being. "I'm sorry. I'll call you Thumper if you want me to," I said, trying not to sound like I was reading from *Bambi*.

She rolled her eyes and blew a cloud of smoke through her nose. "Thanks."

"Who gave you the name Thumper? Was it the man who came looking for you?"

Thumper tossed down the cigarette butt and walked away.

"What did this used to be?" she asked as she climbed the wooden steps to a dilapidated structure behind the Abernathy House. She was determined to change the subject.

"It's where the slaves used to live—and it's dangerous, so you shouldn't go in."

Thumper pushed open the door and eased her way into the small space. The air in the room was ten degrees warmer than outside, and the dust was so thick I had to rub my eyes before I could find the spot where she'd hidden.

"We shouldn't be in here. This place could cave in at any second."

"Look, there's a tunnel," she said, pointing to a hole in the floor.

"That's because this used to be the kitchen. The help would cook the food and carry it through the tunnel to the main house."

"I like this place," she said as if she planned to live there forever.

"Well, maybe we can come back sometime, but right now we need to go. Beeny and my husband are waiting for us."

Emma Sue eased herself to the floor and crossed her legs.

"I'm not going back to the Refuge House."

"Why not?"

"Because if Jerry comes back, he's gonna kill me. Me and everyone else that gets in his way."

"I'm sure he's long gone by now, Thumper. I promise you'll be safe."

Emma Sue closed her eyes and rubbed her belly again.

"Is he the father of your baby?" I asked, trying to regain her attention.

"Why do you ask so many questions?" she snapped between her rocking and rubbing.

"I'm sorry, I just want to get you out of here."

I twisted the top off the water bottle and discovered the ice had melted as the blind man had promised. "Here, you need to drink this."

She took the bottle and thanked me under her breath. After she took a sip she wiped her mouth with the back of her hand. "I'm not leaving."

"Well, I am." Dried pieces of floral wallpaper chipped and broke under my fingers as I felt my way back to the door.

"Don't leave," she said once I reached the open doorway.

"It's hot. I'm leaving."

"If you leave, I won't be here when you get back, and you'll never see me again."

Something in her voice made me believe her. "I know you don't want to hurt your baby, so why don't you come with me?"

Emma Sue looked down at her belly. "My mama was the one that called me Thumper."

I turned and sat in the entrance in hopes that someone who could help would pass by.

I'd assumed Thumper was a stage name or something her pimp called her, but I never thought it was a name given to her by her mother.

"What made her choose that name?"

"My hair wasn't always dark and curly like this. When I was a girl, Momma used to pull it back in a little white puff on the back of my head. I was the only kid who lived at Lost Rabbit, so she called me Thumper Rabbit. Name just kinda stuck."

"Is Lost Rabbit the name of your hometown?"

"It ain't a town, really."

"Does your mama still live there?"

"No." I could tell she was holding back tears behind her curls. "She died when I was a little girl."

"Same time as your daddy?" I asked.

Thumper sniffed and straightened. "No."

"I'm sorry. I know how hard it is to grow up without a daddy."

My comment made her let out a sarcastic burst of laughter.

"Oh, I didn't grow up without him." She pushed her hair out of her face and wiped her tears with the front of her shirt.

"I spent every day of my life taking care of that man. I spent my childhood wishin' he'd die a slow and painful death, and my teen years wishin' God would hurry up and get it over with."

I tried to understand.

"When I first met Jerry, he offered to do it himself."

"Offered to do what?" I asked.

"Kill my daddy."

I wiped my forehead and looked to see if anyone was headed our way.

"Did he do it?" I asked, even though I was afraid of what she might confess now that she'd started talking.

"No, but that doesn't mean he won't kill me."

"Is he your husband?"

Thumper shook her head. "No, and he ain't the father of this baby neither."

"Does he know that?"

The tears came back in her eyes. "God, I hope not."

"If you think this guy could hurt you, then we need to let the police know. We can find another place for you to stay until the baby comes."

At the mention of the baby, Emma Sue started rocking and rubbing her belly like before. A cloud of dust fell from the ceiling and settled on the old makeshift mantel above the fireplace.

"But we need to get out of here and find Beeny and Frank first. Please come with me."

While she considered my request, I took off Frank's hat and used it to fan my face.

"I ain't like you and Beeny. Y'all are good people. I used to be, or at least I tried, but ain't like that anymore."

I wished I was as good and noble as she made me out to be, but there was no denying how far I'd fallen. All of my hidden sin and brokenness surfaced as I stared at Thumper. I couldn't imagine some of the things she'd suffered from life and from men.

"I'm not any better than you."

"Yes you are. You have a family and a husband. I don't have anythin'. The only person that ever loved me was my mother, but she didn't love me enough to keep from—" Thumper stopped rubbing her belly and looked up. "You think you have it hard, but you have no idea."

I took a deep breath as we stared into one another's eyes. She was right. Something in her cried out the dark things she'd lived through. I stopped pretending to understand.

After the air between us softened, she tilted her head a little and studied my face. "What happened to your eye?"

I stopped fanning and put the hat back on. "I got hit."

"By who?"

"By my old boyfriend's wife, that's who."

For the first time, a smile crossed Thumper's face.

"Did you deserve it?"

"I guess I did. See, I told you I'm not perfect."

She smiled and nodded, seemingly pleased that I'd shared my brokenness.

"No one's perfect, Thumper. If we were then we wouldn't need forgiveness, and that's something I need every day." I wanted to make her understand what I'd somehow forgotten. "And we wouldn't need God either."

"Sometimes I feel like God doesn't listen to me. It's like He's answerin' everyone else's prayers, but He's ignorin' mine. I know I've done lotsa bad things, but still. If He loved me, He wouldn't have taken Mama away."

Thumper turned away so I couldn't see her face anymore and pounded her hand on the floor until a cloud of dust rose and covered her body.

"I know what you mean about sometimes feeling like He doesn't listen, Thumper. I feel that way all the time. God let my daddy die when I was nine, and now I'm afraid he's gonna let Frank die as well. Trust me, I know what it's like to be angry with God, but the truth is He loves you no matter how you feel about Him."

"You don't know the things I've done."

"But what I'm telling you is that it doesn't matter. All you have to do is ask God to forgive you. Then you'll be God's child just like that one." I pointed to Thumper's belly.

"You think it's bad if I give my baby away?"

I considered her question before answering. My heart had changed a lot over the last few days, and I needed time before I could give an honest answer. Thumper fanned the cloud of dust aside as she waited for my answer.

"No, I used to think that, but now I see that giving your child up for adoption can be one of the most wonderful and selfless things you can do."

Thumper started rocking again. "It ain't because I don't love her."

"I know." I stood and offered my hand to Thumper. "It's because you do."

.

Out of immemorial chaos He wrought us.

HELEN KELLER

Chapter Thirty-seven

Thumper and I walked shoulder to shoulder until we made it to the place where I agreed to meet Frank. By the time we got there I was almost an hour late, but I was still surprised to see that he and Beeny weren't waiting for me at the corner of Main and Third.

Thumper sat on a rusty iron bench and finished off the last of the water. "So where is he?"

"Well, we're late. Maybe they decided to go looking for us. Let's give them a few minutes. If they don't show up soon, we'll walk to the mission house. It's only a couple of blocks from here."

Thumper looked uneasy. "What's the mission house? I ain't goin' to another house full of women."

"It's not full of women. Actually, it's empty. That's why my mama's living there right now." As I spoke, I began to worry. It wasn't like Frank to stray from the plan. Something was wrong. "Maybe we should borrow someone's phone and let Pen know we're okay."

"I don't want to go wanderin'. Jerry might still be lookin' for me."

"For all he knows, you never left the Refuge."

Thumper stood and began pacing back and forth in a shady spot behind the bench.

"Frank will be back in a second," I promised as I sat in the spot she'd abandoned. "Frank always does what he says."

Thumper tried to keep up as we hurried our way toward the mission house.

Maybe Beeny went into labor? That would explain why he didn't show up.

"Maybe Jerry killed 'em," Thumper offered as she stopped to catch her breath.

"Thanks a lot. All I needed to hear was that your crazed boyfriend killed my wonderful husband."

Thumper wiped her brow and started walking again. "Explain that to me."

"Explain what?"

"How come you got hit by your ex's wife if you've got a wonderful husband? Why didn't Fred stop her?"

I quickened my pace. "Frank. Frank wasn't there."

"Where was he?"

"He was asleep at the mission house. I'll show you where if you'll hurry up."

"Why are you so panicked? I'm the one that should be worried. I'm the one bein' chased."

"I'm afraid something's wrong with Frank. He's sick, and he shouldn't be on a wild goose chase while everybody looks for *you*." The words escaped with more blame than I'd intended.

"Well, I'm sorry, but I didn't ask y'all to come lookin' for me." Thumper stopped again and grabbed the under part of her belly. As I waited, she lifted her stomach and let out a little moan.

"Just come on," I pleaded. "We're almost there. Can you go a little farther?"

I could see the side of the mission house, but I couldn't tell if anyone was parked in the driveway. Thumper grumbled something under her breath before she started walking again. Once we passed the church, I saw that the car parked catty-corner in the driveway wasn't Beeny's Buick. Instead, there beside the long row of red and white impatiens, sat my gray Accord. Before I had time to guess who'd returned the car, Sam stepped out of the front door and yelled for us to get in the car.

"What's wrong? Is it Frank?" I asked as I jumped into the passenger seat.

"Frank's fine—long as you consider the fact that he's 'bout to deliver someone's baby as fine."

Thumper climbed in behind me, her eyes big like a scared cat. After she slammed the door, Sam turned and nodded as he backed down the driveway. I wanted to introduce them, but I couldn't decide on which name to use.

Before turning back around, Sam extended his hand to her, "Hi, I'm Sam."

Thumper went back to being bashful. "Hi."

"Is Beeny in labor?" I asked, trying to interrupt the awkwardness.

"I didn't catch her name. She was a big black woman—looked a lot like Radella when she was pregnant with Cecil. I was sittin' in the waiting room when they came in. I tried to mind my own business, but when he started tellin' the receptionist they needed to call Pen at the Refuge House and let her know you were wanderin' around downtown, I couldn't help but jump in."

"How did you fix my car?" I asked.

"Some woman showed up with Pen, said your keys and purse were in her car, and that I could take it in case we needed room for a third person. The thing started right up on the first try. I knew you'd come back here eventually, so I decided to wait. I was only inside for a second before I saw the two of you walkin' up the road."

"Is Frank okay?"

I tried to read Sam's face as he took hold of my hand. "Yeah, baby-girl, he's all right—I guess." Sam gave my hand a gentle squeeze. "He looks pretty sick though. At first, I thought she was the one bringin' him to the hospital."

Something caught in my throat and made me want to explain that Frank was going be all right, but instead I pulled my hand free and buckled my seatbelt.

"We're gonna be okay, Sam. Don't you worry about us."

Sam topped the hill at Cave Street going so fast that Thumper and I lost our stomachs. My car didn't stop bouncing until Sam parked it under the awning near the hospital's entrance, where Lada stood talking to someone on her cell phone. When she saw me get out of the car, she told the person on the line that I was there and Thumper was with me.

"Is that my mother?" I asked, helping Thumper out of the backseat.

"Yes, she's worried about you. Are y'all okay?"

I spoke loudly in hopes that Mama could hear me through the receiver. "We're fine, Mama. I'm gonna run in and check on Frank and Beeny. I'll call you soon."

Sam and I rushed through the automatic doors and into the half-empty waiting area. I wasn't surprised to find Frank sitting with his hands folded and his head bowed. When I reached him, he struggled to stand and hug me.

"I was so worried when you weren't where you said you'd be. I knew something was wrong." I kissed the side of his cheek—relieved to be near him again. "I thought you'd died."

Frank laughed and extended his hand to Sam. "Thanks for finding her."

"Aw, she's not that hard to find when she's home."

"How's Beeny? What happened? Did she already have the baby?"

Frank removed his hat from my head and placed it back on his. Smiling, he wiggled the brim as if he was the soon-to-be father.

"We were waiting on you when all of a sudden Beeny's water broke. She was scared to death, and the longer we waited on you, the more panicked she got. We decided to go to the mission house first so we could make sure the door was unlocked and leave you a note. When we got here, this nice man told us he was a friend of your mama's and that he'd love to help."

"You mean you don't know who this is?" I asked.

Sam put his arm around my shoulder and pulled me into an uncomfortable sideways hug.

"I'm the best sideline football coach to ever cheer the Deshler Tigers into the playoffs. Everybody 'round here knows me," he said.

I smiled nervously at the two of them, feeling certain that at any moment Frank would realize who the helpful stranger was.

Lada made her way over to us after she settled Thumper into a blue chair near the window. "How's Beatrice doing?" she asked Frank.

"Pen's back there with her now. When we came in, the nurse told us she'd already dilated six centimeters. I guess it won't be long before the baby comes."

Frank was glowing with excitement. While Lada and Sam talked, he leaned in close to me. "Is that the girl we were looking for?"

"Yes, that's her," I whispered.

"Where'd you find her?"

"It's a long story," I whispered. "Is Beeny's real name Beatrice?"

"Yes. Beatrice Jones."

Sam started to excuse himself from the group. "Well, I better get outta here before somebody sends a search party out lookin' for me."

I tried to pretend like telling him goodbye was no big deal, but the question I'd been carrying around since Cecil's accident began to burn in my heart again. Maybe Sam really did know what I'd been holding when Cecil saw me under the water.

As I watched Sam walk down the hall toward the elevator, I decided not to let him go without finding out.

"Sam!" I called out just as the elevator doors were about to close.

He slid his hand between the doors and forced them to stop. "What is it?"

"I need to know something. You told me that when Cecil was about to drown, he saw me holding something under the water. What was it? What was I holding? I know he told you."

"You mean after all this sneakin' around, you still haven't asked him?"

"Please, Sam—if you know, then I need you to tell me. Was it a baby?" The doors started to close again, but I forced them open with my foot. "Was I holding a baby when Cecil saw me?"

Sam shook his head. "No, baby-girl, you weren't."

"Well then, what was it? Because I've been thinking about it, and I think maybe Cecil did die for a second and that maybe he saw me—in the future, or even in heaven maybe, and that I was holding the baby we lost."

Sam pulled me into the elevator and waited for the doors to close. "Amanda, it wasn't a baby. Cecil told me he saw you and that you were holding a—a big rock—like a boulder—up close to your chin, near your chest. He said somethin' inside him knew if he died you'd keep holdin' that boulder until you drowned and died too."

"Another rock. I should've known it would be another stupid rock."

Sam pulled my face to his shoulder. "Maybe he's right, baby-girl."

"Right about what?" I wanted to hit something. I wanted to pound the walls of the elevator until they crumbled.

"If he'd died that day, maybe a part of you would've died, too. 'Cause you wouldn't have had a chance to put down the boulder while you were both still alive."

"That's why I wanted to see him. I wanted to tell him goodbye."

"Cecil can't help you let go, Amanda. You don't need him for that. Only God can lift that burden from you. You gotta ask God to carry the boulder for you."

"I don't want God to carry it. I just want it to go away!"

"Your loss ain't ever gonna go away, baby-girl. It's part of you. But if you give it to God, He can make it one of your strengths. That'd be a whole lot better than what you're allowing it to do now."

"I don't know how losing you, and Cecil, and a baby can ever be a good thing."

The doors opened to the second-floor hallway I'd crept down the night before. After Sam pushed the button on the keypad to send me back down to the first floor, he stepped out.

"Amanda, if you'll put down that boulder and trust the Lord, what you'll gain will be a lot better than what you've lost."

I wanted to believe him. I wanted to let go, but I was still afraid.

"I love you, Sam."

"I love you too, baby-girl."

I pressed my finger against the button so the door would stay open for a few more seconds. "Thank you for being like a father to me."

For the first time, tears began to fill Sam's eyes. "I know the Lord's gonna do better than I have."

And [the blind man] looked up and said,
"I see men, but they look like trees, walking."

Then Jesus laid his hands on his eyes again;
and he opened his eyes, his sight was restored,
and he saw everything clearly.

Mark 8:24-25

Before me I saw a new world opening
in beauty and light,
and felt within me the capacity to know all things.
HELEN KELLER

Chapter Thirty-eight

After two hours of waiting, Pen finally emerged to tell us the good news—Beeny gave birth to a healthy little boy. We were still rejoicing when a couple walked in carrying a yellow blanket and an armful of flowers. The woman wore diamond earrings and a tight blonde ponytail at the nape of her neck. When she saw Pen, the woman started to cry.

"Can we see them?" she asked. Her husband never took his hand off her lower back. Even as they hurried down the hallway toward Beeny's room, he stayed glued to her.

Pen hugged each of us and told us she'd see us later. It was her way of letting us know we needed to leave. My heart ached for my new friend and for the child I feared she'd never see again. Frank pulled me over and kissed me on the forehead. "It's gonna be all right," he promised.

I looked over his shoulder to the spot where Lada was quietly talking to Thumper. Lada reached across the arm of the chair and patted Thumper's hand. They looked like mother and child sitting next to one another. Seeing them reminded me of what Lada said in the garden about love not being self-seeking. She was right—love doesn't take advantage of situations without regard for other people.

Instead, love is what's present when imperfect people are shown grace and forgiveness.

I knew Frank was right. Everything was going to be okay.

I could tell by the circles under Frank's eyes that he was exhausted and hungry. We agreed to pick up some dinner and get the kids before packing up our things and heading back to Memphis.

"Why do you think Beeny wanted to give her baby away?" I asked as we drove in the direction of the river.

Frank lowered the passenger window and let the noises of the city fill the car. Crickets sang in the distance as we waited for a cargo train to cross Montgomery.

"She told me the woman adopting her baby has been her best friend since childhood."

"The woman with the diamonds and the perfect hair is Beeny's friend?" I asked.

"Beeny said she knew the second she found out she was pregnant that the baby belonged to that woman and not to her." Frank turned the knobs on the dashboard. "I didn't ask any questions, but I think Beeny's been through a lot. She's come through it pretty well."

As the train disappeared into the distance, the light turned green and allowed us to cross the tracks. Frank settled on a jazz station and reclined his seat a few inches.

"Do you wanna go by and see the house before we head back to Memphis?"

I shuddered at the thought of seeing what remained of the place I'd grown up in.

"I'd be surprised to find anything left."

Frank leaned forward and stretched his back. "Maybe it'd be good for Honey to have someone go with her. Has she been back there?"

"Honestly, I don't know. I've been too distracted to care."

"Maybe she's avoiding it because she knows how hard it'll be. Maybe you're avoiding it for the same reason."

"It's almost dark. It won't do any good to drive out there in the middle of the night," I said.

"Well," Frank tried to massage away the pain in his lower back, "maybe we should wait and leave in the morning after the two of you have had time to go to the house and look around."

I parked the car in the driveway at the Refuge House and noticed three woman congregated on the porch around Beeny's weathered Bible. They stopped reading as we got out of the car and walked toward them.

Frank was the first to speak. "We're sorry to interrupt. We're here to pick up our kids."

"They ain't here," yelled the heaviest of the three.

"Do you know where they might've gone?" I asked.

The woman on the swing nodded. "Your mama said somethin' 'bout takin' cookies to a play."

"They went to the rehearsal yesterday. Are you sure they said they were going back tonight?"

A young girl in her early teens pushed open the screen door and placed a bare foot onto the porch. "Yes, ma'am. We made some cookies for the actors. Ms. Tilly said they were gonna drive 'em over to Ivy Green and come right back."

"Do you know how long ago they left?" Frank asked.

"Yes, sir. 'Bout five or ten minutes."

Frank grabbed my elbow and pulled me back in the direction of the car. "If we hurry, maybe we can catch them while there are cookies to spare."

"No, let's go get something to eat and wait for them to come back."

"Don't be silly."

I started the car and pulled away from the Refuge. "I'm not being silly."

"Yes you are. You're avoiding a trip to Ivy Green."

"That's not true."

"Come on. You've got to go back sometime."

I parked the car on a small patch of grass near the gated entrance to Helen Keller's childhood home. It was the same way I remembered it: a small patch of land, twice as long as it was wide with perfect landscaping. Before we got out of the car, I finished the last of my French fries while Frank ate the last of his yogurt smoothie. When our stomachs were full, we made our way past the tall iron entryway and up the driveway toward the two small wooden houses.

"The larger house is Ivy Green, and the cottage to the right of it is where Helen and Anne Sullivan lived for a while," I explained as Frank took my hand, encouraging me to slow down.

I could see the glow of stage lights filling the area behind the cottage where the outdoor theater was.

Frank looked up through the leaves and into the starlit sky above our heads. "These are some of the most beautiful oak trees I've ever seen."

"One of the things I miss about this town is the way the stars seem to hang a little lower than they do in Memphis."

Frank rubbed the top of my hand with his thumb. "I love you, Amanda."

My heart rate sped up after hearing him say those words. Amazingly, Frank did still love me. Even after the multiple ways I'd hurt him—he still loved *me*. And not because he was sick or scared—Frank loved me because God loved me.

I watched as he walked through the darkness with his ball cap still covering his head.

"See that tree?" I asked, pointing over the house to the top of a loblolly pine. "Guess how old it is."

Frank studied the tree for a second. "I have no idea."

"Just guess."

"Okay, I guess...it's a hundred years old."

"Nope. Now, guess how far it's traveled from Tuscumbia."

Frank seemed slightly annoyed by my quizzing. "Trees don't travel."

"That one did," I laughed. "Now guess how far."

Frank let go of my hand and crossed his arms over his chest.

"Okay. I'm gonna guess that you and Honey brought that tree here from your land and buried it behind Helen Keller's house while no one was looking."

"No, but that was a really good guess. Actually, that tree is a few years older than me, and it's traveled farther than anyone I know."

"How far is that?"

"To the moon and back," I said as I looked up toward the stars again.

"Really?"

"Really! The seed that grew into that tree flew to the moon over thirty years ago. After the seed began to grow, it was planted here. It's a Moon Tree."

"Is that true?"

"I promise. I remember when it was no taller than the house. Wow. Look at it now." I grabbed Frank's hand and led him in the opposite direction of the stage lights.

"Where are we going? I thought we were gonna grab the kids and leave."

"I want to see the tree up close." I stepped off the brick walkway and made my way around the house, past the fountain, and through the wet grass.

"Can't we get in trouble for this?" Frank asked.

"Just stay close to me. I know how to get back around to the stage." I could hear the actors rehearsing their lines, and I knew that Mama and the kids would be sitting in the front row. Frank and I stopped once we reached the base of the huge pine tree. "I can't believe how much it's grown!"

"When was the last time you stood beneath it and looked up like this?" he asked.

I couldn't remember. From the looks of it, the tree had been growing for a thousand years. Frank put his arms around my stomach and pulled me close to him.

"I love you, Frank," I said as I stood looking up, the back of my head resting against his chest.

"I know you do."

"I'm sorry that I haven't been a very good wife lately."

Frank kissed me on the top of my ear. "You can't do anything to make me love you any more—or any less—than I already do."

I turned and smiled at him. "How is that possible? How's it possible for you to love me regardless of what I've done?"

"Because I don't love you based on the things you do—good or bad. I love you because God loves you—and because He loves me."

Frank followed me down the walkway and past the house where the cooks once lived, but when we reached the spot where we could see the side of the stage, he stopped and turned back toward the garden.

"Where are you going?"

Frank quickened his step. "I think I saw something."

"Where?"

"Over by the house. I want to see—" Frank stopped and pointed into the darkness. "Is that it?"

Looking through the shadows, I understood what he was seeing. Under a small covered pavilion sat the iron well pump where Helen first learned that objects have names, and names are made up of letters, and letters can be formed by using your hands.

"Yes, that's the well," I answered.

"I remember learning about it when I was in school. Isn't this where she first learned to speak?"

"Yes, this is where she learned to use sign language. Someone was pumping water at the well, and as Helen touched the water, Anne began signing the word 'water' into her palm. That's when words began to make sense to Helen. In a way, after years of living in darkness, she began to see."

I realized the irony of what I was saying and how much I remembered. "Helen learned thirty other words that day as well."

"That's unbelievable."

I agreed. "After that, I guess you could say she started growing at the rate of a Moon Tree."

"It's no wonder they called Anne a miracle worker. She was an incredible gift to Helen."

I nodded. "Did you know Anne was once blind too?"

"No. I just thought she taught blind and deaf children so she came here to help Helen."

"It's true. Anne was blind until a doctor fixed her eyes. She learned sign language so she could talk to a deaf friend. I think Helen was her first and only student. They stayed together until Anne died." I put my hand on Frank's back and felt him breathe. "I guess they were kind of like us."

"What do you mean?"

"You were right when you called me blind and deaf. I've been blind to so many things. I thought for a long time that God wasn't talking to me because He was angry with me or something, but I think the truth is that I didn't want to listen. Will you help me, Frank? Will you be my teacher?"

Frank held me in the darkness for a long time before he answered. "I'll do everything I can to help you grow closer to God." Frank lifted his hand to my cheek and turned his hat backwards. "Close your eyes."

"Why?"

"Just do it."

I closed my eyes and relaxed as he pulled me closer, then felt his lips touch my swollen eye. As he held me, I felt both fear and relief. I resisted the urge to pull away. For the first time in my life, I didn't want to run.

"Will you promise me something?" I asked, after Frank kissed my other eye.

"It depends."

"Promise me you'll live forever."

"No one lives forever—not on this side of heaven."

"Then will you try to live longer than me?"

"I promise I'll do whatever it takes to try and get better. We can go see more doctors, if that's what you want, and I'll do whatever treatment they believe will help." A tear rolled down Frank's face. "And I promise that no matter what happens—I'll see you again one day." I knew what he meant, but I couldn't bear thinking about living a lifetime on this side of heaven without him.

Frank looked over at the water pump. "It doesn't surprise me that her first word was water."

"Why is that?"

"Because in one of the first sentences of the Bible the Spirit of God is described as 'hovering over the waters.' I think He was hovering over this water the day Helen's spirit was awakened."

"Do you think He's hovering over it now?"

Frank laughed and lifted my hand to his lips. "I sure do."

For one wild, glad moment we snapped
the chains that bind us to earth,
and joining hands with the winds
we felt ourselves divine.

HELEN KELLER

Chapter Thirty-nine

Mama gasped and applauded when she saw us walking toward her. The actors were still rehearsing their lines—otherwise she wouldn't have had an excuse for jumping up and clapping her hands together. We apologized to the few people scattered throughout the bleachers and to the actors for interrupting the performance.

"I can't believe you're here!" she said as we slid in next to her and the kids.

Lilah crawled across my lap and settled into Frank's, but Christopher's wide eyes never left the stage.

"I'm glad to be here, Mama. This place is incredible. I can't believe how big the Moon Tree is."

"You saw the tree?"

"Yes. And the landscaping looks better than ever. Someone is doing a great job of keeping this place in tiptop shape."

Frank leaned across me to Mama. "I saw the pump."

"The pump?" Mama looked confused.

"The well pump," I explained. "Frank's excited that he saw the well."

Mama threw her head back and laughed. "Oh, I'm so glad. It sounds like you two have been wanderin' around out there in the dark for a while."

"It was kind of fun," I admitted.

Mama patted me on the knee. "Thank you, Amanda."

We watched the action on stage. A woman and a young girl sat together on the floor. When the woman took the girl's doll away, the child started silently flailing her arms about in every direction. When the small actress seemed to calm down a bit, Christopher smiled and made room for himself between me and Frank.

"Mommy, why did that lady take her doll away?"

"Because she wants her to learn how to ask for it," I answered.

We continued to watch in silence until the scene ended with Helen locking Anne in the upstairs bedroom. When we started to leave, someone announced that the crew could take a break to enjoy the cookies Mama made.

"Everyone," the man yelled into an area off stage, "Ms. Tilly brought us some of her famous cookies. If y'all want one, you better come now or else they'll be gone." Almost a dozen people hugged Mama's neck before we left. They were all eager to tell her how sorry they were about the house and to shake hands with Frank and me. Mama seemed proud to have me by her side. Even with the house gone, she seemed happier than I'd seen her in a long time.

The front door was still unlocked when we got back to the mission house, but so was the front door of every other house in Tuscumbia.

Mama helped me get the kids into bed while Frank collapsed onto the sofa. He was already sleeping by the time I got back to the living room. I took off his shoes and hat and placed them in the chair near the door. He looked peaceful with his mouth slightly opened and his head surrounded by a dozen embroidered pillows. I took an afghan off the back of a nearby chair and covered his legs with it.

God, this man loves You so much. Please let him live so that others might see the miracle You've done in him.

Frank turned onto his side and mumbled something under his breath. I waited until he'd settled before I continued.

I know You've already done so much for us, but I need Your help. You're the only one who can heal him, so I'm begging You. I can't promise You that I'll be a perfect wife or a perfect mother, but I'll try to do better. I really do want to know You and serve You. Please forgive me for putting my own selfish desires above Your desires—and please forgive me for making Cecil a false god.

I clasped my hands together and squeezed until I could feel my bony fingers start to shake.

And please have mercy on me and on my family.

I released my hands and tucked them behind my back.

And thank You that You've given me a husband who loves me and loves You. I know without You our marriage would have ended a long time ago. Thank You that You've answered Frank's prayers for me and for this family.

Father. I was amazed by how easily the title breezed through my heart. Like a child testing a warm bath with the tip of her toe, I whispered the word once more in my mind. *Father.* It felt good, natural.

Father, please help me be obedient. Show me Your ways.

I closed my eyes and tried to remember the words the blind man used to call out to Jesus from the roadside. Finally, they came to me. "Lord," I whispered, "have mercy on me."

I felt something inside my soul begin to fizzle the same way Alka Seltzer causes water to bubble.

I swallowed hard and strained to hear the simple question forming in my mind. *What do you want Me to do for you?*

I thought about that question as it filled my heart and poured across my body. Was Jesus really asking me the same question he'd asked Bartimaeus?

Rabbi, I answered. *I want to see.*

I'd almost fallen asleep leaning against the couch where Frank was snoring when I heard Mama on the phone in the kitchen. While I stood and stretched my legs, I listened to her gather information about how Beeny and the baby were doing.

While she talked, I eased into the kitchen and closed the door so we wouldn't disturb Frank.

"Did Lada and Thumper make it back to the house?" she asked, tapping out a rhythm onto her thigh with a ballpoint pen.

"Well, that's good," she replied. "Okay, then. Call me in the morning. Love you, Pen. Bye."

"Is Beeny okay?" I asked as she hung up the phone.

"She and the baby are both doin' great."

"Well, what happens now?"

"You mean with the baby?"

"Yeah, but I'm also curious about what will happen with Beeny. Does she go back to the Refuge?" I thought about the photographs along the hallway and the birthdays on the walls of the prayer porch.

"Beeny will probably go back to the house for a few days, and if she doesn't want to add today's date to the porch then your sister will do it for her."

"And her photo? When will that happen?" I asked with more judgment in my tone than I'd intended.

"Her photo is already hanging in the hallway. It's been there for several weeks. Most women like to have their photo added right away. I guess it makes 'em feel more like part of the family."

"What about Thumper? Is her photo already on the wall?"

"I think Thumper's only lived at the house for about a week. I don't know much about her."

"Do you think she'll stay until the baby's born?"

"Most women who show up late in their pregnancy and are running from something don't stay more than a couple weeks.

Something won't allow them to believe they've found a place where they're loved and respected. Most of 'em find—or make up—an excuse to leave. I'm sorry, but I'm afraid Thumper's going to be one of those cases."

"You mean even though we found her and brought her back, she'll leave again? Even if she's safer there than anywhere else in the world?"

"Yes. And especially now that she thinks that man knows where to find her. Most of the time we spend a few weeks taking care of girls like Emma Sue, and then right before the baby's born, they walk away from it all."

"That's crazy!"

"No. It's heartbreaking, but we can't make them stay."

I bit my bottom lip, wishing there was something else I could do for Thumper.

Mama warmed some milk on the stove while I tried to envision a scenario where leaving the Refuge House and returning to the streets, or poverty, or an abusive relationship would be a better option than staying in a place where you're loved and cared for.

"Don't worry yourself about it. Just pray and believe that God will protect them wherever they are. The Refuge House wasn't meant for everyone. Your sister's only trying to do what she feels God has called her to do."

"She's much better at that than I am," I admitted.

Mama smiled. "Where's Frank?"

"He's asleep on the couch. That's why I shut the door."

Mama poured the warm milk into two coffee mugs. "Are you sure Frank wants to sleep in there?" she asked as she handed me a cup.

I dropped a cube of ice into my drink before answering. "I think he's fine. He'll come to bed if his back starts to hurt."

Mama put down her glass and leaned against the counter. "I have to be honest with you. Frank doesn't look well. And I'm not just talking about his hair and weight loss. What have the doctors told you about his progress? Are the meds working?"

I lowered my voice and tried to avoid looking Mama in the eyes. "No, the doctors don't think the chemo's working."

"Well, what's the next step?"

"I don't know. I think we're going to go see some new doctors when we get back to Memphis."

"New doctors?" she asked once I looked up.

"Yes." I fought back tears. "Honestly, I don't know what we're going to do. Maybe we'll go to Nashville and get a new opinion, or maybe Little Rock. All I know is that we're not going to give up."

"Is that what they're sayin' in Memphis—that you should give up?"

"I don't know what they're saying because I let Frank go to his last appointment by himself. I'm so stupid."

Mama put her glass down again. "You're not stupid. You're scared, and sometimes when people are scared they do stupid things as a way of dealing with their fears. Frank certainly doesn't think you're stupid. What did the doctors tell him?"

"That the tumors are getting bigger instead of shrinking like we'd hoped."

"Well, maybe it's time to switch chemo treatments again. The radiation therapy helped. Can't you do that again?"

"Frank almost lost his kidneys when he was getting the chemo injections. And I was afraid he was going to die of renal failure during the last radiation treatment. So, no. After two years of trying to reduce the size of the tumors so we can even *begin* to discuss the possibility of removing them? No, I think it's safe to say that we're not going to start another batch of pills. Not until we've spoken to someone new who's willing to do something more aggressive than what we've tried in the past."

Mama pulled open one of the kitchen drawers and shuffled through a stack of papers. "I need to ask you something."

"What?"

"I found something that I want to show you." She pulled a magazine from the bottom of the pile and flipped the pages.

"I found this yesterday. It talks about how most spinal cancers actually metastasize from other parts of the body." Mama held the page up for me to see. An image of an elderly man holding his lower back and wincing in pain stared back at me.

I pushed it away.

"Frank has had at least six CT and PET scans, and the only cancer they show are the aggressive tumors growing along his spine."

"But what if the scans are wrong? This says that 70 percent of malignant tumors found along the spine usually start in another part of the body. What if that's why his kidneys can't take the more aggressive chemo? What if it's because the cancer started there?"

"We've asked Frank's doctors that question, but they've assured us that his tumors are primary and that he doesn't show any signs of cancer anywhere else in his body."

"Have they done a biopsy since he was first diagnosed?"

I put my cup in the sink and ran cold water into it until the milky liquid poured over the sides.

"Look, I'm glad you love Frank and that you want to help. But there's nothing else we can do unless a new doctor can find a way to shrink the tumors enough to operate."

Mama placed her cup in the sink next to mine. "Well, then—I guess there's only one thing we can do. We're going to pray. And we're going to ask other people to pray. And we're going to pray specifically for things like new doctors, better treatment, and for those stupid tumors to get smaller." She put her hand on my back and leaned in until her chin was almost to my shoulder. "And we're gonna believe that God will provide everything we need—no matter what that means."

When I thought I could speak clearly enough to be understood, I asked Mama if she believed God knew how much I needed my husband. While she held me and let me cry, she assured me that He did.

"God knows what you need better than you do. You just have to believe that He's gonna take care of you."

Before I settled into bed, I thumbed through Frank's Bible and read some of the scriptures he'd highlighted and words he'd scribbled along the pages. I'd gotten used to reading his tall, nervous script over the years, but it was a little more challenging to read his handwriting when it was tucked in the margins of a book.

I spent several minutes reading bits and pieces from the book of John. Frank had underlined almost every line, but it was the tenth chapter that stood out the most. In the corner, where the number ten sat larger than anything else on the page, Frank had drawn a tiny sheep peering through the wooden beams of a closed gate.

The sheep looked like a little white cloud—the kind a child would draw. It had a head with tiny slits for eyes and black ovals for its feet. I read through the rest of the chapter while his little eyes watched my every move. Something about that sheep reminded me of the rocking horse I'd tried to bury in the prayer garden.

Where did Frank put it? Did he throw it away?

I looked around the room at the various pieces of clothing tossed over the foot of his bed and piled on the floor. His duffel bag was lying open in the corner, near the wooden dresser. Maybe he put it in his bag.

In John 10, I tried to focus on the parable Jesus was telling about the sheep. "The thief comes only to kill and destroy," the book said. Again, I looked at the open bag and wondered if the rocking horse was smothered beneath his clothing.

I don't want to steal it. I just want to know where he hid it.

I put down the Bible and tiptoed into the hallway. Frank was still sleeping soundly with his head buried beneath the pile of pillows. I watched his chest rise and fall a few times before I went back to the bedroom. It looked like a tornado had blown through my half of the room. Scattered pieces of clothing were flung across every inch of the floor. I picked up a few of my things, folded them neatly, and placed them in my suitcase.

It won't hurt to get some of these things packed—we'll need to leave here as soon as Mama and I get back from seeing the house.

Frank's jeans were folded and resting on the bedside table, so I placed them on the chair near a stack of his polo shirts.

I don't want Frank to have to organize our bags.

The bag he'd packed my toiletries in was empty, so I decided to use it as a dirty clothes bag. Once I was through filling it with things we'd already worn, I decided to return some of Frank's clothing to his duffel.

If he did throw the horse away, then I won't have to worry about finding it. But if I come across it while I'm trying to help him pack, then it'll be his fault that he left it where I might find it.

The theory sounded good, so I opened the bag and pushed his clothes around in order to make room for the others. I took out some of Frank's shorts and T-shirts and refolded them to make more room, but still there wasn't enough space left for me to put everything back where it belonged.

Well, I guess I'll have to start over.

I flipped the bag over and dumped its entire contents onto the bed. Loose change spilled onto the quilt and rolled to the floor as boxer shorts, ankle socks, and three different types of granola bars mounded on top of each other. I counted four pairs of perfectly folded socks before placing them in the corner of the bag.

My hand rubbed against something hard in the lining of an interior pocket.

I knew it wasn't the horse—it was too large and square for that—so after a brief hesitation, I unzipped the small pocket and looked inside. There, wrapped with multicolored paper, was a tiny package. I remembered what Frank said as the kids and I backed out of the driveway in Memphis. He'd said something about a birthday gift.

I counted back the days on my fingers. Everything, from the time we'd left Memphis until that moment, seemed like one, long, unending day, interrupted only by brief periods of restless sleep. I counted with my fingers the number of nights we'd slept in each place, and by my calculation, tomorrow was my birthday.

Tomorrow I'll be twenty-eight. I could hardly believe it.

I zipped the bag shut after replacing all of Frank's things and climbed into bed. Lying there, I thought back to the many birthdays I had celebrated in that town as a child.

If Helen were alive, I imagined Mama saying, *she'd be one hundred and twenty-eight years old today.*

With the dropping of a little word from
another's hand into mine,
a slight flutter of the fingers, began the intelligence,
the joy, the fullness of my life.

HELEN KELLER

Chapter Forty

Frank pushed back the hair from my face and kissed me on the temple until I reluctantly opened my eyes. The first light of morning shone through the curtains and filled the room with shades of blue and green. Frank got on his knees by the bed and brought his face close to mine.

"Good morning, Sunshine," he said as he ran his finger along the curve of my ear. "It's time to wake up."

I closed my eyes and enjoyed his touch.

"You have to get up," he whispered.

"Why? Are the kids up?"

"No, but I have to show you something." Frank placed the brightly-colored package between our faces. "Happy birthday, Amanda."

I let out a surprising giggle and sat up. "What is it?"

Frank seemed overjoyed by my reaction. It had been a long time since I'd been happy to receive a birthday gift.

"Open it," he said as he climbed up next to me on the bed.

I shook the box and listened as something tiny rolled around inside.

"Is it a diamond?" I playfully asked.

Frank grabbed the box and pulled at the ribbon.

"No, it's not a diamond, but I think you'll like it just as much.

"Okay, okay," I said, snatching the box. "I'll open it."

I untied the ribbon and tossed it to the floor. In my hand was a tiny white box. I hesitated before lifting the lid, remembering the day Grandma gave me my first rocking horse.

Inside was a silver chain tangled around a square piece of cotton.

"Go ahead. Take it out," Frank said. The chain was so delicate that it was hard to grab hold of at first. Once I'd wrestled it free from the cotton, I lifted it from the box. Frank pulled the necklace closer for me to see. On the end where I'd expected to find a cross was a glass bead like the one Daddy gave me.

Frank gave the glass ball a little shake.

"You told me once about the necklace your Father gave you before he died. I just thought—"

Something inside me broke free.

"I know you lost the one he gave you in the wreck, and I don't want this to be a reminder of that, but—"

I let out a staggered sob.

"—I just wanted to give you a reminder of how much Jesus loves you."

I tried to speak but couldn't.

"In the book of Matthew, Jesus tells his apostles they can move mountains if they have faith the size of a mustard seed. That's all you need—a speck of faith the size of this seed, and God will use it to move mountains. All you have to do is believe."

Frank opened the clasp and fastened it around my neck.

"Does that mean God will heal you if I ask?"

"I don't know what God's going to do with my body, but I know he's going to rescue my soul. He's already moved that mountain for me."

I looked down at the yellow seed and watched it bounce around in the ball.

"It sure doesn't seem like much faith."

Frank laughed. "I think that's the point. All He needs is for us to put a little trust in Him, and then He'll do the rest."

"Can I say it?" Mama asked first thing.

"Say what?" Frank wanted to know.

"Oh, she knows what I'm talkin' about." She tilted her head in my direction.

I added a package of sweetener to my coffee and rolled my eyes.

"Come on, Amanda. Let me say it."

I stirred in the cream and tried not to smile. "Okay, you can say it, but first you have to explain to Frank what you're talking about."

"Okay. We had a tradition when Amanda was a child that every year on her birthday, her father and I would say, 'You know, if Helen were still alive, she'd be turning—'" Mama counted out the years in her mind. "'128 years old today.'"

Frank laughed and looked at me.

"Yeah, nothing makes a girl feel special like hearing she was the second-best thing that ever happened on her birth date," I said.

Mama dismissed my comment with a wave of her hand. "Oh, please. We did it because we wanted you to feel special. Do you know how many people are born on the fourth of July? I bet none of them get upset because people shoot fireworks on their birthdays—and they share a birthday with a whole country. You just share your day with a kind, little old dead woman who spent her entire life tryin' to make this world a better place."

"Yeah, but I wanted my birthday to be *my* day. And don't act like Daddy said that stuff. He never said it—that was your thing."

"What do you mean, he never said it? He invented it! The day you were born he wrote it in your baby book. He thought it was the greatest thing—you being born in this town on the same date as our most famous citizen."

Mama slammed the refrigerator door and almost dropped the carton of eggs.

"It's in your baby book right above the place where the nurse made your footprints. I'll show—"

Mama realized what she was about to say and let her words fall short.

We stood quietly for a while, wondering how many moments like that lay ahead of us—moments when we'd want to look at something or see something, then realize it'd been turned to ashes. I still had a home in Memphis filled with my favorite keepsakes, but Mama lost *everything*.

I couldn't imagine.

Mama pushed at her red bangs and tried to ignore the pain. "Well, I guess I can't show you."

"I'm sorry, Mama. I believe you. I remember seeing those words when I was a child, but I thought you were the one who wrote them."

"Your daddy reminded me six times before we left the hospital that I was the only one in town to have a baby on Helen's hundredth birthday. He stood in the hallway while I was in labor because he wanted to make sure no one else checked in. Your daddy probably sent the other laboring mothers home so you'd be the only one."

Frank's laugh reminded me he was in the room.

"I never knew Daddy cared about that stuff."

"I guess it's my fault for not telling you." Mama took a mixing bowl from the bottom cabinet and placed it beside the sink. "He believed your birthday was a sign that you'd be an amazing woman one day. He was right, Amanda. He'd be real proud of you."

"He'd be proud of you too, Mama."

Frank winked at me as he peeled back a banana.

"For burning down the house?" Mama asked.

I put my hand on her shoulder. "No, he'd be proud of you for always persevering."

"Well, we'll see if you still think that after we go see the mess I've made of the house."

"Have you been back since the fire?"

Mama dropped an egg to the floor and mumbled something ugly under her breath before bending down to pick it up.

"No, I haven't been to the house, and I don't wanna go back today either. It seems like a terrible way for us to celebrate your birthday."

"Well, we can't put it off forever."

"What time are y'all going?" Frank asked as Lilah and Christopher rushed into the room.

Mama dropped the metal whisk into the bowl and turned to welcome the kids.

"Good morning, Honey!" Christopher yelled as Mama picked him up.

"Good morning, angel," she said. "Are you hungry?"

"I'm always hungry."

"Well, then you're in luck, because today we're gonna fix your mama a huge breakfast in honor of her birthday."

"Today's Mommy's birthday?" he asked excitedly.

"Yep, it's *my* birthday."

After a second, he squirmed away from Mama and joined Lilah and Frank at the kitchen table.

While Frank shared his banana with Lilah, Christopher whispered something into his daddy's ear that made him laugh. "Yes, I gave her the pretty necklace she's wearing."

Christopher asked me to bend down so he could see it better.

"Don't worry, Christopher, I know this necklace is from all of you."

"No, that's from Daddy."

"Well, then, how about you give me a big kiss for my birthday."

"No," Christopher said. "I got you something else."

He hurried from the kitchen and trotted down the hallway toward the room where he'd slept.

"Did you help him buy something for me?"

Mama shook her head and continued beating the eggs. "No, and what I got for you burned up."

Christopher flew into the room again and almost fell. "Here it is," he said after he regained his footing.

In Christopher's outstretched hand, he held what looked like a wadded-up piece of red tissue paper. I took the package from him and looked at Frank, figuring he knew something about this. But he seemed just as clueless as I was.

"I wrapped it myself," Christopher said as I folded back the thin pieces of paper.

"What is it?"

"I can't tell you, but I know you're gonna like it."

As I pulled the last bits of paper away, I realized what Christopher had saved for me.

I am the vine, ye are the branches.

The tiny metal sign filled me with joy. This time I let the words sink in, and suddenly it was clear—I was no longer a rocking horse or even a rock collector for that matter. I wasn't an unhappy wife or dissatisfied daughter either. And I certainly wasn't a resentful mother. Or blind. Or deaf.

I wasn't any of those things—not any more.

It is an unspeakable boon to me
to be able to speak in winged words
that need no interpretation.

HELEN KELLER

Chapter Forty-one

Mama and I stood in silence near the hood of my car for a long time as we stared at the pile of smoldering ash and wet garbage that was once our home. A small billow of smoke was still rising from the back of the pile and up through the trees when we'd first arrived, but the gray puffs of smoke disappeared as we stood watching.

From where we stood, the only upright structure we could see was the dilapidated workshop that mocked us from the horizon.

Mama folded her arms and dropped her chin to her chest. "I thought the fire would've burned out by now so we could salvage a few things."

"I don't think you're gonna want anything from that pile of wet mess."

She kicked at the ground with her sandal. "I made a million promises about the things I'd hand down to you and Pen one day. Now I don't have anything to give you when I die. You were supposed to get the twin beds my daddy made." Mama glanced up at the pile of nothing and then back down at her feet again. "I just don't understand."

"Maybe God wants you to stop depending on yourself and start depending on Him instead."

"What is that supposed to mean? Since when did you become the one to hand out godly advice?"

"Mama, I love you, but you always try to fix things. I know you do it because you care about people, but sometimes you just complicate things."

"That's not true," she said, rolling her eyes. "I take everything to the Lord, and then I trust that He'll show me what to do."

"But sometimes you pray and then hurry off to do what you think is best without really considering how other people feel."

Mama let out a huff and started walking toward the area where the back porch once stood.

"Okay, give me an example."

I followed in step behind her.

"Okay, how about your need to have a hand in raising Pen?" I thought about Cecil, but I didn't dare say his name.

"Lada asked me to raise Pen. If I hadn't stepped in, you wouldn't have a little sister."

"I'm not saying you made the wrong decision, I'm just pointing out that you sometimes have a tendency to be overly involved and in the end make everything about what you want."

"You should be thankful you have a mother who's always willing to help."

I watched as she pushed a large piece of wood with her foot and leaned down to pick up something from the rubble.

"I *am* thankful for you. I'm just saying there could be a lesson in this for you too. You won't be able to rebuild this house without making a lot of changes."

"Like what?"

"Like you're gonna have to let people start helping you for a change."

"Fine. You can start by digging."

Mama lifted a sterling silver fork from the ashes and pointed it at me. "Aha! See, I'm gonna be just fine."

"That's exactly my point. That's the same fork you put out every year at my birthday party, regardless of the fact that I didn't want a party. What I wanted was you, but you just did what you thought was best and kept going. You can't rebuild this house with a fork, Mama."

"Well, you gotta start somewhere." Mama laughed.

"Whatever. I should've known you wouldn't listen."

Mama picked up another fork from the rubble and waved it above her head. "Oh, I'm listenin'! I just think you're being ridiculous. I know I haven't been a perfect mother, but I tried my best. Yes, maybe I was gone too much when you were a child, but now that you know about Pen you should understand why."

I looked down at the place where she'd uncovered the forks. "I know now. I just wish I'd known when I was a little girl. I thought you wanted to be with a bunch of pregnant women more than you wanted to be with me. I spent a lot of lonely days in this house."

Mama stepped toward me and hugged me. "I'm really sorry."

"I don't care about the house."

"I'm not talkin' about the house. I'm sorry that I wasn't there for you when you needed me. And I'm sorry that even though I forgave your father for the affair, I was still angry for a long time. I know you remember, baby. I'm so sorry if for one second you thought I wasn't around because I didn't love you. I do love you—maybe too much. I just wanted to be a part of something. I just wanted to be needed."

"You *were* needed. I needed you then, and I need you now. And if something happens to Frank, I'm going to need you more than ever."

Mama pulled away so she could see my eyes. "If you'll forgive me, then I promise this time I'm gonna be there."

As we drove away, Mama reached behind the seat and grabbed my phone out of my purse. The phone rang three times before she was able to flip it open and hand it to me. We were almost to the end of the gravel driveway by the time I got it to my ear and said hello.

I heard a cough and then a long pause on the other end. It was a local number but not one that I recognized.

"Hello," I said again, shrugging my shoulders at Mama.

"Hi."

The voice sent chills up my legs. I stopped the car and stepped out.

"How did you get this number?"

"I've known it for a while."

I swallowed hard and stretched my back. I searched for the right words, but my heart was beating too fast for any of my thoughts to make sense. I stepped further away from the car and ran my fingers through my hair.

"What do you want?"

Cecil's voice sounded hollow.

"I just wanted to tell you I'm sorry."

"Me too," I said. I felt as if I was flatlining.

"And I wanted to call and make sure you were okay."

I turned around and waved to Mama through the windshield to let her know everything was fine. She made a confused face, but I ignored her and turned away again.

"You shouldn't have called me," I whispered, as if someone else might hear.

"I know. But you checked on me, so I just wanted to do the same for you."

"I shouldn't have gone to the hospital. I'm sorry I did that."

"It's okay. I liked getting to see you. I just wish it hadn't ended the way it did."

"You mean with your wife almost losing the baby after pounding me with her fists?"

Cecil got quiet.

I imagined him lying in the hospital bed with the phone I'd used to call 911 pressed against his ear.

"Please don't ever call me again."

"Ever?" he repeated.

I looked around at the beautiful countryside and then up toward the clouds. I imagined how lonely my life might be if I lost Frank. I thought about how much I might need the comfort of an old friend, someone to talk to when things got hard.

Lord, help me.

"*I will strengthen you and help you.*"

Who will help me when I'm afraid or alone?

"*Do not fear; I will help you.*"

"I'm sorry. I won't call again." Cecil's words startled me back to reality. "Happy birthday."

I lifted my hand to my necklace and felt the mustard seed bounce around inside its glass bubble. When I was about to thank him for the birthday wish, I lifted the charm to my lips and looked at Mama.

"I can't talk to you."

"Well, then I'll call you in a few days—after I get out of the hospital."

I moved the phone to my other ear and looked up through the trees again. "No, what I mean is I can't talk to you...ever again."

"So you came back here, turn everything upside down, and now you're just going to leave like you did last time?"

"Goodbye, Cecil."

"Why do you always do this?"

"This isn't like the last time. This time I'm walking away because it's the right thing to do—because it's what God wants me to do."

"I just want to be your friend. You're the only one who understands."

"That's not true, and you know it."

"This is so typical of you."

"No, trust me—it's not. Goodbye, Cecil." I folded the phone and slipped it into my front pocket.

"What was that about?" Mama asked after I got back into the car.

"That was about being obedient, Mama. That was about putting God first."

Mama patted me on the knee as I buckled my seatbelt. "Then you did the right thing."

So in the heart of man shines forever a beam
from the everlasting sun of God.

HELEN KELLER

Chapter Forty-two

Frank insisted on driving to Memphis so I could entertain the kids. They were both sleeping peacefully before we made it across the Alabama border.

"How did Honey react when she saw the house?" Frank asked as he propped his hand over the steering wheel and steadied the car with his wrist.

"Better than I expected."

"How long before she can start rebuilding?"

"I'm not sure. She's meeting with her insurance agent next week. I guess we'll know more after that."

Frank refocused his attention on the road. There was an undeniable awkwardness between us. I adjusted the air vent and leaned in close enough for the wind to push the hair away from my ears.

"Are you hot?" Frank asked, adjusting the temperature and turning the dial until I felt like I was sitting in a wind tunnel.

"I'm fine," I said, leaning back in my seat.

"You don't seem fine." Frank lowered the air again. "Is there something you want to talk about?"

"No," I answered too quickly.

Frank shifted in the seat and adjusted his hat.

"Are you ready for me to drive? Because I can drive if you want."

Frank saw right through my charade.

"Are you sure you're okay?"

I leaned against the car door. "Actually," I said, biting my bottom lip, "I have to tell you something."

Frank grabbed my hand and pulled me closer to him. "Okay. What?"

"Cecil called me."

Frank stiffened and squeezed my hand a little tighter than before. "When?"

"While Mama and I were looking at the house. I didn't know it was him or else I wouldn't have answered."

Frank let go of my hand and grabbed the wheel instead.

"What did he say?" He was wringing the wheel with both hands as if it was a wet rag.

"He said he was sorry."

Frank's jaw tightened.

"I asked him to never call me again."

"What did he say to *that?*"

"He got annoyed, so I hung up."

"If he ever calls you again, I want to know." Frank forced a smile. "Is there anything else I need to know?"

"No, but there is something I've been wanting to ask you."

"Okay," he said cautiously.

"How old were you when you first put your faith in God?"

Frank relaxed a bit.

"I've always believed in God, but I didn't really put my faith in Him until my father died."

"How old were you then?" I was ashamed that I didn't already know the answer.

"He passed away the winter I turned thirteen, three weeks after Christmas."

"Because of a stroke?"

"Well, yes. But it was more complicated than that."

"What happened?"

"Dad started complaining of a headache the day I got out of school for Thanksgiving break, but after he took some medicine he felt fine. We spent the rest of the afternoon tossing the football around in the backyard. He was moving a little slower than usual, but not enough to make anyone concerned. Then on Thanksgiving Day he started complaining that he couldn't see very well out of his left eye."

Frank rubbed the top of my hand with his thumb and let out a short breath.

"Did he go to the doctor?"

"He went to the ER. They did a CT scan, but they couldn't see anything that indicated he'd had a stroke."

"Did they do an MRI?"

"There was no such thing as an MRI back then."

I felt slightly embarrassed at my assumption that his father would've had the same medical treatments as the patients I worked with. "What did the CT show?"

"They told us he'd probably had a transient ischemic attack—a 'warning stroke,' as the ER nurse called it."

"Caused by what?"

"Mom says they did every test possible, but after a day or so they still hadn't found the cause, so they let Dad come home. They'd ruled out every blood disorder and vascular disease known to man, and none of the tests showed any blood clots. Then when I came home from school a few days after Thanksgiving, my aunt was there waiting for me. When we got to the hospital Mom told me that Dad had a stroke.

"I don't think I really understood how much danger he was in until I saw him lying in that hospital bed—unable to speak. I could see the things Dad wanted to say behind the pain and confusion in his eyes, but I never heard him say another word."

"How long was he like that?"

Frank massaged his forehead. "A few weeks. They finally discovered he had a clot in a chamber of his heart. Part of the clot broke off and went straight to his brain. That's what caused the stroke. They let him come home the week before Christmas, but he still couldn't walk or talk. Mom tried to make things cheerful, but it was hard.

"Someone from our church stopped by every day to bring us food, and Dad's best friend came by every afternoon to sit and read Dad's Bible to him. I loved his visits. While Smith would read, I'd curl up next to Dad's wheelchair and pray for him to get better."

"Did he ever get better?"

"No, but he did draw a little cross for me before he died. I have it at home if you want to see it sometime."

"I'd love to."

Frank pulled my hand to his lips.

"I think he drew the cross because he wanted me to know where he was going. The next morning when I came downstairs our living room was full of people. Dad had died in his sleep."

"I never knew he died at home. Did you see him?"

"Yeah. Mom tried to stop me at first, but there was no way I was going to let them take my dad away without telling him goodbye."

"Oh, Frank. I am so sorry. I never knew any of that. I've always wished I could've seen my father."

"I always assumed you *had* seen your father. Were you unconscious when they took you to the hospital?"

I pulled my hand free of Frank's and rubbed my palms against my knees.

"No, but I wasn't in the truck when I woke up."

"That was probably best. You know that, right?"

I fiddled with the vent again.

"Yeah, but I always wished I'd been able to tell him goodbye. Mama decided not to have an open casket, so the last time I saw my daddy was when he turned around in the truck to give me a nasty look about something I'd done. I can't even remember what it was, but I still remember the look in his eyes. I just wish I could've had a chance to tell him I was sorry."

"But you didn't cause the wreck."

"Yeah, I know, but still. Aren't you glad you saw your father?"

"Sure, I was glad I saw him. I mean, that's when it became clear to me that our bodies are only temporary—like shells that we live in for only a small amount of time. My father was not in that room when I ran to the side of his bed, just like your daddy wasn't in that truck after the crash. It was just a body, an empty shell. I believed in God before then, but that was the day I realized that there was something other than this world—other than this life. That's when I believed my dad had gone to be with Jesus. I believed it that day, and I've believed it every day since."

"I'm so sorry."

"About what? About my father?"

"Yeah, but also that I've never asked you about any of this before."

"All of that happened a long time ago. I don't expect you to know everything about my past."

"Yeah, but I should've cared enough to ask."

"It's okay. I'm just thankful you care enough now."

We stayed with our hands tangled together for the rest of the drive home. Christopher and Lilah slept most of the way, while Frank and I enjoyed just being together in the stillness. Noisy traffic and the occasional eighteen-wheeler flashed by us as we drove along Highway 72, but inside the car there was only peace.

I felt the warmth of Frank's hand in mine. I hated that I'd been so caught up in myself that I'd become blind to all the blessings that surrounded me and deaf to the words of hope and love that whispered at every turn.

I knew then that what I needed was grace. I needed God to unveil my eyes and open my ears.

Sing how the ages, like thrifty husbandmen,
winnow the creeds of men
and leave only faith and love and truth.

HELEN KELLER

Chapter Forty-three

June 21, 2010 / Closer to Home

Two years have passed since that unforgettable week in
Tuscumbia. I planned to go back last summer for Pen's wedding, but
Frank was too sick for me to leave so I decided to stay with him and
miss my little sister's wedding. He argued that I should go and take
the kids, but in the end my strong will prevailed.

Pen understood.

Three months after the wedding she and Billy called to tell us
about the baby. Now she calls every time she feels the slightest bit tired
or nauseous. I figured after all the pregnant people she's helped, the
whole baby thing wouldn't be an issue, but Pen's proven to be just as
scared and uncertain as every other first-time mom. And, yes, Billy
thinks the sky is falling every time she mentions a little discomfort.

Kids are going to be good for them.

Mama's throwing a big baby shower for her this weekend at the
new house, so I've already started packing our things to go. It's kind of
late in Pen's pregnancy for someone to be giving her a baby shower, but
Mama insisted on having it at her house after all of the construction was

complete, even though she knows it's not proper for the grandmother to be the one hosting the party. Especially in the South.

"Some things have to be overlooked—even during festival week."

Some things never change.

I'm hoping my niece will be born on my birthday. On *our* birthday. Pen has promised to name the baby Amanda Helen if she's born on June 27, and I can't wait to see if she'll really go through with it.

Mama decided not to rebuild the house in the same spot. She said she was afraid one of the big oak trees might decide to fall and cut a seam right down the middle of the new house. She said she was unwilling to take any chances with that, so six months after the fire, a construction crew poured the foundation of her new bungalow, complete with a wraparound porch, only twenty yards from the cemetery. And, of course, it would have been a little weird to have my old workshop in her front lawn, so she told the workmen to go ahead and remove it.

I thought the whole plan sounded wonderful, but Pen argued that there should be a law about how close you can build a house to dead people. Either way, there was no talking Mama out of what she wanted to do.

Rachel and Megan plan to attend Pen's shower and their kids as well. It will be the first time we've gotten all five of our children together. Afterwards, we're going to the Helen Keller Festival and meeting the new group of women from the Refuge House. I hope they've been busy making ornaments and weaving together vines for Christmas Village, because I know one little girl who's looking forward to expanding her collection of cornhusk angels.

Every Southern lady needs to collect *something.*

I've been hoping I'll run into Beeny in Memphis, but that hasn't happened yet. I'd like to see her again. I'd like to know that she's well. It took some time, but Pen finally told me some of Beeny's background and what brought her to leave Memphis.

Pen reminded me about something we'd seen on TV while she

was visiting our house for Thanksgiving the fall before Mama burned the house down. There was a story that aired on several of the local channels about a woman—a pastor's wife—who had been beaten after she and some of the women from her church finished delivering food baskets to the needy families in their neighborhood. It turned out that Beeny was the woman the news station had been talking about, and what happened was worse than anything printed in the newspaper.

Pen said before that day Beeny had been praying for God to provide a baby for her friend, and because Beeny already had three children of her own, she felt like the child growing inside her was an answer to that prayer. Beeny wasn't living at the Refuge because she didn't have a good family. She was there so she'd have time to heal, and so her children wouldn't hurt for the baby she planned to give away.

Pen also told me that, unlike Mama had predicted, Emma Sue stayed at the Refuge House until her baby was born. She said they were finalizing some of the adoption papers when Thumper decided to keep her baby. Pen said she knew the second she saw Thumper hold her daughter, she wasn't going to let her go. The last time Pen heard from her, she and her little girl were living on a farm just outside of Jackson, and Thumper was getting married.

Whoever he is, I hope he's better than the last guy.

I already miss having someone around to criticize the amount of coffee I consume and the amount of junk food I eat. It gets pretty quiet in the house when the kids are sleeping or away at school.

Frank died the week after Christmas, after I'd finished taking down the decorations and stowing them away in the attic—all except for the ornament Christopher gave me for my birthday. That one I leave out year round to remind me to cling to the Vine and not the branches.

Frank never did any more chemotherapy after we got home. He was patient with me as always, as I dragged him around to every cancer doctor in Memphis and Nashville demanding that they tell us about new drugs and procedures. But after a while, we both gave in to the fact that Frank was either going to die of cancer or he was going to die from fighting it.

We decided to spend the time we had left together doing the things that we loved the most. For Frank, that meant going to church, being at home with the kids, and reading his Bible. For me, it was watching him draw closer to the Lord.

The cancer eventually spread to his lungs, and he was forced to wear an oxygen mask most of the time. He tired easily, but he never complained—not unless I tried to feed him something with too many carbohydrates or not enough proteins.

A few months before Frank died, he asked me to start reading his Bible aloud to him the way his father's friend had done. I wanted to start in the New Testament, but Frank decided we should begin in Genesis where the Spirit of God was hovering over the waters. The more I read, the more I began to understand how close the Lord was to us as we sat together and waited for Him to take Frank home.

Sometimes Christopher and Lilah would sit at Frank's feet and listen to us talk about God and heaven. It comforted them to have quiet times with us. Frank never tired of hearing their prayers.

God's Spirit filled everything: every moment, every staggered breath, and every relived story Frank asked me to write down and pass on to our children. God was a part of us, dwelling among us and filling us with His promises of hope and love.

One morning before Christmas, we awoke to find our yard filled with tiny sparrows. Frank put his arm around me and pulled me over to where he could run his fingers through my hair. We watched as the birds danced around on a thin layer of frost and snow.

"Do you remember the words you read yesterday?" Frank asked as he fought for breath.

I nodded and watched the sparrows bounce around and peck at the frozen grass.

"Please read them again."

I reached for his Bible on the bedside table as he struggled to sit up. Once he was settled, I found the verse in Psalm 84 and read it aloud again: "How lovely is your dwelling place, O Lord Almighty! My soul yearns, even faints, for the courts of the Lord; my heart and my flesh cry out for the living God." I struggled to continue. "Even the sparrow has found a home, and the swallow a nest for herself, where she may have her young—a place near your altar."

Frank took the Bible from me and placed it on the bed beside him.

"You've found a home, Amanda." Frank held the oxygen mask to his face and breathed in before continuing. "But it's only temporary."

That was one of the last things he said to me, but he let me hold on to him for another ten days—until I was ready to let him go.

A day doesn't pass when I don't thank God for sending Frank to me. And a second doesn't pass when I don't consider how lost I'd be without him.

Frank was a gift, and without his strength I would have continued to fight against my own weakness. Without his forgiveness, I never would have learned to forgive myself. I guess that in a lot of ways I'd still be blind and deaf.

Frank believed that people are here on earth for a blink of an eye, and because of that, our faith and hope shouldn't be placed in the things of this world. He agreed with Helen: *Only people count.* That's part of the reason why I don't make rocking horses anymore. Instead, I make wooden crosses—simple wooden crosses—held together with a little glue and a few nails. The kids and I love to paint them with bright splashes of color and small pieces of glitter. Building them has become one of our favorite things to do since Frank's death, and even though I know he'd love to see us throwing paint around in the backyard and arguing over whose turn it is to use the hammer, I believe Frank is in a better place than the one the kids and I live in. He's with his Father now—the one he found when he was a child, and the one he was given before the creation of the world.

Until I see Frank again, I'm going to stay near to the Lord and remember the words that a very wise woman once spelled into the hands of her beloved teacher: "Death is no more than passing from one room into another. But there's a difference for me, you know. Because in that other room I shall be able to see."

I'm thankful the Lord has begun to open my eyes and ears while I'm still living on this side of heaven. I know I won't see everything until I'm in that other room, but God has shown me what true love and forgiveness really is. I've heard His voice, and now I see the gifts He's given me in a whole new light.

My journey home is just beginning.

About the Author

Kimberley G. Graham grew up in Madison, Mississippi along the banks of the Pearl River. In 2000 she earned a BFA in Photography and Graphic Design from Memphis College of Art. Kimberley now lives in Memphis, Tennessee with her husband and three wonderful children. This is her first novel.

You can follow Kimberley on Twitter: @KimberleyGraham
Facebook: https://www.facebook.com/KimberleyGGraham
Or visit her blog: www.SparrowRefuge.com

Discussion Questions for Book Clubs

1. Which character did you relate to the most? Why?

2. Amanda's mother doesn't support her dream of becoming a wood-carver. How might a different reaction from her mother have changed Amanda's behavior?

3. When Amanda is a child, she predicts her father's death. Have you ever experienced a time when you felt like something bad was going to happen to a loved one? How did you react? How might you react to a similar situation?

4. Do you think Cecil and Amanda would have been a good fit for one another? Why or why not?

5. What perspectives does *The Rocking Horse of Tuscumbia* offer about the realities of life and human nature?

6. Do you think Tilly is a good mother?

7. What did *The Rocking Horse of Tuscumbia* teach you about Helen Keller? Did anything surprise you?

8. In reading this book, did you compare your childhood to Amanda's? Has this book changed the way you look at obstacles in your own life?

9. Did this book reveal to you a new aspect of God's character?

10. Do you think Amanda will pursue Cecil again when she returns to Tuscumbia?

Acknowledgements

Above all else, I am thankful for the love of my Lord and Savior, **Jesus Christ**, who has walked me through every minute of writing and publishing this book. My hope is that He's exhausted all of my God-given talents for His glory.

If someone had told me when I was Amanda's age that one day I'd write (or even read) a novel, I never would have believed them. Thankfully, God has used the challenges I faced as a child to strengthen me as an adult. For that, I am eternally grateful.

This book is dedicated to my grandmother, **Beverly Gardner**, who embedded in me a love for reading and writing. As a child I struggled in school and by the time I was nine years old I had already experienced my first case of stress-related shingles. I wanted to give up, but when things seemed unbearable Nanny would rub my back and read to me. She loved me to the point that I couldn't stop trying. Still, she was always honest about her dream that one day I'd become either an artist or a librarian. I think Nanny would be proud.

To **Susan E. Richardson**: You are a gift from God. Most writers are lucky if they can find someone to give an honest critique of their work. You have done that while encouraging me, challenging me, strengthening me, teaching me, laughing with me, coaching me, and loving me...over and over again. I am so thankful for you.

To my copyeditor, **Marcia Ford**: Thank you for the endless hours you spent combing through every line of this book. I know any blunders are a result of something I messed up after your edits.

To my friends in Tuscumbia: **Janice Williams**, what a gift it was to find such a special friend the first time I wandered into the Colbert County Tourism and Convention Bureau. Thank you for all of your support and encouragement over the years. Also, thank you, **Eleanor DeYoung,** for introducing me to the amazing **Keller Johnson-Thompson**. And, Keller, thank you for trusting me with your great-great aunt's words. Helen Keller would be proud of you and your work with the American Foundation for the Blind. I'm proud to call you my sister-in-Christ, and hope you're pleased with this story.

To **Helen Selsdon** at The American Foundation for the Blind: Thank you for your tireless effort in helping me locate and gain permission to use Helen Keller's inspiring words. It's been fun, right? Right?

To my writer-friends: **Michael Ehret, Jim Hamlett, Clarice James, Peter Leavell,** and **Terrie Todd,** I can't imagine this journey without each of you. Thank you for experiencing all of the ups and downs with me, and for loving me regardless of my shortcomings. **Jennifer Erin Valent,** when I grow up, I want to be just like you. **Erin Petterson,** thank you for your honesty, unique perspective, and willingness to help.

To my family and friends: **Amy Carson,** thank you for standing beside me when I couldn't even spell my own name, and for insisting that I finish the race. **Erin Lockhart,** thank you for inviting me on the trip that started it all. **Mom and Dad,** you always allowed me to follow dreams. Thank you for never suggesting that I pursue less than what God was calling me to do. **Ed and Sally Norton,** thank you for all of the meals and for graciously leaving your door unlocked when I needed a place to send the kids.

And to my husband, **Howard,** thank you for sharing the love of Christ with me and for making His love the center of our marriage. Without the love of our Lord poured out daily through you, this book might just be the story of a spiritually blind and deaf girl written by a spiritually blind and deaf woman. **Elijah, Lilly,** and **James,** you are all my greatest blessings and the three greatest kids in the whole wide world. Thank you for letting Mommy claw after her dreams. I'll try to write the next book a little faster.

Epigraphs

1. Chapter 1 epigraph: "I am glad to take you by the hand and lead you along an untrodden way into a world where the hand is supreme." - Helen Keller (The World I Live In)

2. Chapter 2 epigraph: "Many persons, having perfect eyes, are blind in their perceptions." - Helen Keller (The World I Live In)

3. Chapter 3 epigraph: "If you wish to be something that you are not, —something fine, noble, good,—you shut your eyes and for one dreamy moment you are that which you long to be." - Helen Keller (The World I Live In)

4. Chapter 4 epigraph: "Whatever moves me, whatever thrills me, is as a hand that touches me in the dark, and that touch is my reality." - Helen Keller (The World I Live In)

5. Chapter 5 epigraph: "The silent worker is imagination which decrees reality out of chaos." - Helen Keller (The World I Live In)

6. Chapter 6 epigraph: "The earth seemed benumbed by his icy touch, and the very spirits of the trees had withdrawn to their roots, and there, curled up in the dark, lay fast asleep." - Helen Keller (The Story of My Life)

7. Chapter 7 epigraph: "One can never consent to creep when one feels an impulse to soar." - Helen Keller (Address to the American Association to Promote the Teaching of Speech to the Deaf at Mt. Airy, Philadelphia, Pennsylvania (8 July 1896), quoted in supplement to The Story of My Life)

8. Chapter 8 epigraph: "All life is divided between what lies on one hand and on the other." - Helen Keller (The World I Live In)

9. Chapter 9 epigraph: "No child ever drank deeper of the cup of bitterness than I did." - Helen Keller (The Story of My Life)

10. Chapter 10 epigraph: "They laid their treasures at my feet, and I accepted them as we accept the sunshine and the love of our friends." - Helen Keller (The Story of My Life)

11. Chapter 11 epigraph: "I walked in the stillness of the night, and my soul uttered her gladness." - Helen Keller (The World I Live In)

12. Chapter 12 epigraph: "It makes me happy to know much about my loving Father, who is good and wise." - Helen Keller (The Story of My Life, letter to Rev. Phillips Brooks, July 14, 1890)

13. Chapter 13 epigraph: "Remember that you, dependent on your sight, do not realize how many things are tangible." - Helen Keller (The World I Live In)

14. Chapter 14 epigraph: Once I knew the depth where no hope was, and darkness lay on the face of all things. Then love came and set my soul free. - Helen Keller (Optimism) p.13, IN COPYRIGHT

15. Chapter 15 epigraph: "I think of days long gone, flown like birds beyond the ramparts of the world." - Helen Keller (The Song of the Stone Wall)

16. Chapter 16 epigraph: "Everything has its wonders, even darkness and silence, and I learn whatever state I am in, therein to be content." - Helen Keller (The Story of My Life)

17. Chapter 17 epigraph: "If the eye is maimed, so that it does not see the beauteous face of day, the touch becomes more poignant and discriminating." - Helen Keller (The World I Live In)

18. Chapter 18 epigraph: "Joy deserted my heart and for a long, long time I lived in doubt, anxiety, and fear." - Helen Keller (The Story of my Life)

19. Chapter 19 epigraph: "God is love, God is our Father, we are His children; therefore the darkest clouds will break and though right be worsted, wrong shall not triumph." –Helen Keller (The Story of My Life)

20. Chapter 20 epigraph: "Toleration is the greatest gift of the mind; it requires the same effort of the brain that it takes to balance oneself on a bicycle." - Helen Keller (Story of My Life, Letters Part 3: A Supplementary Account of Helen Keller's Life and Education)

21. Chapter 21 epigraph: "We could never learn to be brave and

patient, if there were only joy in the world." - Helen Keller (The Story of My Life, letter to Dr. Holmes, published in the Atlantic Monthly's "Over the Teacups"- May, 1890)

22. Chapter 22 epigraph: "And that faith, the rock not fashioned of human hands, be the stability of our triumphant, toiling days." - Helen Keller (The Song of the Stone Wall)

23. Chapter 23 epigraph: "Love always finds its way to an imprisoned soul, and leads it out into the world of freedom and intelligence." - Helen Keller (The Story of My Life)

24. Chapter 24 epigraph: "I am not discouraged, nor am I afraid." – Helen Keller (The Story of My Life, letter to Charles T. Copeland, December 20, 1900)

25. Chapter 25 epigraph: "Surely there are hearts and hands ever ready to make it possible for generous intentions to be wrought into noble deeds." - Helen Keller (The Story of My Life, letter to the Great Round World, Cambridge, February 16, 1901)

26. Chapter 26 epigraph: "I think if this sorrow had come to me when I was older, it would have broken my spirit beyond repairing. But the angel of forgetfulness has gathered up and carried away much of the misery and all the bitterness of those days." - Helen Keller (The Story of My Life)

27. Chapter 27 epigraph: "The witchery of love is in rock and tree." - Helen Keller (The Song of the Stone Wall)

28. Chapter 28 epigraph: "I never fight, except against difficulties." - Helen Keller (The Story of My Life, quote in conversation with Mr. Joseph Jefferson)

29. Chapter 29 epigraph: "I do not remember when I first realized that I was different from other people; but I knew it before my teacher came to me." - Helen Keller (The Story of My Life)

30. Chapter 30 epigraph: "Thus I came up out of Egypt and stood before Sinai, and a power divine touched my spirit and gave it sight, so that I beheld many wonders. And from the sacred mountain I heard

a voice which said. 'Knowledge is love and light and vision.' " - Helen Keller (The Story of My Life)

31. Chapter 31 epigraph: "When we walk in the valley of twofold solitude we know little of the tender affection that grow out of endearing words and actions and companionship." - Helen Keller (The Story of My Life)

32. Chapter 32 epigraph: "Any teacher can take a child to the classroom, but not every teacher can make him learn." - Helen Keller (The Story of My Life)

33. Chapter 33 epigraph: "I little dreamed how cruelly I should pay for that birthday gift." - Helen Keller (The Story of My Life)

34. Chapter 34 epigraph: "I felt so cold, I imagined I should die before morning, and the thought comforted me." - Helen Keller (The Story of My Life)

35. Chapter 35 epigraph: "Whenever I enter the region that was the kingdom of my mind I feel like the proverbial bull in the china shop." - Helen Keller (The Story of My Life)

36. Chapter 36 epigraph: "I knew there were obstacles in the way; but I was eager to overcome them." - Helen Keller (The Story of My Life)

37. Chapter 37 epigraph: "Out of immemorial chaos He wrought us." - Helen Keller (The Song of the Stone Wall)

38. Chapter 38 epigraph: "Before me I saw a new world opening in beauty and light, and felt within me the capacity to know all things." - Helen Keller (The Story of my Life)

39. Chapter 39 epigraph: "For one wild, glad moment we snapped the chains that bind us to earth, and joining hands with the winds we felt ourselves divine." - Helen Keller (The Story of my Life)

40. Chapter 40 epigraph: "With the dropping of a little word from another's hand into mine, a slight flutter of the fingers, began the intelligence, the joy, the fullness of my life." - Helen Keller (The World I Live In)

41. Chapter 41 epigraph: "It is an unspeakable boon to me to be

able to speak in winged words that need no interpretation." - Helen Keller (The Story of My Life)

42. Chapter 42 epigraph: "So in the heart of man shines forever a beam from the everlasting sun of God." - Helen Keller (The Song of the Stone Wall)

43. Chapter 43 epigraph: Sing how the ages, like thrifty husbandmen, winnow the creeds of men and leave only faith and love and truth." - Helen Keller (The Song of the Stone Wall)